FRICTION

ALSO BY ELOY URROZ IN ENGLISH TRANSLATION

The Obstacles

FRICTION

ELOY URROZ

TRANSLATED BY EZRA E. FITZ

DALKEY ARCHIVE PRESS
CHAMPAIGN AND LONDON

Originally published in Spanish as *Fricción* by Editorial Alfaguara, 2008
Copyright © 2007 by Eloy Urroz
Translation copyright © 2010 by Ezra E. Fitz
First edition, 2010
All rights reserved

Library of Congress Cataloging-in-Publication Data

Urroz Kanan, Eloy, 1967-
[Fricción. English]
Friction / by Eloy Urroz ; translated [from the Spanish] by Ezra E. Fitz. -- 1st ed.
    p. cm.
ISBN 978-1-56478-549-7 (pbk. : alk. paper)
1. Mind and reality--Fiction. I. Fitz, Ezra E. II. Title.
PQ7298.31.R73U7713 2010
863'.64--dc22
                            2010029731

Partially funded by the University of Illinois at Urbana-Champaign and by a grant from the
Illinois Arts Council, a state agency

La presente traducción fue realizada con apoyo del Programa de Apoyo a la Traducción de Obras
Mexicanas en Lenguas Extranjeras (ProTrad)

This translation was carried out with the support of the Program to Support the Translation of
Mexican Works into Foreign Languages (ProTrad)

www.dalkeyarchive.com

Cover: design and composition by Danielle Dutton, illustration by Nicholas Motte
Printed on permanent/durable acid-free paper and bound in the United States of America

To Nicolás

I ask the indulgence of grown-ups for dedicating this toy to a child only three years of age. I have a mediocre explanation aside from the fact that, of course, he is my son: For years I thought I was making wind-up toys for those serious adults who never learned how to play; now, however, I don't know why I make them.

And so I correct my dedication:

For Nicolás:
this friction-powered toy
so that he can have fun
when he grows up
and wants to play.

I shall speak a double truth; at times
one alone comes into being;
at other times out of one several things grow.
Double is the birth of mortal things and double their demise.
For the coming together of all both causes their birth
and destroys them; and separation nurtured in their being
makes them fly apart. These things never stop changing
throughout, at times coming together through Amity in one whole,
at other times being violently separated by Strife.
Thus, on one side, one whole is formed out of many,
and then again, wrenched from each other, they make up many out of one.
Thus they come into being and their life is not long their own,
but insofar as they never stop changing throughout
insofar they are forever immovable in a circle.
But come, listen to my words, for knowledge makes the mind grow.
As I said once before, revealing the outer limits of my thought,
I shall speak a double truth; at times one has grown out of many,
at other times many grow apart out of the one,
fire and water and earth and the immeasurable heights of air.
Then dire Strife stands away from all, while Love
reigns in their midst, equal in length and breadth.

—EMPEDOCLES

So, dare it! Your inheritance, what you've earned and learned,
The narratives of all your fathers' voices teaching you,
All law and custom, names of all the ancient gods,
Forget these things courageously; like newborn babes
Your eyes will open to the godliness of nature . . .

—FRIEDRICH HÖLDERLIN, *The Death of Empedocles*

Disclaimer

Any resemblance to events that occurred at James Madison University between the fall of 2000 and the spring of 2005, and/or any similarity between characters appearing in this Empedoclean novel of Love and Strife and my conspicuous former colleagues in the Department of Foreign Languages and Literatures at the aforementioned university is pure coincidence, and a result of the unchecked flow of *Tyche* (Chance) and *Ananke* (Necessity), which distort and pervert everything. Any actual facts are the product of the exaggerated fantasies of the author and nobody aside from me, Professor Cardoso, is responsible for these writings and inventions.

FRICTION

PART ONE
ERIS

I

Love and Strife, Eusebio, what are they? Perhaps the forces that move the earth, as the famous Empedocles asserted some five centuries before Christ? The philosopher wisely intuited that Love unites while Strife divides and disintegrates. The hatred that Strife imposes becomes part of our own nature. It's a case of like attracting like, while Love, on the other hand, attracts things *unlike* itself. How could that be? Aphroditic Love is, shall we say, a magnetic force—gravitational, if you like—that seeks to mix the four elements, the deepest roots that constitute all things. At least that's what the eccentric aristocrat who dwelled in the ancient, flourishing Sicilian colony of Akragas thought. On the other hand, it can be argued that Eris—Strife—tends toward hate and dispersion which also conforms to a separate group of truths belonging to a separate body . . . but not to the Set as a whole. Kypris, Philia, and Love, is, then, the force that brings about goodness, rest, an apparent state of peace or stasis. Strife and discord, however, cause evil, volition, and *kinēsis*. And this is the universe in which I'm moored, along with my wife Irene, my son Emilio, my ex-wife Fedra, my beloved daughter Dulce, my colleagues in the Department of Foreign Languages, Tino and

Javis and Stefano Morini, my devoted enemies at Millard Fillmore University, Jeff Davis and Gaudencia Gross-Wayne, and everyone else who spends his daily life in constant, deranged arguments . . . all of us form part of a perfect, eternal sphere where all things are in constant flux, and where nothing is ever destroyed but rather combined and mixed, just like the paints on an artist's palate.

But would it not make sense, then, to bring all this tripe together under the single word, friction? The friction between the colors or the chafing of bodies, the friction between ill will and desire, or the friction between treachery and friendship? The galling friction of jealousy, dreams, and the stubborn concupiscence of men. Is it not a fact that we are all brought into being via the same desperate corporeal friction between a mother and a father on one fateful night? Is it not true that, in the end, we all come to be born into or migrate towards a happier or more fucked up life? Was Empedocles right after all?

2

(THURSDAY, JUNE 15TH)

Close the book. I'm talking to you, idiot! Yes, you, the one who's reading, who just now started reading this page; in other words, the one who's falling, hurrying, sinking . . . so close the book, dear Reader, or don't, for it doesn't much matter at this point, because what could happen? More specifically, what could happen to you? Nothing, or not much, at least, maybe a little, almost nothing really, so keep on reading, and hurry up, since you're dying of curiosity, right? Throw yourself into it, yes, jump right in, immerse yourself in it for all eternity, fulfill your infinite desires for knowledge, calm your insatiable hunger. From now on, nothing really matters, because whatever is going to happen will happen . . . it's the way things go in life, or didn't you know that? It's all about falling, slipping, stumbling unconsciously . . . or, at least, if not unconsciously, then without basic regard for simple vigilance, for insomnia, for the spurious nap of life.

Now you are the one who is stumbling, dear Reader, the one and only . . . stumbling over the words, so what gives? It's a fucking miracle that you're still here, entangled, clambering, reading your way through this . . . but enough! Put the book down, yes, put it down and take off, run, get out of that insulated shelter of yours, flee from your late-afternoon office, because you're dying to know, it's so obvious, I can see it in your face, so get out of that ostentatious office on Avenida Reforma, because it's got to be at least four o'clock by now, right? You can see the golden statue of El Ángel de la Independencia through your window, you can't stand waiting anymore, you need to get out of there and find out how that portrait you ordered turned out, escape from that strongbox, that caisson, that vault of an office you're in with the leather chairs and the luxurious gray and sepia carpeting which you're so proud of, that space there at the heart of the world, the center of the universe, in the middle of Mexico City, and go see if Arturo has finished with the oil painting you ordered a couple of months ago, if not longer.

The haste—your haste—is that of love and passion, and Aphrodite is to blame. Didn't you know? Your urgent need to see the painting of your wife at your old friend's studio is called desire, and it's one of the ill-fated forces which moves the universe. Escape from this book, tell your secretary that you'll be going out for awhile, make up any excuse you need, because what you're feeling right now is exactly what Kypris sent down from the heavens, damn it, because even though you don't know it or even care that much about it, at least recognize that you're the big boss man, and nothing but a con artist, and you can say or do whatever you please, your secretary is there to listen to you, to obey you; it's not her job to ask questions, for after all, you're the attorney. And now, dear Reader, you must ask yourself: what does it feel like to have all the power? To have it all right there in the palm of your hand, in your fist?

Have one last sip, damn it, the coffee grounds filtering through your teeth and gums, but pay no attention to that, nothing is perfect, nothing is harmonic; the old man from Agrigento knows that not even big boss men are perfect, not that virile weapon, you bastard, not life, and you less than anybody, dear Reader, so put down your cup, push it to the side, and stand up, because life isn't perfect (of course), and yet you still don't know so you're dying (not really) of impatience, yes, it's you, being consumed by haste and love as if by an army of ants . . . and a glorious fire has been running through your veins, burning you down to the bone (yes to the very *marrow* itself) for many months now, more than a year, perhaps two, since you first laid eyes on your wife, your queen, Matilde, Matildita, Maty, the one who made you feel more like a prince than ever, you above all others, the emperor, reigning over the tumultuous masses that throng Avenida Reforma near El Ángel which you're currently staring at through your polarized glass window, trying to decide whether to continue reading this filth or to go and see your good friend Arturo at his improvised rooftop studio which he fashioned out of two-by-fours and plywood, and again, suddenly, you want to see how that painting is coming along, but you still don't want to put *Friction* down, especially since there will be no more interruptions, and you have the whole fucking afternoon to yourself, to see if Arturo is close to finishing the portrait or if the bastard has gone and gotten stoned again like he used to, so you end up asking your secretary for another cup of coffee for you to slowly nurse as you read, you read, you read gradually, getting more into it, and so you press on, more quickly now, because you realize that you have the book and therefore you have the power, I'm telling you, you have the keys to the kingdom, you're the branch manager, the head honcho, and you don't answer to anybody except for that asshole American who, of course, lives hundreds of miles away in Gringolandia, far away from the third-world misery, the ball-and-cup game of life here in downtown Mexico City, where you're in charge of the Mexico branch of a foreign bank, with your Columbia MBA hanging on the wall, speaking perfect

8

English save for a slight accent and absolute understanding that you are the young up-and-comer . . . well, not so young, maybe, but definitely in what the old timers call "the prime of life," with everything in front of you, of course, Christ, even your health, and love through it all, the love or infatuation belonging to the newly married, which runs through your veins, warming you from time to time like a canorous song, like that eternity of tiny, Velardean ants teeming and crawling and coursing over your arms, your legs, your chest, your brain . . . and how happy you are, how happy you always are, man! You can't ask for more than that, and so you make your decision, you resolve to leave the office, checking your watch (it's just after four) as you abandon the book—this damned book, *Hypocrite lecteur!*—convinced that that bastard, your friend Arturo, will be stretched out in his workshop with a peyote joint between his lips while Tamara, his poor wife, on the other hand, will be hard at work, as he should be, but as you're reprimanding him (half seriously, half in jest) the son of a bitch just laughs, laughs at you, the fucking catechist that you've become, dear Reader, because you're all just a bunch of sorry bastards, Arturo says with a haughty snort, people who just work in order to keep working . . . but hey man, does it really have to be that way, especially since the world has been quite the opposite since the beginning, since the time of the ancient Greeks (now he's acting like a know-it-all)? I'm a painter, buddy, and you, dear Reader, have to admit that yes he paints great, which is why you asked him to do a portrait of your wife as a surprise gift for your anniversary . . . and that, dear Reader, is why you finally decide to loosen the tie which she gave you (after you mentioned once that you needed a pearl-gray tie), put on your coat, and leave your office, telling your secretary on the way out that you'll be back in a little while, not long, and just then your cell phone begins to ring, as if there were some pressing matter, but of course you know that nothing important would be happening that Thursday, the one on which you have the whole afternoon to yourself, to go check in on that idiot Arturo, holed up in his asbestos-filled studio, and urge him to finish the painting which you commissioned over two months ago.

You get in your Mercedes E 2025, avoiding a couple of Indians who had surely just arrived in Mexico City from somewhere like Hidalgo or San Luis Potosí, for they obviously haven't yet learned the traffic laws here in the *Distrito Federal*; in other words, the inexorable law of the jungle, the law of those in power (like you, chief), the law of the luxury car that says *back off* to other models and *fuck you* when they cut you off in traffic … and since you're almost always in a rush, dear Reader, then every single one of them can go and fuck themselves, you say to yourself without loosening your grip on the wheel. San Luis Potosí, which you just saw on the news the other day with Maty, while the two of you were embracing in bed, and such sad news it is, the desperate plight of the local *campesinos*, somewhere up in the mountains, and neither you nor your wife (of course) could have even imagined the water shortages, the utter lack of rain during the past three months, the hunger, the devastating poverty, the unemployment, or the bureaucratic corruption in that shitty little state, children on the verge of death, helpless and abandoned, sick with consumption, dysentery, AIDS, and who knows what else, the women making stews (but no tortillas) out of rats they catch in the streets, because there aren't even any dogs around to do that sort of thing (they either left or were already eaten), and Matilde was so disturbed by it all that she began to cry, unable to tear her eyes from the TV screen, and so that is why, dear Reader, you assumed those two Indians whom you almost ran over were from San Luis Potosí, but they also could have been from the hills of Guerrero or some fucked up little town in Oaxaca, because you, the modern urbanite through and through, neither know nor care about those differences, because you only concern yourself with cities like New York and Paris and this, the heart of the world, the place where you were born, where you learned to live life and routinely screw over your fellow man, the old *Distrito Federal*, the familial cradle where your parents, your grandparents, and your great-grandparents now rest in peace.

You decide to take Insurgentes to Viaducto, where you'll turn off and head for the Narvarte neighborhood where that bastard Arturo wastes all his time painting and painting; that is, when he's not high on the peyote that he smuggled in from Sonora or Chihuahua, whichever it is. Sometimes, yes, he would tell you about his bus trips with the group of artists known as the Agros, his bizarre rituals out in the middle of the desert, his hallucinations out there in the elements, the orgies, as you run a stop sign, remembering the search for the sacred nourishment, pressing down on the gas pedal, digging tubers out of the earth to clean and slice, the nights in camp listening to animals in the distance or walking out into the darkness to see what the hell they really were, coyotes, hyenas, pacas, all in the name of procuring the sacred sustenance of the gods, of the artists, and you accelerate, because they believe in such bullshit, those Agros, you say to yourself as you hang a left, those gods, every painter feels like a poor little misunderstood god and that's why they're only able to paint their resentments and frustrations, but you grit your teeth and instead speed up yet again while they paint their deep-seated hatred and ill will towards others, all the others, a very refined and biased hatred, of course, hatred of those who consider themselves bourgeoisie and working class, *campesinos* and landowners, priests and lawyers, women and children and the elderly, all (or nearly all) of them are targets of the anger and frustration of the fucking Agro artists, but then again you're here, you've arrived, and you don't even have to search long for a place to park, it being Thursday, and thus the traffic isn't all that bad, though it could have been hell, of course, but you're wasting time with these ridiculous musings, so just forget about them, dear Reader, driver of this Mercedes E 2025 with the digital readout and navigation screen, director of this improbable history of love, your own predictable history which you choose not to read (or perhaps you do—who knows—with a nice cup of coffee in hand) but, in the end, it's of no real importance, since here you are, right in front of the old, run-down building where Arturo lives and works, Arturo, your friend since you were a teenager, bohemian to the core, who rejected wealth and political privilege, the son of the famous statesman Roberto Soto Gariglietti, Arturo, the patently macho figure who exploited and mistreated his wife with his boastful attitude as she, Tamara, remained proud and supportive of him while he painted and experimented with the peyote he got on his long trips to the north where he eventually found meaning and satisfaction in the great Capirucha, the Mexican Big Apple, along with fifty-six million other people inhabiting the capital city, according to the last census, taken in 2022.

You park the car and straighten your tie, a move which you regret almost immediately. Why on earth would you do that? For Arturo, who's barely ever worn a tie in his entire adult life? What an absurd custom it is to wear a properly knotted tie wherever you go! You want to take it off, and do so. Much better. You get out of the car, and not just any car, mind you, but your beloved Mercedes, and as you do, two little kids run up to you to tell you that they'll take care of the car, sir, two shoeless kids, probably from San Luis Potosí again or maybe just Hidalgo, one of whom had no shirt, but could they really be surviving on rat meat like the news report that had Matilde to the point of sobbing had said, the one that left her shocked and wondering how she could live in a country as—what's the word—as unjust as this one, and now you're on the verge of asking these street urchins about it, but you stop yourself, deciding that it's better not to know, that it would be better just to pay them to take care of your car, lest they scratch it up with a bottle cap, and so you smile, showing off your perfect dental work, hypocritical dear Reader, director of this excessively predictable tale of love, and once again the eternal ants of Kypris begin biting you, burning your skin, your veins as you think about Matilde, your baby, your hot mama, and you're dying to give her the portrait as soon as possible even though there are still five days left until your first anniversary, Tuesday, June 20th, and the only thing that's missing is the painting because that bastard Arturo is probably behind schedule, so you'll simply crucify him if that's the case, you swear you will, swear you'll kill him, because you're not about to screw up the series of surprises that you have planned for Tuesday, and as you're walking up to the door to his building you're thinking about how it will all kick off with a Brazilian emerald necklace that will perfectly match her sea-green eyes, and you don't even have to ring the bell, then there's the dinner at Maxim's, because someone's just leaving the building and you slide in before the door closes, and of course the seven-day cruise up to Alaska, you've done it before, during all those years when you'd come here to Arturo's studio to watch him paint, and finally, the best present of all: the oil on canvas portrait, and now all you have to do is climb the five flights of stairs up to the roof where your friend lays around and paints and meditates and coughs up peyote, there in his and Tamara's house, if you can call it that, there on the roof of that beat up ramshackle old building, which the philanthropic owners kindly rented to them for a modest amount, because even though he looked like a ragged old bum, Arturo was nevertheless the favorite son of the politician who died near the end of the twentieth century.

Two floors to go, then one more, and finally, as you make your way up the last few steps just before you reach the landing, you can see those indescribable canvases which Arturo hangs all over the place, paintings which adorn (or cover up) the broad walls, invading nearly every space, some of which he's never sold while others you've never seen before, probably his more recent works, and you examine them, examine and admire them, these sinister, dark and dismal works, destroyed phone lines and satellite dishes, phantasmagoric ruined buildings, sickly, meager pedestrians, starving dogs and monstrous spiders, enormous factories, lakes teeming with scraps of metal, old tires, and mangled parts of dead animals, innumerable nightmarish scenes, and you walk down the hall, awash in ochers, grays, and reds, walking towards the door that opens onto the rooftop, the penultimate door, and you open it, dear Reader, understand? you open it because the time is at hand, and when you do, there's the sun! It inundates you for a second . . . nothing happens, though you cover your eyes, the light searing your retinas, and for a moment you can't see, of course, but it doesn't matter because you know this rooftop like the back of your hand, just forty-five steps or so, straight ahead, and then there, on the right side, up against the edge of the roof, you'll find his studio, which you know, as well as the filthy shack where he lives and sleeps with Tamara, and now your eyes are beginning to adjust to the light, it's terribly hot (and what a great idea it was to ditch that pearl gray tie which Matilde gave you for your birthday last year!), you're one step away from the asbestos-and-plywood studio which Arturo hammered together himself when they rented the roof, and now here you are, pushing on the door even though you should really knock first, you think, but at this point it doesn't much matter, dear Reader, because it's too late to worry about that, since your innocent eyes have just now fallen on your wife there at the opposite end of the studio, there she is, it's her, your woman, your baby, the love of your life, but then again, is it really her, or is it merely someone who at first glance simply appeared to be your wife, dear confused, dear stunned and stupefied Reader? Could that really be your naked wife there in the arms of your old friend Arturo? You think so, you could swear that it's her, but, then again, who knows . . . You can see her right now, you're scrutinizing this woman so similar, so like yours, with a man whose face you can't quite see, just his back, his hairy ass sunk into a quilt, his hairy arms around the waist, the back of this woman, Matilde or whoever she is, because you still don't know, dear Reader, the sleek skin on your beloved wife's back, so you continue to observe her with increasing curiosity because you're still not sure, what with so many paintings propped up against the walls making it impossible to focus on any particular detail, or could it be the oppressive heat and humidity which does that, or could it just be a woman you've seen somewhere else, perhaps Arturo's own wife or even a beautiful model who happens to look like Matilde . . . could that be it? Who the hell is that naked body, that precious, carnal object? Damn it! Of course it can't be Maty, because she's at home; or rather, at this time of day, she'll be at the café in Polanco with her graduate student friends, gossiping, eating a slice of *pastel de tres leches*, discussing Latin American politics, all the changes, especially the big change that took place barely a year ago with the election of the new president, Gilberto Rendón, which had left the world totally dumbstruck, so yes, she's there having coffee with friends, but then all of a sudden you wonder whether she's not, you wonder whether these clear, green eyes are those of Matilde, because you seem to recognize them, don't you, dear Reader, just above the left shoulder of your friend Arturo, the artist, who right now has your magnificent and lovely wife here in his studio whether you're reading or not, since what does it really matter at this point anyway, what the hell could possibly matter now that you're seeing this with your own eyes, crystal clear and real, the pain and the hurt burning through your corneas, you, the suffering voyeur, the little man, suddenly feeling as if an invisible object were drilling or boring into you, a hard, stabbing sensation, a stiff jab, a little chocolate-covered pepper that tastes sweet and then burns you from within, but it's not love that's doing it; rather, it's a lascivious burning, a burning sense of disgrace, a crushing, overwhelming sense of pain, like an eternity of hellfire, continuous, fluid, cutting, throbbing inside your head, refusing to let you breathe, refusing to let you blink in the face of what you're witnessing though sweat is running into your eyes, you're sweating like a hog on its way to the slaughterhouse, and man, you think, it's a good thing you left your tie back in your Mercedes, otherwise you might have hung yourself with that sopping wet thing!

And now you clearly hear, as if from beyond the grave, the lovely voice of your dear Maty, she's moaning or startled or saying something to you, dear Reader, something you can't make out, but you feel your stomach clenching up anyway, preparing to retch, but just as you double over in pain you see there, along one of the walls and jumbled in with the other paintings, the portrait you ordered from Arturo two months ago, the portrait of your wife, which, it appears, he was finishing after all, or at least would be finishing it if it wasn't for your wife—and now you vomit

15

at the thought—who is right there fucking and fucking him on top of a patterned quilt, just fucking and moaning with delight there on top of that hairy artist, on top of the god of color, straddling that goddamn Agro artist's legs, clutched by his thick, powerful arms, her fingernails digging into his shoulder blades like she does to you when she's about to orgasm, although this time there is no way of knowing if the clawing was being caused by an orgasm or by the terrible scare that you gave the poor little thing by finding her in such a position, so pompous and blissful, sweetly tortured by the painter's primitive cock, his turgid penis running through her while you vomit and get the hell out of there, terrified, breathless, unable to say even one damn word, still tasting the coffee grounds stuck in your teeth, and you're choked up, you've gone numb, you've lost your bearings, your compass, your mind; your sad eyes have glossed over, your soul feels overcast and dirty despite the intense sun, despite this rust-colored light that cleaves through the sky this Thursday afternoon in the capital city, this 15th of June, this day in which your whole life twists and changes, my dear, amiable and distinguished Reader, my burgeoning friend, my traveling companion.

III

I haven't written so much as a line for over a year now; in fact, this is the first time, that is, unless I fall victim again to the unimpeachable forces of boredom and bitterness. Well, I'm exaggerating: what I'm actually talking about is the first line turned out by a mechanism of words, something which most people, out of habit, call "fiction," though a more appropriate name would be "friction." Ever since I finished my last work, I haven't been able to sit down and write something that even remotely resembled *that*, it was nothing at all like creating sick, neurotic characters who dream that they can speak and make love and madly create friction between their limbs and lips, create it with an almost immoral sense of desperation.

Of course, there were the two articles I had accepted by an academic journal published by a famous Texas university, which not even my friends read, but I haven't written anything that ever approached a factory of words, a thick tangle of human nastiness and vicissitudes. In fact, I don't even know if these words are beginning to look much like a work of friction (though, at some level, it is) since, at this point, all I've said is that I haven't been able to write one damn word until today, more than a year after stamping the final period at the end of that saga which, I suppose, left me deflated, exhausted, with nothing left to give and an unpleasant taste in my mouth, a sad and unpleasant taste. *That's just how it goes, Eusebio,* I say that to myself every day and night when, inexorably, a sort of innate fear or insane terror arises from deep within me because I've yet to sit down and try it again. When I say it out loud, when I brood over it like an ass, I console myself with a glass of whiskey while I watch, from my window, the well-planned streets of this damn college town, morosely reading what has become my passion (or my excuse) over the past two years: the Greek philosophers, especially the pre-Socratics. *That's just how it goes,* I've repeated to myself every one of those last five hundred days, as I finish correcting that never-ending stack of essays which aren't worth the paper they're printed on and return them to their rightful owners—my students—as if they're burning my fingers. *That's just how it goes, Eusebio,* it's the natural order of things, so don't worry yourself over it, or . . . well, at least, don't worry more than necessary; after all, wise men say that moments of sterility are, deep down, moments of future fertility, that those awful moments of infecundity are also moments of profound reflection. And there are those who console themselves with the argument that every day—every hour—that passes without writing, a new idea is incubating . . . settling, perhaps, waiting for that impossible day when you can finally sit down and leave the stupor of whiskey behind you, along with the stupefying monotony of Millard Fillmore University in Virginia, where you and your family happened to end up via the ominous possibilities of fate.

In any case, it was last night (or was it the night before?) when, after grading the last of my students' essays on the Novels of the Mexican Revolution, I sternly told myself, *Eusebio, just start writing about what's happened to you.* Why the hell not? What do you have to lose? What's stopping you? Tell us about that awful combination of sterility and laziness, about the unbearable sense of blandness that's haunted you for over a year here in this fucked up little town in Virginia's Shenandoah Valley, reading (when your son Emilio and the damn revolutionaries permit you) the Eleatics and the Atomists, studying Anaxagoras and Empedocles, and somewhere amidst all that—who knows—maybe you can use some of that as fodder for a work of friction, a black, tar-like work, like an unpaved road, a towpath . . . at the very least it will be a chronicle of the awful pallor of those five hundred days and their pale, Dostoyevskian nights; it will offer a cynical reflection on the virtues of silence, on the various stages of silence that every artist unfortunately suffers from time to time. Damn it: laying whiteness upon whiteness upon still more whiteness. Isn't that what I've been doing here? Mixing evaporated milk with powdered milk with skim milk? Steadily making my way to shit?

To make matters worse, just today, when I finally decided to sit down and start writing again—pushing through the doubts which had plagued me the night before—just a few minutes before I was about to wade back into those muddy waters, I cut the first two fingers on my right hand, the two that I need to write with (I admit, I never learned to type . . . I blame it on love; or rather, I blame it on the distractingly beautiful teacher who visited us every Friday at our school in the Chimalistac neighborhood of the *Distrito Federal.* Suffice it to say that when she arrived and sat down next to us to observe our progress, I had to excuse myself and run to the bathroom to masturbate to the images of her long, fine nails, her pleated skirt revealing a bit of thigh, and her splendid brown-skinned body rubbing up against mine. Maybe I didn't mean to, but who knows; in any case, the fact is that I could excuse myself two or even three times during the course of a single, two-hour class, with the end result being that I never learned the proper way to type. To this day, I still peck away with just my index fingers, though my cock isn't so red and swollen and sore anymore).

Such details notwithstanding, what I would like to say is that I had scarcely even set out to cross these waters—had barely begun to dip into that fecund (abundant) sterility—when, in a moment of carelessness, I cut the tips of my first two fingers on the coffeepot that I'd shut off, intending to clean it and then brew a nice fresh cup with which to celebrate having graded my last essay while my son and wife were sleeping. Some five hundred days and nights went by where I could have sat down to write, and only today, when I finally do so, my fingers are cut up and bandaged. Damn it! Now all I can do is tell the story of my revelation or whatever this absurd thought is called—*well I need a good cup of coffee in hand before I can begin*—the fact that moments or stages of inexplicable fertility can necessarily arise from the most grave periods of sterility—*nice and hot with no sugar, as if I were having it with Irene*—in other words, those barren stages are not, in fact, permanent, though they may appear to be so at the time—*urgently*—indeed, they are an integral part of the overall creative process—*that nearly burns my throat as I drink it, and at the very least gives me the chance for one good stretch*—and difficult moments of incubation—*poiesis*. A reassuring comparison can be made to the curious type of Japanese bamboo that does not grow like other plants; instead, its seeds, when planted, will remain in a completely dormant (perhaps infertile?) state for seven long years, after which, in only six short weeks, the plant will grow to a height of thirty meters or more. So perhaps, for all this time, I myself have unwittingly been this dwarfish little bamboo plant on the verge of awakening from its interminable American lethargy, without a cup of coffee in hand to start off this snowy morning in the empty streets of this sad, dead, planned city. The Sicilian gods willing—Nestis willing—let the mortal springs be moistened with tears, and so let this be true: a simple, quick little nap from which I'm waking up without a cup of coffee ready because I couldn't make a new fucking pot.

That is the revelation (*nous*, as Parmenides and Anaxagoras would say) and at this point, I simply don't know if I'll piss myself laughing, sobbing, or just pondering recent events with a sort of philosophic acquiescence, pondering that which was and is no longer, meditating on those Japanese bamboo plants or those *Distrito Federal* denizens who are on the verge of reaching the summit if they don't screw up or find themselves the victims of a malicious, unfortunate trick played by Hera, the dispenser of life.

4

(TUESDAY, MAY 2ND)

"Look, the first thing I remember about my father . . ." Arturo says with reluctance, almost irritation, as if it were a huge effort to look back in time, a task which—while not an unpleasant matter in and of itself—still wouldn't result in anything remotely *artistic* and therefore wouldn't add one thing to the work he was painting or wanted to paint . . . It's just that Arturo defines each and every ounce of energy he invests (whether it be thinking, moving, or even smoking) in terms of how it could benefit him artistically. He wasn't what you'd call a pragmatic artist, even if he did consider himself a staunch bohemian, an aesthete, a naturalist painter: everything else bored him, unhinged him, or didn't matter one whit to him. To summarize: why drag yourself back through the fields of introspection when you have neither the need nor the desire to do so, merely because that's where he encountered Matilde, the wife of his former and now newly reunited friend. Why the hell would he go and pleasure a refined, bourgeoisie, political science student when so many others had asked the same favor and been denied? The answer jumped to light: it was because the banker had, after all, been his friend since they were teenagers, because he bought paintings from him, because he brought in other yuppie bankers and lawyers to his ramshackle little studio on the fifth floor of that building in Narvarte where they also bought his works, and—above all (why deny it?)—because his wife truly was a thing of beauty, with a firm (but not too large) backside, a nice balance between the shoulders which were set neither too high nor too low (and well-suited to her graceful neck and the shape of her thorax), and only slightly (though tantalizingly) visible collarbones.

Just then Arturo edged a few inches over to get a better view of her, to examine her again, to take in her fullness from his vantage point there on the three-seat sofa the two of them were sharing, resting in one corner of his plywood workshop there on the roof which he and Tamara, his wife, rented. There, in profile, he once again confirmed what he first thought when Maty entered his studio earlier that afternoon: that she was a beauty in her blue, close-fitting skirt and thin, white, nearly transparent blouse. He confirmed that her hair was indeed a deep chestnut color and that she wore it loose, free-flowing, barely grazing the tops of her lithe, alabaster shoulders. She wasn't wearing any makeup, either. Her eyes were green, but not intensely green, he thought: eyes that appeared to be on the verge of catching fire or dissolving in their own sockets. Chartreuse-green, or greenish-gold eyes. Matilde had a rather finely drawn profile, though her lips seemed gathered and her forehead slightly wrinkled . . . those slight lines came from that particular sort of avidity which she displayed as if to prove she really could take something invaluable from Arturo, something which not even he himself could have imagined. He did understand that she was here strictly for the purpose of talking about his father, to see if he'd been able to discover anything about Roberto Soto Gariglietti, the creator or founder of the Partido de la Naturaleza y el Fuego Mexicano which he was beginning to talk about after two decades of relative silence, despite the fact that he was the one who had given the party their original stature and strength some twenty-five years ago when he aided the successful campaign of Mexico's first opposition candidate for president. Now, twenty years after his death, much more attention was being focused on other political leaders, but none more than his illegitimate successor, old Gilberto Rendón, the anarchist bastard with whom (when he was still alive and young) he'd had irreconcilable differences such that, in the end, he ended up handing the fame and absolute control of the party over to him. All things considered, what's certain was that the PNFM had won elections on its own (without forming any alliances) and by a surprising margin of victory, and that the interest in the early days of the movement—and the subsequent political party—had been growing. Maty, of course, wanted to dig up some unknown, redeeming information about his life, and if such information did still exist, it was Arturo who would be able to bring this underground past to light . . . even if it went against his will.

The heat at that time of day was devastating, and it felt even worse in a place like that which was being inundated with light, a benign light necessary for working, Arturo told everyone who entered his studio and immediately became drenched in sweat, necessary for capturing every line and every pore of the models who appeared at his door at noon or in the evenings, whom he transforms, with painstaking meticulousness, into monsters or reptiles, into Gorgons or damsels fatally enveloped by flames, into cosmic vortexes or, sometimes, even into flesh that's been torn apart by teeth and bullets.

"Yes, Arturo, tell me," Maty insisted a few seconds later, when she realized that her host had drifted off into contemplation, apparently having forgotten all about that first snapshot of his father. That little "Yes, Arturo" was not a deep-seated one but rather a subtle snap of the fingers, a tap on the shoulder, a call back to reality, but what damn reality was it? The reality of the two people sitting there in the studio owned by the painter, her husband's friend whom she barely knew herself, and who was suddenly interested in this investigation, or was it this other reality into which Arturo had, in fact, suddenly sunk against his will: the reality of San Nicolás, a poor, dirty neighborhood, on an already distant day, by his father's side, after a political meeting with two or three hundred people, listening to him say to the other children his age, *hop in the van, we're going to find each of you a present*?

While trying to reconstruct the scene in his mind in the midst of the shame and the withering heat of that studio, Arturo realized once again that words don't communicate even a hint of the emotions that were roiling around inside of him, couldn't even begin to describe the vortex of memories that were whirling ever faster, one after another. Could it be that he simply didn't have the words to describe them? That everything was rushing back to him at disorienting speed? Or perhaps it's that only a painting can articulate what was or is felt with a few simple brush-strokes, with a single image brought up from deep within the gut, or a palate of well-mixed colors eloquently spread across the canvas?

"And you were jealous, Arturo, or maybe angry . . . ?" Matilde pressed, intrigued, tossing her hair back, wiping the drops of sweat from her forehead with the back of her hand, examining a pair of nudes that were propped up across the room from her and coated with a thick layer of dust.

"No, absolutely not. It's just the opposite," Arturo replied, lighting a cigarette without bothering to offer one to Matilde, obstinate, serious, almost a mournful, majestic iconic figure. "I feel more proud than ever of my dad . . ."

"But you haven't finished telling me about your first memory of him?"

"Right, well that's why I'm telling you that I get a sense of pride and joy from knowing that the man who gathered up those kids in his van to take them shopping for toys was my father, and that in some uncertain way I contributed to all that, since I had so many toys and they didn't, and ultimately that man was my father and I, magnanimously, loaned those kids my dad for awhile, understand? Because they loved and admired him like I did . . ."

"Hey, your *papá*'s a really great guy! I wish I had one," said a kid stuck there next to him in the back seat of the van, which was now leaving the unpaved streets of San Nicolás behind it, tires drumming over every pot-hole and twist in the road.

"What, you don't have a *papá*?" Arturo exclaimed, embarrassed, twist-ing in his seat as much as he could to see the boy with whom he was speaking, shocked to see that his upper lip was nearly connected to his na-sal fossae, something that, of course, he had never seen before in his life.

"No, he left us a long time ago. I don't even remember him . . ." he re-plied, and, by dint of some unusual mental apparatus that Arturo knows nothing about, the boy with the harelip seems wholly untroubled at the disciplined, matter-of-fact statement about his horrible tale of life with-out a father—any father—which, to Arturo, suddenly seems absolutely intolerable, the sum of all sadness . . . he just can't stand the thought of not having a father at his side, playing, talking, releasing iguanas and parrots into the Chiapas jungle, visiting Teotihuacán during the sum-mer solstice, falling asleep to stories of Greek mythology, listening to tales of Aztec and Mayan gods and witches which his father always re-cited, without being asked or begged, each and every night, those pre-Columbian and pre-Greek gods in whom he believed (Tezcatlipoca, Xi-uhtecuhtli, Tláloc, Quetzalcoatl, Zeus, Hera, Apollo, and the rest) and who had the strength to carry on, to change the face of the earth, the rotten and wormy face of Mexico.

"You felt a little like his right hand man, like your father's personal assistant," Matilde affirmed before finally taking a drink from the glass of water that Arturo had offered her when she arrived, which she had left untouched, careful not to miss a single detail, syllable, or relevant, revealing gesture.

"More or less, I suppose . . ."

"And that's why you don't feel jealous . . ."

"I already told you: it's quite the contrary . . ."

"And how old were you?"

"I don't know." Arturo, the Agro painter, the aesthete, took a deep, fearless drag off his cigarette, and held it in for a good long while.

"You must have been around . . ." Matilde did the calculations in her head, intently focused, as if the number were a matter of life and death, information vital to the thesis that she was about to start writing, and which, eventually, she would show off to her friends over coffee at the café Polanco on some future Thursday afternoon.

"Six or seven," Arturo cut in. "Yes, I must have been about seven."

"So what you're telling me happened more or less around 1992 or 1993," Matilde said, making a note of the dates; then she paused and turned more to her left so she could better see the face of her gracious host. "How old are you, Arturo?"

"Thirty-nine. The same as your husband."

"And how long have you known each other?" Matilde was surprised by her own curiosity, for it took her to a place she didn't want to go; or rather, it took her away from the fundamental issue which had brought her to that claustrophobic, oven-like studio with a blank notebook in her lap and a mini tape recorder switched on. She was sweating; her translucent blouse was clinging to her brassiere. She tugged at it ever so slightly, as if to allow the winds of Zephyr or Boreas between her beautiful breasts, not wanting to distract Arturo now that words and memories were beginning to emerge from the catacombs of the past. But why had she so foolishly shifted the focus of the conversation? She couldn't now retract or reword the question. When he began to reply, it was already too late . . .

"Why don't you tell me how the two of you met?" Arturo responded with a question of his own, playful though with a touch of malice in his words. Once again the painter was struck by Matilde's appearance, even though this was the third or fourth time that he'd seen her: first at a party held by a mutual friend, followed shortly by a wedding, and once by pure chance at a gas station in Colonia del Valle. And each of those times she was at her husband's side. But the fact of the matter is that—in spite of everything, in spite of having seen her on all these occasions—he still hadn't taken in everything about her; or rather, he hadn't been prepared for the fact that, besides being an attractive young woman, she intrigued him because of some memory or simple association of his . . . But all that notwithstanding, it all became clear to him when Matilde, without needing or intending to, moved slightly in her seat, crossed and uncrossed her legs, perhaps nervous under the painter's gaze, perhaps from her particular odor which she was beginning to notice, or perhaps from the heat in that room which had her damp with sweat from her head to her toes: beads were forming on her forehead, droplets were running down her back, her inner thighs were damp, sweating in their close confinement. Arturo stole a glance between the folds of her skirt, and he knew instantly that it wasn't just her legs and ankles which were well-defined, but also her thighs, since the slit in the fabric (like fast-moving fish) revealed something that just so happened to remind him of a certain typing teacher back at the Chimalistac school in Mexico City.

It was then that Arturo subconsciously decided that he would paint Matilde naked, open, with the Popocatépetl volcano between her legs and the town of Atlixco behind her, fading into the mist. Yes, of course, that's how he would paint her; ardent and pensive, with her green eyes examining the hem of her skirt and that aquiline profile, looking bold and impudent, like a Siena Madonna. There was something of a metaphysical fixation there, an insight that suddenly grabbed hold of him like an incubus from the stories his father used to tell him as a child.

"I'll tell you the story later," Matilde answered, taken aback yet laughing, evasive, unassuming, and important.

"Do you promise?"

"Yes, but now tell me, why did your father do that? Why did he all of a sudden load up his van with children and take them shopping for toys?"

"You know . . ." The painter seemed to be responding to the effects of time on memory, to a new account being formed, a simultaneous revelation, something that separated him from that well of light out of which they were both trying to dredge up memories of a famous dead man.

"Now that you say it, I guess that one little act left quite an impression on me . . ."

"What are you talking about?"

"About my attitude, my character or whatever. You know what I mean . . ." He stopped, drifting into thought, staring straight ahead, off towards a wall filled with nothing more than unsold, destroyed, or simply forgotten paintings: a few ocher nudes, a couple of haggard faces, the Temple of the Moon at Teotihuacán, an unfinished portrait of the German filmmaker Carl Gustav Gruber, another of the expat poet Greg Bruchner, a group of frogs devouring an immense crocodile.

"I'm sorry, but I'm lost," Maty murmured, taking a sip from her glass of water and wiping her neck with the palm of her empty hand.

"Let me put it this way: it's a moral question, something that defines you or defines what you do, Maty. It suddenly occurred to me that my father knew then that no matter how much he wanted to, he would never be able to solve the problems of those children or of the thousands of children without families or other means, living in total misery, some of them sick, without clothes, education, or even a future. What could he possibly do in the face of all that? Not much, of course. Barely anything. He wasn't president, and even if he had been, he still wouldn't have been able to fix the country's problems in a day, right?"

"Of course, but I'm afraid I still don't understand . . ."

"Just wait a minute and you will," the Agro painter said as he got up from the sofa and stretched his arms in a wide arc until his shoulder blades popped. "What I'm trying to say is that my father was, more than anything else, a guy who, like Aristotle, believed that happiness was one of the ultimate reasons for man's existence. But what did Roberto Soto Gariglietti find happiness in? Things that can be had and felt in the now, Matilde. That's it. Everything else is evanescent, so to speak. After the meeting that afternoon in that miserable neighborhood, he felt that the only solid, decent thing to do was to take those kids toy shopping and bring them some happiness for that hour or two. To take some time out of his life to make theirs happier, understand? Look, it wasn't at all about the old 'teach a kid to fish' kind of thing, which would have been more of a moral code than immediate action, no free medicines or scholarships or clothes or anything that you'd call a 'long-term solution,' because ultimately such things don't involve immediate love and affection, which was an essential part of my father's philosophical and political theories. It was all quite the opposite. He decided to load them all into the Partido's van along with me, his son, and instructed the driver to take us to a giant downtown mall to shop for something that the children had never had before in their lives: a toy, a worthless little knickknack that nevertheless somehow manages to overwhelm a kid more than anything else in the world. So he drove them to a toy store, and even gave them a ride back to their neighborhood afterwards, because something as simple as a ride in a car was something that many of them had never before experienced. Just imagine the excitement, the euphoria, the sheer joy they all were feeling . . . I even felt it myself, even if I didn't yet understand the reason for it all. I don't know how many managed to pile into the van; maybe fifteen or so. In any case, what I do remember is a mass of smiling faces all around me, sweaty, filthy, eager faces with runny noses, a throng of shouting voices and waving hands, cries of joy and jubilation, and above all I remember what came next. Just imagine it! The presidential candidate surrounded by a mob of half-naked children, his bodyguards standing by, buying all of them the toys they were never able to get on their own: the capitalism, the consumerism, the pleasure and the power of owning a doll or a toy car or whatever, the power to change the whole universe and dispel all the frustrations of life with something they've seen every day of their lives and yet haven't ever had. Because my father, despite all the filth they put out about him from time to time, was hardly a Communist. He was far removed from Proudhon and Marx, or any sort of rough Buddhist or Christian sense of dispossession. He believed in supply and demand, competition, free trade, private property, consumption and savings, but above all he believed in prosperity and material well-being. Yes, you heard me right, for without that there is no way to be happy, no way to become something. That's why he despised film culture and those Mexican telenovelas that glorified poverty, that glorified a lack of responsibility, that repeated the same tired Christian messages of humility and servility that we were already well aware of. He detested the church, of course, which he considered to be the root of many evils, one of which he said was the distortion of Jesus's message to the forsaken: cast off your worldly possessions, give up what little you have, live on shit alone and endure it without complaint, because yours is the kingdom of heaven." At this point in his harangue, Arturo suddenly stopped cold. Then he returned to his seat before continuing. "Those children never got anything—not for Christmas, not for their birthdays—like what my father had given them, and they weren't going to forget it. More than just a toy, more than just the magnanimous beauty of trivial things, he gave them a sense of ownership, they actually *had* something . . . at the very least, my father gave them the opportunity to get what they wanted when they wanted it. They could choose any toy in a store from which they hadn't been able to choose anything ever before."

"I want this ball and those goalkeeper gloves," the boy with the cleft palate said to Arturo, his gums visible to all, juggling a soccer ball there in the toy store along with a presidential candidate, his bodyguards dressed in civilian clothes, and a swarming mass of children running up and down the aisles, shouting with glee, euphoric, carrying dolls, remote controlled cars, puzzles, and coloring books. Some of them were parading around with their selections, showing off the gifts Roberto Soto Gariglietti had promised them, while the *patrón* himself was about to pay the astonished cashier. "What are you gonna get?"

Until that moment, Arturo hadn't even realized that he still had yet to choose a toy of his own. He was absorbed in thought about all these San Nicolás children whom he'd just met for the first time today and whom he would never see again for any one of a number of reasons which, of course, escaped him then: things like social injustice, class distinctions, education, racism, discrimination, genetics, destiny, and so much else. Nevertheless, the fact was that he didn't even *want* to select a toy. Why would he? What good would it do? And then he realized why—oh the bitter surprise!—he already had them all.

"I don't want to disagree with you, Arturo, but doing what your father did with all his money and power . . . more than anything else, it must have given him a great sense of satisfaction."

Emerging from his daze or whatever it was, stuck to that shabby sofa and fixating on that distant visit to the toy store which only today, after so many years, he was remembering, Arturo responded to Maty indifferently, perhaps irritated at having to explain things to this damn petty bourgeoisie woman . . . things which, to him, were clearly evident:

"Don't confuse yourself, Matilde. That doesn't detract at all from the importance of what he did, which was to make us feel better about ourselves, more satisfied, less ashamed of what we were. If what you mean is that deep down, to him it was little more than an act of egoism, well yes, perhaps it was, but tell me this: what act is not? Even the most generous things we do give some pleasure back to the giver. Even sacrificing your life to save another would, to some degree, be a self-satisfying act; otherwise we simply wouldn't do it. Don't overlook that point, Matilde, regarding those false presumptions of Christian generosity. Look . . ." there Arturo stopped suddenly and went over to a corner where there were several stacks of books, looking more precarious than the Tower of Pisa. He selected one, letting the others tumble to the floor, and made his way back over to Matilde as he searched hastily for a particular passage. Upon locating it, he began to read excitedly: "'The belief that *altruistic* and *egoistic* are opposites, while all the time the *ego* itself is merely a *supreme swindle*, an *ideal* . . . There are no such things as egoistic or altruistic actions: both concepts are psychological nonsense . . . Morality, the Circe of mankind, has falsified everything psychological, root and branch—it has moralized everything, even to the terribly nonsensical point of calling love *unselfish*. A man must be firmly poised, he must stand securely on his two legs, otherwise he cannot love at all.' Do you know who said that over a hundred and forty years ago?"

"I have no idea."

"Nietzsche did, in his autobiography. Look: the issue here isn't to determine whether he acted altruistically or egoistically; rather, it's to acknowledge his actions, and the existence of love *in and of itself.* So what you have to see is that it's not so much the reasons or motivations behind Roberto Soto's rather unusual act, but the form of the act itself, the shape of this particular sort of love. Why take those children to buy some trivial gift instead of donating that money to a community leader? Why do that instead of giving a hundred-peso note to an old man on the street, or to a retirement home, for example? His caring or philanthropy or egoism or whatever you want to call it arose from his connection with the other; it took shape there, right in front of your very eyes, if you were looking for it. And do you know why? Because it strengthened him, it gave him a sense of self-reliance, just like Spinoza and Nietzsche. We are always moved by our own accomplishments, Matilde, by the intimate pleasure in accomplishing what we set out to do in life, by our will and desire to affirm ourselves—our power—in the eyes of the world. Nevertheless, what's really impressive is the notion (if you will) that you can make yourself happy while simultaneously making others feel that same way (instead of the opposite), and above all you can do it at a political level, in a truly democratic manner. Like he said, it's not about equality, it's about fairness and justice, about balancing pleasure, all of which (by the way) is profoundly anti-Nietzschean, because Nietzsche himself never believed in fairness, let alone democracy. Look, Maty: my father differed with Norberto Bobbio's opinion of equality even though he read and admired him. He believed in diversity and fairness, in the plurality of mankind and in respect for the other. Fairness and equality are not, you see, the same thing. Of the two concepts, equality is the more complex and subjective. However, he did believe (as Bobbio and Isaiah Berlin did) in liberalism at any cost, in genuine liberalism as the enemy of authoritarianism mired in tradition, although he wasn't quite sure that, in order to be considered liberal, you necessarily had to be a leftist. In that respect, my father was very much like Empedocles, leaning neither to the right nor to the left. He was more Dionysian . . . like Nietzsche, but mainly like Empedocles . . . everything that, to his ignorant contemporaries, of course, seemed to be the most absurd and grotesque way of doing things. A tauromachy of the Hellenic tradition. But that's a whole other story . . ."

"I think you've lost me there."

"What I'm trying to say is that only now, in 2025, having this rather odd conversation with you, am I learning that that afternoon after the meeting in San Nicolás, something I can't quite describe changed inside of me, and that until now, I either didn't realize it or simply didn't want to. Many of my own actions, and perhaps even my entire life, have something to do with that afternoon, and only now am I beginning to understand. Do you see? And thanks to you . . ." Arturo stopped here, waited for a moment, and then went on, a note of contrition or confession in his voice: "But I do know that you're not here to talk about my life; you're hear to learn about my father and how he founded the Partido del Fuego, about how difficult things were in the beginning, the signing of the petitions, the campaigns of the poor, their tiny political and labor rallies in the most distant, remote towns of Mexico, their ideological Syncretism, their philosophical vision, and all that sort of thing. Isn't that it?"

"Well, yes, but that doesn't necessarily mean that I wouldn't be interested in listening to you, in learning about what happened to you or how Soto Gariglietti influenced your manner of being . . . and about your painting, of course," Maty said with a conciliatory tone, trying to demonstrate to Arturo that it wasn't just his father who was important, but also himself; the painter of obscene, deformed figures, of monstrous, pre-Columbian masks, of recurring nightmares, of Chimeras, wild fantasies, oxen, dragons, of empty and shattered cities, of wounded, dismembered women or impossible whirlwinds and snowstorms like those of Joseph Turner, though all of that would of course be difficult to explain at that moment, there, in the improbable case that they should even be explained.

Maty took advantage of the pause in conversation to stand up, and—after casting a quick glance around the room—asked the painter with a smile:

"Would you show me your works?"

"If you like . . ." Arturo replied, unenthusiastically, and with that, the Agro artist took her hand and led her into the center of his studio, a movement to which Maty reacted as if she were shedding her own skin, though this made it rather difficult to seem unsurprised or unafraid, and also to not give the impression of being bothered by the painter's excessive sense of self-confidence . . . Ultimately, he was an old friend of her husband, someone in whom she should have the utmost confidence, just as You, dear Reader, were assured yesterday morning when she woke you with a tender kiss and told you that her first interview in Narvarte was in the morning, which is to say, today.

The workshop measured roughly 220 square feet, and it was built on the roof, up against the interior façade of the building. Its walls weren't actually walls; rather, they were fashioned out of plywood and sections of sheet rock, with a few uneven windows looking out over the avenue below. The floor was the same as the building's roof: reinforced concrete. Inside the workshop was a plethora of paintings spread out any which way, some leaning up against others, back-to-back, forming rows. The frames were covered in dust and some of the paintings simply did not seem to enjoy each other's presence; they lay there, unfinished or sometimes completed but always with a sense of infinite nostalgia or careless arrangement about them, a sort of human slime or rictus, a slack-jawed laziness that their author had impressed upon them perhaps even before they were born. In any case, canvasses upon canvasses occupied the entire room, from the standing rows on the floor to the ones hanging over each and every square inch of the walls, save the interior façade of the building itself. Since there were no skylights to be seen, it was impossible to know exactly where so much light was coming from, but it was clear that invincible beams of photons had flooded the entire room, leaving not a single corner in shadow, at least at that particular time of day. Along one edge of the studio, directly across from the spot where Arturo had stopped to display his works, was the one place where someone could sit down with relative comfort: a broken old sofa where he had had Matilde sit during this first visit.

"And you paint here?" Maty asked, gesturing to a couple of feet of empty space in front of her where an easel stood alongside a smallish table cluttered with brushes, charcoal, rags, plaster, bottles of turpentine and tubes of paint with their colorful contents spurting out: cobalt blue, Prussian blue, green cinnabar, scarlet, magenta, gold, ivory, carmine, vermilion, violet naphthol . . .

"Yes," Arturo said. Then he smiled before adding, "And that's where the women who model for me sit."

"They come here to model for you?" Maty asked, surprised.

"Yes, does that seem strange to you?"

"No . . ." she said, smiling. "Not at all."

After a short silence, Maty asked:

"Isn't it rather difficult to get them to come all the way up here?"

"As a matter of fact, it is," Arturo said with a chuckle, not quite knowing where his guest was going with all of these questions. "But if you really want to know, it ends up costing me nothing."

"How," she asked hesitantly. "And why?"

"Because the models who come here to pose for me are almost always my students from the Centro Cultural Helénico at the Universidad Nacional Autónoma de México, and that saves me a fortune, since I don't have to pay them. I suppose they consider it a privilege to come here and undress in front of me. Let's just say that they believe in my painting. They believe in what I do."

"So your father didn't leave anything to your mother and you?"

"Yes, he left us quite a bit, actually, but it's gone now. Or rather, we spent it all."

"Ah," was all that Matilde could bring herself to say as she went in search of the water glass she had left on the other side of the workshop, on the concrete floor next to the long, broken-down sofa. Suddenly, whipping around to once again face the naturalistic painter (as Arturo was often wont to call himself), Maty dared to ask:

"And how do you know so much about philosophy?"

"My father studied philosophy after he studied medicine and gave up the profession. It was some time after that when he got into politics, a fortuitous blessing late in his life. Were you not aware of that?"

"Honestly, no, I wasn't," Matilde admitted, a bit embarrassed, because—as she had recently learned—there were many things she was as yet unaware of, and it would take several more sessions with him in order to be able to formulate a clear, more precise idea of the man about whom she hoped to write her thesis: Roberto Soto Gariglietti, Arturo's father, and the founder of the PNFM.

"Yes, it's true, before dedicating himself to politics, before I was even born, my father taught pre-Socratic philosophy at the same university you're currently attending."

"That much I did know, yes. I mean, I studied it at UNAM. What I didn't know was that he also studied medicine and that he taught there . . ." She paused for a moment to reflect, and then suddenly asked, "The pre-Socratic philosophers, you say?"

"Yes, Parmenides, Anaximenes, Anaximander, Democritus, Empedocles, Anaxagoras, Heraclitus, all of them."

"Then perhaps we should start there. What do you think?"

"Study them, you mean?" Arturo asked, himself a bit flattered. "I suppose we should . . . I can't see any reason why not. It depends on how you want to focus your thesis; it depends on whether you're as interested in these philosophical aspects as my father was. I can only answer what you ask me, but if you really want my opinion, I suggest you do a little reading. Especially Empedocles of Agrigento, the philosopher who established the four ultimate elements. He is fundamental. And so is Parmenides, whom he once tried to refute, despite having been his disciple."

"Of course . . ." Maty remained thoughtful, hesitating, as if she were on the verge of formulating an idea that nevertheless would fail to summon up life, its forms, or anything else for that matter. It was a stammering that ultimately never came together; in fact, she had never even heard of those names; perhaps, in some distant manner, she could relate them to a few streets in Mexico City, though she didn't even know where they were. Finally, she simply said, "I think I should be going, Arturo. I'm already running late . . ."

"As you wish."

"When can I see you again?"

"I don't know, whenever it's convenient for you. I'm always here . . . painting. The models usually come around noon or a little before, but after lunch I'm usually alone, free . . . for you . . ." He laughed; Maty, though, didn't seem to notice (or perhaps she overlooked) the painter's deliberate slip, because she replied with a serious, expeditious question:

"How about Thursday? Could we schedule interviews for Tuesdays and Thursdays?"

"That sounds fine." The fact was that at this point, any day of the week would have sounded fine to Arturo, since although Tamara could drop by some afternoon, she would never enter his studio without knocking. He had learned this the hard way, because on one occasion, he had his nude model sitting on the sofa with her legs spread wide, and she was furious when Tamara suddenly entered unannounced. After that, his wife had promised that she would never interrupt him in his studio unless it was absolutely necessary.

"Well, good-bye and good luck. Maybe I'll get a chance to meet your wife next time."

"Yes, of course, if she comes by . . ." The painter smiled. "Give your husband my best: tell him that he needs to take a day off work and come buy a few paintings. He must be swimming in money, the bastard!"

Having said this, he accompanied her across the roof (a sort of broad, open, sunny terrace) to the landing that led to the stairs of the building. There they said good-bye with a kiss on the cheek, and Arturo—half in jest and half serious again—said, point blank:

"Perhaps one day you'd like to pose for me, Maty. I'd love to paint you."

Matilde laughed from the stairwell, two floors down, out of sight from one another, when she had a timid (or perhaps cautious) thought:

"Oh, I'm not much of a model, Mister Agro Painter."

"That should be up to me, shouldn't it?"

"That's what you think . . ."

To Arturo, she was already sounding very far away. The young woman's voice and laughter were blurring, running together, almost imperceptible from down there at bottom of the stairs, but they had already invaded his thoughts and piqued his curiosity, his fixation or perhaps his transgression: the thought of seeing foreign skin, with its sandy, marble tones, that contrast between Matilde's pubis and the pale, ermine whiteness of her crotch, her little feet which—truth be told—he wanted to gobble up like a tiny, hungry dog.

V

My name is Eusebio Cardoso and I am a novelist. Well, I'm off to a bad start. I am a professor of Mexican Literature, specifically of the so-called Novel of the Revolution. Such is my life, such is how I am able to support two families. The truth of the matter, though, is that I've only written two or three slim volumes which only a very few people have read in my own country, and even fewer still here in this other country, where

I write for nobody. However: I must also make it clear that I open the file on *Friction* only when I can or wish to do so, because sometimes months will pass during which I won't be able to get one goddamn line down on paper. I've already stated that my great discovery or consolation was knowing that even though I'm not doing what I most enjoy in life (to write, to fantasize), something uncomfortable has grown inside of me, something that has acquired both form and voice almost without me noticing it: perhaps it is that series of questions and prophetic moral dilemmas into which I bottle my faded characters—or should I say—into which they are bottled until the things they say and do suddenly and inevitably bubble up out of me, much to my own surprise. What's certain, though, is that these three substances (biography, morality, and prophecy) produce the books I have published and which very few people in my country have read, a country where—I must say in my own defense—nobody reads anything at all, save for gossip and rumor magazines about film and television stars. Here, on the other hand, in the Department of Foreign Languages and Literatures at Millard Fillmore University where I teach, my books have found three friends: Stefano, the Italian, and Javis and Tino, two Galicians who teach language to the same students who, two years later, will register for my class, in which they will learn the bitter ups-and-downs of the Mexican Revolution through the works of Azuela, Romero, Guzmán, Vasconcelos, and Campobello. But which one is my country now, if I do, in fact, still have one? At this point, I would have to say that it's Mexico. So what am I doing here? How the hell did I end up in this remote, isolated place? That's another story altogether, but I believe that—considering the way that these sorts of biographical things often go against my will—it would be better if I begin here (or stop here) at the beginning, with that fateful or blessed day (I don't know which) when I pulled up roots and left my first wife, Fedra, and my daughter Dulce, in Mexico City to attend a series of conferences on Mexican narrative organized by the Department of Romance Languages at the University of San Francisco, a place to which

I did not take my first wife, Fedra, though she desperately wanted me to. I didn't want her to think that I didn't bring her with me because I wanted to have fun without her in that marvelous city of art and perdition; rather, it was simply because I honestly wanted to spend just a few days on my own—perfectly, completely at ease and alone—reading Kerouac and Ferlinghetti, drinking nightly martinis, taking a random walk down a random street, visiting the Wharf, and above all to be free of the anguish of having to wake up and fix the baby's bottle every night at two and then again at six in the morning, the way it used to be, though now, in fact, I'm doing the same thing again with Emilio, my son with my second wife. But if you read carefully what I have just now written, you will see that I'm lying, because my first wife never even mentioned the possibility of bringing our daughter Dulce with us. In fact, it was quite the opposite: her mother (read: my ex-mother-in-law Dulce) was—according to my first wife—willing to take care of her for a few days if we needed her to. That's how it was, and lacking anything else to unload, all that remains to be said is that I went searching for myself; that is to say, I went looking for what ended up happening just a little bit later, and therefore I can honestly say that I simply wanted to go on that trip alone, perhaps because (though I don't know for certain) I wasn't on very good terms with Fedra at the time, or because I desired something that just wasn't there . . . and I found it. Who knows. Time has passed, and I still find it difficult to give a precise answer to this last question; I don't remember well the minutiae of the case—my conjugal case, I mean—with its roller coaster of daily fights and arguments. In any case, the fact of the matter is that I flew to San Francisco with the intention of spending five or six unforgettable days, and then returning with my arms filled with gifts, gifts which of course were meant as compensation designed to palliate the egoism which, in the end, resulted in my decision to make the trip alone, without my wife (by which I mean, without my first wife). And this brings us to the end of the story which I've postponed until now; that is, the origin or genesis of why the hell I'm in the United States, in this fucking country, working shoulder to shoulder with my colleagues, the Ecuadorian Gorgon and Santiago, the Chilean Nazi, trying to earn a living by teaching Mexican Literature to a group of novices who can barely even stammer out a word in Spanish, and even worse: going to great lengths to send a little money back to my daughter Dulce who was staying with her mother and her grandmother Dulce, which always rubbed my new wife the wrong way because, although she swears to the point of perjury that she understands why I have a moral obligation to send a few dollars to my daughter and her mother, deep down she detests the fact that I do it, turning into something of a moneygrubber every month when it comes time for me to send that check back to Mexico City. It's truly a laborious, frightful thing: I can't even describe the pressure and torture I go through each and every month. That notwithstanding, let me repeat: this is what I was looking for, and so as not to belabor the point here, I'll move on to describe how I met Irene, my current wife, at the conference organized by the Department of Romance Languages at the University of San Francisco, to which I was invited as the keynote speaker, to give a talk about Pancho Villa and how he was on the verge of perishing from being poisoned with very bad milk provided by a Japanese cook, an incident that very few historians are aware of, by the way.

I'll begin by confessing that seeing the shape of her ass (Irene's)—the perfection of that ass combined with the perfection of her body—was a determining factor, an incentive, but not the only one, for I don't want to give the impression that I focused solely on that, because in my heart I didn't fixate on that part of her at all (those of you who know me know this). I would also incur accusations of blatant hypocrisy, I think, if I didn't admit some attraction to Irene's thick, luxuriant backside, which—I must add—is perhaps just a bit too large for her svelte, sculptured body. But what is one to do? That is her body and that is her ass and I've always been attracted to both, which is to say, the apparent or real disproportion, which is fundamentally a perfection, from a certain point of view.

But again, so as not to delve too far and lose myself in the details that contradict the intimacy of writing and also that of this woman, her beautiful ass was the first thing that I saw as she walked into the conference hall, her hips swinging back and forth, always showing me her back (or her buttocks), but that alone would not have been enough. In fact, it was only when she turned around right in front of me, and I could finally see her round face and dark eyes, that I found myself struck, perplexed, and even a little bit scared. Actually, I was very scared. "But why?" you will ask. "Scared of what?" you will of course want to know. This is the hardest part to explain, but I will cut to the chase and not fall into the litany of digressions that have made so many contemporary novels and short stories unbearable to read, especially when I am forced to read them against my sovereign will. I was terrified because Irene, my current wife, looked identical (or almost identical) to the one person I love most in the world: my daughter Dulce, with the patent difference in age, of course. What I mean is that Irene could more or less be a perfect portrait of what I always imagined my young, sweet Dulce would look like as a young woman; that is, when she was twenty-four years old, twenty years after the day when I saw Irene for the first time at that conference in San Francisco, since my daughter was only four at the time and now she is eight and looking more like Irene than ever.

The situation, though, gets even more complicated, but here, yes, I will stop, so that we are not lacking in some Flaubertian sense of objectivity (if such a thing even exists) and similarly I will abound in everything that is exact and precise in certain details which, otherwise, would not permit an understanding of how I was finally able to abandon my adorable little girl and her mother for a young Cuban-American woman and for another country, which proffers little more than dollars while my colleagues, my students, and (most importantly, of course) those stupid academic committees in which I customarily participate, despite the fact that I detest them with all my soul, keep me from creating and teaching the things I enjoy most: frictions . . . Right now my only concern is recalling those insufferable, bureaucratic committees in which hundreds of hours are wasted while people like Gaudencia or Marco Aurelio Vasco-Osama—once so young and innocent, and still lovers of literature—have, as the years passed with ever-growing monotony and boredom, been reduced to mere bureaucratic academics living miserably at the expense of that same literature and on the exorbitant tuition paid by parents of students who want to learn Spanish: yes, of course, it's my own fault, I've been a member of the Departmental Curriculum Committee, a liaison for Multicultural/International Student Services, an honorary member of the Latin American Studies Committee, and a member of the Departmental Curriculum Committee's Internal Self-Study Team, and—just in case that weren't enough—I served as director of the Search Committee for the Foreign Language Department along with several other committees, the result of all this being that I was left without even the desire to sit down and write for a minute . . . if I ever actually had a minute to do so. But I did all this myself. *Mea culpa, mea culpa.* In these things—and only these things—I invested hundreds of hours during the past five hundred days and their respective white nights with good whiskey and cigarettes and landscapes of well-traveled streets invaded by snow, after putting the final touch on that long saga which left me deflated, having only read, (that I know of) three muddled works (one of them by a benevolent, autistic giraffe, who I'll tell you about soon enough). My brain very nearly boiled over, it atrophied, and it might even have been transformed without my knowing into a head of lettuce or flan, something shapeless and gelatinous, something in a pathetic state, a state of putrefaction.

But let me return to my story with Irene, because the rest of it (the part about the departmental politicking and machinations) will take some time to tell, though it is quite amusing, to the point of pissing yourself in laughter . . .

It was during one of those comings-and-goings, in the midst of one of those formidable swings of the hips, that Irene and I made eye contact, smiled to one another, and introduced ourselves; in fact, she took a long, expeditious look at the name tag hanging around my neck before telling me that I had the same name as her father, and that, of course, it was a very unusual name indeed: Eusebio, Eusebio, she murmured, barely pursing her beautiful crimson lips. But the chitchat was interrupted when we noticed that a conference session was about to begin, and all the other invited professors were returning to their seats in the lecture hall. She said it was a pleasure to meet me, and then she went away. It wasn't until later that afternoon that I approached her again and invited her out for a bite to eat. But the truly odd thing was that she replied with an absolute directness that she was not, in fact, hungry, but that she did want to go out because there was something truly quite important that she needed to tell me. "To discuss," actually, is what she said, leaving me astonished, since we hadn't even gotten to know each other yet, and already there was something we needed "to discuss," something quite specific, hence her need to advertise it in advance. Although I had specifically asked her out "to eat," she suggested we go out for drinks in the city, and that is how, at eight o'clock that night, we ended up in a lovely little restaurant by the bay on Fisherman's Wharf, where we ordered (again without coming to an agreement) a bowl brimming with exquisite clam chowder which we quickly dispatched along with a plate of fried calamari and a bottle of red Napa wine which I ordered myself. It was during dinner that I began to realize, little by little, why Irene had agreed so readily to go out with me despite having a number of reasons for not doing such a thing. I'll list them here. First, the fact that I never removed my wedding ring; I either forgot about it, or perhaps it simply didn't matter to me, but then again, maybe I did so on purpose (although I very much doubt this latter explanation, as it isn't exactly my style of doing things, so I prefer either of the two former options, though I must admit I'm not certain about either of them). Second, Irene had a fiancée, a Gringo who loved her passionately and had received his PhD in literature from the same university as she. The third thing working against us (or, as I should humbly say, against me) was the fact that there was (and of course there still is) a twenty-year difference in our ages, as well as the fact that—whether it's nature or my own ancestors who are to blame—I am not what some would consider a particularly attractive man; however, it was precisely my physical appearance and the circumstances we found ourselves in which, in the end, prevailed against all the probabilities—or, as they say in English, "against all odds," which is much more linguistically precise than the Spanish term *probabilidad*, which is ambiguous and can signify any one of a number of things—and I ended up with a beautiful, young, sexual woman like Irene, with an ass and a body as amazing as hers, who ordinarily would never have paid attention to an unattractive (though not incredibly ugly) married man twenty years her senior. But what aspect of my physical appearance have I confessed to, other than my mild ugliness? Nothing, save for what I've already mentioned, and the fact that I was—as Irene said, holding her glass of wine in a trembling hand—exactly like her father, even in age. I was astonished by the revelation, so much so that I couldn't help but contemplate her there, sitting across the table from me, witnessing what I could swear was my daughter Dulce twenty years into the future, listening to her silky voice, looking into her eyes, observing Dulce's mouth and neck, and her hand gestures, because even then, and despite the twenty years between the two of them, the similarity was already quite astounding. I couldn't contain myself (though perhaps the wine had something to do with that) and so I showed her a picture of my little girl that I kept and still do keep in my wallet, and Irene—without so much as a word between the moment I showed her the photo and the moment she accepted it with her thin, tremulous fingers—was petrified . . . or nearly so. She dropped her nearly empty glass, spilling a few drops of wine onto the tablecloth, and the first words out of her mouth were: "We're almost identical; I mean, she looks exactly like I did when I was her age." And then she opened her purse and took out a photo of a young girl, five or six years old, embracing a man of perhaps twenty-seven who was clearly her father, and who (I must confess) looked extremely similar to me—at least, similar to me when I was that age, since I've grown a bit in the waistline, thanks to alcohol and the Wendy's hamburgers which I love, despite Irene's protests to the contrary. But one other detail is missing, and perhaps it is more important than I led you to believe when I mentioned it in passing, and that is the issue of our then-current circumstances. This doesn't have to do with the common things we've found in our life from time to time; rather, it's a very different thing which I'll tell you about now: my lovely Irene had only recently (no more than a year before we met, I believe) lost her father who of course was still a relatively young man at the time (my age, in fact, forty-three years old) in the most tragic circumstances you might imagine—in the strict sense of how I understand the term today, after having read the Greek legends—which is to say, it was the result of a bee sting, something which nobody, not even he himself, knew he was allergic to. It happened during a family vacation, and so his daughter was unfortunately present for everything, or almost everything, up to when he was admitted into the hospital. After that, the next time she saw her father, he was in a coffin. With tears welling up in her eyes, though she didn't let a single one fall, she told me that night at the restaurant in San Francisco:

"And besides the name and the physical similarities, Eusebio, you have his sense of humor. How can I say it . . . it's in your gestures, your tics, everything. Strange, right? Don't you think?" And then I, impelled either by emotion or alcohol or the ardor between my legs, took her hand underneath the table and the wine-stained tablecloth and squeezed it, despite the fact that I knew full well that I hadn't yet had the opportunity to demonstrate my true sense of humor or any of my many tics (all of which are quite irritating, by the way). But what did my action imply? Solidarity? Compassion? Affection? Pity? Concern? Desire? Love? The urge to fuck? I suppose it was all of the above, a mixture of everything that my beloved Empedocles would simply consider Love, and which I will discuss further in the upcoming pages.

However, for those who are paying attention, there is (or could be) an objection to the conclusion that my own life is the reason why I ended up teaching here, in the United States, married to Irene with a son, a second little sprout, as attractive and astute as his mother. And the objection is thus: if Dulce, my daughter, is as beautiful as I've said she is, and she doesn't even remotely resemble her father, which is to say, me, who is ugly or at least somewhat so, then by default, she must resemble her mother, and if that were the case, then logically my first wife Fedra should look very similar to Irene, which simply isn't the case. If what I'm drawing up for you in a matter of sentences is really the case, then who the hell does my daughter look like? Quickly, I believe she looks most like her grandmother Dulce, whom I previously mentioned in passing: my handsome ex-mother-in-law, who at some providential moment was willing to take care of her granddaughter Dulce but didn't end up doing so on account of me, who chose to run off to a conference in San Francisco all by myself, which resulted in the subsequent ups-and-downs of this particular case.

To the aforementioned (and patently evident) objection, I'd like to add another one, dear Reader: the fact that if Eusebio, Irene's father, looked so much like me, and therefore wasn't very handsome, then Irene should look rather like her mother, something which (I knew at once) also wasn't the case. So the only solution to this part of the riddle is that Irene had, in fact, been adopted by Cuban-American parents, and that she (I would later learn) had actually been born in Mexico.

To bring this sketch to a close, I will simply say that after that encounter on Fisherman's Wharf, which was followed by a long stroll along the bay, things continued to happen, one after another, leading (inevitably, of course) to my separation from Fedra, the supremely difficult decision to leave my daughter Dulce (not my mother-in-law Dulce) and eventually to my marriage to Irene in San Francisco: a strange substitution (I know) of a young girl for a young woman, because even today, when I return home after spending three hours in one of those abominable committees,

I am always amazed to see the incredible similarities between the two of them . . . and that, of course, results (for better or for worse) in bringing back many memories of the two of us together, my daughter and I chasing each other down the hallway of our house in Coyoacán, playing hide-and-seek among the rattan furniture, spending hours sprawled out on the spongy carpet putting together a Sleeping Beauty puzzle, wrestling and horsing around, listening to songs by Cri-Cri the singing cricket, going hand in hand for ice cream at Siberia, buying a globe at the plaza and smothering her with kisses, perfectly happy with the heavenly gift which today seems so very far away from me.

6
(THURSDAY, JUNE 15TH, CONTINUED)

You leave the fifth floor of the building in Narvarte, the building you've known for years now, dear Reader, the site of so many memories of drunkenness and poetry, that studio fashioned out of asbestos and plywood and situated on top of a roof in the *Distrito Federal*, that pigsty in which Tamara and Arturo have lived for so long that you can no longer remember exactly whether you would come to visit your friend, the Agro painter, there before he married Tamara, or if his wife had always been a presence there, along with that son of a bitch who right now is balling your wife though he'll still call you "brother" and look "happy" when you're sharing a bottle of Hornitos tequila, the bastard, the traitor. But what's happened? How did it all begin? How could it have happened? Since when? Why has Matilde done this? Why, since it was only yesterday that she told you she loved you with a kiss and a tender squeeze of the hand? What does this whole, tangled mess mean, dear Reader? Are you going a bit crazy? Is it perhaps real? Is this nausea—this story that you're reading—real? And the viscosity, the headache, the hell that's populating your brain, your chest, your ears . . . is that real? And the tears staining your face? Are you crying? Dreaming? Are you certain that you're not dreaming, dear Reader? Would you swear to it? Are you quite sure that you're not reading? Are you not stuck in some sort of depraved, sickening friction, stuck in a story that some son of a bitch is writing for you, about you, or against you, right at this very moment? What the hell is going on, my unwitting friend? What is happening at this exact time and place in the universe . . . out there . . . or in the universe . . . here within? Have you continued reading, voraciously, in a daze, or have you simply watched as your woman is lifted up, seized, grasped, bound by the robust arms of your friend the painter, the traitor himself whom you've seen with your own eyes, panting, moaning, though not in pain but in pure, unadulterated pleasure, his face flushed with bliss, the way you never did, you impotent Reader of *Friction*? Are you still reading this? In spite of everything? Yes, I'm talking to you . . . perhaps you've looked over these lines or even gotten into your car and driven off to your luxury apartment without knowing exactly what is impelling you to do so, why you're taking this route and not another? But where else could you go? Nowhere, that's for sure; there is no way you could go to your parents' house or a church or a theater so you can cry in silence, wallow in your own compunction, coat the armrests of the seat next to you with the snot pouring from your nose . . . You have to—you must—return home (the place you both call home, of course), to your little house, your love nest in Las Águilas, that hideaway where you and Matilde have lived your smug little lives ever since you were married, and which (of course) her dying father left her in his will. Well, he was dying then (when the two of you were engaged), and today he is very dead, buried even, but that is another story altogether, one with which you need not concern yourself, since right now a taxi driver is passing in front of you on Avenida Universidad and you're about to hit him with a defensive honk of the horn, but instead you avoid him with a skillful maneuver borne directly from the perplexity of pain, the instinctive jabs which you feel pounding away at your ribs. But, of course, you still don't quite believe everything you've seen, you're skeptical, and meek as a lamb because you're faced with this horrific, appalling, ruinous thing, isn't that it? And because human beings do not have it in their nature to be so vile, so despicable as that (though a German philosopher with a deep knowledge of the subject once said that the human being is an abyss). But haven't you just seen it—or perhaps read it—with your own eyes? Think. Think. Sit at this traffic light and think. Take advantage of the pause. Think. Did you see it with your own eyes or did you perhaps read it with your own eyes? In any case, it is the truth, and at this point the end result is the same: it doesn't matter, because it's you and only you who knows, you're the one who's collapsing, you're the one who's beaten down, you're the one who's fucked. In the end it's all about you, furious Reader, and the vehicle of your discovery (whether your seeing eyes or your reading eyes) changes absolutely nothing, nothing at all, because ultimately the only thing that matters—the only thing that counts—is the fact that they've made a cuckold out of you less than a year after your wedding, when you felt happier, more exuberant, and more powerful than ever before . . . right?

VII

The spring semester is the most difficult time during the academic year, at least in the southern United States. With all the other universities in the world (with the exception of UNAM, which never paid me a cent), this does not to seem to be the case, but here, at Millard Fillmore University in Virginia, that's the way things are. First and foremost, it's difficult because it would seem that the students have been counting down the days of winter to the point where suddenly, from one day to the next, they shed the heavy corduroy pants, wool sweaters, and gloves of January, February, March, and April and replace them with whatever skimpy items they have on hand: short miniskirts that reveal everything, from the turquoise, violet, and coral painted toenails to the hem tight around the femur and the supple curves of the greater trochanter, tight cutoff shorts that expose a thin slice of the lower gluteals, spaghetti-strapped shirts or thin cotton blouses that show off bare navels and bellies the color of golden sand dunes. Starting with spring break, and even before that, the students flood the well-manicured lawn of the quad where they stretch out on the grass to nap or read, play frisbee, or simply toss a ball back and forth for hours, absorbing every last particle of sunlight as if it were necessary for life itself. Perhaps scenes like this are not uncommon in the United States, but to a Latin American man forging a home in this northern land (or should I say the southern part of North America), it is a sight to see, in both senses of the verb; first as a classic spectacle (a typically American folk tradition) but also for the sight I've just described: toasted bodies, young bodies, thin, elastic, majestic bodies, scattered across the quad, offering themselves up to Inti, the venerable Incan god of the sun. Sometimes I even fancy myself as Constantine Cavafy, with notebook in hand, sitting on top of the rocky outcropping there on the quad, amazed and hungry for the light, describing in detail what I observe through my tiny binoculars, my prick hot and swollen, my hands sweaty and sticky. The only difference, of course, is that Cavafy watched the boys whereas I observe the girls.

Stefano, the Italian, and Javis and Tino, the Galicians, and I await the season with delight, vehemence, and a Greek sense of *enthousiasmos*, after having endured the southern winter with partisan stoicism. This past winter, especially, was a nightmare that wore on and on to the point where, on two occasions, a couple of days of sun were hit—pow!—with a blizzard that left the sky cloudy for a week or two.

Every half hour or so, Tino and Javis will drop by my office and make faces and hand gestures that simply mean, run, you idiot, come with us, get out of there, out of this hovel of academic bureaucracy (which is little more than a bunker filled with books) and come see something absolutely extraordinary, though of course I already know what it is, or I can at least hazard a guess. And that, dear Reader, is how one comes to contemplate all these astounding and astonishing things at Millard Fillmore: there are students here who choose simply to lounge around the quad in string bikinis and thongs which (in the best of cases) are flesh-colored, girls rubbing themselves with suntan oil in plain view of their classmates who, by the way, seem completely comfortable with the whole situation. But what about their siblings, cousins, relatives, and fellow church members? I find myself wondering as I watch these young men, lounging around the lawn, absorbed in their notebooks or chatting with one another as if nothing at all were going on, as if having a headless, life-size inflatable doll lying next to them on the grass were a perfectly normal thing. So of course I am constantly intrigued by the following question, one which I have turned over in my head time and time again: are they really such assholes? Do they not even realize what is lying there on the ground next to them, or—having seen it on an almost daily basis—do they simply regard it as unimportant? Have they forgotten what they are, and what they can become; which is to say, the arcane pleasures and possibilities of a much sweeter amorous education? Are they not aware of the temple—the golden pavilion—that hibernates there between the iliac crest and the posterior inferior pelvis? The peculiar thing (I don't want to call it contradictory) about the case of these beautiful Viking-like women is that some of my own students and former students also frolic in the grass like a herd of hogs in the mud; the odd mishmash of their genetic Puritanism, liberalism, and feminism at any cost—according to university gossip—makes them the hardest ones to bang, to screw, to *coger* as I would say, or *follar*, which is the word Javis and Tino use in their own particular brand of Spanish (the intersection of nomenclatures always being an interest of mine). Irene and I, when we get together with Stefano and Stephany, his lovely wife, and the invariably present Galicians, enjoy intellectual wordplay and punning jokes, which make this relatively tasteless American life a bit more bearable, a bit more passable, as we say. For example, upon hearing a uniquely Mexican turn of phrase (*chingar* instead of *joder*, for example, which is to the American *screw* what *shag* is to the Brits), they will laugh among themselves and say, "Goddamn it, Eusebio! Aren't you required to teach established, normative Spanish?" To this, I will always reply, "Ah, you're mistaken, Tino. The Spanish we speak in Mexico is *enriched*. But you may stick to the standardized version, if you prefer." And then I proceed to explain to them (or rather, I "educate" them, as I told Irene later that night in bed): "What could be more enriching, Tino, than being able to say, with the same natural facility, *milpa* or *maizal*, and know and understand that they mean both maize and corn? Is an owl a *tecolote* or a *búho*? Does *zacate* or *yerba* grow on your lawn? Are those *zopilotes* or *buitres* circling the sky above that carcass? Are those baggy clothes *guangos* or *holgados*? Do you use a pestle with a *molcajete* or *mortero*? When your plane hits turbulence, does it *zangolotea* or *sacude*? Does a man with an enlarged prostate use the bathroom *seguido* or *a menudo*? Do you buy rice in a *costal* or a *saco*? When it's cold, do you throw on a *sarape* or a *manta*? On Thanksgiving, do you eat *guajolote* or *pavo*? Do tortillas *tostarse* or *tatemarse*? Does a running back *zafarse* or *soltarse* from a would-be tackler? Does a homeless person sleep on a *petate* or an *estera*? On a windy day, will a child fly a *papalote* or a *cometa*? And all of this—of course!—according to your whims or desires, silly Tino. In the summertime, do you wear *huaraches* or *sandalias*? Do you go swimming at the *alberca* or the *piscina*? Do acrobats turn *maromas* or *vueltas*? Will untreated lumber *se pandea* or *se comba* if left out in the rain? When you wake up in the morning, is your hair *mechudo* or *greñudo*? Is that a *chapulín* or a *saltamontes* hopping around in the grass? Are those nippers, whippersnappers, *escuincles*, or *niños* there in the schoolyard? If you want some real fun, Tino, I can offer many more examples of the Spanish language's 'rich synonymy.' I'm willing to bet that you don't even know what half of these words mean. I bet you barely even recognize them, and that you certainly wouldn't use them." That seemed to quiet him down for a bit, and he had a pensive look on his face, eager to change the subject. Stefano and I will then have a beer out on the deck, either at my house or his, and sometimes even at Tino and Javis's house. Although they're in their mid-thirties, they're not married and they live together, and—as far as I know—they're not fags, though that is still up for debate: as they say, appearances can be deceiving . . .

But getting back to the subject of spring and the difficulties it presents to professors who, like me, are married though not castrated and therefore prone to strong erections every time we cross the quad, taking it all in, before entering the classroom to find at least five or six girls who could be my daughters (well, I exaggerate) just as easily as they could be stunning Playboy models (and on this last point, no, I am not exaggerating). But returning again to the issue that truly vexes me, the fact is that spring is such a difficult time (April is the cruelest month) because there is, quite simply, nothing at all to do about it, save to watch and endure, for it would never occur to them to say something to you, and they would never dare to insinuate something. Not one coquettish flirt, not one expression of femininity is ever directed at you or your colleagues. Nothing. It's as if you were a forty-year-old eunuch, not unlike (by the way) my colleague Marco Aurelio, who specializes in Golden Age Spanish literature. There isn't even a way to find out whether they like you even a little bit (platonically, of course) or if they simply view you as a homosexual or some second-rate mentor. Everything gets complicated and refined if, aside from being her professor, you're (as I've said) over forty years of age . . . and if they find out you're married with lovely little children (which, to these young students, seems like the epitome of romanticism, heroism, or who knows what sort of madness or conservative delirium), that makes you, their professor, something of an irreproachable angel, a sack of virtues, an unattainable soul who has eyes for no one other than your wife, who's so miraculously fortunate to have found you, of course, before any of them could begin to fixate on you. And look, dear Reader, it's not that I don't adore Irene—don't get me wrong—it's not that I don't love her, that I'm not as excited by her as ever, but I simply cannot prevent myself from observing and confirming what leaps into view every morning on campus in May and June: so much beauty, so many young people scattered across the lawn, though at the same time I see so much accumulated stupidity and myopia, so much incomprehensible Puritanism, which I still haven't gotten used to, given the fact that in Mexico, where I taught before coming here, more than one student flirted with me, and once or twice I even slept with one, but . . . let me clarify: they were former students of mine, and for that reason I'm not embarrassed to admit it. But, even if they were current students, I don't think I would have been embarrassed then either; in fact, there are some professor friends of mine who have slept with many of their students, and often for reasons that don't always necessarily obey the pure impartiality which governs desire and attraction between two human beings. In fact, it is a completely different set of reasons, one which I don't want to get into, as I usually prefer to avoid moral discussions. But all things considered, not even my former students notice me, and at the end of the semester I won't receive anything more than a note full of *bonhomie* and respect that I was their best professor, or that they learned much about Villa and Zapata in my class, something which—but between you and me, dear Reader—I don't know whether to take as an insult or flattery from these sensual, terrifying Viking women whom I've been charged with teaching Mexico's Youth Athenaeum movement and the Novel of the Mexican Revolution. According to Irene, at least one of them had to be in love with me, even if I wasn't even aware of it. Who knows! At best, I'm a sucker, an idiot, a blind and ignorant man, but the fact is that Irene doesn't believe me that nothing ever happens, in my departmental bunker or anywhere else for that matter: no indecent proposals, no appreciative kisses, absolutely nothing, although I have to admit that yes, at times, I would have been happy to receive something. So what can I do if Irene doesn't believe me? Not much . . . or perhaps there is: perhaps something can be done, perhaps (if I wanted to) I could remedy the situation. But how? It might sound barbaric, but right now I'm reminded of a Paul Auster novel where something unlikely though with a sense of probability happens, and if I only dared to emulate it, it could perhaps result in something positive for our already excellent conjugal relations. If memory serves me right, the protagonist of that novel was, like myself, hopelessly in love with his wife and would never have been unfaithful, although she—with her personal code of ethics—believed otherwise. This woman's conviction is so strong that, in the end, it all but overwhelms her own will, and her husband decides to commit adultery so as not to defraud her of her conviction and so she won't leave him owing to his foolish abstention. But I'm exaggerating all of this, of course: Irene is in no way a woman on the verge of jealous rage (although, yes, she is quite peculiar), nor have I had to go to such extremes in order to authenticate my wife's doubts about my own fidelity. I will speak about this burning subject tomorrow or some other time, because now it is time to leave my bunker here at the Department of Foreign Languages to go see Emilio and have a glass of whiskey (actually Scotch, since they like to be specific about it here) on the rocks and to spectate and even participate in the architectural projects that take place on the square carpet lining the floor of their rec room. As we sit there, building a skyscraper out of hundreds of tiny, colored blocks, I think of Mexico, I think of my daughter Dulce, suddenly a stranger to me, and I think about how I would like to have them both (Emilio and her) here with me, but such a wish is so absurd that I might as well imagine myself as a Mormon with two wives under the same roof, or even in the same bed.

8
(THURSDAY, MAY 4TH)

"I'll explain my theory on colors, Maty, which is directly related to the Agro movement, something you've heard about, of course," Arturo said at four thirty that Thursday afternoon when his old friend's wife appeared there on his roof, this time dressed in a thin white dress that reached her feet, in the Oaxacan or Yucatán style, with short, loose sleeves that lent (or seemed to lend) a note of freshness to her armpits, to her alabastrine neck, and to her half-exposed collarbones, exposed because that type of dress was designed to be constantly slipping down off the shoulders, an effect matched by the pretty pair of sandals she was wearing, leaving her small, delicate feet open to the air.

"Well, I have to admit I've never heard of such a movement, Arturo."

"Oh yes, it was a group, Matilde, a group of painters," he said, directing her attention to a couple of the paintings. "At one time, not too long ago, we were all friends. We traveled together through Sonora looking for peyote, but we don't see each other anymore, we don't support each other; in fact, all we have in common is the name, which nobody has seen fit to remove, because it seems to be the only good thing left to us from that bitter adventure and the rituals we organized there in the desert with the Yaqui Indians. Some of them don't even paint, can you imagine? Of course they call themselves painters: Agro painters. But ultimately, everything has to do with Empedocles of Agrigento's theory of color, which I learned from my father when I was a child and which I later passed on to that band of charlatans who haven't completed a single painting for several years."

"And what does that theory consist of?" asked Maty, half curious, half indifferent, since she herself didn't know whether it was of any real importance, or if she should simply let inertia and courtesy take their course.

"According to the philosopher, there are four basic elements or 'roots,' which are never created or destroyed; rather, they are simply engaged in an eternal process of being mixed and separated. All the others that we see and perceive are something like an illusion of the senses. These four elements are the sun, the earth, the heavens, and the sea, although they are also referred to as fire, earth, air, and water. Occasionally, they are known by the gods who represent them; Zeus, for example, would be fire, Hera would be the air, Nestis the water, and Aidoneus, the earth.

These can be interpreted to such a degree that they can appear altered to the point that the elements seem to have changed, although in the strictest Empedoclean sense they have not, because they are indestructible and simply being recycled."

"But that's just basic physics, Arturo: the conservation of matter and energy. Nothing is destroyed, but everything transforms." Maty continued to make her way through the workshop, occasionally stepping over an empty frame or some other unused object lying on the floor.

"Yes, but remember that Empedocles lived in the fifth century B.C., and there was much left to learn . . . For many, he was the Da Vinci of his time. A Greek Newton, even, with the added fact that Empedocles was above all a Humanist and a thaumaturge: a doctor, a mystagogue, an inventor, philosopher, biologist, politician, and astronomer, among many other things."

"Okay then . . ." interrupted Matilde, so that the artist would not have to finish enumerating the network of connections.

"So Empedocles offers a pictorial method of illustrating how an infinite variety of possibilities can arise from these four basic elements or 'roots,' which are—for the Agro painters—the four fundamental colors which you will see repeated over and over again in nearly all of my works." Here Arturo stopped, turned around, and walked calmly over to the same long, threadbare sofa that sat along the opposite wall of his workshop; he lit a cigarette and, again, without offering one to Matilde, inhaled a lungful of smoke and sat down, his legs spread, motionless. "Look, according to this method, which was sort of a guideline for the Agro painters, these four colors can be combined to produce anything that exists in the world, and for that reason, painters are creators in the strictest sense of the word, which is to say, we create and place in the world everything that exists: trees, men, women, wild animals, birds, fish, stars . . . all the monsters and the gods themselves. Everything, Matilde. Nevertheless, similarities with the philosopher take on a much greater precision because in their own time, ancient Greek painters only worked with four colors: white, black, yellow, and red; the same four which—as you've no doubt noticed—are the prevailing colors in almost all of my own paintings . . ." From his seated position, Arturo gestured towards the same two works that Maty had observed herself last Tuesday, right there in front of the sofa where she had just sat down. One of the paintings displayed two women embracing each other about the waist, one of them apparently ashamed, hiding her head behind her friend's back while the other one looked out at the viewer; they both were naked and the color of their skin varied between ocher and a lemon-yellow. The other painting showed some sort of shyster or sleazy bureaucrat with bullish face, seated at a writing desk in front of a yellow sea, probably a minotaur tired of his daily work routine. "The problem would come later, when other philosophers wanted to determine whether Empedocles thought that particles of those four elements actually combined with one another, or did they simply come together, sticking to each other in some imperceptible way."

"And?"

"Well, apparently he believed that they came together but that the human eye alone could not distinguish that union, and for that reason, people like Aristotle said Empedocles had been mistaken, although the fact is that he was only partially mistaken, since his belief was that everything was united or separated according to its passion or movement, and that therefore the four elements, although mixed together, were indissoluble. So Empedocles reduced the changes to a mechanical, colloidal mixture, something more or less limited; something akin to a superpositioning or juxtapositioning of particles. Pictorially, Maty, we could say that even though, for him, there were combinations and mixtures, they extended only to a certain point, one which depended on the degree of porosity that the elements had. For example, water mixes well with wine, but not with oil, because their respective porosities are not symmetrical to one another. Therefore, according to Empedocles, everything in this world depends on its porosity, on a body's actual capacity to penetrate another, and this of course leads to his theory of Love, but that is a separate question which I'll talk with you about at another time . . ." After a moment of silence, Arturo added a caveat, as if to make the origin or purpose of the lesson clear: "This is more or less the pictorial creed of the Agro painters, Maty: the desire to maintain the simplest, mechanical mixing of the colors, among other things, such as the medieval notion foreshortening or decreasing the size of an image in perspective, which of course is nothing new, since it comes from Gauguin and some other Postimpressionists and Fauvists who wanted to maintain objects in their primitive, indigenous appearance."

"But tell me, Arturo," Matilde cut in sharply. "Even though you know full well that the colors are combined, you prefer to believe or imagine that they only join or separate according to their porosity?"

"Exactly. Everything is united. The particles of paint are only stuck together, even if it appears that they've suddenly become mixed, and this is the aspect that we want to stand out, maintaining a certain rudimentary quality, a certain underlying primogenial texture, like the Fauvists, though our subjects are more or less modern; or rather, an arbitrary mix of archaic and modern subjects. That's where the atypical resistance you noted arises." Arturo took out his cigarette case again, and this time he offered one to his guest, who nevertheless rejected the offer, and not before taking a glance at her watch. "It's a matter of having your eyes deceive you, Matilde. They deceive us and all of a sudden we think we're seeing a true mixture there on the painter's palette, as I've said."

"It sounds like an antiquated madness to me." Matilde smiled, still holding her mini tape recorder, which she hadn't even switched on yet, given the fact that she wasn't even sure whether or not to begin the interview (or if she had actually already begun it), which she had intended to conduct with the son of the deceased Roberto Soto Gariglietti. What did all this have to do with politics or democracy in Mexico?

"According to Empedocles, and later Democritus, the human eye is made up of two of the four elements—of fire and water—and these represent the colors of white and black, respectively. Those are the basic colors, while the other two—the yellow and the red—are the simple colors. Are you following me? The sense of sight, then, arises from the basic colors . . ."

"So shouldn't we see everything in black and white?"

"Not exactly, since according to Empedocles, the eye also has a bit—just a tiny little bit—of earth and air in it, which gives it the ability to perceive yellow and red."

"So what you're saying is that the eyes themselves emit those colors, yes?"

"Look: in those days, there were three theories, three schools of thought. One group believed that the eye was the agent that emitted rays—in other words, pure fire—towards objects. Another group believed the opposite; that is, they believed the eye received certain effluvia emitted by the objects themselves. The third group, which included Empedocles and later Plato, believed that both the object and the eye emitted rays and effluvia, which mixed together, creating what we know as sight or vision. He explains this in one of his most famous dialogues."

"I'm not familiar with it, Arturo."

"But, Meno . . . do you agree with Empedocles that certain effluences are given off by all existing things?"

"Certainly."

"And that there are pores into which and through which the effluences pass?"

"Yes, of course."

"And that some of the effluences will fit into the pores, whereas others are too large or too small?"

"That's true."

"So color, then, is an effluence of form, commensurate with sight, and perceived by that sense."

Arturo paused here, took a breath, and reflected for a few seconds before continuing on, a bit more lightly now:

"Empedocles also had a theory that it could be the essence of all thought. He states, and repeats time and again, that like is always perceived by like, and that similarity always attracts similarity . . ."

"And what is that supposed to mean?" Meno asked, moving from her place and looking at her wristwatch again . . . something uncertain but intriguing was going on: she was behind schedule, but fortunately, at that moment, it was neither hot nor muggy, something she had been afraid of, having decided to wear that loose, comfortable Oaxacan dress to her second visit with the painter. Experiencing the heat of the previous afternoon had put her on guard.

"Well, if the eye is comprised with more water and fire than air and earth, then we will see things that correspond primarily to them, things that end up being the most compatible: white and black."

"But that's not the case," argued the young Meno, slightly agitated by what seemed to be a series of trivialities and absurd little things that had nothing to do with her reasons for being there: Arturo's father, his life, his work, his disappearance, his roller-coaster ride through Mexican politics, from standing in opposition to the PRI, the PAN, and the PRD to the founding of the Partido de la Naturaleza y el Fuego Mexicano. "I see many different shades of color, Arturo."

"Well, that may be what you think, but there are only four . . ."

"Of course. Always according to Empedocles . . ." she said facetiously. Then she suddenly stood up from the sofa, a bit annoyed, upset, eager to begin the interview once and for all. "If there are four roots and four colors, then we should only be able to see and perceive those same four things. Period."

Upon seeing Arturo, her mentor, smiling with delight, still watching or admiring her, sitting there, speechless, right in front of her, Meno, the disciple, turned the screw once more:

"What do you say to that?"

"I say that you have a point," Arturo finally replied, satisfied that the student was applying herself, demonstrating more persistence and interest than she had during the previous lesson that past Tuesday in Narvarte. "Theophrastus, another philosopher, made more or less the same argument as you. If like is always perceived by like, as Empedocles theorized, then how is it that we may perceive mixed colors, such as gray?"

Upon seeing or simply feeling that they weren't really getting anywhere (nowhere that Meno considered relevant or even intelligible with regard to the Agro painters or this philosophy that Arturo was so insistent upon discussing), the young woman suddenly resolved that it was simply time to walk away, though not before asking her host (who had demonstrated his words via some of his paintings) merely to verify what he appeared to be hinting at: that the Agro painters were (as her husband believed) truly crazy, and that prolonged exposure to peyote and desert sun had combined to toast their brains a long time ago.

"Well, I have to leave a bit early today, so why don't you show me what you're working on?"

"What a shame that you have to leave!" Arturo said with an almost pained look on his face, or perhaps it was a bit of histrionic helplessness, but nevertheless, in his heart (and almost without recognizing it) he was truly upset: he was beginning to enjoy the student more than the lesson.

"But we'll see each other again."

"Oh I know," Arturo ventured in a hungry, wolfish voice. "The next time, you can pose for me. What do you think?" The question was as smooth as it was cutting; in his demand was a desire to temper it with an indistinguishable (very fine) mixture of command and humor, of seriousness and levity designed to confuse Meno and prevent her from leaving for just a few more moments, moments she might spend walking around the painter's studio a few more times, trying to prove to herself the supposed Empedoclean theories of color in the works of Arturo Soto.

"You're crazy," Meno said, blushing, taken aback by Arturo's sudden reply. At the same time, though, she had to admit that her husband's friend's unusual request had just a touch of flattery and excitement in it—yes, just a touch—his words almost imperceptible, like a whisper, a mist grazing her skin, giving it a slight chill. To her reaction, she could add only the following: "Why do you want me to pose, anyway?"

And since Arturo could not divulge his true reasons for the request, he simply said:

"In order to demonstrate the great Empedocles of Agrigento's theory of color, of course!" He laughed.

"So are you going to paint me in black and white?"

"Have you seen any of my works that have been?"

"Well, no . . ."

"Then what are you talking about?"

"I don't know. The truth is . . ." She hesitated. A moment later, though, some sort of itch—an inexplicable sense of vanity, perhaps—arose out of an inexact, unknown place and led her to say, consciously though almost against her own will: "Only if you promise to tell me more about your father. Everything I want to know. Understand? Look, Arturo, I really need to get to work on my thesis. If I don't, I won't get my degree. I've been avoiding my advisor for months now, and if I do any more stalling, I might as well kiss my master's good-bye."

"I understand," he said, although he could hardly keep himself from touching and kissing those symmetrical shoulders, those insinuating bones, and—even more insinuating still—those razor-sharp clavicles. "You can count on me."

"And how would you like me to dress?"

"However you like," Arturo replied, tossing his cigarette butt on the floor of the workshop and stomping it out apathetically. "Does this Saturday sound good to you?"

"I don't think so. We spend Saturdays with my in-laws."

"Ah, of course . . ." Arturo retracted the offer. "Then you tell me when."

"Next Tuesday at four thirty, the same time as today. As we've arranged . . . remember?"

"Yes, of course."

"I think I'll be going now . . ." And without waiting for an answer, she threw open the studio door and stepped out onto the roof where, fortunately for the both of them, they sky was still laden with clouds, just as it had been when she arrived there in Narvarte, lacking the fiery touch that was there the previous afternoon. The outside world there—at least, the sunken world of Mexico City in 2025—seemed to have coagulated. Perplexed, Maty noticed or perhaps imagined for a few moments that everything had become eternal there, seen through her gray, glaucous eyes, eyes that constantly sought something unattainable on that crepuscular, capital city skyline. Whether it was by inertia alone or by the need to say something new, she stopped there and called the quiet, composed painter to her side. She wanted to find out whether Arturo might perceive the same thing as she did, or perhaps she was moved by the anxious, eager, feminine desire to confirm her feelings. Whatever the case, to her misfortune, her husband's friend took advantage of his discovery to conclude, almost demonstrably, the day's lesson:

"According to the philosopher, the sky is spinning all around us at an incredible speed, although you and I cannot see it."

This time—and only to play the devil's advocate, being a little weary of philosophy—Meno answered without turning around to face him, convinced with her answer:

"The sky looks like it's been detained. Don't you think? There's no wind. It was just a metaphor for telling you that the world was immobilized that afternoon on your roof."

"On the contrary, it's just that you do not see the movement, the centripetal force of the sky which prevents the earth from spinning off the precipice of the universe. We're in motion ourselves, Meno. The cosmos is moving as if in some sort of interstellar eddy. You know? Empedocles compared the phenomenon to that of water in an inverted glass, which will not spill out if it is spun at a high enough speed."

"But that's not how it works. Everyone knows that."

"Of course that's not how it works. But we're talking about the fifth century before the birth of Christ. As far as science in those days, he's not too bad . . ."

"You always say that."

Meno, the disciple, was tired, overwhelmed. Without taking her eyes off the multitude of buildings and rooftop antennas across the city, she allowed herself to become absorbed in her own thoughts for a couple of minutes. Then the painter offered to walk her across the exposed rooftop over towards the door to the landing and the stairs below. Immediately after that, they said good-bye with a quick, impersonal kiss. Meno began to make her way down the stairs in an almost robotic way. After ten or twenty steps, back in the hallway where they had contemplated the hanging paintings, red and yellow, ocher and turquoise, Arturo called out in an almost scolding tone: "I hope you recorded our conversation. Everything I told you today has to do with what you want to know about my father."

"I don't understand . . ."

He could barely hear Meno's surprised, disconcerted voice, now a distant trill in the depths of the stairwell, three or four floors beneath his vantage point there, on the precipice of that earthly abyss.

IX

Long before meeting Irene and coming to the United States, and even before I met Fedra, my first wife, I was the sort of man who believed in fidelity—in strict, to-the-letter fidelity between a couple—without which, it is said, a true relationship could not exist, much less a passionate one (and by passion, I mean of course the capacity to be reflected in the other, to consubstantiate with each other, the way a mirror can see itself in another mirror). I'm speaking seriously here: I believed and practiced that (aberrant) vision of things, that theory of life or (if you like) that obsessive and extreme form of relationship. Now, though, I'll proceed to tell you what actually happened.

I would have been . . . twenty-two years old, and at that time I had a good relationship with a beautiful girl whom I cared for deeply. In those days, I was, as I recall, an idealist to the full extent of the term, a champion of purity. My youth, aligned with my Christianity and goodwill, combined to forge that notion of faith in love to a fanatical degree. I suppose people like Phillip Ritter, our department chair, or Javis and Tino, the normative Galicians, would find it difficult to reconcile or even identify the man I was twenty years ago with the man I've become: someone who tends toward the cynical, blasé, and often skeptical . . . but not in love, in any case, since I retain a sliver of hope for any signs of trustworthiness in the human condition, despite everything it has (at the present time) going against it.

It was at a dinner where I met Gilberto, who was ten years my senior, and whom I'd already heard speak previously. That was the night when things began to change in my life. Suffice it to say that, almost without intending to, he became the guru, the watershed event, the point of confluence of many things that were happening all around me, though without my knowledge. Perhaps it is only now, with the perspective and experience gained in four decades of life, that I can glance back at that strange, memorable dinner and realize the final, definitive change that occurred . . . in me as well as in him, I suppose. So, you will ask, what the hell happened that night?

Well, it just so happens that I took my lovely fiancée to that friendly gathering. There were perhaps four other couples who gathered there at that house on Calle Minerva in Coyoacán, a neighborhood I'd never been in before. I think I knew one or two of the couples; I don't remember exactly, nor do I even remember who it was who invited me there, or why. Today, from this great distance, I can barely even picture Gilberto (who would become a friend of mine years later) sitting there at the end of that pleasant room, smoking and sipping a drink after a sumptuous dinner with the other guests. He might have been the only person without

66

a date that night. All the others (if memory serves me right) were seated on a comfortable sofa or in one of the chairs, while some of the girls had even settled down on the carpet around a coffee table filled with glasses of wine, whiskey sours, and margaritas. It would have been late, past midnight, and we were all probably a bit tipsy from the combined effects of the alcohol, the cloud of incense, candles, cigarette smoke, and the music of Miles Davis, though not yet too tired to carry on a conversation or to become embroiled in one of those debates that light up the night almost anywhere in the world where a pinch of intelligence and good humor come together . . . the sort of debate that is, of course, sorely lacking in the United States, where people say goodnight around ten o'clock and where you will rarely find a pinch of humor (if anything, you'll find a touch of numbness and affected, conceited academic intelligence). But getting back to the matter at hand: I will say that I was—as I still am, though in a different way—a born debater, and whatever my position on life or ideals might have been, as I said, I would have defended them with the dignified ferocity of the adolescent man that I was. Again, as I've already stated, at that time, I was a loving, faithful sort, given to but one woman: that woman was Isabel, whom I brought with me that night, and who must have been sitting there at my feet, leaning back against my knees, while I was proudly boasting (though I don't know exactly why) to Gilberto something more or less along these lines:

"You may not believe this, but in the three years that we've been together, I've never cheated on Isabel. Not once."

"That's too bad," Gilberto (my future friend) responded from his seat. It was patently obvious (though I, at the time, did not see it) that the guy was a schemer, a rebel, a professional provocateur. Then, he asked me:

"What did you say your name was?"

"Eusebio Cardoso."

"Well, I say again, that's too bad, Eusebio, because people your age— surely you're not even twenty-five yet, right?—need experience, they need to get out into the world, to lose themselves a bit."

"And how old are you, then?" I asked, spitefully.

"Thirty."

"And you're still lost?" I pressed on, half annoyed, while putting my arm around Isabel's shoulders, who was surely watching, overwhelmed by this smooth-talking, charismatic guy who didn't mince his words.

"Fortunately, yes, just as I was when I was twenty." He took a drink from his glass, a rum and Coke I believe, and said, sententiously: "As they say, if you don't get lost once in a while, you'll never have a chance to find yourself, but if you start now, with a little bit of luck, you might just discover who you really are, and what the true nature of your soul is, Eusebio. You'll probably find that you're not what you think you are."

"And just what am I, in your opinion?" I asked from my position in the chair, still holding my glass of tequila, though not drinking it. Clearly, this inquisitor had targeted me because of my naïveté, my purity, or whatever it was that he saw; in any case, I had taken the bait.

"A polygamist, like me."

"But if you don't even know me, how can you be so sure?"

"Even if I don't know you, I've read a number of books that speak to such things. There is one, for example, called *Eros and Civilization*. Are you familiar with it?"

"No, I've never even heard of it."

"Then it's up to you to discover it."

"The book?"

"No, Eusebio . . ." He laughed in an all-but-unbearable, strident voice. "The fact that you are a polygamist, just like me. Even though I've only just met you, the fact is that I'm quite sure of it. Now, all that's left is for you to find out for yourself, to corroborate it, and when that day comes, you'll see that I'm right," he said to me with an intelligent and sardonic smile, which was probably directed more at Isabel than at me. Then, he added, "But it doesn't matter what you're saying tonight about infidelity, to me, someone who doesn't know you, someone you've only just met and whom you may never see again in your life. What's important is this beautiful lady who has accompanied you; what's important, Eusebio, is that what you've said here clearly wasn't intended for me; rather, it was directed towards your princess here, who—for obvious reasons—is someone you want to keep and to conquer, and in that regard you're doing quite well."

"You mean to tell me that I'm claiming to have been faithful for three years just to look good, since I'm right here in front of her?" As I said, I'd taken the bait, and now I'd swallowed the hook and been caught in his net, entangled in an absurd dispute which, nevertheless, was driving away my life, my ideals, perhaps even my honor, while he, on the other hand, was evidently some sort of recalcitrant non-conformist.

"I'm saying that if you had been unfaithful—even just once—you wouldn't say so now, right? You're not that stupid. And that's why your words, as frank and transparent as they may seem, are tainted, conditional, slanted . . ."

"Not even . . . You're wrong," I answered, holding back the inklings of wrath as I sat comfortably on the sofa. "I have not been unfaithful to Isabel, and if I had been, I would have told her."

"What about right now?" Gilberto asked maliciously just before taking another sip of his rum and Coke.

"No; if it had happened, I would have told her by now."

"If what you're saying is true, then why not let it all out tonight?"

"Well, like I've already said: because I haven't been unfaithful, because I have absolutely nothing to reveal to Isabel." I was stern, intrepid, irritated, and probably still hadn't taken a sip from my full glass of tequila.

"Ah . . ." he exclaimed, suddenly becoming the thoughtful one, until a moment later when he let loose with an unpremeditated, point-blank shot: "And her?"

"What about her?"

"Has she been faithful to you?"

The truth is that I couldn't believe it, nor in all likelihood could the other guests who were sitting all around us, the other couples sipping a digestif, smoking, listening, but not participating; who knows whether they were embarrassed or amused or bothered as they bore witness to this battle between purity and impurity, between fidelity and infidelity, between monogamy and polygamy, which subsists in every human being. However, as I recall it, I kept my composure, feigning an arrogant, self-imposed naturalness which of course I neither felt nor possessed. I finally took a sip of tequila—my first in quite a while—cleared my throat, and offered a simple, succinct, and accurate answer:

"Of course."

"You surprise me, Eusebio. How do you know this? How can you be so sure?"

"I just am."

"Ah, now I see," he replied, though not without a bitter hint of irony, of cloying, coquettish treacle. "Your bulletproof certainty leaves me a bit perplexed, Eusebio. I hope it stays with you forever. Then again, perhaps I don't."

"Look," I said. "Isabel has been as faithful to me as I have been to her, and I rely on that, understand? It's a matter of confidence, of reciprocity, of transparency. She's been faithful to me because I've been faithful to her. If I hadn't been, I would begin to lose confidence in her . . . That's my logic, plain and simple. Don't do what you don't want others to do."

"But do you think she would tell you if she had been unfaithful herself?"

"Of course," I said, eager to end the conversation but unable to find a way to bring that about.

Throughout this chat or debate, Isabel had not moved from her spot on the carpet where she sat at my feet, leaning up against my legs: she remained there, quiet, serious, mute, looking straight at Gilberto, perhaps taking the occasional sip from her glass of white wine. I don't know. I don't even remember the other guests; I'm sure they were there, mouths agape, inhaling the incense and the dried fruit scent of the candles that flooded the room, but for me it was like being on stage in an absurdist play, in the proscenium, front and center next to Isabel and this guy

Gilberto (my future friend) while everyone else—hidden by the shadows of the theater—watched us, following every movement, every gesture, even the slight inflections of our voices to see if we were mistaken. Yes, that's how I imagine or remember it, that supremely odd night on Calle Minerva in Coyoacán, twenty years later, not enough time for me to have forgotten all the evening's details, but more than enough for me to realize, today, that a number of them have escaped me.

"Would you agree?" This time the question was directed at Isabel.

Before I could intervene, she had already answered in the affirmative, barely moving her jaw, without opening her lips. Then, Gilberto said to the both of us:

"Then I congratulate you both, though I'm afraid to say that in spite of everything, you haven't quite convinced me. And do you know why? Because when you're simply repeating statements in each other's presence, it detracts from the truthfulness of your confession."

"What are you trying to say?" came a man's voice from back in the shadows of the house.

"That I don't believe that either of them has been faithful to the other, the same as everyone sitting here and listening without saying a word . . . But it doesn't matter what I believe, right? We should be drinking and toasting our hosts . . ."

"I agree. To our hosts!" said a female voice from the bank of armchairs like theater seats among grisaille and amorphous bodies, indistinguishable from one another. "The truth is that we don't care what you have to say, Gilberto. We know you too well. Besides lacking any sense of tact, you've got the wisdom of a puppet when it comes to love."

I, of course, did not know him that well. In fact, I didn't know him at all. I didn't know that he was dedicated to politics, or that he was looking forward to a far-off day. And—though I couldn't have fathomed it that night—I would come to know him over the course of those years.

I believe Gilberto remained there in his seat, in the darkened gloom of the living room, without uttering another word for some time, perhaps even the rest of the night (who knows), languishing amidst the tedious chatter that was floating into the air along with the cigarette smoke and the smells of incense and scented candles. I did not speak with him again that night, as Isabel and I moved off to some other conversation.

Even today, that dinner party on Calle Minerva remains a memorable one, at least for Gilberto and I, if not for the others. Even now, as I recall that fortuitous encounter with a man eight years my senior, whom I engaged in that embarrassing dispute. But I will neither dig any deeper nor pause to discuss what many have already intuited at this point in my story: that something might possibly have happened between Isabel and Gilberto some time ago, and that the encounter there at the house on Calle Minerva, in Coyoacán, was neither fortuitous nor by chance. In fact, it was quite the opposite: they were both throwing body blows to my rib cage, and enjoying the fact that they were using me as a punching bag. But in any case, the story doesn't end there, which is fortunate, because the fact is that a year or two later (I won't say how I learned of their complicity, nor of how things ended between Isabel and I), they announced their engagement and were soon married: she was no more than twenty, I think, and he was in his mid-thirties, a war veteran, or at least that's what we all assumed, since in those days most men got married well before they turned thirty. Eventually (as I would later learn), they had three children and ended up very happy together, all but inseparable. But more important than all this is the fact that Gilberto became my friend many years later, after that dinner (when he was already married to Isabel), as a result of an accident wherein I saved his life after finding his overturned car on Avenida de los Insurgentes and took him to the hospital, no questions asked and without even waiting for police or an ambulance to arrive on the scene. But that's a whole other story, one which I'm not about to get into here . . . but nevertheless, it would have been two or three more years after that car accident, I don't know, before he confessed to me, alone, at a downtown café, something which I always thought—and continue to think—is the epitome of irony and paradox:

"Eusebio, you changed my life. Did you know that? I never told you, but you changed my life one hundred and eighty degrees. I'm not talking about Isabel or the children we had together. Or about the accident. I'm talking about something else, something completely different."

"What are you talking about?" I asked him, that afternoon at the café, where we were sitting and waiting for our respective wives, Fedra and Isabel, to return from shoe shopping. So yes, by then, I was clearly married to Fedra, my first wife, and we might even have been awaiting the arrival of our daughter Dulce, but who knows? Events are juxtaposed in the distance, and memories dovetail with time.

"I'm talking about what you said about fidelity that night at the party on Calle Minerva. Remember, Eusebio? When I saw you embracing Isabel with so much affection, you convinced me that it would be well worth the trouble to at least try and give myself to only one woman, like you said with such conviction, yes, to be faithful until death do us part. You hear me? Just one woman. And I did. I've stood by it ever since we were married, Eusebio, even if you don't believe me, and I've done it by conviction alone, pure and simple. Just like you. That's what life is about, don't you think? And now I'm an unrepentant monogamist. Who would have thought it?"

And with that, as I recall, he broke into laughter, either at himself or at life in general.

"Honestly, you haven't cheated on Isabel once since you've been married?" I asked with a glance. "That's a bit hard to believe, don't you think? Knowing you as well as I do . . ." I fell quiet for a moment after this last statement before making the following resolution, hypocritical though it may be: "You know, Gilberto, you can confide in me. That's why we're friends; I'll be dead and buried before I tell anyone anything. Not even my shadow."

I admit, I didn't know where I got the strength to cast off any semblance of aplomb in order to speak to him like that . . . especially to a guy as wrapped up in politics as he was (and continues to be).

"It's true, Eusebio. I'm not lying to you. That's the wonderful thing, the impressive thing . . ."

"What is?" I said, disconcerted, sharpening my glance, pricking back my ears, my skin bristling like a hedgehog.

"That I don't care whether you tell Fedra or anybody else for that matter. That I'm happy, I've been really happy ever since I made the decision, based on pure conviction, to be completely faithful to Isabel, something I'd never been able to do before. That's why I married her, Eusebio. Otherwise, I'd still be a bachelor to this very day. Let's just say that conviction preceded my decision to marry her and start a family. Of course, that conviction plus the infinite love that I feel for her."

I listened, truly stunned, unsure of whether Gilberto was (once again!) pulling my leg, or if he was actually being more honest now than I was. But in any case, from what I could gather, he seemed to be sincere and totally genuine, both in his love for Isabel and in his chaste words. I believe that at the very least he had no reason to lie to me on that particular occasion, and I didn't ask him for any kind of explanation. Needless to say, listening to him there at that downtown coffee shop, I felt like asking him why and for how long they had been seeing each other behind my back, why they had toyed with me in such a way, and why they had organized that false fortuitous meeting and that debate about a couple's love and fidelity on Calle Minerva. Why . . . if it was all just an absurd ruse? But I didn't do it, I didn't ask. I kept it to myself, not wanting to tarnish our friendship.

That ancient afternoon, as we waited for Isabel and Fedra, Gilberto concluded his confession (or whatever this was) with the following words:

"Now I know you weren't lying then, though I swear I didn't believe you, or anybody else for that matter, who would have sworn to me that he was faithful to his wife. I simply didn't believe it; it went against all my principles, all my assumptions, understand? I believed strictly in polygamy, the same way I believe in democracy and capitalism. And now we're a couple, Eusebio."

"Well, I'm happy for you. For the both of you. Congratulations, really," I said immediately, with a broad smile, though still without knowing whether Gilberto was joking around with that unexpected confession after so many years, and the two of us now married to two other women who—to make matters worse—had become true, inseparable friends. But nevertheless, just a short time later, he would be corroborated by Isabel herself, who (at the very least) said that her husband was indeed being faithful, right down to the bone, the way I was a decade or so before. In fact, Isabel went on to tell me a strange and salient anecdote in which she described hearing from a third party about how Gilberto had rejected the repeated advances of a young female member of the Partido. And so it was true: Gilberto had undergone a radical change, either after she broke off the relationship with me, or after they married each other. Plenty of years have passed since all this—a decade, in fact—and the river has run its course.

Still, though, it was her, my cunning, beloved, everlasting Isabel—the one who smiled, tossing pillows at me in the Tuesday morning hotel room—who hadn't changed so much as a hair on her head, and who would never even think of changing, either.

10

Empedocles had a goal in life: to rescue nature, the world that surrounds us, from the immobility and the unity to which Parmenides had submitted it with such irrefutable, overwhelming logic, that ever since the Eleatics, philosophy has been at an impasse. Why? Because Parmenides had, with his conclusions, deprived us from any sense of perception, any true contact with reality, the physical world, making us doubt her while at the same time demanding that we accept the paradoxical notion that nothing can exist with the exception of the Being, which fills and permeates everything . . . to the point where we are no longer able (thanks to him) to move from place to place. Where can you go if everything is full? And if everything is full, then how is it that I can, in fact, move?

The Parmenidean *kosmos* denies the plurality of things in favor of a congruent Monism: all things are, inherently, the same thing, just as there is one Being which is All, because to imagine, on the contrary, that a Non-Being also exists would be blatantly preposterous and absurd. And rightly so . . .

After he had established that the phenomenological world was fictitious and that movement, therefore, was impossible, Parmenides forced the future of philosophy into two, diametrically opposed paths. So, either the implacable Parmenidean logic would go on to construct a *kosmos* in accordance with our senses (one of Aristotelian hylomorphism), with a plurality of physical elements surrounding us, all in constant motion, the way we see and perceive the world (or as we imagine the way we see and experience it), or a person would necessarily be forced to admit the existence of two different types or degrees of reality: an existing one (in other words, immutable and intelligible, as Parmenides stated) and another that changes, that can only be the object of opinion (*doxa*) and never of knowledge, because this second type of reality was not trustworthy, not verifiable.

If nature and the perceivable world (things) do not warrant the name Being, they are, however, not entirely nonexistent, because they constitute something of a third category, the so-called Becoming, an intermediate state (ambivalent and ambiguous) between the Being and the Non-Being in which—at least for now—the senses count for something. It goes without saying that this alternative was the one that gave rise to Plato, and along with him, all the idealism that had subsequently permeated humanity in one way or another for twenty-four centuries.

In order to challenge his teacher and mentor (Parmenides was twenty or twenty-five years older), Empedocles was forced to distance himself from an apparently unitary and static concept, which nevertheless included that same Parmenidean sphere, which contained and conserved the four indestructible roots or elements (also known as *arche* or *archai*), mingling and attracting one another by means of a powerful force which the mystagogue from Agrigento called Eros, Kypris, Philia, or Aphrodite. Love, then, united the dissimilar and therefore its tendency would have remained ineffective without the emergence of its counterpart, the equally powerful force he deemed Strife, or Discord, which had the ability to separate and disintegrate things through quite original means—like attracting like—in other words, the exact opposite path of Love.

These two pugilistic forces circle and struggle with one another, striving to win predominance over the four roots. The great step that Empedocles took, and the giant footprint that he left behind him, was to declare that fire, air, earth, and water were indestructible, and that the movement that caused the continuous and necessary mixing and combining that constitutes the very universe itself was not caused by the elements themselves, but rather by outside forces working upon them: Strife and Love, Eris and Eros. But more original than all that is the fact that this inside-out theory had, more than anything else—yet indirectly so—a decisive psychological and spiritual effect upon hundreds of millions of people. Even upon you, who is reading and living these lines.

XI

It seems that there is something inside of me, a sort of amorous Empedoclean force that tries to unite the dissimilar, the distinct, the things which simply have nothing to do with this world. Let me explain. It was me who, no more than two months ago, had the ridiculous idea to ask Irene about her biological parents, the ones she never met, and about whom I hadn't heard so much as a single word in my entire life. Why would such a foolish idea have come to me, considering that it wasn't my problem, and that it never had been? To be honest, I don't know how to respond: all I can say in my own defense is that there seems to reside within me a sort of magnetic energy that tends to attract and mix with everything around it, almost as if I somehow preferred the massive, crushing, teeming mishmash of humanity, when deep down I really want to be here, in Virginia, more or less isolated, with my wife and my son Emilio, enjoying their company after class, far from the famous carousing, clattering multitudes of Mexican families, just like in the old Burrón family cartoons.

Well, not wanting to stray too far from the matter at hand, I'll say that one fine morning I asked Irene if she had ever felt like trying to find out the identity of her true parents. She answered me, still yawning and bleary-eyed:

"No, Eusebio. Why would I? Why would I want to?"

I admit that I was a bit irritated by such an implacable answer.

"What do you mean, why? To know . . ."

"And why would I want to know, if I still wouldn't be able to do anything about it?"

"Not everything in life has an aim or a reason why," I said, trying to be anti-teleological, to see if that might convince her while at the same time satisfying my own appetite for curiosity. "Sometimes you just do things without having a particular goal in mind. You just want to do them, you know? And in this case, I'd think you'd want to satisfy your own curiosity, that latent desire that you've kept buried within yourself all these years . . ."

"But I'm not curious, I've never been curious, and I don't feel like I'm hiding anything either."

"I honestly don't understand you, Irene; it's absolutely legitimate and natural that you feel the need to find out who your true parents are," I said in one long breath as I lay back on the bed where we were both laying, half naked, crisscrossed by dawn's first light on that clear and lovely Virginia spring morning.

"Look," she said, propping herself with a pillow up against the wall, trying either to console or dissuade me, I don't know which. "Before he died from that bee sting, my father showed me a letter, Eusebio."

"A letter?" I asked, intrigued, inching myself closer to her.

"Yes, you heard me," she replied intuitively. "My mother still keeps that letter that my biological parents gave her when they gave me up for adoption. Actually, they didn't give it directly to them, since according to what Eusebio and Irene, the only people I ever considered my true parents, told me, they never met the other couple, or knew who they were. The letter came via the adoption agency, and now my mother is holding onto it for me, sealed, so I could open it when I turned eighteen."

"But you're twenty-eight, Irene!" I jumped out of bed, wildly excited, thinking that I was still dreaming, or that I'd misheard the enormous revelation that had just escaped my wife's lips. "Why haven't you told me?"

"I've never felt the need to read it. In fact, it never even occurred to me." She turned to face me, almost threateningly, and somewhat bothered. I must admit that the "it never even occurred to me" stunned me. You can't just dismiss, as if they were nothing, such questions as, Who am I? Where do I come from? What am I doing here? Who are my parents, my relatives? Why did they abandon me? Which blood is mine, what are my origins, my roots, my identity? It's the kind of language that leaves an indelible footprint on what one says or recounts or dreams; it is not to be used unless it is truly necessary. So, in the end, it was extremely hard for me to believe her, to trust in her words, her flippant remarks. Rather, she came across as aloof.

"I can't believe it," I responded, perplexed and a bit upset. "I can't believe you never told me."

"There are many things I haven't told you about, Eusebio. Just as there are many things you haven't told me. You haven't told me about your past, other than the fact that you were once married to a woman named Fedra and that you had a beautiful daughter with her, who you say looks a lot like me, and even today you still haven't introduced me to her. You appeared one day in my life, in San Francisco, you liked me, I loved you, I told you everything that I had to tell you about my life, I wiped the slate clean, I laid it all out there for you, Eusebio, don't you remember? To begin a life together, starting at zero, and I've dedicated myself to that, to living without the need to ask for explanations or details."

"Of course," I said, feeling that Irene was slowly but surely changing the subject, making it more about me and our relationship, things which, in this case, I wasn't concerned about. All that interested me was her adoption, her roots, her parents, both adoptive and biological, her childhood, and that sealed letter, which I'd only just learned about after several years of marriage.

"And tell me this, Eusebio; what the hell would I say to them if I ever met them?" Irene got up, as if she suddenly realized she were laying on a bed of thistles, and stretched, lithe as a spring and straight as a lance. I realized that she'd taken the bait: curiosity was doing its ant-like work just when I was facing defeat, ready to concede. Nevertheless, at that crucial moment, I knew in my heart I was right: how could she possibly say something as emphatically categorical as that? How could it not intrigue her, not keep her up at night? The desire to know, for example, who your true parents were and why they abandoned you, why they gave you up for adoption? What could be behind all this? What history, what misunderstanding?

"Honestly, I don't know," was all I could muster, desperate, wishing I had come up with a better response so as to keep her inner investigation going.

"I knew that." Irene was suddenly a bit irascible. She was gesturing and moving from one side of the room to the other, acting out a possible scene with her biological parents, a couple of phantom beings who were not there, but would soon materialize: "Hello, I'm your daughter. My name's Irene. You're my parents, did you know that? It's great to meet you. Could you please tell me where the hell you're originally from, since as far as I know, I'm Cuban—Cuban American, actually—but who knows, maybe I'm Chinese or Korean, and I've come here today to find out. Oh, and by the way, maybe you could explain why the hell you put me up for adoption. Maybe you didn't love me . . . ?"

"I understand," I muttered, getting out of bed myself so I could embrace and console her. And I was surprised by my own intuition: Irene was shaking. Really shaking. The fact is that, for a few moments, I had apparently also taken the bait myself, all this talk about adoption and the sealed letter she didn't care about, and now I could see just how far I'd gone without even wanting to, or to put it another way: looking for her suffering in a certain way, provoking her suffering, causing it, though in no way was I trying to make my wife suffer because of my own curiosity and imprudence. I figured that the subject, after so many years have passed in the life of a human being, would have been something much more foreign, something almost impersonal. While not completely spurious, at the very least I never believed for a single moment that those doubts could become so internalized, so entombed, that they could seem innocuous or even nonexistent. But there they were, right in front of my very eyes. Meanwhile, I continued to embrace Irene, who suddenly began to cry slowly, very slowly, bathing my arms in her warm tears, which shone with an iridescence in the light filtering in through the window that spring morning.

Suddenly, unexpectedly, she pulled away, out of my arms, and said:

"You're right, Eusebio. I don't know why I've waited so long, I don't know why the hell I've been so afraid all these years. Maybe afraid of the truth? Me? Well, no; I've never feared the truth, and I'm going to prove it to you right now. Watch this!"

As she said this, she pushed me aside and headed straight for the cordless phone we kept in the living room (actually, it was the only phone we had) and began to dial (punch in?) a number with one hand while she wiped away her tears with the back of the other. Fortunately, Emilio was still sleeping soundly in his bedroom, without so much as a word, even a peep, completely unaffected by the vortex or cosmic eddy that I had whipped up that immemorable morning.

"What are you doing?" I asked, suddenly afraid, fearing the worst.

"Calling Irene, my mother, in San Francisco."

"Your mother? Why?"

"Why do you think, Eusebio? So she can send me that letter, or maybe read it to me over the phone or something. It's time."

"Wait, wait!" I cried, but it was too late: my dear old mother-in-law had already answered the phone. From East to West, from the Atlantic coast to the Pacific in barely an instant, a thousandth of a second at most, was enough (or even more than enough) for my wife, determined or blinded like I'd never seen her before, to say to her mother on that indescribable morning, one which I'd rather not be reminded of:

"I want to read the letter, *mamá*."

" . . . "

"What do you mean, what letter? You know what I'm talking about . . ."

" . . . "

"Yes, I'm sure. I want to read it. Why would you say that, *mamá*?"

" . . . "

"Yeah yeah, I know . . . It seems strange, but it's really not. I've thought about it for a long time, months even, I swear . . ." Irene was, of course, lying about this part, flagrantly lying, perhaps, although in another way, maybe she wasn't actually lying at all, or at least not in as blatant a manner as I first thought, as I watched her there, gnawing at my fingernails. Let me explain myself: if she hadn't literally been "thinking" about it, as she said, it could be argued that she had been "ruminating" over it, deep down, for years, perhaps lustrums . . . and who knows, perhaps she couldn't even say herself, and in any case, I wouldn't have felt (as I feel at this moment) culpable under any circumstances, since she was the one who decided to call her mother and ask about the letter from her biological parents, which means that in the end I was nothing more than a simple agent, a detonator, a pivot point that over time released the long-delayed "ruminant thought" that existed in the depths of her tempting heart. I was definitely playing the part of what my dear Empedocles called *Ananke*, the personification of Necessary Chance.

"..."

"So, what then, *mamá*?" Irene didn't even turn around to look at me. I could see her there, dug in next to the large lamp in the front window; or rather, I saw an eclipse of her body, her silhouette, darkened, blackened, surrounded by an aura of light, which sanctified her.

"..."

"Yes, just FedEx it to me, or whatever you want. I'll pay you for it."

"..."

"It's my right, *mamá* . . ." My wife's voice was beginning to raise its tone, so much so that I was afraid that Emilio would wake up. But no, he continued on in the dreams of the innocent . . .

"..."

"Yes, I'll wait for it," she concluded with a forcefulness that I'd only heard a few times myself. "I'll let you know as soon as it comes. Yes, yes, I'll tell you, I promise. I swear. I love you, *mami*, and thank you. Bye."

She fell silent, though it was a reverent and almost gloomy silence, one which couldn't help but cast a certain pall over that brilliant, melodious, and cheerful Virginia morning. Irene didn't say another word. We went into the kitchen, made a pot of stiff, black coffee which we sipped slowly and silently, smoking several cigarettes, waiting for Emilio to wake up, waiting for the FedEx package containing the sealed letter from her biological parents to arrive at our front door. And it arrived—it finally arrived—after two or three more days of coffee and cigarettes, after a number of spring-like May mornings. Which isn't to say that, in the meantime—in the interval—I didn't struggle internally between two very different and even contradictory feelings: the first was the desire to know what the letter contained, and the other one was the desire to know absolutely nothing, and to hope that the package had been lost along with Tom Hanks in some barren, remote island in the American South.

12
(TUESDAY, MAY 9TH)

"Will you let me look at you from closer up?" Arturo asked Maty that Tuesday as he approached her without really waiting for a response. They were alone, parked there on the left side of the painter's workshop, right where the models typically posed, either standing or lounging on a couple of sequined pillows that had been scattered on the ground. Although it wasn't as warm as the first time Matilde had been there, one week ago, it also couldn't be said that the place was fresh; in fact, it was far from it, lacking any real ventilation system, despite the windows overlooking the street, which were kept open. The light, however, was formidable; intense bursts of photons permeated the room and illuminated the paintings and unfinished canvasses everywhere. There were, of course, certain advantages to living on the roof of a well-designed five-story building, and even more advantages to painting there, for it was completely isolated and foreign to the rest of the tenants.

There was also, just a few yards from the studio, the tiny little hovel where Arturo lived with his wife, which consisted of an unmade bed, two cast iron chairs, a table with an electric stove, a few tin cups and plates, a mini-fridge, a stand-alone bathtub with no curtain, and—finally—several two-by-fours fixed to the wall where dozens and dozens of books on painters and painting were stacked without rhyme or reason: books on Cimabue, Botticelli, Raphael, Caravaggio, Titian, Rembrandt, Ribera, Gauguin, Bonnard, Picasso, Orozco, Frieseke, Modigliani, Kerrington, Davison, Falques, Kahlo, and Herrán, among others.

"And what is it that you want to see?" she asked, holding her ground just a few feet away from the painter.

"Your eyes, Matilde. What else?"

"And why would you want to see my eyes?"

Instead of answering, Arturo asked a different question.

"Can you see at night?"

"What are you talking about?"

"I'm asking whether you can see better at night than the average mortal?"

"Are you insane? You ask me the most absurd questions," she said before opening up her Louis Vuitton bag and changing the subject: "Look, I brought the tape recorder with me, and now I would like for us to get down to work. We'll get to the paintings and the color of my eyes soon enough. You promised, Arturo."

"Yes, but I didn't specify the order in which we'd be doing things," Arturo replied, with a broad smile that, deep down, was designed to intimidate or even upset her a little. And without even giving her a chance to move, he had reached out and taken hold of her chin, the same way he would do with his regular noonday models, observing her in the light cascading in through the open windows as if she were a talisman or a Tanagra figurine.

It seemed evident by now—and perhaps even since her first visit—that Arturo knew that Matilde knew that he was attracted to her, and this knowledge did nothing to drive him off or intimidate him even a bit; in fact, it had quite the opposite effect: he was even more animated, more motivated to keep pressing forward, step by tiny step, unhurried and quite sure of his position in this strange board game in which, almost by chance, they found themselves facing off, together, body to body. But what Arturo did not know, however, was whether she was attracted to him, and the fact of the matter is that ever since the second Tuesday, Matilde was still not quite one hundred percent sure herself: she wasn't sure whether she was attracted to Arturo or disgusted with him or some mixture of the two. Physically, of course, she was attracted enough; she liked, for example, his brashness, his fearlessness, his lack of modesty, his hands and arms, his virility or crudeness, something quite masculine about the painter that never ceased to clamor for her attention, to provoke and irritate her, and which has little or nothing to do with you, dear Reader, who are—and forgive the excessive frankness here—a very distinct class of man, though one who can't be described or defined, as you know . . . Arturo, the Agro painter, was indeed taller than you, as Matilde herself noticed the first time she laid eyes on him. He also had longer and hairier arms, as were his chest and fingers. Arturo didn't seem to shave (at least, not very often) and his face, the sharp line of his jaw, was always shaded or hidden by his beard which from time to time—and depending on the light—gave him the sinister or tenebrous air of a goddamn second-rate artist. All things considered, though, the interesting fact was that the three- or four-day beard didn't seem to detract from him; rather, it favored him because, according to Matilde, it fit with the typical notion of someone who makes himself a painter *in extremis*, an eccentric bohemian who lives on a roof in Narvarte (a sort of Mexican attic apartment) with no fixed schedule and total freedom, totally at ease, chewing peyote, smoking marijuana, or drinking tequila while at the same time (that is, whenever he feels like it) painting portraits of his young, submissive, doleful models. Arturo's eyes, set beneath thick black eyebrows, were extremely dark, with scarcely a hint of light, like those of a Turk: they penetrated her, she felt their intense pressure for seconds at a time, and this occasionally made her feel uncomfortable, repulsed, although inexplicably she also found herself enjoying the feeling, as if she were submitting to an ancient, unknown totem. In a patently indefinable way, Maty was at once excited and terrified to discover that she was attracted to him, and that he was interested in her (the look in Arturo's eyes, as contradictory as it might seem, made her feel at once sinful and enveloped, shameful and protected, if it were indeed possible to feel sinful without feeling disgraced or subject to divine punishment). Nevertheless, she wasn't sure about how much or why she liked him, or what part of herself the painter found most seductive: whether it was her green eyes, her breasts, her legs, her shoulders, or simply everything; nor could she be absolutely certain that she was the one and only object of his desire, or if Arturo didn't simply desire all of his models, all the women of the world. In fact, she'd never even seen him with another woman, not even his wife Tamara, whom she didn't recall ever having met in her entire life, not even at the wedding of a mutual friend which all three of you had unwittingly attended: her, you, and him.

"So, why would you ask me whether I can see better than other people at night?" Matilde asked.

"Because your eyes are so clear."

"And what does that have to do with anything?"

"It means that your eyes have more fire than water in them. That's all. Mine, on the other hand, are just the opposite. More water than fire."

"I don't understand a word of what you just said."

"I have to warn you, it has to do with Empedocles," Arturo cautioned, directing her to have a seat in a wrought-iron chair (a few feet away) while he positioned himself at an easel which was ready and waiting there with an empty canvas. "Why don't I paint you, at least while we talk? Would that be alright with you? Ask me whatever you want, Maty, but don't move from that spot, please, don't move . . ." He finished his request with a demand, while closing one window and opening another. A new breeze appeared, or changed its course, just like the light itself.

Matilde simply switched on her portable tape recorder and placed it on her lap. She kept her eyes on Arturo; rather, she kept her eyes on those parts of the painter which were visible from behind the easel. Just then, a strong gust of air entered the studio and seemed to refresh her semblance, her neck and shoulders. She felt, for lack of a better term, content. She didn't know why, but somehow she felt truly happy, almost exuberant, to be having her portrait painted that afternoon: after all, she couldn't remember ever having posed for anybody ever before. The models who come here to pose for him must have felt something special, she suddenly thought. What could Arturo, her husband's friend, be painting now, at this very moment: her lips, her neck, or perhaps whatever his imagination dictated. Or perhaps it was both things, what he saw and what he believed he was seeing, the way he imagined her to be? But . . . she felt a moment of doubt: could he really be enamored of her, or was it all just a deceitful ruse conducted by an actor, a *conquistador*, just another Don Juan ladies' man? And was he not even bothered in the slightest that she, Matilde, was married to one of his friends, a longtime friend from whom he had somehow recently grown apart? In fact, what did they even have in common, besides an old, invisible, extinguished friendship? Apparently, all of that (their possible past affection) did not matter to the painter . . . or, at least, it didn't matter much, for he didn't even seem concerned with the possibility that Tamara could suddenly appear there in the studio. But did Arturo have some reason to fear the arrival of his wife, or of anyone else, for that matter? Had he made any moves or taken any steps that would expose him or otherwise act as evidence against him if he were to be discovered? The truth is that no, he hadn't. Arturo knew how to bob and weave, how to duck and dive, how to take small, seemingly insignificant steps which nevertheless ultimately led him to his prey, a fact that—in a vague, indefinable sort of way—she was well aware of. This attack or slow approach, Maty figured, had been going on since their first encounter; she had felt him setting his sights on her, planning infinitely in advance, like a storm brewing in the offing. And despite it all, without knowing why or with what ulterior motive, she let it happen, while he licked his chops like a hungry bloodhound. As she sat there with the tape recorder in her lap, she realized that it was all part of the painter's stratagem: to warn his prey, to give it sufficient and effective, though imprecise signs, signs that he—the lecher, the Satyr, the *macho cabrío*, the symbol of male power and masculinity—was moving in closer, signs that sooner or later he would leap upon her, enveloping her splendid flesh, her neck and shoulders, and that none of it meant anything to him, not his friendship, not his commitment to an interview, not his wife Tamara, and certainly not a sort of moral or philosophical sense of restraint. And if she, Matilde, who was there right now—if she had sought him out and visited him—she had to accept the consequences; if not, then she had better disappear, she had better leave immediately. But what about her thesis? That whole thing about the father of this guy sitting across from her, painting her portrait? What would she do about that? Abandon everything because of sanctimoniousness, prejudice, ideals, fear, or attraction? What would her advisor say? And you, her husband? Why change the subject now, when she was growing ever more convinced that something wonderful, something never before published, could come out of the son of Roberto Soto Gariglietti, the founder of the Partido de la Naturaleza y el Fuego Mexicano? All things considered, the fact was that being the child of the most important figure in Mexican culture and politics of the past century did not seem to be the least bit important to the painter; he was, of course, used to the fact that . . . but, you fool! Who isn't accustomed to their ancestors? That notwithstanding, this was a wholly different case, something unique and distinct, a different sort of disinterest than what Arturo was showing: it was as if his father were not, in fact, dead and were still out there walking around, dropping by the studio for a visit every Friday or Saturday, as alive and affectionate as ever, an unpredictable magician, mad as a hatter.

Just then, Arturo seemed so focused on the lines he was creating and erasing on that canvas that he almost appeared withdrawn, almost alienated; he wasn't there in Narvarte, he was absent, anchored to his *daimon*, fixated on the details of its face, on her face, on the core of her *physis*, on the hardened bones that were his essence, his *archai*, on Matilde's green eyes or her pale complexion, on her legs that were sheathed in jeans, on the sharply defined lines of her naked shoulders, and of course on her mouth, as red and smooth as the fruit of the pitahaya cactus. He drew her, painted her, and this left a strange, vivid impression on her, Maty, a supremely odd sensation which she felt in spite of or despite herself, and the worst thing about it was that she didn't know what to attribute it to: was it the sullen beauty emanating from the pores of this stricken, affected, entranced man who was drawing her, who seemed submerged in the subtle features of her facial structure, or the unprecedented experience of possessing the knowledge of being portrayed? What was it? What did he see in her that she herself could not see right now, that she couldn't find during all those hours spent standing in front of the mirror in the intimacy of her own little alcove, that you, her husband of course, couldn't find either, leaving her absorbed in thought, touching herself, alone, the incipient bags under her eyes, her temples, her maxillary bones, her breasts, her belly which was growing a little less firm with each passing day? Did Arturo notice her eyes, those clear, chartreuse green eyes that could see better in the dark than most mortal eyes, just as a deer in the nocturnal forest? Could they see—could they predict—the future? Could they follow Arturo's movements, those specific, calculated gestures directed towards her? How long would Maty be able to contemplate and interpret his desire?

"Why do you say that my eyes have fire in them?"

"I told you before, remember?" Arturo replied without putting down his charcoal, his head darting in and out behind the canvas in a sort of mechanical, pendular oscillation.

"More or less, but what does that have to do with whether I can see better at night than in the day?"

"Look . . . Empedocles said that light-colored eyes were igneous eyes, and that they consisted of much more fire than water. They are covered in water, and earth and air are also present in varying proportions. But this fire of yours stems from the center of your pupil and moves across the other elements. In other words, it passes through the membranes that surround it. According to Empedocles, light-colored eyes are akin to a candle burning from inside a lantern on a stormy night, which is to say, the rays that they emit are not extinguished by the wind and rain, but rather they manage to illuminate, to perforate the darkness."

"That's interesting," Matilde murmured, perhaps fascinated by the explanation, or perhaps even stimulated by that fascination. She didn't quite know herself. But in any case, she continued to sit there, immobile, with the mini recorder turned on and sitting on her lap.

"Once objects have emitted their respective effluvia, corresponding colors appear, and these are themselves captured by rays of fire; in other words, the rays and effluences meet in the air and thus produce vision. Light green eyes, like yours, Maty, contain more fire and therefore more acuteness when it comes to seeing in the dark. They are more attuned to penetrating the effluences given off by objects at night. Dark eyes, like mine, see far better during the day because they have a higher proportion of water at their center, which is surrounded by fire. The light of day, then, compensates for the darkness of the eye's water, understand? That's why, according to the old philosopher from Agrigento, people like you see better at night than during the day."

"But I see perfectly fine during both the day and the night," Matilde replied without moving from her spot, perfectly static though still awaiting direction from Arturo who, from time to time, would make subtle signals for her to lift her chin, show more of her profile, her neck, or her alabastrine eyelids.

"Or could it be that you have above average vision at night?"

"Yes, more or less. I'd agree with that. I drive almost every night, you know?"

"You see? I knew it, Matilde." He paused for a moment before continuing, the charcoal still in hand: "According to Empedocles, people with higher amounts of fire in their eyes tend to have more debilitated sight during the day, since the fire grows then, blinding and obstructing the water's pores. That disability which people with igneous eyes like yours persists until the fire itself is intercepted by the humidity in the air, or *aer*. In other words, each effect is corrected by the corresponding, opposite element. In fact, Empedocles wrote somewhere that the eye was created by Aphrodite herself."

"Everything you're telling me, Arturo, has a patently magical quality to it, don't you think? I'm surprised that you seem to believe in it so blindly."

"I never said that I believe in it, let alone blindly."

91

"So . . ."

"So what, Matilde?" Arturo replied, knowing full well what his interlocutor wanted to get at with her question.

"So do you believe it, Arturo?"

"You know what? I believe that I'm going to leave you with a little bit of doubt." He winked at her from his seat before adding, with no small amount of coquettishness, "Let's see if, after getting to know me, bit by bit, you can figure that out."

"That's not fair."

"Of course it is. In fact, it's you who wants to know more about my father, and I'm sitting here telling you about him. Think about that!" He said this, preemptively insinuating that his new model, his friend's wife, would not have understood that herself.

"Could you possibly be a little less cryptic and speak more clearly to me, please? I don't see the connection there at all."

"What I've wanted to say to you since your very first visit here—and which I've been putting off until now—is that my father's life underwent a hundred and eighty degree turn when he had his big revelation at the age of eighteen, when he was visiting Sicily for the first time with his best friend from prep school. More specifically, he told me himself that they were visiting the southern coast of Sicily, where he'd always wanted to go since he was a child. As I said before, Maty, my paternal grandmother was Sicilian. Well, even though she was born here, in Mexico, her father, Enzo Gariglietti, was Sicilian, where the city of Agrigento is located. Yes, the same beautiful coastal city where all this philosophy we're discussing comes from. You see how simple it is? Do you see the connection now?"

"I still don't quite understand. Not completely," Matilde said, uneasy, gently shifting her tape recorder in her lap, on her pants, as if turning it slightly would somehow impart greater clarity to the voice and story that Arturo was telling her. "What does one thing have to do with the other?"

"Well, nothing except for the fact that my father visited his great-grandfather's home city when he was eighteen years old, and it was on that visit that he discovered his true vocation . . ."

"Politics?"

"No, look, I already told you. Medicine." The painter replied in a mildly impatient tone although he wasn't entirely sure whether or not he had, in fact, told his friend's wife, and if it really was her memory that had failed. "Roberto, my father, first studied medicine at the Universidad Nacional, right after he had returned from his first trip to Europe which, of course, his parents—my grandparents—had sent him on as a graduation gift."

"We're talking about 1962."

"Around then, yes."

"And Empedocles, from what you told me . . . wasn't he also a student of medicine?"

"He wasn't just a student of medicine, Matilde. He was nothing less than the father of medical science in Italy. He founded the so-called 'empirical' school, and he taught Filistion of Sicily. Even before Hippocrates and Galen, whom they say were influenced by him. Did you know that?"

"And that's the reason for this lecture on eyes and sight and colors?"

"No, as a matter of fact, that part is of particular interest to me, as a painter. Theories about color and sight have always interested me, starting with Goethe's famous thesis, and then there was the crazy Turk, Mani Velibi-Zumbul-Zadi, you know?" At that moment, he doubted whether to continue discussing the theories, or if he had better leave them for some other time. In the end, he decided to end the confession with a thin, twisted, oblique smile: "Something I learned from my father, in spite of it all, you know?"

"I see that, yes." Although she was moved, the more important fact was that Matilde was beginning to feel mildly nauseous. Was it fatigue? Weariness? But neither of those made sense, considering that, for some time, she had barely moved. Had she really been sitting erect all this time, simply watching the painter working there at the easel, moving only when he directed her to? Maybe it's just the posing, she thought in her own personal, tired, exhausted mind; but she never would have expected that. Nevertheless, the fatigue was stemming from something more nondescript than the simple fact of sitting there quietly and having her portrait drawn; it was as if the accumulation of scattered information—which vanished just as quickly as it came—was too difficult to apprehend. Not completely, at least. Arturo was fulfilling his role, yes, but not exactly in the way that she needed; he had an exceedingly strange, ambiguous, and even mysterious manner that kept slipping through her fingers. It felt like she was following a never-ending thread, the thinnest of strings, and was never able to catch up, as if she were engaged in the eternal pursuit of something unattainable. But in spite of it all, she felt content; something told her that she was on the right path and that maybe, from that point onward, she had to consider each comment—absolutely everything, down to the last detail—as potentially a part of her master's thesis. She couldn't discard anything yet. She needed to pay attention to even the most absurd theories that the painter spat out.

"On the other hand, my father's father, who was completely Mexican with almost no Sicilian in him, was a tall, robust, dark-haired man with thick eyebrows and a Pancho Villa-style moustache. That grandfather of mine was also an important political figure, Matilde. In fact, he was trained as an engineer who gave up constructing dams and bridges in the country to put an end (as he put it) to the corrupt PRI and Miguel Alemán who, by the way, was a man that my grandfather knew well and harbored a personal disagreement with, according to what I heard him once tell my grandmother. Since my paternal grandfather was so wealthy, he had the luxury of doing what he wanted: to throw himself, for example, into the fledgling government, among many other rash excesses that he could involve himself in since I was not yet born. I suppose that's where my father, Roberto Soto, inherited part of his latent democratic rage, his controversial, contrarian, detractive personality. He was an impossible, frantic man. Pedro Soto, my paternal grandfather, started out as a member of PAN, but he soon grew disillusioned with those staunch, dogmatic Catholics; he never believed for a moment that that was the path Mexico should take, despite the fact that the vast majority of Mexicans are Catholic. According to him, it was like going back to the days before Benito Juárez . . . and how does one march one hundred years into the past when, during that time, you've managed to achieve separation of church and state, something that certain European countries still haven't been able to do, despite their claims to the contrary? That's why any sign or even a hint of something that would mix politics with blind Catholicism would instill him with a sense of doubt and immediately put him on edge. Well, from there, my grandfather moved towards the Left, but I don't have to tell you, Maty, how easy it was for Pedro Soto—just like it was for my father after him—to become disillusioned with that other political orthodoxy. In the 1940s and '50s, you could find truly idealistic sorts, like the Revueltas family, ready to immolate themselves for this or that abstract cause, be it God or Communism, it didn't matter. Or you had those corrupt, lukewarm, faux Marxists, who were only involved with the movement because deep down they believed in the triumph of the Left at any cost: even the cost of having their brothers and sisters and parents lined up before a firing squad, like what happened in Mao's China. Two extremes which, of course, didn't jive with my mustachioed grandfather, Pedro Soto, and which jived even less with my father, who went, as you know, to yet another political extreme, one that was almost impossible to imagine at the time, to the point where he decided to take the millions he inherited from my grandfather to create the Partido de la Naturaleza y el Fuego Mexicano, the PNFM, which now has us all transfixed here with the absurd hope for change in Mexico. Isn't that right?" Arturo smiled and loosed a dreary and rather ironic laugh. "But ever since the turn of the century, when Vicente Fox won that famous presidential election in 2000, the Mexican people have been waiting for a change, a miracle, really, and nothing, absolutely nothing has happened during the past twenty-five years, just as my grandfather foretold (despite his vigor), and just as my father, Roberto Soto Garigli-etti, as temperamental an idealist as ever there was, tried to carry out . . ." Here the Agro painter paused, put down his piece of charcoal, exhausted and indifferent, and said to Matilde, "You know what? I'm getting tired. Why don't we finish the portrait another day?"

Caught by surprise, absorbed as she was in Arturo's overlapping story, Matilde took a moment to recover and consider what the Agro painter was asking of her. Finally, and with no small degree of difficulty, she gradually awoke from her sleepwalking state, switched off her mini tape recorder, stowed it back in her crocodile purse, and got up from the broad, broken-down sofa. Dusk was beginning to fall. It was probably seven o'clock, or even eight. The heat of the day had dissipated from the study, and in its place a sort of temperate, lukewarm sediment had settled in, just enough to stick to the skin and smear it with algal chloro-phyll. Maty stretched her arms and then calmly cracked each of her fin-gers. Strange: when would Tamara, the wife of this singular man, arrive? Did he actually have a wife? It didn't much seem like he did. She tried to approach the canvas, still under the effects of the drowsiness, but Arturo interposed himself, saying that she would see it soon enough, when it was finished. They left the studio and together they walked over to the stairwell, where Matilde was suddenly able to overcome her timidity and ask him a question:

"Arturo, if your father and grandfather had so much money, then . . ." She suddenly realized that her question was very poorly worded, and found herself at a loss as to how to complete it. Could she correct her-self? Either way, what was patently obvious was the fact that she wanted to know how a guy from a family as wealthy as Arturo's was supposed to be could wind up living in a dilapidated little hovel in Narvarte, on the roof of a five-story walkup, selling paintings to prosperous accountants and attorneys like you.

Arturo came to her rescue and answered without so much as a hint of shame:

"My father spent a good chunk of it, and my mother spent what was left. I did too, for awhile. And believe me, there was a lot of money to begin with. A lot. But I have no regrets. I love the way I'm living my life."

"And Tamara?"

"She likes this lifestyle too. If she didn't, she probably wouldn't have married me, don't you think?"

"Of course," Maty replied automatically, although something about all this still didn't quite fit, at least not with her own social expectations; in other words, earning money to gain social status. There, Maty figured, was where the chasm between them existed; that was the origin of the sense of rejection or malaise that had been pestering her despite the opposing sense of attraction or fascination she felt for this strange character with the angular face, dark eyes, beard, heavy eyebrows, and generally coarse features. Nevertheless, Matilde was scarcely able to discern this thought, coming as it did just when Arturo—in order to say goodnight to her there in the violet half-light of dusk—decided to plant a kiss squarely on her lips: quick and luminous.

XIII

The FedEx mailer arrived, and along with it, the sealed letter. It was, obviously, a very old, yellowed letter, and evidently it had never been opened, as evidenced by three distinct wax seals which had kept the contents of the letter safe until the day—if such a day would ever arrive—when Irene would decide to read it. That afternoon when it arrived, my wife decided to wait until Emilio was bathed and ready for bed; later on, we ate dinner together, silently, with scarcely a word between us, just a comment or two on the wine, perhaps, or about the salad I'd prepared just the way she likes it: with raisins, almonds, pears, grated coconut, honey, feta cheese, and a dressing made from ginger and Thai soy sauce. After that, she got up from the table, asked me to disconnect the phone, and locked herself in our bedroom with the letter and a glass of water. I followed her with my eyes (I'm sure I looked rather like a sad, supplicant old hound dog watching his elusive love walking away from him), watched her disappear behind the closing door, and remained there in our living room, trying to read a bit of Greek philosophy in order to distract myself from the sense of curiosity draped over me. Which isn't to say that I wasn't paying attention to what I was reading: the four phases of Empedocles' cosmic cycle. I suppose this wasn't the proper time or place; far from it, in fact. I don't know how much time passed—perhaps it wasn't much, only twenty or twenty-five minutes—when I saw her emerge from the room with a broken, ashen look on her face, the likes of which I'd never seen before . . . not since we've been married, not even during the exhausting labor of childbirth, which left her flat and drained there in the hospital bed, as livid as a distended zombie.

Irene sat down on the sofa next to me, contrite, and spoke in a voice that that could have been coming from beyond the grave:

"According to this letter, Eusebio, my biological mother is . . . Dulce."

I still hadn't fully comprehended what I'd heard, let alone reacted to it, when she spoke again, slowly and emphatically:

"Yes, Dulce, your mother-in-law."

"What the hell are you talking about?" I demanded, drawing my feet up onto the sofa and underneath my forty-seven-year-old body, which made me look vaguely like a squashed lotus flower.

"I'm talking about my mother. About my biological mother . . ."

"Dulce?"

"Well I'm certainly not talking about your daughter," Irene said, raising her voice to an exasperated, almost feverish level. "I'm talking about your Dulce, your mother-in-law, or rather, your ex-mother-in-law, Eusebio. Fedra's mother."

"Fedra? Dulce?" My head was reeling, and I admit to feeling a powerful wave of nausea. I was too confused and overwhelmed with the revelation that I had unintentionally brought about: What did those women from my past have to do with my present wife, with Irene? What the fuck was she talking about? Was I dreaming? Could Irene have been hallucinating? "Explain it to me again, a little more clearly. I just don't understand you, and honestly I'm starting to feel a little bit crazy."

"I don't know how I can be any more clear, especially since I don't quite understand it myself. If your ex-wife Fedra's mother's name was Dulce Mallea, then it's her. It can only be her. Now do you understand?"

"Yes, of course, Dulce Mallea . . ." I repeated after her, like a stupid, drugged-up robot, sitting there during that loving month of May, that May of dung and rage.

"And your father?" I asked, just to be saying something.

"The letter didn't say anything about my biological father. It was written and signed by her. Just her."

"Can I see it?"

"It's in the bedroom, you can go read it if you want to," she replied with a slight gesture and a nod, gently closing her eyes.

I jumped up off the sofa and ran into the bedroom. I was sweating profusely, or at very least, the palms of my hands were. On the bed lay the opened mailer and the old, yellowed, slightly wrinkled letter. I went over to the lamp and started to read, quickly, skipping over whole sentences at a time, trying to uncover the essential, revelatory elements in a flash; immediately after finishing, I went back and reread it in a much calmer manner, with the careful deliberation of a drunken hermeneutic philosopher.

Brief, affectionate, it came across as a note begging forgiveness from an unknown daughter, a baby girl who, one day in the uncertain future (right now, actually), would become an adult with many unanswered questions. Unfortunately, the letter did not offer any answers (I don't know if I was just supposing or guessing that it might have been designed to urge Irene to investigate the questions more, and ultimately seek out her mother, Dulce, in some uncertain, improbable future). It did not say, for example, who Irene's father was, nor did it explain what motivated my ex-mother-in-law (if that's who the author truly was) to give her little girl—and my current wife—up for adoption. What it did say was something we already knew anyway: that Irene was, yes, of Mexican descent, and that she had been born in Puebla de Los Ángeles. There was nothing Cuban about that. Yes, Irene and Eusebio, her adoptive parents—her authentic parents, she called them—were Cuban, and that led to the beautiful accent she shared with that island, and there were the exquisite stews she'd learned from my mother-in-law, the *ropa vieja*, and of course there was my favorite—the *sancocho*—which she prepared for me every year on my birthday alongside all of my beloved friends from the university, Stefano and Stephany, Javis, Tino, and Ritter: the roasted suckling pig with garlic encrusted fried yucca. The letter offered neither explanations nor details . . . and from that fact I was able to deduce that she, Dulce, my ex-mother-in-law, had no more idea than we did about who had adopted her baby, nor what they had named her or where she ended up residing. Zero information. Nothing. All things considered, those must have been some of the adoption agency's strict requirements, the conditions to which my ex-mother-in-law had to agree almost thirty years ago, before they would permit her to give up her little baby for adoption. So, now what? That decision was clearly up to my wife. From then on, my position would be a subsidiary one: support her, keep my mouth shut, listen to her, wait, and hope. At least, that's what I tried to do, but nevertheless, a few short minutes later (once again sitting next to Irene on the living room sofa), I understood everything with perfect clarity: the Homeric *noein* took hold of me, that selfsame sudden illumination that Hector and Helen felt. At that moment—how stupid of me!—I was finally able to see clearly that which had been right in front of my very eyes this entire time; in other words, the obvious substitution of a false impression by a new, veritable impression. I don't know quite how to explain, but I felt out of breath, as if I were in a vacuum. It was as if one of Apollo's rays had penetrated my head. I saw Irene sitting there, alarmed, asking me if something had happened. And evidently, something had, for I blurted out, point-blank:

"Do you see?"

"See what?"

"The tremendous similarity you have with my daughter," I replied, anxious and annoyed, my mouth dry, my lips chapped. "Now do you see why?"

For a moment, or perhaps it was seconds, she didn't seem to understand my words (she seemed absorbed in thought and a bit disturbed and concerned, as she should be), but then, a moment later, she turned to me with wide, crazy eyes:

"So Dulce Mallea is my mother, then; there can be no doubt whatsoever about that, Eusebio." She took a deep breath and then added, for emphasis: "Yes, your ex-mother-in-law from Mexico is my biological mother, do you see?"

"That's exactly what I was trying to say: that both my daughter and you are spitting images of Dulce Mallea. She, my daughter, looks like her grandmother, and you, of course, look like your biological mother."

"So does this mean that Fedra is my half sister?"

"I think so." There was nothing I could do but agree with that question, though I wasn't sure whether I wanted to accept my destiny, as if we were characters in a puppet theater being performed in an empty theater, isolated in the universe there in Madisonburg, the ass of the world.

We had exhausted the discoveries, the revelations. That was all that could be said. Nearly thirty years of silence and ignorance were being revealed, were coming to light, in just a few short minutes, just like any other thing, and the world didn't stop turning, nobody was struck by lightning, nobody fainted in the middle of the scene. We had been able to bear it; especially Irene, my beloved wife, my angel. Or that's how it seemed to me at the time. I suppose that if someone had been watching us at that moment, they would have seen our faces marked by a look of perplexity, uncertainty, of not knowing what the hell to do, where to go, or what course of action we should take: the face of someone who has seen the monstrous face of Medusa, also known as Professor Gross-Wayne, alias Hydra of Lerna. But not everything was spelled out; there were some things left to clarify, and the path we would follow depended entirely on Irene, on how willing she was to investigate this, or if, on the other hand, simply knowing the true name of her biological mother would be enough for her. In my own personal code of conduct, I promised to shut up and wait for that time to come. When enough time had passed, I said to myself, my wife would sound it out in her soul, and I would wait for the path she wanted to take to reveal itself in the next couple of days: her decisions, her changes in mood, her curiosity, her will. I would not participate in her process. No, absolutely not . . .

I offered her a cigarette, and I lit it for her. I lit one for myself as well. I got up to open the back door leading to the deck: I desperately needed a bit of air. The night was an unfathomable talisman, a mixture of cobalt and purple, and it hung silently over the forests and fields of Madisonburg. Emilio slept, unaware of the surprises and vagaries of life, the very same vicissitudes which I would know and experience in my own flesh from time to time, just like my daughter Dulce, in Mexico, whom I imagined was also asleep and dreaming the dreams of the innocent, something which I hadn't dreamt in a long, long time.

Watching the bruised, purplish May sky, feeling the fresh night air on my temples, and taking a third drag on my cigarette, I turned to Irene. At that point I could no longer contain myself, and I suddenly asked her, breaking my previous oath to keep my trap shut:

"Don't you think you should call her?"

"You know I like to go to sleep early," she replied, not paying much attention to me, exhaling scrolls of smoke as if they were Hesiod's *peirata*, staring into space, far from the deck where I had stopped. "I don't want to wake her up; I'll call her first thing in the morning. Please, just leave the phone disconnected, okay?"

"As far as calling Dulce Mallea is concerned . . ." For some impossible reason, I simply could not say, "calling your mother." The fact was that, come what may, I didn't have God's forgiveness. I frankly just didn't have it. Was I really unable to keep my mouth shut, to leave my wife in peace and not meddle with her life, her decisions? What motivated me, why the hell couldn't I just bite my tongue? I justified and explained my actions (as I usually do) by arguing that Irene's life was inextricably linked to my own, and that I was just now realizing that it had been and always was linked in ways that I never could have imagined.

But Irene didn't respond to me. She was probably furious. She stubbed out her cigarette and locked herself in the bedroom without wishing me good night. I was forced to sleep in the living room, not because she had ordered me to, but out of some basic feeling of respect or prudence . . . but what do I know? Maybe I even made the decision because of the sense of mystery that is instilled by the sudden appearance of Chance in our monotonous and boring lives. In fact, I couldn't sleep very well, and could only lie there and think, turning over my wife's situation in my mind eleven thousand times, her identity and destiny so inextricably linked to my own life, and that of Emilio and my daughter Dulce. In that sense, the powers of *Tyche* and *Ananke* exceeded my intelligence, my predictions, my analytic abilities. Of all the many women in the world, I happened to meet—and end up in a second marriage with—the half sister of my ex-wife, completely without knowing it or knowing who they were. And to make matters worse (or perhaps by the Grace of Providence), my son Emilio was the half brother of my daughter Dulce! Should I therefore be elated about this coincidence, or should I be terrified? If this were not the work of *Tyche*, then who could it have been, dear mystagogue from Agrigento? Perhaps it was one of the Sicilian goddesses reborn? Kypris? Or Eris?

14

(THURSDAY, MAY 11TH)

"So tell me, Maty, is your husband still the voracious reader that he used to be?"

"You mean the way he was when you knew him?"

"Of course. Ever since high school, he was devouring books, and nothing else. He loved to read and imagine himself in the character's—the hero's—role. I was surprised, then, that it was he who ended up dedicating his life to making money while I work to perfect the art of starvation. Who would have thought!"

"He doesn't actually make as much money as you might think, Arturo. It's true, he works like a slave, from dawn to dusk, for a Dutch bank, all the while swearing and lying to himself about being the boss. Strange position for a boss to be in, don't you think?"

"Have you considered the fact that back in prep school he was the intellectual and I was the son of a wealthy candidate, groomed, in the world of politics, to become a future Mexican statesman? Ha!"

"He never told me much about the two of you, though I admit, he hasn't had time. He never does. Nor do we talk about politics . . . just what he studied. Deep down, I don't really believe that he was all that interested in my career or what I did, but at least he tries to pretend that he is, you know? He's a good husband, caring and faithful, but always absorbed in his own things. What can you do? That's just men . . ."

"Well, not all men." Arturo laughed again. "Some of us live, paint, and do not read."

"I see him so late in the day that we just plop down to watch TV and have dinner in bed," Maty continued without paying any attention to Arturo's retort, her tongue perhaps under the control of some demon or other mechanism that rainy afternoon, causing her to go on and on about herself, undressing in front of the man who was there to undress and reveal himself to her, not the other way around. "That's about all we do. Otherwise, he's always walking around with a copy of that book *Friction* in his hands, always reading, like you said."

"I see how that could get boring . . ."

"No, I'm used to it by now. In fact, I like to read too. As soon as I see him open *Friction*, I start reading something myself . . . you have no idea how many overdue books I have!" She paused for a few seconds, calibrating a thought, before finally speaking again: "Only those that have to do with my thesis, Arturo, but they really pile up. Which reminds me, I wanted to tell you that this weekend I'm going to reread some parts of the book that your father wrote."

"Which one?"

"*Eros, Eris, Politics and Teratology in Mexico.*"

"Ah," he said as he recalled it. "You have no idea how many problems that essay caused him, something which I doubt anybody ever really understood, beginning with the title, which for him was already something of a sublime provocation. His whole theory was ridiculed and torn apart by his contemporaries."

"I can imagine. But would they have understood it? I have to admit, I don't. At least not very well."

"Right from the start, Maty, they were put off by the title. Imagine a member of the PRI or the PRD reading something like that back in those days. Their motto was the complete opposite: screw them now, screw them later, and screw them thoroughly."

"I think we're still practicing that sort of thing today, no? But anyway, what do you think about the book?"

"Did you read the snippets of Empedocles that I recommended?"

"No, I'm afraid not."

"Well then, switch on your tape recorder, and I'll explain the relationship between the two; or rather, where it was that my father differed from him in order to develop all his political, philosophical, and human lucubrations . . . A true madness, if you like, but a coherent one. Perfectly coherent."

Without waiting for more of an invitation, and happy to be getting down to business, Matilde removed her recorder from her Louis Vuitton purse and sat at the ready, her eyes and lips open, waiting to absorb and capture the voice of her host. Yes, she was prepared. Of course she was. She had been waiting two, three days now for this latest encounter. She had skimmed over a few excerpts from Roberto Soto Gariglietti's book, barely taking any notes in her haste, and much of the philosophical content had escaped her. She understood that a sort of cosmogony or general theory of the universe was the basis for the politician's obtuse principles. More than messianism or Utopia, which Soto Gariglietti scorned, his thoughts consisted of a complex reflection on the psychic-political phases through which the Mexican people had passed and through which they continue to pass, dating back to pre-Hispanic times.

Before he began, and without saying where he was going, Arturo exited the studio and headed over towards his room on the other side of the roof. It was pouring rain. Maty was left perplexed, with no idea quite what to do. Should she turn off her recorder, pack up her things, and leave? Or just wait? Before she could resolve this question, the painter had returned to the studio carrying two opened bottles of Bourgueil and two tin cups with handles. He set them down on a small table in front of Matilde and wiped the rain from his face and hair with his forearm before sitting down next to her.

"Forgive me; the glasses are all dirty and I don't want to waste any more time." He poured the wine and handed a mug to his guest without bothering to ask her if she wanted any, and then he clanked his against hers in a toast that produced a strange sound, a dry and crisp blow devoid of resonance. Maty couldn't help but think—as she took a small sip—about the advantages that come with drinking out of a tin cup rather than blown glassware, since the clinking of glasses produced a dreadfully strident sound which always drove her to the point of hysterical laughter, though she didn't quite know why. She should make the switch to tin cups, for sure. But wouldn't that be absurd? she immediately said to herself. What would her parents think? What about her friends at the café in Polanco? What about you, dear Reader? Without noticing, sinking deep into both her own ponderings and the lone, sagging sofa in the studio, they turned to be able to face each other as they talked, having decanted half the wine between the two of them, which served to facilitate the winding explanation being offered by Arturo, still damp with rain, an explanation which was filtering in through Matilde's open pores and permeated her bones just as the wine melded with the tin of her cup, even into her very *archai* itself, drawing her towards the sort of madness or alchemy elaborated by Roberto Soto Gariglietti thirty years before.

In his lengthy and systematic essay, the politician declared that—in accordance with the cosmic cycle theory described by Empedocles—four distinct phases of government have existed throughout Mexican history, phases which are incessantly repeated. The first takes place when all the elements are reunited in a limitless sphere. This mixture, when it achieved perfection, gave root to the existence of the divine; nevertheless, in the physical realm (or in the human dimension), the most perfect mixture that can be obtained was one of intelligence and knowledge, said Arturo, pouring more wine for him and his guest. What gives this sphere cohesion is Love, Eros, and up to this point, Strife, Discord, Eris, and Hatred are external, alien. Only peace and rest existed in that *Sphairos*, which is the entire universe and beyond, Matilde. It's important to clarify, Arturo stressed, leaning closer to his guest, that even when the elements are inextricably mixed, with desire and attraction between them, subsumed in a sort of unsung harmony, which the Greeks called *Philia*, each retains antagonistic characteristics which will later come to light. Up to this point, Maty felt that she was able to more or less follow the threads of the explanation. She did not interrupt, did not open her ruby-red lips glazed with alcohol; she simply limited herself to listening to the painter and to taking sips from her cup, which Arturo diligently refilled. The Golden Age, which my father identified as that of the Toltecs and their form of government, would correspond to this first stage. We're talking about the time of Christ, can you imagine that? According to him, the emergence of Teotihuacán signified the second phase of the Empedoclean cosmic cycle, and this happens precisely when Strife penetrates the sphere and Love slowly loses its predominance. It comes across as—how do I put it—a sort of exclusivity among the elements, which disperse and separate from the mass, from the roots. The process is gradual, very gradual, and it is precisely there, this phase, that our world, today's Earth, has settled into. But even so, Matilde, each element conserves traces of the other elements; the disintegration is not a total one. It is a clear refutation, as you might expect, of those so-called experts who, at some point in the history of philosophy, believed that, for Empedocles, our world is the world of ever-increasing Love. It's not. It's completely the opposite. Currently, in this second phase, Love is in a process of declivity, of weakening, in the face of the predominance and might of Strife, whose force, by the way, is rotary, helical, like that of an eddy or what the Greeks called *dyne*. To this point, Maty did not know whether it was the wine from Loire or the philosophic discourse that had left her in a foggy, unreal, maddening plain, a place of pure, fermented vertigo: it was as if the painter's studio and the objects packed into its corners were made of plastic or rubber, expanding and contracting according to their own will, independent of anybody or anything. She was not entirely sure that she understood the argument, but something deep within her—a tiny light which she grasped with desperation—assured her that she needn't worry too much, that she was recording the painter's entire lesson, and therefore she could listen to it again, tomorrow, when she was more relaxed, and break it down and reconstruct it as she wished. She said this to herself, of course, as an initial reaction, in the cove of her thoughts, which she wasn't quite able to articulate thanks to the wine or the rain outside. And so, unable to verbalize them, she nevertheless was able to intuit them, to spell them out: she did not have to worry, she had only to listen, to let herself be led by the cadence of the sentences, by the Empedoclean cycle, by Roberto the father and by Arturo the son and by the Spiritūs Sancti itself; but above all by the second of these, the son, so sullen, dark, and virile as he led things, gradually and imperceptibly, towards the phase (so arduous) which both of them desired to reach, yes, she already knew it, she knew it then like a bolt of lightning that splits a white cedar, like a shot from an harquebus piercing the skin, like a wound you'd want to staunch with Lysol, borax lotion, or petroleum. The intuition, the clairvoyance, frightened her, surprised her for almost a minute, but soon enough she recovered and settled in to listen, intently, to the words of the Agro painter, which were telling her that the third phase was the most problematic of all the phases that make up the Empedoclean cosmic cycle, and although the separation of the elements in concentric circles over all the Earth is due to Discord, the total process of separation takes place in an instant, a flashlike moment of transition wherein that which is completely separated suddenly begins again to unite, to congregate itself. Thus, all things, the cycle itself, can be divided into three equal periods, Matilde: Discord-Love, *Sphairos*, and Love-Discord, while the fundamental relation could be described, then, as a quadruple—completely united, separating, completely separated, and uniting—although the third step would be exclusively represented as a pure moment of transition. This supremely brief moment, when it exists, would be comparable to the sort of government the Aztecs had, and its best metaphor would be, all doubts considered, the *Guerra Florida*, the Flower Wars. You've heard of that, right? Of course she knew what the Flower Wars were, she thought. They were a horrible, idiotic, act of cruelty . . . until Arturo stopped her train of thought by placing his hand gently upon her mouth and adding: no, Maty, a necessity, a cosmic, ontological Necessity, the sort of thing the Greeks called *Ananke*. Without these ritualistic deaths and sacrifices, without these wars, these hunts and massacres, the Aztecs feared that the firmament would collapse upon the world, understand? They feared that everything would disappear. The palm of Arturo's hand was no longer covering Matilde's mouth, her ruddy lips; it had imperceptibly slid towards her hot cheek, and now,

109

pausing there, it grazed the arched, sweaty hollow that formed between her hair and the nape of her neck, the neck and the hair of his friend's wife, the beautiful woman who was letting him caress her without offering any real resistance, perhaps protected and sheltered by pre-Socratic philosophy or the warmth of the wine from Loire that lent an imaginary feeling of suffocation to the studio, in spite of the incessant rain falling outside. Without the separation of the elements, without Discord, we would not be present for the inverse process, that of unification, the creation of the world and of mortal beings by the work and grace of Eros, the famous Kypris or Aphrodite of the Greeks. The fourth phase, then, is the one that corresponds to the Conquest of Mexico, but more than a simple Conquest, Maty, it was a bloody phenomenon of miscegenation, at least, that's how my father understood it to be in his book: this fourth phase is, of course, about the union of the sphere, but the process does not, however, cease to intrigue, as you'll see, because it is not Love that takes the place of Discord; rather, Love is forced to contract as a result of the entrance of a new factor, Hatred, which compels Love towards the center. In accordance with this advancing process, Eros, thanks to the *dyne*, the eddying forces of Strife and Discord, is locked up in the exact center of this mass. At this precise moment, without even a hint of hesitation, Love begins to extend itself once again, always starting from the center, and unite the elements in order to form another world with mortal beings. And Discord? Matilde whispered, which proved, even to herself, that she was indeed following things, despite the fact that Arturo's hand was still caressing the back of her neck, following the difficult Empedoclean lucubration, the heteroclite theory of history and philosophy propagated by Roberto Soto Gariglietti. Discord, the painter replied, is defeated, relegated to the outskirts of the sphere, and with that comes a period of rest, just as there was at the beginning, like I said, a calmness that subsumes everything in an ineffable, serene, marvelous state, and having said that, he pulled her smoothly yet firmly towards him and he kissed her. Maty knew it was coming, she had been waiting for it, but she couldn't have been sure about when, exactly, it would happen; in fact, for a time, she thought that the painter was simply delaying the inevitable, or perhaps he had forgotten about his true objective, but on the other hand, there were other moments in which she felt that everything, ultimately, was going to start moving quickly, and because of that, it would be better to wait for another day, one without rain, another minute, or better yet, perhaps, she would never return to the studio, never finish her thesis, and save her marriage. It was that uncertainty, that delay, which, in the end, distracted her and allowed her to receive, without even thinking about it, that fierce, uncontrollable kiss: she anxiously thrust out her tongue, as Discord and Hatred thrust out Love, and she assured herself that yes, this was what she wanted, that cowardice or infamy was indeed worth the pain and trouble, that she could not control herself at this point, that fate had been cast to the wind, and that you, dear Reader, would be betrayed that afternoon before even reaching your first anniversary . . . Union miscegenation copulation or sex, fuck intercourse fornication, confusion confluence conjoining mixing amortizing of blood, forge bay cave yawning open sore, a widening and contracting and widening and contracting chasm, shell spider scorpion, junction perforation crack chrysanthemum or everlasting carnation that suddenly closes up around a dolmen or stinger: Love penetrated by Discord, the expansion of Aphrodite due to that helical, rotary, myrtle sipping hummingbird force of the sovereign Discord: Eros penetrated by Eris: she suddenly understood everything via *nous* or at least she believed she did with Arturo plunging diving joining driving in a flash with the leptosomatic macrogenitosomia sting in the blink of an eye without her even noticing or realizing as he was lifting up her dress digging his nails and pulling off her Victoria's Secret panties while they both continued to kiss, sucking on shared saliva with avarice clutching clawing grasping at her gluteus maximus, her ass as wide as the Argentine *pampas*, riding her like a *gaucho* atop his bucking bay mare the way her husband her cuckold had never done before, chomping at the bit, fervently sinking her teeth into the shoulder of the painter riding her because she could not bear that lascivious cosmic eddy and his tendril or lingam so deep inside of her oh so incredibly deep the *sperma* or nacre syrup from the man with the black, lightless eyes or jet-black like a dog since now yes she was inebriated satisfied content with Arturo's index finger (or was it the ring finger?) *per angostam viam* and because Matilde desired at that very moment to be reincarnated as the prostitute of Cibola the mare the priestess of Bacchus or whatever: whore of Hesperides or happy immoral canephora driven mad and subjugated while just outside the rain continues to fall the sky remains occulted as the gigantic clouds continue to thicken over Narvarte . . .

XV

The other day I found the answer to the question that had kept me up in quite a state that night: were the events taking place the work of *Tyche*, or what the hell was it in reality? Since Irene was still in an introspective state the likes of which I'd never seen before (to the point where I almost didn't recognize her), I though it the opportune time to go to the grocery store with Emilio, leaving her alone for a solid couple of hours, in silence, with only her thoughts. I would buy tomatoes, lemons, garlic, onions, butter, aromatic herbs . . . everything needed for a good pasta with white wine sauce, which was one of my specialties.

The Virginia afternoon was beautiful, clear, with a slight breeze at your back, buoying you up; you felt light, aerial, almost happy to be alive. As for myself, all this that I'm telling you is not the least bit important, or it wouldn't be, if—just when I stepped out of the enormous grocery store—I hadn't had one of those so-called epiphanies, a strange revelation which later becomes quite difficult to describe or relate, even with a few drinks, your head spinning in a cloud of cigarette smoke and the strains of Miles Davis's trumpet.

The fact is that when Emilio and I left the grocery store with bags in hand, we found ourselves face to face with a group of Mexican compatriots. Upon seeing that trio (a father, a mother, and a boy about the same age as my son, or perhaps a bit older) I had an impression that I'll translate more or less thusly: what does this small Mexican family have to do with me, with my son Emilio, Irene, and I? In the strictest sense, they have absolutely nothing to do with us—nobody introduced us, nor were we neighbors or acquaintances—just as I have nothing to do with the black family getting out of that car over there, or with that albino Gringo family, or the Korean or Chinese family from down the road. To the eyes of most Americans, the trio of compatriots have quite a bit in common with my own family—given that we both speak Spanish and come from the southern side of the Río Bravo (or the Rio Grande)—yet in our hearts, and even superficially, there is little if anything that binds us, in the same way that there is nothing that binds, *sensu stricto*, the multitude of American families scattered throughout or packed in across the nation. In other words, being Mexican, sharing the exile's experience (as hundreds of thousands of others do), and sharing a country of origin doesn't make me feel somehow united to them, any more than I feel united with the checkout lady at the grocery store or with one of my students at Millard Fillmore University. In fact, I probably felt closer to my students (despite the difference in age) than I did to that family of Mexican immigrants trying to make a better life for themselves, just as I was trying to do with Irene and Emilio. I know that, at least in principle, what I'm saying doesn't make much sense, and that it might sound a bit ridiculous or hollow, despite the shared necessity of living the life of an exile (whether imposed or not), which involves, first, understanding how others often try, in spite of themselves, to homogenize or situate you in some category that's as restrictive as a corset, and, secondly, the sheer amount of time it takes before you can, bit by bit, even start to assimilate, despite what your government (which one?) says, despite what your church says (which one?), despite what others say (in this case, it's the Gringos you run into on a daily basis). You have nothing to do with those other Mexicans (or Latinos or Hispanics or Chicanos or Pochos), just as if, for example, I were walking with Emilio down the streets of Mexico City, we would have nothing to do with the thousands and thousands of other people we passed on the street. I neither love them nor hate them; in other words, they don't matter to me. That family and ours speak Spanish, we're all Mexicans, but what of it? That coincidence or similarity doesn't necessarily imply that we have to have something in common. Where does that impulse come from? Some call to identity? No, it's completely misplaced, as is the case, I imagine, with those monolingual Americans I so often encounter: is it the case that, from their point of view, they have something in common with each other? In essence, no. They might even desire or believe in things that are diametrically opposed. In any case, it's just me and my own foolish prejudices that imagine or create networks and connections by sight alone (maybe because certain people have the same blond hair or speak English), since the only certain thing is that there is nothing that unites people *a priori*, simply because one sees or intuits it in that manner.

In summary, what I wanted to get across with this parenthesis while my wife was deciding what to do with her life is the fact that my relationship or identity with another Latino in the United States needn't be better or worse, greater or lesser, than what I have with any other person, whether Gringo or Russian or Chinese or Peruvian. But if, on the other hand, if I happen to exchange a few words with the cashier (whether she is Mexican or Ukrainian or Japanese), then the beginnings of an *ipso facto* relationship, whether voluntary or not, would be established: one which might (with a variable, x, as potential) or might not gain a foothold in the future.

All this mental circumlocution I did that morning at the store led me to another, no less important question: With whom do I want to establish a relationship? Who are the people most similar to me? With whom do I want to have contact, friction, or even a friendship? And since each and every time I confirm that the world is a giant ball of shit, or a sphere, as Empedocles would say, a *Sphairos* of immeasurable human stupidity (also known as ignorance, myopia, narrow-mindedness, small-mindedness, provincialism, egoism, nastiness, prejudice, convenience, wickedness, maliciousness, envy, jealousy, viciousness, or poor faith), then I can do little else save try, little by little, to conform to my own paltry sphere, my close circle of relationships, my network. This should not affect other, similar things, which I may or may not encounter, though, in fact, I must encounter them in order to create that parallel, substitute world. (Although here it is important to clarify the fact that it's not really about a full-scale substitute world and that we're not being evasive or looking for a way out; rather, it's simply about creating a small subset within the greater Set at large, which is the world. It's an attempt, then, to construct a more or less *ad hoc* atmosphere, a place where people have roughly the same anxieties and interests, with the random happy few who agree in principle with you and make for a more amiable, more bearable life.) All this, of course, sounds like a universal truism, but in fact it is not: it's about understanding once and for all that this is the way the world is, like Baroja said. It's an infinitesimal sum of sets and subsets jammed together like toes in a shoe two sizes too small, struggling to share a habitat where nobody wants to be or participate in another set or subset or sub-subset, but where people desire quite the opposite: where each one wishes, as much as possible, to maintain and preserve his own small, fragile set. His own little nest. Nevertheless, there occasionally arises a madman or a nation or even a proselytizing religion that attempts to rise up, to expand the strength of its set, to impose itself on the others, agglutinating other subsets without respecting or even understanding the most elemental thing: that we are perfectly different, that diversity and plural worlds are necessary. All social utopias (especially the powder keg utopias that brought down the nineteenth century and continued their devastation into the twentieth) have taught us is that it's an act of acute stupidity and a waste of energy to try to change the world, to change those millions of sets and subsets that inhabit and share the Earth with one another, because ultimately it means bringing an end to dissimilarities, about imposing law of the strong upon others using the false sophism of the *telos* of History, those "necessary ends" which, since the days of Aristotle and through the age of Hegel, try to point to a goal, a happy conclusion, as if someday we would simply decide to consider ourselves as equals, to bring us all into line, homogenized, and become a single Set. This sort of expansive search, this universal Necessity or *Ananke* of integrating the disparate and dissimilar, was something that Empedocles imagined as a cosmogonic and beneficent force which he called Love, Philia, Aphrodite, Kypris, Eros.

And now, back to my epiphany that morning: Eris, Strife, Discord exists, and it also has, in my opinion, a very beneficial function, a profound and much-maligned reason for being: I understood that we aren't here, in this world, to be as one (the way Friedrich Schiller and George W. Bush dreamed of) or to assimilate with the other, but on the contrary, we are here to try to conform, time and again, throughout our lives, to a sort of small redoubt, a tiny sphere of the similar—barely even a sub-sub-subset—with the unique aim of not only finding Fourier's Harmony or the unattainable Love in Empedocles' *Sphairos*, but also that more or less indescribable thing, which I discovered that afternoon, holding my son Emilio's hand as I left the grocery store: that the great central mass, the sphere, will not be able to include us all forever, will not be able to eternally contain—whether in distinct or indefinite proportions—the four basic elements or roots, since it is that very same magnetic or centripetal force which—just as we have entered the phase of Love—brings about Discord, the disintegration, dispersal, and separation of things before turning them (once again) into new and varied subsets. It is, let's say, the *raison d'être* of the sphere: its own, intimate nature.

The infinite succession of worlds which is the Empedoclean cycle (and therefore the source of my revelation) must divide itself, according to Empedocles, into three equal phases: Discord-Love, *Sphairos*, and Love-Discord, with a mere infinitesimal moment of rest in the middle. And, delving even deeper, the relation could be described as quadruple—completely united, separating, completely separated, and uniting—although this third stage or period would be represented by an incredibly brief moment of transition. In fact, just as Aristotle keenly observed in making his teleological critique of Empedocles' anti-teleological thinking, when separating the dissimilar in the sphere, Discord reunites similar substances (though in small subsets and sub-subsets), and it is precisely there that I find the true genius of the man from Agrigento. I was able to corroborate this for myself barely a minute later when, right there in the grocery store parking lot, I saw a group of young black people in a friendly gathering, chewing gum and smoking cigarettes and listening to the same unbearable song, and I thought, "Here it is, Eusebio, proof that like attracts like . . . it's a space into which neither Emilio and I nor anybody else would be invited to participate or coexist." But no more than two minutes had passed (my son and I were in the car by then and ready to leave) before we saw two of those same young black people (both of them, as I said, reunited in their intimate sub-sub-sub-subset created in advance by the paradoxical and beneficial force of Discord) come to blows, falling to the asphalt, smeared with blood, watched and cheered on by their partners, their friends, the ones who I thought belonged to that irreducible sub-sub-subset. In the time it takes to blink your eyes, two police officers arrived on the scene (one white and the other Chicano, by the way) to separate them, handcuff them, and take them back to the police station or wherever. As I started to pull out of my parking spot, I said to myself, "That's how it begins, with a quarrel and an immediate separation of equals, the inevitable, unifying process of Love: the dissimilarities, which are just about to be precariously reunited, are now left to be united, integrated once again, to form and shape the sphere, which condenses and mixes (in differing proportions) everything that is different, everything that is distinct, everything that is not equal.

Outside the parking lot now, and on the way home, I thought again: perhaps I have to create my own reduced circle in which, by any means necessary, I would prohibit things like vanity (Fedra), idiocy (Dean Whitehead), wickedness and inferiority complexes (Gaudencia), provincialism (Wynn), the false cleverness of innocence (Vasco-Osama), racism (Bormann-Smythe), the hidden cowardice of Christianity (Ritter), hypocrisy (Fazzion), reticence (Javis), brownnosing (Tino), and the millions of prejudices that exist in the beastly, imbecilic world today. Perhaps I will be something of an *Ananke* for my wife, a conscious and necessary agent of Hatred and Discord? If that were the case, it would include the fact that Eris doesn't remain static and immovable either. On the contrary, the phase that the world is experiencing is, according to Empedocles, one of incredible tension between the supremacy of Love and the increasing power of Strife, which is disintegrating unity bit by bit. With regard to Irene, it may not all be due to *Tyche* as I said earlier; rather, to plain and simple friction.

16
(TUESDAY, MAY 16TH)

"My father was born in 1944 and he died in 2004. He was sixty years old, just as Empedocles is supposed to have been. I was born in 1984, Maty, just after my father turned forty. I don't have to tell you this, but honestly, his death hurt me deeply. As you know, I was in the middle of my adolescence, a maladjusted, insufferable, snot-nosed brat, desperate to find his way; in other words, a boy desperate to become something different from his famous, beloved father. I didn't want to be his continuation, a bad imitation, a parody. The ironic thing, as you know, is that the harder a kid tries not to become his father, the more he ends up repeating or perpetuating him . . . His exemplary death moved me to reconsider the antagonism I felt towards him, to reconsider my naïve rebelliousness, and for the first time, I was able to recognize which elements of his character had been passed on to me and which had not . . . and—what a surprise!—it was much more than I ever thought, you know? But first, Matilde, let me get back to Roberto Soto Gariglietti and my maternal grandparents and great-grandparents . . ." Arturo didn't wait for his friend's wife to respond. He wanted to speak, to talk, to tell her everything he knew; it wasn't just his acquired commitment, his promise, but now it had also become something of an uncontrolled necessity, an obligation that was quickly sweeping over him as he caressed Maty's brown hair and chin as she looked up at the smoke-stained ceiling of the painter's studio. "My father's mother was named Ana; she was Mexican even though her father, my great-grandfather Enzo, was a Sicilian man who came to Mexico almost by mistake. He was born in Agrigento, the illustrious land of Empedocles. The ship carrying Italian immigrants to New York never reached her destination, and instead the passengers disembarked at the port city of Veracruz a year and a half before the Revolution began. My great-grandfather, a young and inexperienced man, started his life there from rock bottom, without so much as a penny. He knew nothing of Mexico and her tribulations. In just a short time, however, Enzo Gariglietti came to know the country's internal battles and wheelings and dealings like the back of his hand; better, even, than some of the natives he met. He got involved in the machinations and elaborate plottings of power-hungry politicians who promised the imminent fall of Porfirio Díaz. Like many young people in those days, and despite being a foreigner, my great-grandfather was inflamed with passion when Madero, that little man exiled to the United States, won the presidency in 1911. It transformed him overnight into something of a revolutionary; or rather, it was his admiration for Madero and the subsequent treachery by Victoriano Huerta in 1913 that turned him into a true, diehard revolutionary, a Garibaldi figure fighting for justice in a country that wasn't his own, but was quickly adopting him. In fact, did you know, Maty, that the grandson of Garibaldi himself was in Mexico at the time, but he turned out to be an upstart puppet who was using his grandfather's name to gain power for himself. On the other hand, after just over two years of working on behalf of Madero in Veracruz, my great-grandfather had become something of a patriot—well, perhaps not exactly—but a man committed to justice and equality and the future of Mexico, things which he hadn't, of course, been able to find in Southern Italy. During those years, still living on the coast there, he met a timid, young, broke orphan from Durango. The parents of my great-grandmother Josefa had been assassinated by a landowner, and an old boss sympathetic to her father ended up giving her a small inheritance, which Josefa used to flee Durango for her distant relatives in Veracruz. There, at the famous Gran Café de la Parroquia, Josefa met Enzo Gariglietti completely by chance, when he gave her a few *centavos* for a *café con leche* which she had ordered but couldn't pay for. Shortly thereafter—and without making a *telenovela* out of it—they fell in love and got married, despite their mutual poverty. Enzo improved his Spanish, and Josefa began learning Italian. But it wasn't until several years later, in 1922, that she gave birth to her only daughter, my grandmother. But before I tell you about Ana, you need to know something very important, Maty: how did a Sicilian man named Enzo end up being one of the most hated supporters of Pancho Villa of that period? The reason is simple: the same landowner from Durango, a man named Domínguez, was, among other things, one of the hundreds of bloodthirsty enemies Villa had, swearing time and again that the man had robbed him of a few head of cattle some time before the Revolution, around the turn of the century, when the man once known as Doroteo Arango was still a young, unknown *bandido* from Northeastern Mexico. Domínguez hated him with the same fervor that the wealthy hated Villa and his Dorados. I suppose that was the reason why Domínguez had been pursuing him for quite some time, always on his tail though never quite able to lay a hand on him. Villa, on the other hand, said that Domínguez was a no-good dirty swine, a dishonorable man, a man who had done nothing but exploit his laborers for decades, including some of Villa's own relatives, or relatives of his wife Luz (well, one of his many wives). In the end, when the powder keg blew up and spread out across several states, Villa returned with a handful of men to personally recover damages that the landowner had caused him, his wife and her relatives, as well as the laborers themselves. This was around 1912 or 1913, I think. As he redistributed the goods from the *hacienda* among the orphans, *campesinos*, and widows—something he did every time he took over a property—Villa found a decent sum of money that belonged to one Josefa, who, as I said, was living in exile in Veracruz with her husband, my great-grandfather Enzo, barely able to earn enough to eat while they worked on behalf of Madero. After two or three months, at Villa's personal request, they both returned to Durango and the same tiny house on Domínguez's property that Josefa had once called home. There, my great-grandfather Gariglietti first met the general and immediately became enamored with him and his revolutionary will, his sincerity, and his commitment to the helpless, downtrodden, underdog class which reminded him so much, he said, of people in his native Sicily. He did not delay, then, in joining the armed uprising against the tyrant Huerta. As the years passed, though, Enzo became one of the most loyal foreign delegates that Villa had. He served him primarily in Europe, where the general sent him on a number of occasions, with the task of convincing other nations—especially the Vatican—to refuse to recognize Huerta's government, and later, that of Carranza. It was all in vain, though, for as you know the Vatican has always sided with those who hold the power. It knows the chameleon's art better than any other state. My great-grandfather spent the better part of the decade engaged in this business of lobbying, in this game of struggling for power, until, in 1922, at thirty-odd years of age, he had his one and only daughter. Ana, my grandmother, was a very beautiful young woman, according to some photos taken during her youth in Durango, which is why, since the age of thirteen or fourteen, she began to attract the attention of the wealthy men in town. It seems that my great-grandparents sent her off to Mexico

City to study, partly because they wanted to keep her from falling for someone they considered undesirable, but also because she had a real affinity for languages. She spoke perfect Spanish, Italian, and English, and wanted to continue on into French and Russian; something which would have been quite impossible there in Durango. But in the capital city, around 1941 or 1942, she met a strapping young man from Veracruz, my grandfather Pedro Soto, who was studying law and had his sights set on one day becoming Interior Secretary or even President of the Republic. He only rose as high as senator, but the fact is that Pedro, my paternal grandfather, was a natural born politician, and since he was a teenager, he had been set in the path of that same vocation as the man who would, shortly thereafter, become his father-in-law. My grandfather Pedro Soto had family money, so it wasn't much of a problem for him to devote his entire life to his passion and true calling: to bringing democracy to the country, to social reforms, to defeating the PRI, and—above all—to bringing an end to his political adversary, a young man from Veracruz by the name of Miguel Alemán, whom he knew all the way back to their days as students at the old Jesuit school. Yes, Matilde, my grandfather Pedro, the father of my father, bet poorly. In other words, he always sided with the losers, the humiliated ones, just like his father-in-law, my Italian grandfather, had done. It appeared to be a family defect, one of those genetic diseases that are passed from generation to generation. The curious thing, though, is that it never seemed at all important to either of them, and even less so to Roberto, my father. Their *modus operandi*, so to speak, was to be contrarians, to make life impossible for as many corrupt politicians as time would allow them, instead of accepting political handouts, which they always declined. Both of them, Enzo and Pedro, father-in-law and son-in-law, were unrelenting to the fullest extent of the term, and both insisted on the need to create a true democracy, with rotating powers, and freedoms based on progress and education, as the only possible solution for Mexican government. But that was just the first link in a little chain, wherein a lack of democracy meant that there would be no freedom, and without freedom there would be no education, and without education there would be no fairness, and without fairness there would be no justice, and without justice there would be no economic prosperity either, and that was something about which they both concurred. In this sense, according to them, democracy itself isn't worth a damn thing other than as a tool for garnering certain benefits of well-being and prosperity that everyone ultimately wants: potable water, electricity, a functional sewage system, urbanization, and a minimum threshold for quality of life, including health, education, security, purchasing power, freedom of the press . . . basic things, which even today, in 2025, do not exist. I suppose that's why father- and son-in-law got along so well. They believed in these things to the letter. They were bloodthirsty enemies of the state, or better yet, enemies of that sort of Cardenist-Populist state that, instead of promoting foreign investment and the free market system, obstructs them. Instead of privatization, it promotes state intervention. Instead of stimulating the economy, it asphyxiates it. If we don't start securing political transparency, if we don't start demanding honesty and rectitude at the highest levels, if we allow the slow bureaucratization of the country, if the judicial system is not solidified and legitimized, if we don't respect and value minorities, we won't get anywhere, and every single Mexican man, woman, and child will be fucked. According to Pedro Soto, the so-called Caudillo Syndrome—pure oligarchy, corruption, and nepotism—is present in all Mexicans, infected deep within their marrow like Catholicism or Castilian Spanish. He felt it necessary to eradicate the disease, and that it could be done, with enough time and the proper example. It would take at least one hundred years . . . but in the end, we would have it. Needless to say, he was an optimist. It would have to begin with children, with the education of children, with schools, with transforming their minds and spirits; it would have to begin with the dismantling of the pernicious colonial mind-set, with its defects and vices. He didn't create a political party, he didn't align himself with the PAN, but he was able to become a senator in the fifties and left his mark, scattered the seeds, the generational idea which, as you know, his son would continue. It is my father, then, who would later rewrite the history (let's say) of his father's truncated or bankrupt destiny. It would be Roberto Soto Gariglietti, and not Pedro Soto, who created the Partido de la Naturaleza y el Fuego Mexicano back in the nineties, and who—thirty years later—rose to become a presidential candidate . . ." Here Arturo paused to take a breath, before reaching down to take a cigarette from a pack lying on the floor of the studio and lighting it. Immediately after inhaling, he offered one to Maty who rejected it, though without disengaging herself from the painter's body, which she was leaning against, languid and attentive. "I already told you the other day that my father had his revelation in Sicily, right? In Agrigento. My father was visiting there around 1962 or 1963 with Pablo, his best friend. Some other time I'll tell you what happened there, about the unexpected thing that shook up his life, turned everything on its head, changing his life forever when he was a mere eighteen or nineteen years old. In any case, he retuned to Mexico a changed man with the firm conviction to study medicine. Which he did, though he didn't finish his degree. In the final semester of his brilliant academic career—October of 1968—his life took another radical turn. Pablo, his best friend, the same one he'd traveled to Europe with, was slaughtered right in front of his very eyes, and this drove him irremediably into politics, something that he'd previously avoided out of fear of repeating the life of his father. In a way, the Night of Tlatelolco opened his eyes for the second time . . . though in a terrible sort of way. After that unexpected discovery in Sicily, the event that had initially steered him towards a career in medicine, the second revelatory moment occurred during that horrific massacre, which he witnessed when he was twenty-four or twenty-five years old. So again, that is the reason he left medicine, choosing instead to study philosophy, an apparently radical change in course . . . though not really, if you examine it closely. He believed that we had not only inherited our ideas of democracy and justice from the Greeks, that our concept of justice and our search for the truth came from the ancient Greeks; he also believed that our perceptions of humanity and our scientific stammerings stem from them as well. He believed (or he said he did) that the profound study of the Greeks would lead us unfailingly to an understanding of the Romans, of Seneca and Hadrian; a process not unlike the one that led him to follow his own father and my great-grandfather Enzo . . . though each, as you now know, took a different route. All that notwithstanding, I think that what really happened was that, first, the dramatic political events in the fall of '68 shook him deeply, and second, though he was ready to leave medicine behind, he certainly wasn't about to start studying law. He was more interested in the philosophy of law, which was a much more abstract concept, one he wasn't able to define at the time. He deeply despised shysters, he scorned litigants, he had no sympathy for attorneys or people who took degrees just to further their blossoming political aspirations, but mainly he detested the whole legal bureaucracy because, as he said, it was the swamp in which Mexico was mired. I suppose that's why studying Greek philosophy was the best alternative, for he had finally found something that he loved, and it was the only thing that helped him out of the existential sense of discouragement into which he had fallen since the death of his best friend. All this considered, his extravagant point of departure, so unlike that of any other politician, was more political-philosophical and even more so purely philosophical: it was the point of view from which a philosopher perceives nature, the way the pre-Socratic thinkers came to know and understand things . . . It was also around this time that a marvelous article fell into his hands purely by chance, one written by a man who would soon become a true mentor and friend, despite their significant difference in age. This man was one of the twentieth century's great philosophers: an Austrian Jew named Karl Popper. He was a rationalist to the extreme, and he taught my father what he had already fully inherited from his own father and grandfather: the importance of swimming against the current, of taking on the job of criticizing the foundations, any form of unchallenged truth, any type of episteme, especially those pertaining to scientific knowledge, which would soon carry my father (who was a pseudomystic at heart) to the other edge of what, in principle, Popper was predicating. Anyway, what my father read during the winter of 1968–69 was a long—a very long—transcript of a lecture Popper had given at a conference a few years before (around 1965, I think) to inaugurate the Colloquium on the Philosophy of Science at Bedford College. It was entitled "Rationality and the Search for Invariants," and its primary thesis was none other than that of the pre-Socratic philosophers; in particular, his favorite philosopher, Parmenides, the same Eleatic rationalist who would devote many more works on the subject from that time until the end of his life. So, anyway, the fact is that my father, fed up with Mexico and the orangutan running the country, decided it would be best to first go and study at the London School of Economics, where Popper taught, and leave everything else behind . . ."

All of a sudden, an unexpected creaking, cracking sound stirred them from the state of historical ecstasy they'd been in for over an hour now, one reclining upon the other there in the painter's studio, on the same cushions on which the models posed from time to time. Matilde, unsettled, thought she heard the sound of faint steps, barely a whisper of someone passing outside, on the roof, near the separate room where Arturo slept. She jumped to her feet, hands clasped to her chest, as if someone were suddenly watching her. She turned around (inquisitively) to see the painter's face, which, to her surprise, simply smiled and offered a wink to calm her down, to settle her with an ambiguous movement of the eyebrow. She didn't react, as if she didn't understand the gesture. Arturo, as if in response, began to softly caress her naked back, the way one might stroke a horse or a cat in heat that had curled up against his ribs. She didn't say anything. Not even a word. Finally, unable to hold it in any longer, made desperate by the unbearable silence of her lover, Matilde whispered, afraid that someone might hear her:

That same night, after we'd polished off my pasta with white wine sauce (I should clarify: after Emilio and I polished off the pasta, for Irene didn't have so much as a bite), my wife announced that she would need a few days for serene reflection. My surprise was evident in the strong, simple belch which I could not control and which left Emilio in peals of laughter that immediately gave way to imitations of his uncultured and idiotic old man. This, along with the lack of patience Irene possessed that day, simply hastened the hour of our anxious conjugal ritual. Not exactly the one involving the desire of love, but rather the desire for rest at the end of a long and complicated day: get Emilio into his pajamas, brush his teeth, read a couple of stories to him, simulate a prayer, and then wait for sleep to come to you in the warm and cozy penumbra of your bedroom. That was my task, and I admit, I loved it.

However, I missed doing all that with Dulce, my daughter, now so far away from me, so distant from her dear old foolish *papi*. Needless to say, not having her by my side was a silent sadness, which ate away at me like a termite chewing through rotting wood. The curse of nostalgia does not wane with the years, though I thought it would (or hoped it would) at first, when Emilio was born and filled this old exile with joy.

But let's not get sidetracked. I had to put my son to bed because it was clear that Irene wanted to talk that night, that she needed to tell me something, and she did once we were sitting down on the comfortable couch in the living room, which was the best part of our American-style home:

"I hope this doesn't upset you, Eusebio, but I called my mother again, and she invited me to go and spend a few days in San Francisco. I still haven't gotten the whole truth. Why keep deluding ourselves? Why should I delude you? I need to know what to do, and I'd rather be alone, to meditate . . ."

Although unnerved, I still had the experience born of my one and only divorce, and I replied without revealing my sudden surprise:

"You know I support you. I'll wait for you here. I'll take care of Emilio. Take as long as you want."

"I'll take him with me. That way you won't have anything to worry about. My mother hasn't seen him, and this would be a good opportunity for both of them, don't you think? Emilio is a stranger to his own grandmother. She promised to take care of him while I decide whether to go to Mexico in search of my real mother, or whether I should leave things as they are."

"So you're thinking of going to Mexico?"

"Honestly, I don't know. I'm confused. Very, very confused."

I must admit that I didn't know if the frank, abrupt news I got from my wife that night felt liberating or depressing. I didn't know what to feel because, in all honesty, to this day I still don't know how to feel, I'm still not sure how to calibrate my emotions, if I even have any. Suffice it to say that I was confused, just like her, but evidently my confusion was a pittance when compared to the mental and emotional jumble that my wife must have been working her way through. So I kept quiet. I was trapped. We were trapped. I accepted the trip, her inner trip, her anabasis or whatever you want to call it. That same night, Irene went online and bought the plane tickets, and the next day, my little family—the only one that I had, and the only one I had known during my entire Madisonburg existence—was gone, first to spend a few days with my mother-in-law in San Francisco, on the complete opposite side of the country (a place which, for all intents and purposes, is another country altogether), and then perhaps on to Mexico City, the wicked Capirucha, home to thirty million savages.

Before saying good-bye, as Irene was about to enter that aseptic labyrinth of an airport with Emilio, I was able to tell her (though I don't know whether it constituted a sulking, vengeful response to her hasty departure) that I also might leave town and spend a few days in New York, if that was alright with her. The spring semester had just ended, and summer classes were yet to begin. As always, she responded with a great big hug, and said:

"That's a great idea, love. Of course that's okay. I don't want you to be in the house all alone. That would be so depressing. If you want, invite Stefano or Javis to go with you. Whoever you want to keep you company." She sounded so jubilant about it that I couldn't help but feel a bit deflated. Didn't it matter? Even a bit? Wasn't she worried that I, her husband, was heading off to New York, possibly with Stefano, my raucous, bawdy, Italian friend from the department? *No, Eusebio*, I told myself, trying to maintain my sanity. *It's not that it doesn't matter to her. Take it easy, man. It's just a little time for her, some space, an opportunity to figure out what she (relaxed and on her own) really wants to do about solving this cosmic biological mystery. Wait for her, man, just give her a few days or a couple of weeks, and everything will clear up fine.* So, to make a long story short, I will simply say that a couple of days later, though still not completely calm, this man (me) left for New York, though without Javis or Stefano, whose wife, Stephany, a rather jealous Quaker, didn't really appreciate my invitation. Nevertheless, once I arrived in that imposing city of pinnacles and skyscrapers, dazed and disoriented in the crowded bowels of Penn Station, I once again realized what I'd always known and yet seemed to forget with each new visit: that New York does not exist, that New York has never existed, that New York is like Cairo or Mexico City or even a bit like Paris, though it's also quite different . . . How do you put it, Irene? None of these cities exist in principle, or they exist in part, or perhaps New York is simply the only one that has never existed, even after it was invented or dreamt up. I corroborated that truth again during those five days in which I strolled by avenues and squares, streets and parks, bridges and museums, suddenly understanding—like a García Lorca fresh off the boat—that I didn't exist either, despite the fact that I was there, watching so many people at arm's length. And that's what really happened: suddenly, in the span of time it takes to blink your eyes, nobody noticed me, I didn't mean a thing to anybody for those five solitary, ill-starred days I spent roaming and rambling all over Manhattan until I crossed the Brooklyn Bridge and reached the other side and Brooklyn Heights, where I could contemplate, dazzled in the late afternoon light, the buildings piercing the reddening sky just across the water.

New York City, Irene, is a crowded island, but it is also a city of millions of individual islands jammed together and stacked upon one another, which makes the process of alienation complete and immediate as soon as your plane touches down at JFK or LaGuardia, or as soon as you set foot on the chaotic platforms in Penn Station. Perhaps you could prophesy that I wouldn't meet or even exchange so much as a word with anybody during five insufferable days in New York? But perhaps I'm exaggerating, perhaps I did speak with the manager of the little hotel I stayed in for eighty dollars a night, or with the man hawking papers at the kiosk, or the young woman in an apron who served me coffee every morning in the corner of the hotel . . . but aside from those three, Irene, plus a crazy man I ran into one night, I couldn't have a friendly conversation with anybody else. The point is that I walked and walked and walked. But where? I don't know. In fact, it's not even important; you simply walk up and down Manhattan, along Broadway, past Union Square, Second Avenue, Fifth Avenue, 14th Street, Central Park, SoHo, the East Village, Astor Place, Times Square, St. Mark's Place, Lexington Avenue, everywhere, everywhere, all the while thousands and thousands of faces are passing you by, thousands and thousands of fleeing, transient bodies passing your perfectly invisible body. But maybe they do see you? Did they see me? Apparently, we see each other, or at least it seems that our eyes meet, our gaze occasionally collides for an instant, sometimes for a second or two, who knows, but then . . . nothing. They disappear, they are no longer there, completely dissolved, leaving no sign, no track, no trace of human reminiscence, recollection, or memory, and all because immediately after, in the blink of an eye, almost consecutively, really, you have passed through the gaze of perhaps two or three or four more people, crossed paths with hundreds of fugitive faces, just like that, *ad nauseam*, which is a truly terrible and promiscuous thing. The retina cannot fix itself on anything, the reticle cannot focus its crosshairs, damn it . . . nothing solidifies, nothing congeals, no frame is frozen, as they say dogs are incapable of doing in their stupid canine memories. It was, believe you me, like playing a game involving an infinite series of intentionally lost canine glances, a sort of limitless, bottomless well of endless, fleeting looks: to see and not be seen, to cross paths and not have your path crossed on a congested sidewalk. A macabre game played at a breakneck pace whose primary axiom or rule was the impossibility of recognition, the freezing of body or sight. There was something actually quite debilitating about it, something overwhelming, because if you suddenly wished (let us suppose) to turn the classic New York rule on its head and just once fixate (for example) on a face, a nose, a frown . . . but it was as clear to me as a metaphysical slap in the face that this rule would nevertheless remain inflexible, indestructible: there would still be no correspondence, no reciprocity, no human contact. Glances, yes, there would be many, many glances. Looks would abound. But recognition, no. That would be impossible, Irene, and do you know why? Simply because you cannot recognize what isn't there, what does not not exist. You can't see the unseen; you can't even dream of it.

So, after that new epiphany, I began to realize that if I did not exist to any of those thousands upon thousands of beings who saw me, whose field of vision encountered my own as they hurried down the street, then nothing should exist there, everything had to be an illusion, an act of prestidigitation performed by David Copperfield . . . but, of course, on a much grander scale. And further still: I understood that New Yorkers, though they might seem like robots or zombies with open eyes and completely alert reflexes, do not even exist because they have, at their core, such an acceleration of particles—with such a high velocity of displacement—that the molecules which comprise them very quickly begin to disperse themselves, to disintegrate to the point where they are scattered into the ether, ending up in a sort of stain or residue or *arche*, something not unlike an essence or clothed entelechy, a human nebula with eyes, skin, teeth, and a nose full of hair and snot.

It is perhaps that acceleration itself—ultimately converted into an incredible centrifugal force and combined with the conglomeration of the city and the crevasse or bottomless pit that lives and feeds there in New York—that is the root of their nothingness, their emptiness. Even if I know you today, for example, tomorrow I may not recognize you, I may not remember you because, a split second later, I have met another and another and another one still; in other words, I don't know anybody, I never knew anybody, which only confirms what I've always known: that New York is the synecdoche for the world, it is everything reduced to nothing, it is the megalopolis where, if I copulate with you, I copulate with nobody; where, if I have a child with you, I have never had any children with anybody; where, if I grow old with you, I do not age because I have never aged or because I simply haven't been born or because I don't recognize my own father, or never had one, let alone a mother or brothers or sisters. How can you be related to someone who hasn't been born, somebody who doesn't have a birthday? How can you age if you don't exist? How can I exist in New York if I can come and go from this city without giving a damn about anybody, if nobody notices me when I fall onto the subway tracks or get hit by a car while the teeming multitudes continue to walk past, impassive, as if nothing had happened, hurrying (as always) down the sidewalk? I do not exist, Irene, because there is no recognition, because there is no reflection in the other's eyes, because there is no reciprocity, thanks to the ineffable Empedoclean Love, thanks to that damned Kypris, who mixed everything together and bound it with concrete, I suppose.

18

(TUESDAY, MAY 16TH, CONTINUED)

"Did you hear that?" Matilde said, startled and growing impatient with Arturo's silence and apparent lack of concern.

"Of course I did."

"Who is it?" she demanded, jumping back from the painter to whom she felt so attracted because of his charm and lightheartedness, though she also felt his imposing will, the strength of his calm confidence.

"Tamara, who else?"

"Your wife Tamara?"

"She's the only Tamara I know, Maty." Arturo smiled, unconcerned, as he lit a cigarette and inhaled with delight, well aware of his young interviewer's combined embarrassment and astonishment.

"But you told me—you assured me—that she wasn't here in the afternoons. Any afternoon . . ." Maty almost dared to raise her voice while at the same time moving to gather her clothes and get dressed, something which Arturo quickly put a stop to, saying in a gentle, obliging, warm whisper of a voice:

"She never comes by in the afternoon, Maty. It's not my fault she's here today . . . I don't know, she must have forgotten something. But don't worry. She never comes into the studio. Never. It's part of the deal."

"What deal?"

"The deal that she won't interrupt me while I'm painting, because some of my models are upset whenever someone other than me sees them posing. It happened once, and it was a disaster. I suppose it's not easy when the painter's wife walks in while his models are posing there, stationary, with their pubic hair and tits hanging out, right? Sometimes I ask them to spread their legs or touch themselves with a finger or the handle of a paint brush, things like that."

"What in God's name are you talking about, Arturo?"

"Keep your voice down . . ."

"I'll be quiet, but you'd better have a good explanation . . ."

"Just don't worry. Tamara never comes in here, and it wouldn't surprise her anyway, for the simple reason that she already knows what's going on . . ."

"And what the hell is that supposed to mean?" Maty was out of sorts, stunned, really, by this information. She couldn't just walk out of the studio, but then again she didn't want to remain there for a moment longer and be found, naked, on top of Tamara's husband's body.

"She knows that you're here with me."

"What?"

"Tamara knows that you've been by the studio a couple of times. On Tuesdays and Thursdays, to be specific."

"But she thinks that I'm here to interview you, right?"

"No, Maty. She thinks that you're posing for me, not interviewing me." With that, Arturo took another drag on his cigarette, scattering a dash of gray ash on the dark, curly hair of his chest. After a lengthy exhalation, he spoke again with absolute serenity, with a sense of tranquility which he tried to impart to his lover as the thin scrolls of smoke drifted up into the dark, charred air of the studio: "Yes, don't be alarmed Matilde, please. She thinks you're posing nude for me just like the other models. That's all. Don't worry. I told her that you were coming. She knows that our sessions started two weeks ago, and that I'm working on a beautiful portrait of you."

"But there's no portrait, Arturo."

"But there will be . . ." her delighted lover countered, insufferably sure of himself.

"But I only posed once for you, and that was for a charcoal sketching, right? And you weren't even satisfied with it . . . or were you lying to me?"

"Believe me, it will become a lovely portrait . . . It will."

"But what if Tamara suspects something and suddenly just comes in here. Think what would happen!"

"I already told you that's not going to happen. Now look, stop worrying and come closer."

"How can you be so sure?"

"Because she knows that you are my friend's wife, and it would be humiliating for the both of you if she suddenly burst in here as if she were sniffing something out, understand? That's basic female psychology:

reverse pride. She's not going to come in here. I know that like the back of my hand. She knows that you are my friend's wife because he gave her the advance himself the day I wasn't here."

"What advance, Arturo? What are you talking about?" she asked, astonished, feeling another gust of airless heat wash across her numb, sweaty body.

This time, Arturo seemed upset, a bit irritated, but only for a second or two, a momentary flash in his opaque eyes. He had mentioned the payment, yes, but a moment later he recovered and—whether with real or feigned calmness—he replied:

"Look, I shouldn't have said anything . . . because it was supposed to be a surprise. Your husband wanted to give you a portrait for your anniversary. At least, that's what he said the last time I saw him."

Maty was overwhelmed with confusion. Had she heard him correctly, or was she dreaming? Of course, she had no idea about the gift, about the portrait, or about the surprise you were plotting, dear naïve Reader. She'd first gone for the interviews and only for the interviews; but now, though, she was there for him, for the body of that Agro god, for the love to which she had succumbed two days earlier, for the madness of sex, like a stake driven between her legs, which she knew how to lick and manipulate with alternating hard and soft and hard and soft hands to the point of vertigo, the point of exhaustion. Although she desperately wanted to secure that interview with him and learn the secret history of the subject of her thesis, right now (and against all previous predictions) the reasons for her visit—for her repeated trips to the painter's hot study—had been slyly combined. It was the sex she got and the information he gave her. Yes, they were two different things, of course, and if they were mutually exclusive in the beginning—if they inhabited exclusive spaces—things have now changed: both motives became intertwined, became a single, insoluble, double-faced object whether or not she wanted them to, which at any rate is no longer important. In fact, she wasn't sure about much of anything at the moment; she couldn't think, not anymore, she just couldn't, not in the heat and accumulating new revelations that were making her feel nauseous, her thorax bending in submission, while his masculine arm clasped her to him.

Just then a door squeaked, and once again slight little footsteps crossed the burning plain that doubled as the roof of an old building in Narvarte. The sound grew more distant, more diffuse, until it disappeared altogether.

"Is she gone?" Matilde asked, no longer mute, now sitting next to the painter, covering her chest with a cushion, bathed in the purple hues of twilight, or perhaps she was just protecting herself from the attack that was sure to come if his wife suddenly burst into the apartment with a knife in her hand.

"Yes," Artuto replied without looking away from her, admiring her, desiring her once again, filled with calmness and peace. He took one last drag on his cigarette before extinguishing it in an ashtray already overflowing with discarded butts. It was warm in there, in the fifth floor studio, despite the window—with no sill—that was open to the streets of Narvarte below. A minute or two passed, their arms and shoulders laden with pearls of sweat as a sense of serenity and well-being once again reigned over the ramshackle studio. Then Maty emerged from her daydream-like state, perhaps taken by inspiration, and asked:

"So that's why you wanted me to pose for you right from the beginning, yes? Because my husband asked you to do a portrait? That was it, wasn't it, you asshole?"

Slowly, without losing his composure or showing even a twinge of nervousness, Arturo answered, unmoved and affectionate:

"It wasn't just that, Matilde. It was because I wanted to see you that way, I wanted to see you undressed, naked, and alive, because I had a feeling that I was already in love with you . . . Because to turn you into a statue, even for a couple of hours, was almost to take you, to have you, to possess you, do you understand? It was as if I appropriated you. It's a disease we painters share."

"But you don't love me, Arturo, don't even kid yourself," Maty said, almost flattered to hear him speak in such a way . . . however false or dishonest it might be, but then again, how could she be sure? How could she know if he were lying? Perhaps he was speaking the truth. Could he really be falling in love with her?

"This is the second afternoon that I have loved you. And if not, then what the hell would you call it?" Arturo asked, smiling covetously, turning to her again, drawing her to him with her forearm.

"Well, in that sense, yes, we have loved. So you win," Maty replied, jokingly, playfully, letting herself once again be drawn into the arms and body of the painter.

"Don't kid yourself, Matilde. There is no other feeling," Arturo replied, embracing her, pulling her body towards him. "Others call it *caritas* or *amistad*, but the Greeks called it *agape*, and that, of course, has nothing to do with the love that you and I have here."

"Again with the Greeks, Arturo."

They both stopped speaking. The devastating silence of the afternoon glided across the workshop and the terrace, leaving waste and ruin in its vaporous wake, along with beads of sweat on their foreheads and shoulders. The footsteps of Tamara or whoever was outside (maybe a tiger or giraffe) had evaporated, converting themselves into infinitesimal particles of water vapor, into *aer*. They could be calm now, almost content, even proud of their sex and their secret; now Matilde could relax and start kissing him from head to toe again, until suddenly—surprised by her own intuition or perhaps the illumination of the final *anaklasis* of the afternoon that filtered in through the window—she asked:

"And how are you ever going to finish the portrait in time if we continue making love here in your studio instead of having me sit and pose for you?"

"That's already been solved."

"I don't understand . . ."

"It's quite simple, Matilde," Arturo answered with his almost insuffer-ably mysterious tone of voice on that afternoon of truth and discovery. "You know what? I'm almost offended that you haven't seen it from the very beginning . . ."

"What are you talking about? Is this another riddle?"

"Let's see . . . tell me this: does your husband think that you've come here to pose for me, or to interview me in the hopes of getting some valuable information about my father? What does he believe? What have you told him?"

"That I came here to interview you, of course. That's what he thinks, and that's what I've been trying to do all this time, Arturo, even when we're lying on this quilt here, among all your old pillows."

"What I mean to say is that the last time I saw him, he gave me some photographs of you, and I've been working from them . . . Without you, of course. The condition is—or rather, it was—that you not find out about the secret surprise he wanted to give you for your anniversary."

"So you're saying that you don't need me to pose for you at all."

"No. I already told you that. I've been trying to tell you that all after-noon . . . but you don't listen or you don't dare to listen when someone finally decides to ante up and tell you the truth. I wanted to possess you, I wanted to have you quiet, alone, for me . . ."

"You wanted to seduce me . . ."

"Yes, although to be honest . . . I didn't know if it was going to work," Arturo admitted, laughing, squeezing her tighter.

Nothing that the painter said, however, seemed to upset Matilde; on the contrary, she was pleased to see how much she liked him, corrobo-rating what her intuition had told her during her first visit to that roof. Secretly, in her heart, she felt full, radiating with the knowledge that the painter had succumbed to her just as much as she had succumbed to him. They were, then, on a level playing field, faced with an apparently equal set of circumstances, or at least that's what she believed; there-fore, there was nothing else to add to the discussion or internally debate about, since in a certain way she had already cast her fate to the wind and because, aside from that one unique, two-faced goal (sex with him and the information on Soto Gariglietti he offered up while lying there on the quilt amidst the scattered cushions), nothing else really mattered at that point in her life. At this moment she had no more words with which to explain that skein of feelings in which she'd been caught up, blinding her from the memories of her first year of marriage; in fact, she couldn't think about anything beyond that roof, nothing more than an arm's length away, nothing beyond her own, fiery body, beyond the needs and desires of that body . . . it was like sinking, sleepless, into the waters of a fishbowl, or into a darkroom developing pan, liquid, float-ing, swimming. Her ideas or premonitions ran down a dead-end alley, where they suddenly crashed into a violet or orange point beyond which she could no longer think about or foresee anything, let alone predict her own future, her conjugal future. She felt surfeited, her flesh was at once sated and flaccid, a perfect combination. Now all she needed was to indulge herself once again in physical, epidermal joy, to indulge her-self, even, in the disastrous effects of her treachery and surprising im-pudence, of her shame. From that moment onward, if not forever, she wanted to continue to feel him, to possess him, Arturo, now that she had risked everything—her marriage, her faithfulness, her first conjugal year—with an inevitable, irrecoverable roll of the dice. Right now she was simply happy leaning up against his side, against his flank, his flesh, and she did not want to reflect or meditate on the consequences of her actions . . . she wanted only the ardor (the burning, the carbonization) inside: that was the inextinguishable truth. Her legs burned yet again with impatience and the need to put out the flames creeping up around her, the bonfire incinerating her innards and sex. Of course, there wasn't a single fiber of shame or remorse tying her down, holding her back. In fact, as strange as it may seem, the opposite was true: the restraints and restrictions had been amputated, not a hint of modesty or inhibi-tion affected her, she needed something, anything, urgently, and for that reason she set about fucking, skillfully and adroitly, with the talent of a goldsmith or butcher, and Arturo's cock was in her hands whether he wanted it there or not. Almost immediately, unbounded and feverish, she began to lick, to suck voraciously, until the moment came when she felt the need to mount him, to squeeze him, exploit him, to gather up all of his desire, his impetus, and that made her at once blind and impatient: she reached the summit, agonized, and fell back, livid, like one of Rossetti's dead, floating ladies . . . without concern for anything else, with no interest in anyone, not even a possible appearance by Tamara or her thesis or her wedding anniversary, and not even so much as a thought for her loving husband, you, dear conspicuous Reader of *Friction*.

XIX

It was a few days after I returned home from my hallucinatory and solitary visit to New York when it all began, when everything in my routine life suddenly became more complicated; or rather, when I myself complicated everything there at the university, the town, and the world. If Irene and Emilio had been there, perhaps the end result would have been different. But the fact is that they weren't, they had gone to visit my mother-in-law in San Francisco and then on to Mexico to unravel the thread of her own life, probing her other mother—in other words, her biological mother—my ex-mother-in-law Dulce Mallea, and gradually getting to know her impulsive biological half sister, my ex-wife, Fedra. And I have to add (as if all this wasn't enough) that my son Emilio had just discovered that he had a half sister, somewhat older than him—my daughter Dulce—and both of them were, of course, becoming quite fond of their respective aunts, my wife and my ex-wife. But all of this, as wildly hilarious or insanely Rabelaisian as it might seem, paled in comparison to what happened to me (to me and my gargantuan surroundings) while I was alone, sullen, in Virginia, preparing for my upcoming summer course on the Novel of the Revolution (more precisely: *Memorias de Pancho Villa* by Martín Luis Guzmán) and caught in a hellish net from which I still haven't managed to escape. Nevertheless, before I describe the scope and circumstances in which the lamentable events I participated in (either in an active or honorary manner) developed, I must try, at least, to provide a superficial sketch of the characters who played roles in this drama, the human beings of flesh and bone and shit who were involved in the ill-fated events there at Millard Fillmore University.

First, and at the epicenter of all the disasters to come—the sinister black hole or Erebus that was our Department of Foreign Languages— we find my Ecuadorian colleague, the Gorgonian woman Gaudencia Gross-Wayne, the undisputed expert on the works of the Icaza Prize-winning and vastly underappreciated Ecuadorian writer Marcelo Chiri-boga. I must say that since I first set foot on campus at Millard Fillmore University, Gaudencia has not let a single day go by without boasting about her intimate friend Chiriboga, and on more than once occasion she has shown me her collection of photos, which she guards like rel-ics, as if they were strands of hair or grungy fingernail clippings from the writer himself. In them, Gaudencia is standing in a group of four or five strangers in a circle around Chiriboga, who is sitting (bored? overwhelmed?) in a wicker chair situated in a large, colonial-style liv-ing room. I should also add the fact that Gaudencia was quite proud of being the author of eight or so published works about her Ecuadorian compatriot. Among them, the notable ones (though I confess I haven't had the time to read them) include *The Use of Color in the Works of Mar-celo Chiriboga*, *The Rainbow in the Works of Marcelo Chiriboga*, *Primary Colors in the Works of Marcelo Chiriboga*, *Secondary Colors in the Nov-els of Marcelo Chiriboga*, *Picturesque Colors in the Narratives of Marcelo Chiriboga*, *The Use of Red in the Later Novels of Marcelo Chiriboga*, *The Use of Green in the Short Stories of Marcelo Chiriboga,* and finally, her most recent publication, *The Use of Blue in the Poems of Marcelo Chiri-boga*. In a rather curious way, all these incisive and extensive essays (they are clearly extensive, but I can't speak to their incisiveness) have been published by the Ecuadorian press Qohelet, which, according to recent rumors, only publishes works by authors who'll pay a hefty subvention. But all that is pure gossip, Gaudencia sternly argues, spread by other, envious members of the department who know full well that she has money—plenty of money, in fact, according to her. The scandal, though had reached as far as the Qohelet offices in Guayaquil, when it was discovered that Gaudencia's last book—the one on the color blue—was a crock, a work of pure absurdity, because as far as anyone knows, Chiriboga has never written a single poem in his life . . . though yes, he has used the color blue, of course, when he needed to describe the oceans or the magnificent Ecuadorian sky. My colleague never offered an explanation on the subject; once, months later, she muttered sulkingly that the fact that nobody knew about his unpublished poems didn't amount to an atom of proof that they didn't actually exist, to say nothing of what she so cleverly referred to as "Chiriboga's sublime, poetic prose." But moving on to another subject, one that I believe is more relevant, and still equally related to my colleague, is the fact that the Gorgonian Gross-Wayne received her doctorate some lustrums ago from the University of Wichita, in Kansas, where her mentors were the famous Avellaneda and Macpherson, with whom she never slept for the simple reason that they both rejected her offers (this according to one of Macpherson's former students whom I know rather well and trust completely). The next logical question that jumps out at you, then, is this: how the hell did they decline the advances of their Ecuadorian student and budding professor without offending her, considering the fact that she was (and yes, I know what I'm talking about here) ugly, horrifying, really, beyond your wildest imaginations: the bulging eyes of a toad, a bit of non-incipient fuzz growing on the chin, deep, spongy bags of wrinkles for cheeks, and a beakish nose as porous as a garbanzo bean? The answer was quite simple: whenever she presented herself at their offices at the department there in Wichita, they were able to drive her off with the argument that—despite the fact that she was so young and attractive—they simply couldn't put their academic reputations or their professorial integrity at risk. And that was, without a doubt, the best excuse they could have offered, for I've learned that if you try something like that in the Yankee academic world, you'll lose not only your job but also your reputation. Then and only then did the Lernaean Hydra stop harassing them, according to what my informant told me. But what was most surprising of all was the fact that, six months later, a story appeared in several newspapers all across the country reporting that Avellaneda had been expelled from that very same university for an eccentric fixation on zoophilia: apparently, in the desperation brought on by his abstinence, the Extremaduran professor had, for the better part of a year, been keeping a pet, some sort of orangutan or other related simian which, according to the article, had fled from a local zoo because the zookeepers there were starving or otherwise mistreating it. This, I believe, should be sufficient confirmation of the degree of monstrosity that my colleague Gaudenica represented: that Avellaneda, rather than taking the opportunity to sleep with a young student, preferred, despite everything to the contrary, to engage in aberrant sexual behavior with none other than a fugitive ape. To this already patently unusual and abnormal case, I'll add yet one more thing: the fact that Gaudencia suffers from color blindness . . . a condition which, if I'm not mistaken, she's had since she was seven years old. That, of course, proved to be no obstacle to her supreme goal of a profound investigation (as I've gathered) of such a delicate subject as the pictorial range of the Ecuadorian author. (It wasn't poor Avellaneda's job to authorize an ophthalmological exam for each of his graduate students.)

The fact is that this woman and I have never understood one another. No matter how hard she first tried to win me over with flatteries about how lovely it was in Cuernavaca and Acapulco, about how much she admired Laura Esquivel and Guadalupe Loaeza, I never allowed myself to get caught up in slick, nonexistent compliments. She has an arrogant, authoritarian personality that just doesn't sit well with me, and she blatantly pulls rank whenever she has the opportunity to do so. Her students detest her even more than her colleagues, and many of them have complained to me personally about the offensive and despotic manner in which she treats them, something which I, unfortunately, have never been able to do anything (not much, anyway) about, for one primary reason: I haven't been granted tenure at MFU, and I didn't want to put my already precarious position in jeopardy with other colleagues who did have tenure and could easily fuck up my status there at the university. So I, proud Eusebio, like my friend and colleague from Turin, Stefano Morini, and the Galicians Tino and Javis, about whom I've spoken before, have had to take a deep breath, bite the bullet, support her, and listen to her rail against every conceivable thing for the past five years, always with smiles on our faces, always ready to applaud her harsh remarks or her worn and hackneyed reminiscences of her youth alongside her maestro Chiriboga in their native Guayaquil. Of course, none of us wanted to lose our jobs or risk our chance at the cherished and aforementioned tenure . . . something that, now that I'm writing here, has already been lost. I have to admit that teaching at Millard Fillmore University offers good pay and a good amount of free time, which can lead one into simple idleness or alcoholism, or into the alienation of writing, which is what I'm trying to do today (however unseasonable it might be) and which I neglected to do during the past two or three weeks when I found myself alone in the house without Irene and my son Emilio.

Just to finish up vivisecting the Gorgon, and before I get into what's happened here, I'll simply add that just last summer, Gaudencia was able (through sheer perseverance) to throw an inexperienced professor of translation, Marion Siegel, out of Millard Fillmore. She hadn't secured the much-desired tenure because, first, the Ecuadorian just wanted to screw with her career, and, second, she wanted to show off her influence and machinations when the time came for poor Siegel to take the next step in her career path. The motivation behind this desire or imperious scheme to toss out the professor of translation was not antipathy or mutual personal incompatibility between two women of different nationalities and ideological beliefs, but something much more sinister: the furtive desire to secure that position for her own daughter, Katrina, which she was eventually able to achieve with the permission and support of Dean Whitehead, despite the fact that I tried (secretly) to prevent the appointment after contemplating Marion's unjust dismissal. I should add that ever since we arrived in Madisonburg, Irene—with her wonderful feminine intuition—warned me about the kind of woman the daughter was (according to her, she was much worse than her mother). Also, my wife tried to dissuade me at the time from getting involved in the delicate matter of the Dean wanting to allow Katrina to skip over the established protocols of advertising the position on the Modern Language Association job lists. Early on (that is, during our first year there), I failed to fully grasp the sense of antagonism Irene held against Katrina since, although she was just as surprisingly horrific and horrendous as her mother and Otus, the giant, she was still a *gringaecuatoriana*, an Ecuadorian American, which implied a certain degree of acculturation or common civility, as opposed to the barbarism and despotism of her mother. Soon, though, I discovered the intrinsic truth about her frightful character, but it was too late, and now both Katrina and her mother suspect—or have it on good standing—that I opposed her promotion to Marion's vacated position. It goes without saying that this played a part in screwing up my career, my tenure-track position, despite the fact that the Ecuadorian Gorgon was not on the committee of veteran professors who wisely evaluated my case.

Secondly, and to continue with this sketch or departmental flow chart, I must mention two of my colleagues on the other side of the aisle, my two extremely effeminate friends, Marco Aurelio Vasco-Osama, who specializes in Golden Age Spanish literature, and Santiago Bormann-Smythe, a Chilean expert on opera and vaudeville. I don't have anything against homosexuals—I never have—and in fact, to this day, one of my best friends is a fag back in Mexico City, but these two individuals were not your average, everyday fags. Along with Gaudencia, they formed a secret conclave, a lurid guild, about which Stefano, the Galicians, and I knew nothing, and which we never would have thought existed. Nevertheless, I will not speak about that conclave now. The important thing is to know the ambiguous moods of these two colleagues, who—though they seemed similar, or at least similar in sexual preference—detested one another, just as they detested me, although (I must admit) they always maintained a degree of courtesy and innate goodwill, inherent in their refined queerness, which certainly wasn't the style of choice for Gaudencia, who was a chip off Doña Bárbara's cruel old block. The Gorgon will either love you passionately (which she always shows by not making you a target for attack or the object of her infinite disdain), or she dislikes you passionately (which is her usual custom: she'll dislike you if you don't have a doctorate, if you don't have two or more published books, or if you aren't white, even if you're just off-white, olive-toned, native-looking, or otherwise not a part of what she arrogantly considers "high class" Latin America).

On the other hand, I must admit (as I always do) that ever since Irene and I arrived in Virginia, I underestimated Marco Aurelio Vasco-Osama's Machiavellian capacity, owing to the fact that he is clearly the most reclusive and timid person I have ever met in my life, and quite the opposite of Gaudencia or Santiago Bormann-Smythe. For example: soon after our arrival, Irene and I invited him to have dinner with us at our house, an offer he declined at the last moment, owing to a stomachache. A couple months later, we invited him over again, and he again declined, that time owing to a toothache. The third and final time, we extended an invitation for Sunday brunch. He called us that morning complaining of a migraine that had him laid up in bed, exhausted. But the fact was that the only bed he had was a couch in his office at Millard Fillmore's Department of Foreign Languages. He could be found holed up in there at any hour of the day, whether morning, noon, or night, and even if the door was closed, you could still hear the faint sound of his fan, which he uses despite the air conditioning units that are installed in every office. On one occasion, Marco Aurelio told my taciturn friend Javis (who later related it to us) that he never had the slightest inkling to leave his office and go out into the campus or the town, because he could go out into the world through his computer screen, he could come and go at his ease without ever leaving the comfortable recliner he had set up in his office. He felt, I suppose, like a sort of modern-day Parmenides, denying himself the reality of movement in his own virtual way. And if that were not enough, Marco Aurelio didn't have a car. Why would I, if I don't even know how to drive? was his retort. But not having a car in a town so completely sprawling as this—with extensive, deserted streets and perfectly laid out avenues, completely lacking in pedestrians—is entirely ridiculous. This place is the complete opposite of a small- or medium-sized European city, where everything is within walking distance and there is no need for a car. Here, you can't even buy a Coke without one. Early on, from what I know, Javis and Tino, being the decent and thoughtful people that they are, and completely devoted to Marco Aurelio, offered to take him places like the grocery store and the pharmacy, but after three or four occasions (when they finally realized the way he was using them without offering them so much as a glass of water in return), they stopped helping him; which is to say, they stopped chauffeuring him around. Since then, I believe Marco Aurelio does all his shopping by phone or Internet. Of course, such a thing is only possible in this ultra-modernized American society.

So as not to get bogged down in Marco Aurelio Vasco-Osama or get into the inextricable complexities of his pubescent years, which had a picaresque effect on his life ever since, I'll move on to Santiago Bormann-Smythe and his complicated operatic and vaudevillian habits. Yago is a sixty-something (or seventy-something; I have no idea) man without a hair on his head; a good-natured sort with exquisite and sumptuous tastes, a lover of Wagner and Verdi who taught foreign languages for reasons nobody could understand, not even himself. At one point, they said, he had been an outspoken opponent of Gaudencia, but then, when he was inducted into the mysterious conclave, they became inseparable, as thick as thieves. Suffice it here to say, for the sole purpose of summarizing the ruthless character and boundless cynicism of this man, an expert in departmental politics, that he once told me (years ago, when I still trusted him and he still trusted me) of his unconditional admiration for Pinochet, "who between you and me, Eusebio, was the only man *macho* enough capable of bringing order to the chaos of communism that has overtaken my country." Santiago lives in the United States not because he fled the dictatorship, but quite the opposite: he was sent here to study on a scholarship offered by his own government, and in the end he decided not to return because he had nothing to return to, he told me with tears in his eyes on that distant afternoon not long after my arrival: "My mother, my last link with Chile, passed away some time ago." Of course, the Chilean community in our county (which consists of eighteen individuals and a dog) hasn't to my knowledge had anything to do with him. This doesn't seem to bother Yago in the slightest. In fact, it's quite the opposite: he is (or appears to be) quite happy in his provincial mansion with the operas of Wagner playing at full volume, with his twenty-year-old Romanian fiancée, with his trips to the Salzburg festival every summer, and with focusing the rest of his energy on the trickery and political entanglements that roil within the Department of Foreign Languages. He is, without a doubt, the complete opposite of Marco Aurelio. If the latter is a timid, introverted, antisocial misanthrope, the former is extroverted, social, extravagant to the point of absurdity, and always pleased with himself. They both share some characteristics, though: both are refined and cultured in their own, quite peculiar way, they are exquisitely neat and tidy, elegant, crafty, bald, of slim build, and above all they are both part of Gaudencia's nefarious sect, along with (of course) our censured former dean Whitehead, our new dean Davis, and his intimate friend, Professor Wynn, from Texas.

But we'll proceed case by case.

Dick Whitehead is a fat, inflated, jowly faced sort. His pink cheeks hang down from his temples like Play-Doh, that amorphous mass Emilio plays with for hours on end while Irene and I talk out on the deck. Those Plasticine cheeks always seem on the verge of falling off his face . . . though they never do, they simply slide and shake from side to side like pendulums, whether Dick is laughing or looking serious. They say he coached the football team back in his younger days, and from there he began a constant, capable, step-by-step climb through the ranks until he had become Dean of the College of Arts and Letters at our prestigious university. There is not a single professor at the school (that is to say, no historian, no musician, no anthropologist, no philosopher, no sociologist, no political scientist, no general humanist) who does not despise him deeply, though they wouldn't even dare to whisper such a thing. Nobody understands what the hell an old football coach is doing in the dean's office of the College of Arts and Letters. Whitehead speaks nothing but English, and of course it is a provincial, hillbilly, redneck English, a sort of dialect where words like "vicissitude" or "gratis" or "affable" don't exist for the simple reason that they do not appear in the dictionary given to him by his wife, who is a very likable country bumpkin, by the way. His contraction-filled slang is worse than that of my students. This supersized dean—who, by the way, I saw on more than one occasion furtively dining at the local Wendy's, as I did—was, as of a few days ago, in the last stage of his career. Although he had announced to the five hundred or so PhDs who made up the university's faculty that he was excited about the upcoming year, a bout of indigestion had forced a last-minute retirement. Though we knew he was an intimate friend of Gaudencia's, we weren't sure of when, exactly, he'd entered into the Gorgon's conclave, or if he was actually a founding member dating back to the time before Javis, Tino, Marion, Stefano, and I had even set foot on those alien shores. I should add one very important detail here, something to help clarify this sketch I'm drawing up and to conclude my rather unflattering (indeed) description of

El Gordo Dean Whitehead. I'm referring to the fact that Dick held the strings of probably the most astute member of Millard Fillmore University's faculty, the Associate Dean, his own personal Cerberus, Professor Jeffrey Davis, who is temporarily occupying the dean's office since it was vacated, *sensu stricto*, after Whitehead's retirement, according to the announcement distributed among the faculty and staff, which I've already described. In other words, he was forced into early retirement due to indigestion brought on by overindulging in hamburgers. After that, Professor Jeffrey Davis, his guard dog, took over the reins as our new, interim dean. It was with him, then, that I filed my complaint, even though it all started under *El Gordo* Whitehead's term. But the fact is that the story would have ended up the same way with either of them: it was a disastrous comedy. What happened would have happened no matter who the dean at MFU was. But, as I've already said, I'm determined not to go any further without first having painted an Orozco-like fresco, an *ad hoc* mural that depicts our sinister Department of Foreign Languages, which Dick always referred to—not without a grain of truth—as an insufferable Tower of Babel.

Now, before I tell you about my close friend and accomplice, Stefano Morini from Turin, I feel it's a good time to briefly mention the two chairs of the Department of Foreign Languages, two indispensable characters in this tangled web of a tale in which I've found myself and in which I will be caught up again soon; sad, solitary, and idle—an idleness which, of course, got me a bit hot and bothered and that, in turn, led me to put my nose in it to the extent that I did. If it sounds odd that I spoke about "the two chairs" earlier, it's because first there was one, and then, subsequently, another one, not because there were two chairs at the same time, which is neither compatible nor possible . . . but sometimes it happens, despite everything going against it, as will be demonstrated.

So I'll speak first, then, about Professor Phillip Ritter, who has been the chair ever since Irene and I got here some five years ago. Ritter is without a doubt a good and decent guy, a bit strange and quiet, perhaps, but a good Christian man whose appearance calls to mind a big-eared giraffe with soft, crystalline eyes. Tall, lean, and as translucent as goat's milk, Ritter smiles every time you greet him, with eyes that resemble those of a dozing giraffe; then suddenly he seems as if he's drifted off and become engrossed in thought, absorbing what you've just said to him, but this is not due to a lack of courtesy: it's simply a lack of certain social skills, common sense, or perhaps a bit of autism. Ultimately, you're never quite sure whether you should wait for him to respond, of if the conversation has already finished. He is the epitome of chivalry, to be certain. And despite our differences, there are two things that unite us: our genuine love of literature (something sorely lacking in this department) and our mutual scorn for the two fags and Gaudencia, whom he simply cannot stand, though he's been able to tolerate her for five long years for two simple reasons: one, because he is nothing if not a Protestant gentleman, and two, because the Ecuadorian Gorgon never ceases to remind him (whenever she has the opportunity) that she has an extremely tight friendship with Dean Whitehead, which of course scares the shit out of him and leaves him completely disarmed and unfit for intradepartmental combat. The intimate camaraderie between those two was enough to force Ritter, for five full years, to endure her arrogance, her fits, and her nefarious initiatives which, by the way, were not at all infrequent, and which always had a single common denominator: to block any moves initiated by the other members of the department. If Santiago Bormann-Smythe is, in this sense, a ruthless architect of political machinations, the referee of a shitstorm, then the Ecuadorian Gorgon is the Hydra's other head. She can deliver a cutting remark *par excellence*, representing unabashed tyranny and class discrimination with a viperous tongue that lashes out like a whip. If, for example, you happen to show up one day wearing lightly scuffed shoes, she will find the most opportune moment to pillory you in front of everyone. If you don't arrive on the dot to one of those insufferable departmental committee meetings (while she, however, is anything but punctual), she'll toss out some comment about your legendary tardiness, which should come as no surprise to anyone by now. None of this, of course, was tolerated by the magnanimous, lanky, big-eared Phillip Ritter who, like a good Germanist, had a deep sense of civic and democratic duty, a limitless (and exaggerated) respect for other people's freedoms, and in my opinion an innate decency that bordered on an obtuse love for his fellow man, which was dictacted by his strict adherence to the tenets of Protestantism. The problem with Ritter, then, is utter pacifism, his Kantian passivity, his autism or what Stefano blatantly deems his cowardice. Not once during his time as chair of the department did he pull in the reins on Santiago or Gaudencia. He would have defended himself with the argument that it wouldn't have been an easy thing to do with a powerful dean on the side of the Gorgon, and this was half true, though only half: he could have at least proposed it, he could have proposed putting on the brakes and slowing, to a certain extent, the incommensurable exigencies of Gaudencia and Yago who, by the way, is the professor with the most seniority in our department, which in turn grants him certain useful privileges. I'll offer an example. As you know, the semesters at Millard Fillmore consist of sixteen weeks: the spring semester runs from the second week in January to the final week of April, and then—after the optional summer courses, which run from May to June and from July to August—the fall semester begins the last week of August and ends the first week in December. That leaves a month around Christmas and almost four months during the summer where one can do whatever his heart desires: stay or leave town, teach an intensive summer course (for additional pay that's nothing to sniff at), or hole up in the library and do research, which is something nobody at Millard Fillmore ever did . . . not even me, since I get the fuck out of here and go to Mexico City as soon as my May/June course is finished to see my daughter Dulce, who is getting bigger every day, though not enjoying it as much as I had hoped. To summarize, each semester is less than four months long, which (for administrative reasons) are divided into two segments or blocks of eight weeks each. In the time I've been here, Santiago and Gaudencia have managed to finagle their way into teaching only one segment instead of two, using the other eight-week block as a chance to vanish from the university town like hares fleeing the warren and return to La Scala and Guayaquil, respectively. But how is this possible, and why the hell haven't I done so myself? It's very simple: they offered to teach double the number of hours during the first block, and were approved by the chair (in other words, by Ritter, who never denied their requests), though in the end they didn't actually end up teaching the agreed-upon number of hours. The obvious question, then, is why doesn't anybody else do this? The answer is simple again: if I were to approach the giraffe and ask about doubling up on one segment so I could got to Mexico during the other one, Ritter would apologize most sincerely, almost ashamed by his subsequent ergotism: "It's just that Gross-Wayne and Bormann-Smythe acted early. They put the request in to me a long time ago . . . And you know, Eusebio, we can't all go and leave the department here empty! What would our colleagues think? Above all, what would the Dean think?" I suppose, apart from his timidity and his lack of balls, he has to reconcile himself with his fear, his pacifism, his Christianity, or whatever the hell else has left him so paralyzed. Of course, if you are his friend—and Javis, Tino, Stefano, and I are his friends—then you have to understand him . . . and not only that, but you also have to feel sorry for him, for the awful yoke he shoulders, and even feel united with him in his fucked up destiny of subordination to a Chilean fag and a insane woman from Guayaquil. At a *petit comité* meeting of the four friends, held at a Barnes & Noble café, we asked ourselves: what advantages were there to be had from being friendly with the chair the past five years? The answer was absolutely none; in fact, there were disadvantages. But I swilled my espresso and continued to try to justify and defend the good Ritter. Was it not an advantage to speak intelligently about the work and whereabouts of Benno von Archimboldi over a few ice-cold German beers? I asked, to which Tino *ipso facto* replied with equal parts annoyance and sound judgment:

"But he doesn't even drink. Phillip Ritter has to be the only German in the world who doesn't drink. So what the hell are you talking about, Eusebio?"

The fact is that there was nothing I could do. Defending Ritter was like defending Innocent III or Alexander VI.

The breaking point was, as I already said, when they dismissed Professor Marion Siegel, whom he liked and admired. When Stefano, Tino, Javis, and I saw what had been perpetrated—and what was going to happen because of it—we decided to go and speak with him to put a stop to it. But ultimately, it was only me, Cardoso the Innocent, who was fearless enough (or perhaps reckless enough?) to go to Ritter's office one afternoon to tell him about the unjust situation we saw, and the indignation we felt about it. He told me that there was nothing to be done about Siegel, though he thought quite highly of her. In fact, it wasn't more than two or three months after Marion's dismissal that Katrina arrived to replace her, as if the expulsion of one had nothing to do with the appearance of the other. When it was clear to me that the giraffe wasn't going to do so much as lift a finger on behalf of Marion—owing to his fear of the Gorgon and the Dean—I had the awful idea of sending an anonymous letter to the Office of Affirmative Action, exposing what had happened in my department. The African-American attorney in the (allegedly independent and autonomous) office took no action, not even opening an inquiry into what my colleagues and I considered a gross example of nepotism, bias, and personal misconduct. Only Stefano knew (unfortunately for me) that I sent that anonymous letter, in October or November of last year, as I recall. Of course, ever since then, I've been walking on eggshells; I couldn't, under any circumstances, engage in any unusual behavior. Accusing a dean of anything can come with very expensive consequences. I knew it then, and I know it now more than ever.

In order to conclude this departmental sketch, I must mention the other ringleader, Porzia Fazzion, Stefano's *paisano*, who became Phillip Ritter's successor overnight—just when Irene and Emilio left me here, about to begin my first intensive summer course on the *Memorias de Pancho Villa*. She's currently the *de facto* chair of the department, since Ritter (who is technically still the chair of record) was demoted by Davis, once Whitehead took leave to recover from the overingestion of hamburgers. And that, then, is how there currently are—contrary to the established norms—two departmental chairs.

Porzia is a single, fiftyish woman with a kind manner about her; quite lovely, though a few incipient wrinkles belie her years. Despite a not entirely successful nose job, she's what you would call an attractive and mature woman, an elegant lady with pointed breasts and pointed heels, always quite nicely perfumed, which is why (I confess) I was always quite pleased when we shared an elevator together or exchanged a pair of friendly kisses when we greeted each other in the halls of the department or on the campus quad. A *ciao* here and a *ciao* there . . . *arrivederci*, we repeat in singsong voices despite the fact that my Italian is all but nonexistent, and because we avoid speaking English unless absolutely necessary. It was as if I had met the long-lost and unmarried sister of my own mother, who could have been quite attractive in her youth. Nevertheless, Porzia, just like almost everybody else in the department, didn't give a damn about literature; still, though, she was well liked by everyone . . . or almost everyone, I should say, with Gaudencia being the lone exception, for she detested her for being attractive, if not exactly for being intelligent. Porzia was possessed of an indescribable mixture of charisma or kindness which—despite what you might think—was actually quite hard to read, to penetrate. It's almost as if, in the end, she was always hiding something from you, a secret from her youth in Rome, or what do I know, perhaps some truculent passage taken from one of Alberto Moravia's books that had affected her to the bone and which she would never forget. If, for example, you approach her, trusting in the good-natured smile she unexpectedly flashed you that morning, you will quickly discover an invisible shield that, however it may seem, is simply impenetrable. So, despite the attraction her weathered Italian beauty could provoke, you're in for a rude awakening if you hope to become her friend, or anything more intimate than strictly a departmental colleague. Yes, we went to have dinner with her a number of times; she always had a little gift for Emilio and a bottle of Chianti for us, but nevertheless it was patently obvious that she only really felt comfortable when her *paisano*—my friend Stefano—and his wife Stephany also came. But above all, she goes truly crazy with joy whenever she sees their daughter, Alessandra, running around. The child has become her goddaughter, the light of her life, not to mention best friends with Emilio, my son. In fact, they were born within a couple weeks of each other, and ever since I first met Stefano, the kids have become inseparable. Well then . . . now that all of this has been said, and the organizational flow chart has been dissected, I suppose I can calmly refer to what happened, to the evil events that have occurred, much to my detriment, during these last few days and weeks. There were, of course, several other professors in that insufferable Tower of Babel, but none of them were directly involved in the events that were growing nigh when Irene was in Mexico and my good friend Stefano's wife Stephany called me at home to say that she urgently wished to speak with me about something of capital importance . . . *It's a matter of life and death, Eusebio, please come now, right away, as I really need to speak with you.*

20
(THURSDAY, MAY 18TH)

"He was cured of fright. As far as betrayals go, he'd had enough. If Orozco was untrustworthy from the moment they met, he simply couldn't believe what happened to Madero. Betrayed . . . and by him? All those fucking months that the president had him locked up in a Mexico City cell, on the verge of desperation and madness, after he—Pancho Villa himself—had offered up his life and proven his loyalty in battle, he was forever embittered and no longer afraid, for he no longer believed in men, in men of any class, but especially statesmen and politicians, which represented the worst in human nature. Eventually, he didn't even believe in his own mother! That's why the power-grabbing Victoriano Huerta didn't surprise him much, Matilde; he was not at all surprised that the sly and crafty general would end up assassinating his boss—their boss—the Baron Saint, the mysterious hero, Madero. It was almost prophetic, a *double entendre*. The president's own brother Gustavo had warned him a couple of days before: "Watch out for Huerta," he said. Nevertheless, what Villa was never able to understand is why the president ultimately trusted and believed in Huerta and that slanderous bullshit that the general sent to the capital via telegraph from Chihuahua, where they were both fighting against Orozco's counter rebellion while he was constantly plotting vile things behind his back. Villa would bellow—*The scoundrel, the mangy dog, the greedy, usurping bastard!*—in a thundering, almost euphoric voice to my great-grandfather, Enzo Gariglietti, while recalling those years of penury. The Sicilian listened to him, Maty, without saying a word, attentive and respectful, weighing each and every one of the general's words. *How was it possible? How the hell was it possible?* repeated the vociferous hero of the Revolution. And, to make matters worse, how could he bow down and beg the drunkard Huerta for his life, to spare his hide, begging like a whore? He couldn't even forgive himself! And in the end, how could Madero have believed Huerta, and then put Villa, the Atilla of the North himself, in jail for seven months, and not even listen to what he wanted to hear? Now, he repeated like a lunatic, he was cured of fright, Enzo: unafraid of everything and against everything, Maty. Yes, immune. To be honest, for years he didn't even trust in his own wife, Luz Corral—that's right!—but ultimately, he trusted women least of all. They were the worst, he said, the weakest and most treacherous. For that reason, because of that deep-seated sense of mistrust, there were years when he took to disappearing, vanishing from headquarters in favor of the mountains or plains. Enzo the Sicilian, who knew what he was talking about, said that he remembered how Villa would suddenly and without warning join the troops for mess and then lounge around in the orange afternoon sun with them. He came as a surprise, when nobody expected it, in the light of the bonfires: he sat down among the peons, the landless workers, chatting with them, coexisting, stuffing himself, enjoying himself for awhile, happy, half-anonymous, half-miserable. And, Maty, there was no alcohol involved. Not a drop. No *mezcal*, no *pulque*, no *sotol*, nothing. And it's not because none of his soldiers or officers ever offered him a swig; it's because if they did, Villa would likely shoot them dead on the spot, or at least flog them like a horse. He hated alcohol as much as or more than he hated men of the cloth, the Chinese, and the cowardly, invading Spanish bastards. On those freezing nights spent in the desert or in the mountains huddled over the red-hot burning coals, Villa asked his soldiers about their lives, their children, their wives, their plows, their fields of *milpa*, their cattle and mules, about everything they had left behind to join him in his campaign to settle accounts with the wealthy, to bring justice to the North, to Chihuahua, to Durango, to Coahuila . . . wherever a foothold could be gained. Villa knew how to listen, it was his greatest virtue, though according to Enzo Gariglietti he could become hopeless at times. He knew how to involve himself with his troops, and he was able to retain everything (or almost everything) he heard, to keep it with him, even the most insignificant anecdote they shared with him. He was perhaps born with that face we all have come to recognize, that we've all seen in textbook photos, Matilde: a good-natured sort of face, bronzed, glowing, and almost always grimy. Pancho Villa seemed to get cheered up when his Dorados told him about their lives, their illusions, their dreams of justice. He almost always seemed content, even when he was angry, which, as many people said, was because the General had the face of a child, a boy with a long moustache and coarse stubble on his unwashed and unshaven chin. But all that aside, he had always been a boy, until he became an adult and a revolutionary. My father once recounted a story his Sicilian grandfather told him, that one night under the stars, shortly after the attack on Columbus, New Mexico, in the open country and in front of one of those enormous bonfires, Nicolás Fernández, one of his favorites and the most loyal of his men, suddenly asked him:

"'Why do you hate the ones with the almond-shaped eyes, my General?'

"Villa was perplexed; the truth is, he hadn't expected such a question. Sitting there in front of the hot coals, he looked fixedly for quite some time at Nicolás, who would accompany him to Hacienda Canutillos many years later, and ultimately to his death in 1923. It was to this man, then, (though the rest of the troops heard him that night, including my great-grandfather) that he replied:

"'I only hate Chinamen, not the Japanese. Don't confuse them, Nico. They are two very different people. The former group came to invade the country and filled it with fraud, opium, and games of chance. The Japanese, however, brought progress, a desire for change, medicine, science, and knowledge. The Chinamen just meddle and make trouble and, except for a few tricky *cabrones* who are only looking to pick your pocket so they can plant more rice, the only things they know how to do are to cook and eat. They can't stand our beans, our maize, our tortillas . . . and what's worse, they don't eat chilis. That's the truest way to judge a Mexican, don't you think? So watch out if you ever run into one of those dirty Chinks.'

"But what Pancho Villa never knew, Maty, was that despite his fawning admiration for the Japanese, he had been an arm's length—a few millimeters, really—from perishing at the hands of one of those people whom he admired, whom he defended from any and all attacks, more than any other race, and who were growing in population in the northern regions of the country. Even though they were small in number compared to the masses of immigrating Chinese, by the end of the nineteenth century, there were thousands of them in Chihuahua, Sonora, Tamaulipas, and Sinaloa. And ironically, he protected them until the day he died, just as he had with the Gringos . . . that, of course, was until President Wilson turned his back on him and bet instead on the wild goat, his other enemy, the worst, most fucked up of them all: Venustiano Carranza. But Maty, are you listening to me? You didn't fall asleep, did you? Maty! Matilde . . . !"

XXI[1]

Ritter, the autistic giraffe and my good Germanist friend, said, with his traditional German wisdom, that you shouldn't be blinded by the myth of monocausality, and that all things happen for many reasons. There is not one, apparent, unique cause behind an event, but rather multiple ones . . . and because of that, he adduced, it's important not to loose sight of the many, varied events that occur in your life, if you suddenly happen to stop and take a look back. This is one of those truisms or apothegms that, I believe, people like me wear as a thimble on a finger, a shoe on a foot, or a muzzle on the snout. And I say that in all seriousness. Even more so now, after considering what has happened. And more so still if I recognize (which takes more effort than it does to accept it) that I often tend to be . . . how can I put it . . . dogmatic, monocausal, and prone to tunnel vision. To put it succinctly: I usually inflate things, whether great or small, within the universe I inhabit; I tend to observe events as if they are an absolute (Parmenidean) and not as a flowing river (Heraclitean), a tendency which, by all means, contradicts reality—the phenomenological world of cause and effect—according to my friend Ritter. And

---

1 Dispensable chapter. Against the author's expressed will, the publisher has decided at the last minute to include this offensive chapter, which—needless to say—is deeply embarrassing to Professor Eusebio Cardoso. Most likely aware of the capital error in judgment that it was to write this chapter, the author changed his mind and wanted to remove it, but the book had already gone to press and there was nothing left to do about the matter.

so I ask myself now, what would Empedocles, my beloved Empedocles, think about all of this?

This digression comes into play in relation to the subsequent effect of my visit to Stefano's house, at a time when only his lovely wife Stephany was there, desperate to tell me what she had called me about, which—in the end—left me stunned, breathless, with my mouth dry, and completely petrified.

"Eusebio, Stefano is cheating on me, I just know it," she said, biting her nails and clearly nervous on that first afternoon when I appeared at their tree-lined house at a time when we both knew Stefano was in class and little Alessandra was at the day care center—at a time when nobody on Earth could disturb us—and if that weren't enough, it was also at a time when Irene was hundreds and hundreds of miles away, breaking bread with Fedra, my ex-wife who also happened to be her newly discovered biological half sister.

"Are you sure?" I asked, unmoved, sitting there in their dining room with a hot cup of chai scorching or scalding my hands, surprising myself by the spontaneity with which I had responded, because my answer was a lie, a lie of omission, committed right there in front of my friend whose husband, Stefano, had not one but two lovers (that I knew of!) in two of the neighboring towns.

"I'm not sure; technically, I'm not certain of it, Eusebio," Stephany acknowledged, sitting there next to me, clutching her own cup of chai, contradicting herself, driving herself crazy, which in turn was driving me crazy, or perhaps she was simply trying to stick a needle in me in order to pull out a thread. "But my intuition—my feminine intuition—is telling me that there's another woman. I already confronted him, but he swore to me that there isn't anybody else."

"That's because you're his one and only," I replied with the aplomb of an actor, though I admit I was embarrassed just the same. I repeated it three more times, defending one friend while at the same time refuting the factually correct feminine intuition of my other friend, his wife.

"Would you tell me?" she asked, suddenly lifting her eyes up from her steaming cup of chai and sinking them deep into me, very, very deep. It was a glance that contained multiple meanings, which I will attempt to delineate, because they are, I think, essential to understanding what happened immediately thereafter when I reached out with my arm, apparently for an extra bit of sugar for my chai. Well then, her eyes shone with an undefined mixture of fixedness, sweetness, sternness, forbearance, corroboration, scrutiny, seduction—or a desire to buy any information I might have about her husband—meekness, seriousness, tenderness, dignity, impotence, and even a hint of coquettishness, though using this last descriptive noun now seems, all things considered, more like a platitude, since everything I've said was nothing more than an undeniable sign of coquettishness, an irrefutable sign of femininity that was perfectly open to interpretation. But (I ask myself) what sort of coquettishness are you talking about, Eusebio? An offering? An offering of what, exactly? My friend's wife? Or was I confounding everything and this coquettishness or idle flirtation wasn't really offering me anything? I want to interrupt myself here and make it very clear that I am many different things, but one thing I am not is a complete imbecile, and that is why I know, in retrospect, that in that look of meekness or sweetness or deep verification in my friend Stephany's eyes there was indeed a subtle, impalpable wink of coquettishness. However, deducing from that flirtatious moment with my friend's wife that some sort of offer was being extended, was that not perhaps going too far, reading too much into it, an exaggeration, an imagination or projection of something that didn't exist, a leap into the abyss of conjecture and nonsense? In any case, I still find myself pondering it to this very day, pulling my own hair out over the question of why she used the conditional tense and said, "*Would* you tell me?" Why put it like that? I am convinced that something must have been behind that incisive question which, of course, was designed to elicit a response from me, to urge me to admit what I knew in exchange for something . . . but what? What was it? What could it have been?

It was then, if my memory serves me right, and without being able to intuit anything else from that inquisitive look and all the meaning it carried with it, that I decided to stand up with the pretext of going to help myself to another cup of hot tea from the pot which was still sitting on the extinguished stove in the blue-tiled kitchen some ten or twelve feet from where we were sitting. Stephany was behind me then, with her back to me, or rather, we had our backs to each other: she was sitting in her chair with her arms propped up on the dining room table while I was pouring a thin stream of scalding water into my cup, thus evading her deep, inquisitive look. It was then, I think, that I first heard the sputtering . . . Of course, I first thought that it was the water boiling in the kettle, but that couldn't be it because the stove was off. But then, a moment later, I listened to the sputtering sound again and turned around to discover that the sound wasn't something sputtering at all; it was a meager bout of tears, an incipient yet curtailed sob congealing in Stephany's sublime throat, who, as I've already said, had her back to me. I, of course, having turned to look, was not about to turn my back on her again. I could see hers (so perfectly straight!) shivering and shaking, inclined as if she were on the verge of collapsing into a burst of sobs but she didn't want to out of shame or simply because a vitamin pill was caught in her throat. But I would be lying if I said that the only thing I saw was her back bent over the dining room table . . . I also saw her arms and shoulders—her naked shoulders—the fine scapulas of a gymnast, her waves of blond hair, and it was then, just then, that the devil took hold of me and I walked over to the dining room table without my cup of chai in hand, an action which, when carefully considered, demonstrates that the old trickster had indeed already sunk his talons into me, because clearly I would need both hands free for the operation that was rapidly developing in front of me. I walked slowly, very slowly, until I reached the back of Stephany's chair, and then I placed my hands on her shoulders in a show of support, solidarity, understanding, condolence, friendship, or mercy, perhaps? Just what the hell was it a sign of, Eusebio? Just because you say it's support, solidarity, or condolence doesn't make it so, and you know better than anyone (though in a fucked up, treacherous sort of way) that Stefano, your best friend, did indeed have a lover, which therefore makes his wife's feminine intuition correct, right? But look . . . that's not necessarily true, or not completely true, Eusebio. Having placed my hands on her naked, bronzed shoulders does not necessarily signify corroboration or understanding at all (you're not to blame!), it doesn't necessarily imply a secret betrayal of my friend (don't beat yourself up over this, man!). I simply wanted to express what it did, in fact, signify at that precise moment: masculine desire or passion (mine!) when one catches a glimpse of a woman's bare back and does not know how to resist. So then, without asking her, and with the devil dug in deep inside me, I began to massage with my thumbs and index fingers her strong, smooth, bronze shoulders, and her collarbones like those of a swimmer or gymnast or something like that. First I applied some deep pressure, before relaxing it a bit, so that Stephany could release her tension, her sadness, her pain. I confess that at that moment my cock grew hard, a bit moist, and that the craving or whatever it was that Stephany was feeling inflamed me more and more: in fact, my balls were on the verge of bursting.

"Thank you," my friend's wife said as she lifted a hand from the table and reached back to hold or pat my own in a gesture of what? Friendship, loyalty, desire, conspiracy? Then she removed her own hand while I continued to massage her muscles without saying a word. My technique was a sort of an applied muscular pressure—think Chinese acupressure à la Cardoso—and if someone were to open a day spa for young women offering (among other services) my so-called "applied muscular pressure," it would probably be a success.

The fact is that after five or six minutes of performing my arduous duty, I said, quite seriously:

"I think you're a little tense." That had two simultaneous implications: first, that her suspicions about her husband, despite what she'd already insinuated, were obviously false, which therefore absolved me of having allegedly suggested that Stefano had possibly betrayed his wife (or, at least, that's how I saw it), and second, that she, Stephany, truly did need to relax, which meant that I would accompany her, allowing myself to be tamely led along; which meant that she would lie down on the long sofa there in her living room, which she did wordlessly and without question; which meant that she would close her eyes, which she did without the slightest bit of resistance, and—finally—which meant that she was allowing herself to consent, right then, finally, for her own benefit. Once all this was all said and done, I—and my devil within—straddled her, without saying a word and without asking her if it mattered to her or bothered her, though with the complete confidence that comes from being an experienced masseur (which I was not!). I settled on top of her as if in a saddle and prepared myself to give her the most professional massage I could imagine these sorts of massages to be. I have to point out—and I am a bit embarrassed to do so—that we were fully clothed at all times. Neither of us removed so much as a sock. Nor did we kiss. For her part, she simply allowed herself to receive "applied muscular pressure" all over her body, while I, for my part, was growing harder, feeling my cock grow more and more turgid, to the point of bursting, pressing it into her turned-up ass as if it were any other bone, my knee perhaps; in other words, as if nothing important were going on there so close—so very, very close—to her inviolate and illustrious anus, her eminent (if not apparent) intestinal orifice. Stephany must have felt that thing, so very hard, rubbing back and forth against her bulging ass, trembling as my hands worked their way over her back, but she continued to act as if she didn't notice, as if it were nothing but a massage that one good friend might give to another after an exhausting game of tennis, with the lone difference being that, at that moment, we were not partners in a doubles match, and we certainly weren't playing tennis.

After the "applied muscular pressure" session which will one day become popular worldwide (at least, I hope so . . . and only, of course, if I open my spa), my hands began to slide down the flanks of the wife of my colleague from Turin, my best friend in all of America. When we got to the point where she had to slightly elevate her torso so I would be able to run my hands between the sofa and her body, Stephany did not offer any resistance; on the contrary, she collaborated, obligingly lifting her torso in a sort of pulmonary contraction so that I—the wise and prestigious acupressurist—could relax her chest and apply friction to her nipples, for the poor things were quite tense. As incredible as it may seem, at no moment during all of this did I attempt to remove her off-the-shoulder blouse, and neither did she. It was as if, with that lone precaution (the fact that we were both fully clothed), we were implicitly agreeing that never, under any circumstances, would we move beyond that point, that we had to maintain certain norms and limitations, to respect our respective and beloved spouses and children, and besides, everything that took place in that house that afternoon was a simple massage, an innocent athletic gesture that one friend or tennis player would commonly offer to another. Finally, just before the end of the session in which I could no longer contain myself, I explored and developed—again, only via "applied muscular pressure"—the pert, upright ass of my Italian friend's wife. Stephany didn't utter so much as a peep when I began my work there with extreme diligence and perseverance. Even when I got to the point where my hands were between her legs and her ass (with clothes on! with clothes!) I had the temerity to whisper, *are you feeling a bit more relaxed, are you feeling a little more comfortable,* and time and again Stephany nodded in agreement, letting it happen, letting me work, by all appearances truly at peace with my massage and my methods. So, obligingly, I continued to knead that delicious flesh wrapped in fabric, absentmindedly taking advantage of the chance to trace my fingers over her cunt, which—as I was beginning to sense through her clothes—was growing more and more humid, almost soaking wet. Once again, in order to assure myself that I wasn't overstepping my bounds, I asked her if she was feeling good, which she again confirmed with a moan, and so, still on top of Stephany, I quite openly placed my right hand on top of her cunt, between the sofa and the clothing which we never took off. My "applied muscular pressure" proved to be quite effective with her sopping wet little pussy, and shortly thereafter I had the feeling that the wife of my Italian friend and colleague was coming, yes she was coming, because she couldn't stop moving up and down and left and right with that gorgeous, prominent ass of hers. As for me, like I said, I had already come in my trousers long before that, staining them. And despite all that, what I wanted more than anything else at that moment was to get out of that house, go take a good bath, and forget about everything that had happened there. Why deny it . . . I was already starting to feel the harassment and persecution of remorse (goddamn fucking devil!). Of all the women in the world, I had chosen the worst, the one I never should have touched, not even in thought: my best friend's wife, the friend of my own wife, Irene, and mother to Alessandra, who was best friends with my son Emilio, who was almost the same age as her.

A bit ago I said that I was many things, but that one thing I was not was a complete imbecile. But in fact that's not quite true: I can turn into a complete imbecile. I was just one more among the multitudes that abound in the world, and the worst (or is it the best?) thing about it is that—apparently not content with my imbecility—I repeated that athletic ritual with Stephany on five or six other occasions. Always at her house, on that same cushy sofa, but without taking the time to drink our tea, which sat there cooling on the table. We never kissed; I didn't try and she didn't look for it . . . fortunately. We never undressed each other, and we always—every session—reached orgasm. I made her come with my applied muscular pressure, and she made me come thanks to the friction between my penis and her round, bulging ass. But remember, though, that it wasn't a penis that I was rubbing with such fervor; it could have just as easily been a bone or my knee or one of her young daughter's dolls, what do I know, any more or less pointed object, anxious to rummage around in a place with no available entrance. Stephany and I carried out our game, our athletic ritual, five or six more times until one afternoon—Irene and Emilio had by then returned home from their trip to Mexico—just before I was about to leave, deeply repentant (as I usually was after leaving my friend's home), his attractive wife suddenly said to me:

"You know, Eusebio, I think what we're doing is wrong. I don't think Irene or Stefano would appreciate it if they found out, and I guess we would appreciate it even less if they were doing this." This latter suggestion, I admit, bothered me, irritated me greatly. In fact, the whole speech was irritating. It made me feel—why not just say it?—ashamed, humiliated, unfaithful, disloyal, like a goddamn fucked up son of a bitch, which is what we both in fact were. If I'm admitting that Stephany's words upset me, it's because—in a way that's quite vague and difficult to explain—I suddenly felt, in a fit of hysteria, that she had demarcated herself, defined herself, or was attributing to me some sort of blame or responsibility for what had happened. It was as if she had suddenly put an end to the feverish ritual in which we had both been involved and immediately returned to being the mild-mannered, judicious wife who realized the incredible stupidity of our relationship.

At first I didn't say anything; I was simply burning up with anger and impotence. Instantly the living room was taken over by an acute silence, full of sharp edges, broken glass, and barbed wire. I pondered the situation for a few moments, trying to alleviate the rage that had invaded me. Finally I spoke, still furious, though I masked it as best I could:

"I think you're right, Stephany. We should put a stop to this right here and now, and forget it ever happened." My emphasis was, of course, on the forgetting: I already felt bad enough about my infidelity, my disloyalty, and I didn't need to compound it with a lack of judgment or sanity.

In some inexplicable way, I left the house feeling relieved, free from torpor, perhaps because I knew that I would never again betray my Italian friend, nor would I be unfaithful to Irene. I was no longer possessed:

the devil had left me. I found some peace in the thought that what had happened on those five or six occasions during the past two or three weeks was finally buried at the bottom of the sea, firmly anchored with cement . . . and forgotten. Unfortunately, the relief or whatever it was that I felt didn't last long, for the Hiroshima bomb would explode just a short time later . . . right above the beautiful, radiant, unshorn head of Irene, my poor wife, who had returned from Mexico with rather chilling news about her biological mother and my ex-wife Fedra.

22
(THURSDAY, MAY 18TH)

"Some time after the frustrating Mexican Expedition conducted between June of 1916 and February of 1917 by Pershing and Patton (the same two generals who would later become famous World War II heroes), a sense of desperation and falling morale began to settle in after so many months in fruitless pursuit of Pancho Villa and his famous Dorados through Northern Mexico. In the end they had all grown weary of the chase— military men of every rank and stripe, American FBI agents, and other functionaries of the Gringo government—but above all, it was Carranza's inept supporters who weren't able to lay so much as a finger on their quarry. What the hell were they going to do, Maty, now that President Wilson had decided, against all signs to the contrary, to give the order to withdraw his troops from Northern Mexico? That's exactly what the bitter participants of that famous Expedition were asking themselves. How do we catch that fat fucking moustached son of a bitch Arango, that miserable killer and bandit, the rapist of Namiquipa? Needless to say, in the end, Villa proudly wore the responsibility for the American invasion of Mexico like a ring on his finger, an expression that my father, Roberto Soto Gariglietti, said that his grandfather (my great-grandfather, the triumphant Enzo himself), used to use. It was Enzo who, years later, would dedicate much of his time to studying archives and investigating the underlying threads of the revolutionary history that he himself had helped to weave as one of Villa's foreign delegates. It was him, Villa, and not President Carranza, who was the true nationalist, the true patriot, the true anti-Yankee, said the Sicilian, laughing roundly, although ultimately it really wasn't quite like that, you know better than me, Robertico, because Villa still harbored the vice of admiration for those he'd been protecting since the beginning of the Revolution. His attack on Texas, then, even with the high costs involved, glorified and popularized the Atilla and his valiant Dorados at the expense of President Carranza, who had been supported by the Gringo Wilson . . . In any case, a few months later, after the Yankee troops had already returned to their side of the border, a civil servant and a military man met privately in an unknown hideout somewhere in Texas. The first, Maty, was a man named Stone and he was the chief of the FBI's field office in El Paso, Roberto. By all accounts he was much more arrogant and cynical than the man he was chatting with. To this man, apparently of a lower rank, Stone said point-blank, without removing the long, thin cigarette he held in his mouth in a cigarette holder:

" 'Look, Captain Reed, we need to eliminate Villa once and for all . . . with or without Wilson's approval, who of course doesn't know shit about what things are like now in Mexico. As Patton says—and I agree with him on this—you'd have to be a complete fucking idiot to think that a half-savage and completely ignorant people like the Mexicans could ever form a real republic. He thinks that Wilson must have the brain of a worm to have decided to withdraw from Mexico. All our neighbors have now is a despot, and that's all they want. The entire Expedition didn't do a goddamn thing, Captain! We can't just sit here like we're scared stiff. What a waste of energy and money, spending all those months in the desert just so that mangy dog could laugh at us as he slips through our fingers . . .' Stone fell silent after his fiery tirade. He waited a moment, taking one long drag on his long cigarette, staring at the other man, his eyes obsessive and almost spiteful, before finally saying: 'You should know that I spoke with Pershing not long ago, and the frustration is tearing him apart. He's humiliated and depressed, shut up in his house, and doesn't want to see or salute anybody.'

" 'Yes, I can imagine. With nothing to show for his efforts, he's become the laughingstock of the Expedition,' Reed replied, firm and expeditious, lighting a cigarette as well (though he didn't use a cigarette holder, Maty) before taking a long, hard lungful of smoke which he then released into the atmosphere, blotting out his face like a cloud. 'It's just incredible that even with the help of the Federales, they still couldn't track down that scoundrel. They say he was wounded and holed up in a cave with only his cousin there to care for him.'

" 'I've heard that too,' Stone nodded, and at that point he finally began to settle down in his soft armchair, with a pensive look on his face. It was hot as blazes that August, and although the rickety old fan in the lounge area of the club they were in lent a bit of relief to the place, making it slightly more comfortable, it was nowhere near sufficient.

" 'So tell me then, what do you need me for?' Captain Reed asked, stretching, emerging from his drowsiness or resentment, the cigarette still held firmly in his mouth. 'What's this all about?'

" 'As I already said, it's about killing Pancho Villa,' Stone replied in an anxious, almost threatening tone. 'Pershing wants him dead. He said so. And he asked me to do it.' Yes, that's what he said, you heard me, Matilde, you heard me, Robertico, said Enzo the Sicilian to his grandson, my father, a few months before he died.

" 'And how are we going to do that?' Reed asked, a bit taken aback, though it wasn't Pershing's request that surprised him, since he had finally been in Mexico now for a number of months. 'Especially since it's going to be even harder now than it was before? Without our troops there, how can we catch him? Nobody's been able to get to him. Not even close. You know that. He up and vanishes; he turns into a ghost every time he retreats into the mountains or the desert he controls.'

" 'We'll do it through the use of some rather unconventional tactics, *amigo*.' Stone lowered his voice and leaned in closer to Captain Reed, though such secrecy really wasn't necessary at that time of day. The club where they had met was devoid of customers; nobody was inside drinking despite the devastating gloom of the street, which irremediably found its way into the establishment through the very interstices of the building itself. 'We're going to poison him.'

" 'What?' exclaimed Reed, truly perplexed, his ash-laden cigarette hanging between his fingers, on the verge of collapsing, falling, and crashing onto the floor of the club where their covert conclave was taking place.

" 'You heard me, Matilde,' the FBI agent affirmed upon seeing the widening eyes of his young colleague; he took another drag on his cigarette and paused for a moment before finally deciding to solve or complete the mystery that had brought them both there to El Paso: 'Gemichi Tatematsu, an old personal servant to Villa's brother Hipólito, has put us in contact with certain compatriots of his who are willing to assassinate the General for a reasonable sum. As you know, Robertico, Villa admires the Japanese and currently has two young Japanese cooks working in his kitchen.' "

"Incredible . . . I can't believe it . . ." Maty exclaimed, this time without yawning or even blinking an eye as she reclined on the painter's naked chest, giving no outward sign that she had fallen asleep again, with her recorder firmly in her grasp.

" 'After speaking with a guy named Jah Hawakawa, an associate of Gemichi, we decided that it would be best to deliver him dead, because to get him across the border alive, as Pershing wants, would be all but impossible.'

" 'Does Pershing know about these . . . rather unconventional tactics, as you put it?' Reed was clearly vacillating, Maty, and you certainly couldn't blame him. 'I ask you this because you know as well as anyone that if any of this were to get out, it would become a huge international scandal. The United States government would be put on trial before the international court of public opinion!'

"'Of course. He authorized the Japanese approach himself. He's agreed that it's worth the risk.'

"'Makes you wonder if the idea to poison him was more their idea.'

"'More or less,' Stone replied, not very sure, rather ambiguous, actually, with the last bit of his cigarette burning down to the cigarette holder clenched between his teeth, as if the thin stripe of smoke offered him some sort of protection, as if his life and the life of General Pershing—or at least their reputations—depended on it. 'And this is where you come in, my old friend.'

"'I'm listening,' the Captain answered as he extinguished his own cigarette, which by then had become nothing more than a little tower of ash.

"'You have less than two weeks to find these Japanese collaborators. A surgeon from Pershing's army will give you the poison so that you can hand it over to the Japanese right . . . here . . . ' he said, pointing to a spot just to the north of them on a smallish map of the Mexican Republic. 'Yes, here it is. September 3rd, at ten o'clock at night. You will find them at the cantina in the center of the town.'

"'What's the name of the place?'

"'I don't know.'

"'And if it's not the only cantina in town?'

"'There's only one, don't you worry. You'll be able to find it. It's a very small town.'

"'And the doctor?'

"'I can't give you his name. You'll meet him in two or three days. All you have to do is go to his clinic, feign a fever, and receive what he gives you.'" Arturo, the Agro painter, paused for a few seconds, perhaps measuring or gauging the effect all this was having on Captain Reed, or perhaps just letting it seep down into him, into his guts, his testicles, into the very core of his being. "'We will know if it was a success on the third day because that's how long it takes for the poison to have its effect, and there are no symptoms or signs up until the moment of death.' Apparently, that was one of the conditions set by the Japanese, Roberto, Enzo Gariglietti said to his grandson, Matilde, and he passed that on to me, his kid, you know? Of course, Robertico: they were nervous and needed time to escape without raising suspicion among Los Dorados, who always surrounded and protected Villa, even when he went to the bathroom . . .

" 'What are the names of the contacts?'

" 'That's not important. They will be the only patrons you see there at the cantina that night. All you have to do is show up.' Of course, getting to that town was a bit complicated, Matilde. 'There weren't any good roads that lead there, according to the reports I've received. It's possible you'll have to spend a night out in the desert before you arrive. Find yourself a good guide and a team of mules. Pack supplies.'

" 'I understand,' was what my father told me his answer was, however uncertain it might have been, to his dear grandfather Gariglietti when he was telling him this tale, more than half a century ago, this anecdote that's straight out of a Hollywood film, and which (though you wouldn't believe it, Maty) is well-documented in the annals of Texas history.

" 'This should help you get there, with a little bit extra for yourself.' He slid an envelope across the table to him containing a stack of Mexican pesos with a stack of U.S. dollars on top.

"And with that, the conversation between Stone, head of the FBI's field office in El Paso, and the young Captain Reed, came to an end on that unbearably hot summer afternoon. They exchanged a strong handshake before taking leave of each other without so much as a backward glance. All that remained were the smashed, trembling, smoldering cigarette butts, filling the air with a whitish, opaline smoke. Which reminds me . . . Maty, could you pass me the ashtray, please?"

XXIII

Before explaining how and why the bomb went off in Irene's head and how the shrapnel from that bomb scarred so many people in that shit-stained southern town, I need to describe what happened during those few weeks in Mexico between my wife and her recently discovered biological family. Not to do so would be like killing off my obsession with realism, with which I've always tried to work in harmony. The realism aspect is, of course, something of a damn neurosis for me, which, deep down, has more to do with the problem of depicting reality than it does with problems of mimicry, of creating hasty reflections of the world . . . problems which, in principle, do not interest me. As a reader of books and watcher of films, I have always been concerned with one thing above all others: verisimilitude, pure fucking verisimilitude, whether it involves Martians, nymphomaniac sirens, or weak-bladdered giants on top of the Notre Dame Cathedral. In that regard, I am Aristotelian, my beloved Empedocles, but only in that regard, I assure you. Everything else emerges from this, from verisimilitude; it is all subordinate to my conviction or faith in the writer's ability to make me believe in what I'm watching or reading, and if they can't do that—if I don't believe or agree with the supposed "truth" of what he is insinuating—then my desire to continue down the path of frictional immersion begins to wane: my attention fades, the act of watching the film or reading the book ceases to have meaning, and I fall asleep in the arms of Morpheus. Why would I continue on, what objective would there be in reading a book or watching a film if I didn't believe a whit in what was happening, in what was to come? Better to close the book, better to leave the theater, better to face reality, which—of course—is occasionally much less probable than any friction. Where does this weakness, this Achilles' heel of mine, come from? Perhaps this urgency stems from the need to put an end to things I've recently left half-told, unfinished: the story of my wife and my ex-wife, the encounter in Mexico City, the great Capirucha, between Irene and her biological mother, the recently created (though ever-present) familial triangle in which I've now unexpectedly found myself nose-deep.

Basically—and to cut to the chase—I have to say that Irene returned home happy, very emotional, and feeling quite the opposite of how she felt when she left (remember?), having learned about her biological roots after getting that damn letter from her adoptive mother (her only real mother) via FedEx from San Francisco. She was so content and so full of herself, so full of new information, that she never (not for one moment) noticed my blushing cheeks, my bright and burning shameful face, the result of my innate inability to hide my infidelity with Stephany, the hot, sexy wife of my friend from Turin. And so I let her explain everything to me; I listened to her day and night for an entire week, between bottles of wine, beers, tequilas, whiskeys, half-drunk, because the story I'm about to relate to you is but a tiny fragment of a long-winded and winding speech, repeated again and again in a number of different ways, with varying states of feminine moods ranging from joy to fear to sadness to surprise to impassivity and resentment, all scrambled together and often difficult to categorize or discern, just as Empedocles describes the fragments dispersed throughout the body before they come to constitute a human being. Let's describe it thus: an Irenesque vortex that I will attempt to unravel, as God grants me to understand.

It seems that after two days of being in San Francisco with Emilio and her mother, Irene decided to call Dulce, her other mother. Apparently, my ex-mother-in-law answered the phone herself. Irene said that yes, her nerves were frozen, and that they froze more solid still when she heard the calm, sweet voice of Dulce Mallea on the other end of the line. She didn't know what to do, didn't know what to say. She realized that she wasn't prepared. According to her, she suddenly realized that she wasn't simply contacting her own biological mother; she was also contacting her current husband's ex-mother-in-law, a fact that unnerved her even more, freezing her words before they were even formed. What could she say? If she started with her name, Dulce would probably think that my crazy wife was calling for some other reason, some complaint or insult related to me, Fedra, or the boy, and that she would simply try to avoid my wife at all costs. Apparently—and according to an explanation she gave me one of those nights we spent drinking on the deck and watching the starry sky above Madisonburg—that was the first time Irene fully comprehended the difficulty and complexity of the situation, but of course it was already too late: there was Dulce, on the other end of the line, asking who was calling, waiting for a response, demanding to know what she wanted, and yet Irene couldn't respond. Her tongue had quite literally gone limp. But there would be no rescue, since Irene's mother (my current mother-in-law) wasn't there; she was in the other room with Emilio, playing with toys I imagine, or perhaps that's what she told me, but in the end it didn't matter at all. My terrified wife hung up.

Irene says that she caught her breath, waited two or three minutes, and then called again. It was time—it was destiny—so why prolong it any longer? she said. Dulce Mallea, my beloved ex-mother-in-law, answered the phone again. Then, my wife, with the complete fluency that untimely things can bring out in a person, blurted out:

"I'm sorry to bother you, but I'm calling because I recently learned that you're my mother . . ."

Irene says that the first thing she heard was silence. She heard the tone, the quality of the silence and listened to it as she'd never listened to anything ever before in her life: she heard it huge and real and encompassing everything, stronger than noise or sound or music, more lasting than words or songs or presidential speeches. Dulce Mallea didn't utter a word, but that doesn't mean she was silent. Had she covered the earpiece? Could she be crying? Would she be assessing the truth or falsehood carried by these otherworldly words? But if she didn't hang up, wouldn't that be some sign of certainty, of an indestructible truth in the voice of the young woman who had dared to say what she had said? It was highly probable, of course, that Dulce had, for many years—lustrums, even—been awaiting that call, with the knowledge that one day, in spite of everything, it would come. Why not, if she herself had written that damn letter, which Irene read and I didn't back in Madisonburg? And now that I think about it (and now that I'm telling you this story), my ex-mother-in-law must have figured that this call from her unknown biological daughter would have been made long before it actually happened. Perhaps she assumed this daughter of hers would have opened and read those sheets of paper as soon as she turned eighteen, and since then a full ten years had passed without a call. Maybe she even forgot about the possible call she had so longed for . . . who knows, but I doubt this last theory very much. The fact of the matter, though, is that Dulce, my ex-mother-in-law, didn't respond. She said nothing, and after a few seconds the silence became a sort of inflammable igneous mass, not to mention an increasingly expensive long-distance phone call. But the other fact of the matter is that neither of them hung up the phone, and that—in and of itself—was worth a thousand words. Irene had to have known that, expected that, even, and so she decided to shut up and not say one syllable more, choosing instead to wait, to wait for the shock or fright or surprise or whatever it was to fade. And that's what finally happened, after six or seven minutes, when Irene heard the same calm and caring voice that my mother-in-law Dulce had always used with me:

"I'd like to meet you . . . if you would," she said, without so much as asking her name. Of course, that response brings up another question: why? Why would it possibly matter whether her daughter were called Irma, Lorena, Petra, Viridiana, or Juana? She was simply her daughter, the same daughter she'd given up for adoption, and that was the one and only thing that mattered. And so clearly she was relieved that she did not have to offer up the fact that her name was Irene, something which would have been incredibly difficult to explain and would have only caused more confusion between her biological mother and her.

"Of course I want to . . . that's why I'm calling you." They were speaking Spanish of course, and I noticed that suddenly Irene had changed from the formal to the informal, from *usted* to *tú*, and believe you me, that's meaningful, more than just a simple device cooked up by an exiled, provincial novelist.

"And where do you live?"

"In the United States," was Irene's chosen response. That sort of evasiveness hinted at something more fundamental: not having to explain that although she was currently in San Francisco, she lived in Madison-burg, Virginia . . . a fact that would, of course, have led to other questions (read: questions about me) which Irene did not want to get into at the moment.

"Would you like me to come see you?"

"No, I'd rather come to you, if it's all the same to you."

"And how did you happen to get my phone number?"

"It wasn't all that difficult . . ." was the only thing that Irene could think of to say, which (of course) put a slight smile on her face, a wry grin which—according to what she told me—was akin to saying, "If you only knew . . ."

"When would you like to come?"

"Whenever it's convenient for you."

"No, no, I'm always available, honey." Irene heard her biological mother's affectionate voice, as kind and loving as ever, I imagine. "I've been waiting for this call for years now, you know?" Here, then, was confirmation of my theory (which I had deduced previously) that this surprise phone call from my wife was something for which Dulce Mallea had been yearning for quite some time. All that notwithstanding, the thing that still begs attention is that not once during the five years that Fedra and I spent raising our little Dulce in Mexico did my ex-wife ever tell me her mother's story. I was equally surprised that Fedra never told me that she had a biological half sister (that's assuming that she knew she had one). It was even less likely that my ex-mother-in-law would have told me about her past. For that reason, let me state for the record that what I'm about to describe came to me from Irene and only Irene, my beloved wife, during the week after her return to Madisonburg, and not via my ex-wife, but you needn't concern yourself with all of that because, thanks to the communicative property, it doesn't matter which way you slice it: not one iota of the incontrovertible past can be changed, nor can the final, beloved product—my wife—be affected.

Dulce wouldn't let her stay in a hotel. She and Fedra picked up Irene and Emilio at the airport in Mexico City and (from what I understand) took them to their home where my daughter Dulce was waiting for them with the nanny. This is much more complicated than it might appear to be as I've related it here; in fact, it was a tangled web of Alarconian proportions since, as you know, my wife had only ever seen one or two photos of Fedra and her mother, and Fedra and my ex-mother-in-law had only ever seen one or two photos of Irene and the boy, so once they finally met face to face, they still weren't sure whether it was somebody else, a mistake, or if it was pure, random chance that Irene and Emilio were landing in Mexico City at the same time but for completely unrelated reasons. But apparently the confusion was alleviated just a bit when my wife—planning ahead—walked right up to them, holding Emilio's hand, and introduced herself:

"I'm here. It's me. Irene."

"Don't I know you from somewhere?" Fedra asked, stunned, suddenly feeling a twinge of recognition, although in fact she did not "know" her in that sense of the word; rather, they simply knew of each other's existence.

"Yes, Fedra," Irene answered. "I'm Eusebio's wife, and this is Emilio, our son."

"Hello Emilio, how are you?" said my ex-mother-in-law, squatting down to greet the boy, or perhaps to lighten the tenseness or whatever it was that had suddenly begun to incubate there like Plasticine or chewing gum.

"You see!" I interrupted Irene as she was recounting the events for me that night on the deck, doing shots of tequila with lemon and salt:

indispensable tools for an exceptional occasion of exceptionally interwoven gossip. "You must have used your last name, and that must have tipped them off."

"When you told me your name was Irene, I admit I never even imagined that you were the same Irene . . . you know, who married Eusebio?" said my ex-mother-in-law, embracing her with tears in her eyes, according to what Irene told me. Then the three women and the boy began to walk down the long, illuminated airport concourse, with the porter carrying their luggage along behind them. "I can't believe it. I mean, how could I? But tell me . . . how is he doing? What did he have to say about all of this? Doesn't he think it's all just quite unbelievable?"

"Well, what would you have wanted me to say, Eusebio?" my magnificent wife replied that night under the full moon, as she leaned on the handrail of the deck, bottle of tequila blanco in hand, her eyes glistening with the combination of moonlight and twice-distilled liquor. "You didn't believe it at first either, you were just as shocked by the coincidence when you read the letter. And—don't forget—you were the one who encouraged me to call my mother in San Francisco and have her send that letter, after all these years of not wanting to open it."

"So we're half sisters . . . can you believe it?" Fedra blurted out, suddenly embracing her too, also with tears in her eyes, according to what Irene said, which came as a total surprise to me. Fedra had apparently emerged from her daze, while I was still stuck in my state of annoyance and embarrassment. "Why didn't you tell us who you were?"

"But when were you going to do it, love? When? On the phone, maybe? Fedra really is a bit insensitive," I responded to my wife that night, whichever night it was, under the moon, recognizing the unusual, delicate nature of the situation, sipping my tequila blanco, understanding why Irene preferred to keep quiet right up until the last possible moment, swallowing the lump in her throat without the aid of a decent tequila to help her during that difficult, critical moment, though she had it now, as she recounted the awful anecdote.

"Well, that doesn't matter anymore, honey," Dulce interrupted, fortunately before Irene could answer. She tipped the porter and once again embraced her newly acquired daughter, her recovered daughter, her Gringo or Cuban or Mexican or unknown, undiscovered daughter who luckily happened to speak Spanish and who was at this very moment standing right in front of her very eyes nearly three decades after she had given her up for adoption. "We're going home, girls, and we have so much to talk about. Right, Emilio?"

"So Emilio was happy? And Dulce, my daughter, how did she look?" I asked my wife this between sips, at some point during the innumerable conversations we had every night that week before (devastatingly) the bomb hit, scattering shit everywhere, which I'd prefer to leave for later. "Dulce really does look a lot like you, doesn't she? Like I always told you she did?"

"But you look so similar to my daughter, you know?" Fedra suddenly said in the car, unable to take her eyes off her half sister, a few years younger than her, exhausting herself as she took all of it in. "In fact, I think you look more like *mamá* than I do. Every once in awhile I see a picture of you, Irene, but honestly it's nothing like having you here in front of me, live and in the flesh. I'm sorry, I'm just so emotional, I don't really know what I'm saying . . ."

"Yes, I really think you look like me too," my ex-mother-in-law said to my wife, examining her as they sat at a stoplight on the way back to the house. "What do you think?"

"Yes, a lot. Really a lot," I said, repeating what I once said, a number of years ago now, at a restaurant on Fisherman's Wharf, to my wife, which I subsequently repeated on a number of occasions, after we were married and had added Emilio to our family, in Madisonburg: her incredible similarity with my daughter and with my ex-mother-in-law, though not with my ex-wife.

To summarize (and so I don't have to go on about the chitchat in the car as they made their way through the congested traffic on Insurgentes), it appears that Irene and Fedra were getting along well enough. Again, I confess, my first fears were that this encounter could turn odious, but contrary to all my pessimistic predictions, the two half sisters were gradually growing rather fond of one another, getting to know each other, and working towards what you might describe as a healthy relationship, helped along—above all—by the amiability and generosity of my ex-mother-in-law, who was always there, close by, as loving and affable as ever, which I know, I truly know. But no matter how many times Irene told me about them, in the warm, dusky nights on our deck, I just can't imagine what those first days there were like, in an unfamiliar house, in an unfamiliar city, with an unfamiliar mother and sister. Though I suppose or imagine that, with the goodwill that animated each of the individuals involved, they would have managed to have a few wonderful days of . . . internalization? Reminiscence? Anagnorisis? Withdrawal? Absorption? Memory? Reunion? Celebration? What the hell do you call it? Basically, Irene went there in search of something very concrete, according to the explanation she gave me before leaving: she wanted to learn—firsthand and face-to-face—why her biological parents had given her up for adoption. While at first, as I admitted *a posteriori*, she didn't want to get to know or even search for her biological mother (and even less so her half sister), the fact is that, in the end, not only did she find the answer she was longing for, but she also gained a new family, new relatives, new friends, new . . . what? What the hell do you call them? How do you ultimately define the aunt and the mother of my daughter Dulce, half sister to our son Emilio?

"And tell me," I finally dared to venture late one night, after Emilio was already asleep, as Irene and I sat out on the deck with beers in hand, lemon slices, and a can of salted peanuts between us, since it's virtually impossible to find spicy peanuts anywhere in Virginia. "What ended up happening? What was it that caused Dulce to give you up for adoption? I'm dying to know, Irene, ever since you came back home. You've probably been putting off telling me on purpose, right?"

"Are you really okay with telling me?" my wife asked her biological mother on her third night there, I think, when she felt that the right moment had come, that now was the opportunity and she didn't want to postpone any longer the chance to have a concrete answer to the question that was the catalyst for this trip with Emilio to Mexico City and even for taking up residence in that same old house I myself knew only too well. "I'd like to know, yes, if it's okay with you. I think I'm ready."

"But who knows, Irene," I interrupted yet again, this time spilling my bottle of beer: a sign of how nervous I was. "Honestly, I'm not sure anybody is ever fully prepared for things like this."

"Well, Irene, Fedra's father died when she was still a child. I was a forty-five-year-old widow, and I never remarried. I tried to remake my life by going out on dates with a couple of potential candidates, but honestly I never felt comfortable with another man after that. I felt strange, used, out of place . . . but what did I know, those were just foolish ideas, cobwebs in the head of a prudish old widow, if you like. The fact is that I never remarried, and that I raised and educated Fedra, my only daughter, up to that point. Her father loved the works of Jean Racine, hence the unusual name, so don't think that I'm the one who named your sister, not at all. I objected to it at first, but later I got used to it. We can say, Fedra, that your father was an extravagant sort, but yes: he left me, he went away and left me . . . But that's not what you wanted to know, Irene . . ."

"Of course that's not what I wanted to know!" I interrupted my wife, anxious to get to the point.

". . . We're not here to talk about Dad," Fedra cut in from her seat in the armchair that third night of confession. "We can do that some other time."

"In other words, you and Irene don't share the same father, right Fedra?" I said, my eyes as wide as hallways, incredulous and morbid, why deny it? I was finally picking up a few important pieces of that story.

"I was never a very thin woman, but I wasn't at all fat, either . . . I only got that way after Fedra's father died. I suppose I was quite depressed, which increased my appetite, and I started eating more and more, especially chocolates. Ugh, you have no idea how much I love chocolate! White chocolate, dark chocolate, milk chocolate, chocolate covered cherries, almonds, or hazelnuts, anything in a box, even mint chocolate and chocolate liqueur. Everything. They're my weakness. Well, they were . . . With many of my friends, it happens the opposite way, you know? When they get depressed, they stop eating, they lose their appetite. But with me, Irene, it's important for you to know that it happened the other way around . . ."

"But what the hell do chocolate and obesity—things I'm already quite familiar with—have to do with this whole adoption thing?" I interrupted my mother-in-law that night because it seemed to me that she was beginning to spiral into hopeless circumlocution, an endless string of pointless wordplay that would never get to the heart of the matter.

"So when what happened happened, I didn't even realize it, you see?"

"But what was it? What happened?" Irene asked, on the edge of her seat.

"What happened, *mamá*?" Fedra asked, apparently also unaware of this unusual story, which—according to what Irene revealed to me— explains why Fedra never mentioned it to me before.

"'What happened happened'? What the hell is that supposed to mean?" I cried, losing my sanity, my patience, on the broad backyard deck there in Madisonburg on a warm June night.

"I mean that when those two men raped me, I never, ever imagined that I would end up pregnant," my beloved ex-mother-in-law suddenly said, now indeed getting to the point, delivering a hard, fast shot to the head, a real knockout blow.

It was as if a thick, viscous silence had suddenly been draped over us, like a sweet, impenetrable molasses. I didn't speak. Fedra didn't speak. Irene didn't speak. My ex-mother-in-law didn't speak. Nobody spoke. The silence was bituminous, a mixture of danger and anguish. Raped? Overweight? Pregnant? Widowed? Finally, emboldened by the fact that

I wasn't there at the time and learned of all this two weeks after the fact straight from my wife's mouth, I broke the ominous silence that surrounded us:

"And how old were you, Dulce?"

"Well, just do the math, Eusebio: if I had Fedra at thirty-five (in other words, not exactly young) and her father died when she was five years old, then that would make me a little over forty when I started piling on the pounds thanks to (as I've said) those chocolates, those goddamn chocolates filled with hazelnuts, peanuts, cherries, raisins, white chocolate, Swiss chocolate, Belgian chocolate, Guatemalan chocolate, bitter chocolate, semisweet chocolate, milk chocolate, boxes of chocolates, chocolates with *rompope* eggnog filling, even that Nestlé 'Abuelita' chocolate (have you seen that?) to the point where I just ate and ate giant chunks of chocolate to satisfy myself, as if the world were about to end, as if the world itself were nothing but a humongous, succulent treat . . ."

"Yes, yes, yes," I interrupted, desperate, almost irate. "But Dulce, what does your weight have to do with all of this, with being raped? And why are you so focused on your size anyway since you're not even that big . . . just thick, or curvy, if you will?"

"Because I didn't realize I was pregnant until the day Irene was born, you stupid numbskull. Now do you understand? Yes, as absolutely incredible as it sounds, it's true. For those nine months, I didn't know I was carrying a child because of what I'd done, which was—as I said— become a pig, a filthy swine, doing nothing but eating chocolate liqueurs and chocolate with puffed rice day after day as I cried my way through widowhood. I asked myself, what am I going to do now, without my daughter's father, without Fedra's father, our support, my life, my angel, the man who sustained me through the good times and the bad? You can't imagine how I felt; I was going crazy, Eusebio, I was on the verge of absolute, devastating insanity, and to make matters worse, I had a daughter who was five years old at the time, precisely the age where little girls need their fathers more than ever. Back then, all I ever thought about was eating chocolate (which I did) and because of that I didn't feel like I could make anybody happy. How could I learn to love another man if I looked like a whale, if I was constantly in tears, stuffing myself with chocolate-covered stuff, and if all I had to offer was the burden of a fatherless daughter, my little Fedra, your ex-wife? Well . . ." She paused to catch her breath, gathering herself and calming down a bit, drying her tears with an embroidered yellow handkerchief she stitched herself, before continuing: "Time passed, ten years in fact, and I became a very irregular woman. In other words, sometimes I would menstruate and sometimes my cycle would stop. It's not as uncommon as you might imagine. I was fat and I was irregular. I worked just enough—the bare minimum, really—to carry on; it was important to provide Fedra with an education, but I also have to say that my parents-in-law were very supportive of me all those years. They always helped me out financially. They had a bit of money, you know? But that wasn't everything. Money couldn't bring back my husband, and it wasn't going to change my destiny either. I don't want to beat around the bush, because I can see you're getting impatient about finding out all the morbid details, so . . . those two men raped me when Fedra was fourteen years old, I think, which means that, yes, I was nearing fifty. And so that's it, you heard me: they raped me, they shamelessly humiliated me. A fifty-year-old woman. An old lady. And a fat one . . . can you believe it? I don't know what they saw in me. I don't know why they were so intent on disgracing me. It was, Eusebio, the single worst experience that ever could have happened to me. Please don't ask me to go on; I've almost never told anybody about this, and I don't want to start doing so now. It's a dead and buried chapter of my life. All that matters is that you know that I am Irene's mother and that those men were complete strangers who jumped me in a park and took advantage of me, robbed me, and threatened me with my life if I said anything or went to the police to file a report. They didn't even have to threaten me, since I wasn't about to say anything to anybody, as you might have imagined. I didn't; all I wanted to do was start forgetting it ever happened . . . and I almost succeeded. Almost . . . because when I stopped menstruating, I simply attributed it to menopause. What else could it have been? In fact, it had happened before; sometimes months would pass without a menstrual cycle . . . and then they would return. So let me tell you: my cycles were often irregular, and it's much more common than men seem to imagine. Why the hell would I think that a woman on the verge of turning fifty might be pregnant? Especially one like me! That was the last thing that would have ever crossed my mind . . . and since I didn't see a doctor after it happened, I was even less likely to have found out. And that's when the unexpected—the unimaginable—thing happened: little Irene, my baby girl, was born. One day, there I am in my living room . . . and my water just broke. I was petrified. Two of my neighbors immediately came to help me, and—along with the maid—they helped me into bed, where I gave birth. Thank God Fedra wasn't there; she was with her grandparents that memorable afternoon, and she ended up staying there for a number of weeks until I was finally able to think and decide what to do with the baby . . ."

Just then I saw the baby crying. My baby, Irene. My beloved little wife could not stop sobbing. Also, I caught a glimpse (at a distance, of course) of my beloved ex-mother-in-law wailing in sorrow while Fedra was sitting there next to her, her mouth wide open. My own eyes even began to tear up and my nose began to run upon hearing this frightful tale. Dulce continued on in her velvety sweet voice, suddenly grasping the hand of her daughter, who had regained some composure.

"Believe me, Irene, I never stopped thinking about you, I never stopped loving you, but I just didn't think I could take care of you on my own. I felt useless, like a fat cow, sad and abandoned and alone in the world, with nothing but bad luck coming down on me from above. One of those neighbors of mine suggested that adoption would be best, and after five or six weeks, that's exactly what I did. Yes, after a lot of bureaucratic paperwork and a litany of doubt that plagued me and kept me up at night for quite some time, that's what I did. The adoption agency had a condition which I'm sure you're already aware of: I was to break off all contact with the child, to forget about her, I would have no right to know about her new family, parents, or anybody else. Blind confidence, that was the condition, and I assumed that I had it. I had to. And then all I had left was memory, the ineffaceable memory of a baby girl who spent nine months in my belly without my ever realizing it, a tiny little baby girl whom I only got to know over the space of five weeks. Did I regret my decision? Yes, very much so. Almost every day. Why deny it? Why didn't I keep you? Who was stopping me? I could have done it. I know I could have. You were mine. I had no justification, and so I won't try to justify myself now. Not even being the victim of rape at fifty years of age justifies it for me, no matter how much my neighbors—the only ones who knew—wanted to convince me that bringing a child into the world under bad circumstances just wasn't the same as doing it under good conditions. Irene, the people at the adoption agency assured me that you would be in very good hands, that you would be placed with a loving couple who couldn't have children of their own, that I shouldn't worry anymore about that, and that—if I wished—I could write a letter to you, which you would have the right to open and read when you came of age, and after that—if you so desired—you could find out who your true mother was. But that couldn't happen until you were eighteen, and when that day came and went without a letter or phone call, I assumed that you had chosen not to know, not to find out, and I understood that perfectly, I even assumed and respected that, Irene, I swear to you. I had less right than anybody to judge you based on that decision. On the contrary, it would have been perfectly fine if you hadn't come looking for me, but now you're here and we don't have to think about that, you're here, with me, with us, and still I just cannot believe it, I still feel like I'm dreaming or hallucinating in my old age. I can only ask your forgiveness, ask that you forget the past. I hope you can, and I hope that we can become good friends, if nothing else . . ."

Then, at the most inopportune time, the phone in the dining room jumped to life (but aren't those damn phone calls always untimely, no matter where you are in the world?), interrupting or putting the finishing touch on the sad and incredible story of my children's grandmother. I left my wife alone there on the deck under the silver-plated moon and walked back inside the house where I paced back and forth, still disoriented, and half-drunk besides. It was much darker there than it was out in the yard, which, as I said, was warm and moonlit that night in June. After some effort I found the cordless phone and switched it on. Snotty and tipsy, I heard the voice of a woman I know say, rather distressed:

"Eusebio? Eusebio Cardoso? I need to speak with you. It's urgent."

My knees wobbled, my head spun, and all I could muster was a drunken stammer:

"Yes?"

24
(THURSDAY, MAY 18TH, CONTINUED)

"So what happened with the Japanese assassins?" Matilde asked, anxious to know how the story ended before she got up, got dressed, and went home—yes, dear Reader—back to the house where you were waiting for her. "And of course, what about Villa?"

"From what we know and according to documents filed at the National Archive," Arturo replied, a bit overzealously, apparently very well informed by his father, who in turn was well informed by his grandfather Gariglietti, "On the 23rd of September, 1917, two men named Dyo and Fusita poisoned General Pancho Villa. They immediately fled Chihuahua without leaving a trace. Apparently, some time later, and with safe-conduct documents, they were granted entrance into the United States, where they met with Captain Reed, the only officer who knew about the mission after that brief encounter in a Chihuahua cantina, and who would file a report on it just a short while later."

"Were the cowards paid for their work?" Matilde interrupted, at once surprised and stupefied by the story.

"Probably, yes. But the poison didn't work."

"What happened? What went wrong, grandpa?" Roberto asked.

"According to Dyo, he put the poison he'd gotten a few days beforehand from Reed into the cup of coffee from which General Villa drank on the morning of September 23rd. But according to Fusita, Villa poured half his coffee into another cup and gave it to an Italian confidante of his sitting on his right-hand side. In other words, me, in other words, my great-grandfather, Maty. Enzo, who happened to be in camp at the time, took a sip from his cup, tasted it, swished it around in his mouth for a moment, and then swallowed, unconcerned and content. Just imagine, both of the Japanese spies must have been trembling in their boots! They would have been strung up by their balls! Dyo feared the worst: what if the Italian died? What if you, grandfather, died right there at the officer's mess, my father Roberto asked of my great-grandfather, the illustrious Sicilian protagonist of this mysterious bit of revolutionary history. *What if the promises Captain Reed made about the delayed effects of the poison were pure lies?* thought Dyo and Fusita, the Japanese traitors, over and over again. *What if Pershing's surgeon's concoction didn't work, and instead of three days . . . the Italian dropped dead right then and there?* All that was possible, Maty, according to what my great-grandfather Enzo said to my father when he asked him about it on that vague and distant occasion back when he was still very young. But none of it happened. What did finally happen was that, just before fleeing, they watched with their own eyes as Villa sipped his own half cup of coffee, as parsimonious and pensive as he always was in the morning."

"So why did it fail?" Maty pressed, looking nervous and upset as she fixed herself up, putting on her smallish wristwatch and stowing the rest of her scattered items in her purse. "Was Villa immune to the poison? Was your great-grandfather?"

"I don't know," Enzo categorically replied, with an obvious smile on his lips, clearly pleased in having saved the day.

"Did it not have the desired effect, grandpa?" Roberto persisted.

"Dyo and Fusita swear, Maty, that two weeks before the assassination attempt, they had taken two tablets from the bottle (which contained twenty) and fed them to a dog in the street, apparently with excellent results."

"So Dyo and Fusita were lying?" Arturo asked his father yet again, who in turn asked his grandfather Gariglietti.

"We don't know, Maty, but on the day when Villa was supposed to die, he didn't, of course, and it wasn't the end of my great-grandfather's life, either. They both survived, and nobody knows why. Villa, on the other hand, as you already know, would live on for another five years and had a number of battles left to fight, until his final defeat or betrayal in Parral, Chihuahua, when he was ambushed in his car on the way home from a baptism to which he'd been invited as the child's godfather."

"But there's one thing you still don't know," Enzo suddenly said to his grandson, dear Reader, and which Arturo repeated to Maty, your wife, taking her by the arm: "The whole conspiracy was silenced, filed away, and forgotten by the American FBI, and—listen to me—it was never uncovered . . . until many years later, when I read the report myself (completely by chance) and learned how close to death I actually was that distant September morning . . . Pershing, though, was able to evade responsibility for masterminding this macabre yet laughable plan when it was finally revealed. Nevertheless, a few days later (just a few days), Pershing achieved his career-long dream despite the setbacks he suffered during the frustrating Mexican Expedition: he was named General of the Armies by President Wilson, the same president both Pershing and George Patton despised with all their heart. How ironic! Pershing was probably never able to forget about Pancho Villa, not even during his glory days as the invincible soldier of World War I, a war which probably ended up saving Venustiano Carranza from an imminent attack or an attempt at annexation by Wilson in November of 1916. Did you know that, Matilde?"

"No, I honestly didn't, Arturo, but now I really have to be going. My husband is going to kill me . . . he's been waiting . . ." Already dressed and perfectly made up, Matilde kissed the painter on the lips, gently biting him with delight before applying another coat of dark crimson lipstick. She checked her wristwatch again: she was running very late indeed. You waited for her, dear Reader, with this Devil's book in your hands . . . almost convinced that what you're reading is friction, pure miserable friction written by an indecent, macabre author . . . isn't that it?

Just before rushing out of the studio with her Louis Vuitton bag and mini tape recorder in hand, Maty asked her lover, as if she were truly emerging from an incredibly long and foggy hallucination about a Revolution that took place over a hundred years before:

"But Arturo . . . what does all this you're telling me have to do with Empedocles of Agrigento, and—above all—what does it have to do with your father? I'm already so lost, I don't understand anything."

"You will, next Tuesday, when we meet again."

XXV

"Eusebio, do you remember me?"

There, in the darkened dining room, a matter of feet from the deck where Irene was still contemplating the soft nocturnal landscape, I felt like I had died, like my legs had suddenly become as heavy as lead, and for a moment I stopped breathing, though I managed to hold on to the cordless phone. *Stephany. It was Stephany.* But what could this woman want? Didn't she say that everything was forgotten and buried at the bottom of the sea? No more massages, no more applications of muscular pressure, not more athletic massage-related visits to her house. Nothing at all. She said so. She had been very clear about that. Nevertheless, now I had to conduct myself with absolute casualness, had to be amiable, invariably courteous, natural, and measured. This was, after all, the mother of Alessandra, my son's best friend, as well as the wife of my friend from Turin, my best friend in the whole goddamn town of Madisonburg, Virginia, so very far away from Mexico, my beloved homeland. What the fuck had had I gotten myself into with her? Good lord. What kind of a mess was I in now?

"Of course I remember you, Stephany. What kind of a question is that?" I replied, forcing a smile to my face in the darkness of the dining room: a patently ridiculous smile, which nobody was ever going to see.

"I'm not Stephany." It was a woman's voice, a familiar voice—distant though still familiar—the voice of an American who spoke very good Spanish; in fact, it was clearer and much more clean and orderly than Stephany's Spanish, who occasionally still struggled with Castilian syntax when speaking. "It's your former colleague, Marion Siegel, the professor of translation. Remember me?"

Still in my cloudy daze of complete astonishment, I forced as much casualness into my voice as I could, as if I hadn't stopped thinking about her since the day the corpulent Whitehead gave her position to Katrina, the toadish daughter of the Gorgonian Gross-Wayne. "Yes, of course, Marion. Why wouldn't I remember you?"

"You thought it was somebody else, didn't you?" she said, poking fun at me, smiling at the other end of the line (I assume) before firing another jab: "Stephany?"

"Yes, Stefano's wife. Do you remember him?"

"Sure," she said, recalling her former Italian colleague, with whom she'd also been good friends during her time in the Department of Foreign Languages. "How is he? Still teaching there, I suppose."

"Yes, he's still here with us, poor guy," I laughed. "They're doing well. Stefano, actually, is doing super . . ." That was hyperbole, of course. Super? What the hell was that supposed to mean, Eusebio? Are your nerves betraying you? Was it the alcohol? Did the potential unmasking precipitate feelings of guilt and remorse? Was that it, or was it the sum of all the news about Dulce Mallea, my ex-mother-in-law, which I was still slowly digesting over the course of the week? To this day, I still don't know the reason for my idiocy, but I do remember that I used the word "super" the way a child or a simpleton might shout it upon meeting Superman in the flesh.

"Super? Oh, that's great!" she exclaimed, perhaps a bit disoriented, but then she changed the tone and timbre of her voice, indicating that it was time to get down to business, as she said to me in authentic Mexican slang:

"Something heavy is going down, Eusebio. Something you're not going to believe at all. But it's something that you—yes you—should know before anybody else."

"What are you talking about?" I started sweating profusely, immediately thinking that this had something to do with Stephany and Stefano, or with Irene, because as I've said, everything that happens around here ominously tends to involve me in one way or another.

"Who is it?" Suddenly I heard a third voice, one that clearly didn't belong to Stephany or Marion, but to somebody else, some other woman. "Who is it, Eusebio?"

"It has to do with Whitehead, Davis, Bormann, and several others," came the voice of Marion, much to my approval and peace of mind, from the other end of the line.

"It's Marion Siegel, love," I called to Irene, who was standing there, still whimpering, in the penumbra of the dining room, motionless, static, watching me with perplexed, grieving eyes, the recent events that had taken place in Mexico with Fedra and her new mother still fresh in her mind.

"Yes, and Marco Aurelio," was the confused response from Marion Siegel, my beloved former colleague who was forced out of the university by the dean and replaced by the toad woman. "Him too."

"No, no, Marion, forgive me. I was talking to Irene . . ."

"Marion?" Irene scratched her head, working back through her memories, trying to recall some image, to put a face on this friend from the not-too-distant past.

"Please tell her I said hello," Marion said.

"Marion says hello, Irene," I repeated, refined, with great care and attention to detail, or should I say: good manners, pure and simple.

"And how is Emilio?" Marion asked, almost good-naturedly, as she remembered my son, which is always worth noting no matter how genuine the words are, or the person speaking them.

"Tell her the same from me," Irene answered, blowing her snot-filled nose into the yellow handkerchief that Dulce had given her before she retuned to Madisonburg, among several other gifts and trinkets that my wife brought back from Mexico City.

"He's looking good, growing, very intelligent . . ."

"I'm going to bed. I'm tired. I'll wait for you there. Don't forget to check on Emilio and turn off the light."

"So look, Eusebio . . ." Never one to wait, Marion returned to the subject of her call after the habitual introductory banter that was much rarer in a standard Gringo than a Hispanicized and cultured one like she was. "As I was saying, there are several people involved, and I only just recently found out about it, including a wealth of details . . ."

"Yes, I'll see you in there, Irene, don't worry." I kissed her on the forehead as a loving father might kiss his ten-year-old daughter.

"But I'm not worried, Eusebio . . ." Marion replied, once again confused, mistaken, and all because I didn't cover the phone when speaking with my wife. "You're the one who should be worried. I don't work there anymore, thank God."

"Me?" I replied, embarrassed.

"Yes, you, Eusebio. You and Tino and Javis and even poor old Ritter . . . you all should be worried, very worried. Or, at the very least, you should be aware of what's going on there in the department, right under your very noses."

"Honestly I have no idea what you're talking about, Marion. Could you start again? Just to be clear?"

"You have no idea because I haven't told you anything yet," my former colleague grumbled, getting a bit worked up and growing even more impatient than I was. "You'll see . . ."

The truth is that I was lost, I was lost and very much on edge; I didn't understand one whit of what Marion Siegel was trying so earnestly, so desperately, to tell me, as if there were an assassin out to get her that very night. Was I drunk or was Marion drunk or had she just gone straitjacket crazy in the past year since I saw her last, when she lost her job at Millard Fillmore? Perhaps it was pure, brutal fatigue setting in, if not in both of us, then at least in me. Yes, in me . . . that much was evident. It wasn't her. In any case, as curious as I am (and have always been), I wasn't about to miss an opportunity to hear some gossip as juicy as this promised to be, another exceptional story in this sleepy little town, so I picked myself up and shook off any signs of fatigue and got ready to listen to Marion, my former colleague. I grabbed a cold beer from the fridge and went out on the deck, taking a seat among the twittering stars and the trembling cicadas, or was it the other way around? All the surprising news and revelations that Irene had brought me back from Mexico and dished out to me over the course of the unforgettable week, which I've already described, was suddenly shuttled to the back, placed in a corner and buried away to make room for the impending story that my dear former colleague Marion Siegel was about to relate:

"I found out from Sofía, the maid, my maid, a great Honduran girl, very reserved, who has been working with us for three or four months. She's sensible, and demure like none other, Eusebio, and just as good as gold . . . you have no idea! Before coming to live here at the house, she spent two years with another American family, the Mongers. She says they treated her very well, but they ended up moving out of Madison-burg, which is true, Eusebio: I spoke at length with Señora Monger before hiring Sofía, and she confirmed that they left Madisonburg for

Pennsylvania, which is why they let her go. But none of that really matters. I'm only telling you so you don't think Sofía is into lies or slander or anything like that. She's a humble girl with no real education, but she's honest, so believe you me, she couldn't come up with what she did if she hadn't seen it with her own eyes and smelled it with her own nose. She'd been keeping it a secret, bottled up inside of her for so long, and only yesterday (in a sort of fit) did she let it all out. It had been eating her alive. For two or three years now, something like that. When she was working for the Gorgon. That's right, Eusebio, you heard me! Before going to work with the Americans I told you about, Sofía worked for none other than Gross-Wayne herself. Can you believe it? Small world, right? Well, anyway . . . she worked for her for two or three years I think, until she just couldn't take it anymore and left—escaped, really—from that damn house, half-crazed and disturbed. It's not that they were holding her hostage or anything. According to her, she needed the job so she could send money back to her family in Tegucigalpa or somewhere around there, I don't know, and the Gorgon paid her well. Too well, even. I'll tell you we don't pay her that much. Maybe half, and that's still a lot. But you'll see, Eusebio! You'll see why Gaudencia and her husband paid her so well! It wasn't out of kindness or generosity or to be a good Christian. We both know it couldn't be anything like that. She was paying for silence. Buying her silence. You heard me. She was paying her off so that she would keep her mouth shut and keep the secret. She never explicitly said it quite like that, not in so many words, but it was clear to any good listener. One thing about Sofía is that she's not stupid, believe you me. She fully understood that she had to keep quiet about what she eventually discovered in the basement of that immense home in the affluent Highpoint neighborhood where the Gross-Wayne family lives, as you know. But in the end she couldn't take it anymore, couldn't stomach the vile stench of the thing. Let's just say that only something as rotten as this could disturb her so much that she almost went insane. Disgusted and horrified, Sofía escaped from Highpoint. Actually, what she told

Gaudencia was that she had to return home to her parents in Honduras, and apparently Gaudencia believed her and even bought her a plane ticket and shipped her off back to Tegucigalpa, far far away from Madisonburg. Just imagine . . . what if she didn't think Sofía would keep the secret, what if she had to take it to the grave with her! It's just atrocious! But in the end, the poor girl didn't go . . . and right there, in the airport, after saying good-bye to the Gorgon and her husband, carrying fake baggage and everything, she turned around and went right back to Madisonburg, where she had already set up a job working for the American family I told you about, the Mongers, with whom she lived for the next couple of years. She worked quite happily for them, decontaminating herself, until they left town. Now that Sofía is with me, and after she found out that I worked at Millard Fillmore for some time before I was fired by Gaudencia and Katrina, she finally had the courage to speak up, and yesterday afternoon she told me everything in a sort of heroic fit. It wasn't easy for her, let me tell you. If only you could see how reserved she really is! It took a lot of coaxing, even after I noticed that she really needed to get something off her chest, that there was something very thick and heavy caught up in her throat . . . and that it had been there for quite some time already. So my job was just to give her confidence, to help push her along, until yesterday, finally, the poor thing finally conceded and let it all come out. And even though this young Honduran girl might not look like a gossip girl or a chatterbox, the poor thing just couldn't hold the secret inside her anymore; she has no family here, although she did say that this was something she wouldn't tell to anybody, not her parents, her siblings, her best friends, whomever . . . *This just runs too deep!* That's how humble little Sofía put it, in her own words. There's nobody else I can talk to besides you, ma'am, she said. You're the only one I feel comfortable with; I wouldn't dare to bring this up with anybody else; the people back home would say I was crazy or dreaming or high on drugs, and my folks might even send me off to the loony bin, what do I know? But since you've told me about your own bad opinions of Señora Gaudencia, then I'll tell you about my own experience so there's someone else who knows about it, plus you can tell me if what went on in that giant house was wrong—if what they and their guests did was really as nasty as it seemed—or if I just don't understand, since I'm just a girl from a tiny little town in Honduras? Yes, I know Señora Gaudencia is from Ecuador, and even though I've never been there, they can't be all that different from the people I know back home: good Christian people, clean, decent, humble, normal people, that's all, and so I don't know if such customs are par for the course in Gringolandia, but at the very least I never saw such things with the other family I worked with for two years, the Mongers, you know, ma'am? But anyway, what happened was that once or sometimes twice a month a group of very well-dressed, wealthy, elegant people—all professors from the university there in town—would come to Professor Gross-Wayne's house for dinner. Señor Santiago Bormann-Smythe was always there; he has such a beautiful name, very resonant, and I wrote it down on a napkin so I wouldn't forget it, but he wasn't as good a person as his name led me to believe; on the contrary, he barely even deigned to look at me, as if I didn't even matter to him. Like I didn't exist. I was a piece of Central American furniture, an old, worn-out piece of furniture that he could just toss his coat and scarf on whenever he entered the Gross-Wayne's stately mansion. But on the other hand, Marco Aurelio was very different whenever he came over for Señora Gaudencia's dinner parties. He didn't have any hair, you know? A bald little man. But then again, now that I think about it, neither one of them had any hair. Neither Señor Santiago nor Señor Marco Aurelio Vasco-Osama. The difference was that, while they were both well-mannered (how do you say it, effeminate or even a little faggoty?), one was always very courteous with me while the other didn't even bother to say *hola*. It's not like that matters to me, or that I was looking for him to acknowledge me in some way, but where I come from they say that you can tell a person's true nature through their manners, not their money. Even Señora Gross-Wayne was polite and well-mannered towards me, as she was with anybody else. True, she was very authoritarian at times, and she could yell like nobody's business, but she never yelled at me. The one she did shout at and insult all the time was her poor husband. Señor Larry had the backbone of a dishcloth. I'm not exaggerating. He never said a word, not so much as a peep; he just smiled and nodded his head in response to everything, and he never complained. Once those long dinners had ended, Señor Larry would bid goodnight to his guests and disappear into the upstairs reaches of the house. Oh, but wait! I forgot to mention Señora Gross-Wayne's bosses. First was a heavyset man with a beard. His name was David Jeffrey . . . or no, my mistake: Professor Jeff Davis. Yes, that was his name. He always showed up with a mint in his mouth, and he always left with a mint in his mouth as well. He stuffed them into every pocket of his sport coat, which was a very nice, checkered sort of thing. He always came with a fat man, a very fat man, with a jolly, reddish face. His appetite never seemed to be satisfied, for he ate more than anyone else at the party, often four or five servings. Everyone was very respectful and even docile around him, and they called him Doctor Whitehead. This gentleman was about seventy years old, and Señor Davis was about fifty, and neither of them spoke a word of Spanish, unlike the other professors I already told you about. Right away I could tell, from the amount of deference that everyone paid to him, the fat old gentleman was the boss, the *patrón* of the university. But once they started dinner and began going through bottle after bottle of wine, they forgot about ranks and seniority, and even Señora Gaudencia softened up a bit, can you believe it? She seemed almost human; I mean, you know how hard and rigid she can be at times, when she looks like she's about to strangle somebody! But during those dinners, she seemed to unwind a bit and was even somewhat kind to me. As for me, I stuck to my task throughout the night (during which time, a strange smell was creeping in from who knows where): serve, serve, serve, and then of course gather up the dirty plates and glasses and clean, clean, clean. And yes, ma'am, I do have to say that Señora Gaudencia was a magnificent cook. She prepared the dinners on each and every one of these occasions, though I was never allowed so much as a taste of her succulent stews, marinade, and paellas. I did, though, learn a number of really good recipes, some of which she said came from her native Guayaquil, passed down from her mother, her grandmother, and her great-grandmother, who had been married to a dictator, she always said. But anyway, I digress . . . The other guest was a professor named Wynn, and he had such a funny accent. Oh yes! He didn't speak a word of Spanish either, just English, like Whitehead, the fat old *patrón* with the red face I told you about earlier. Professor Wynn wore tall, pointy-toed boots and had very long sideburns. One day, Señor Marco Aurelio smiled at me, lowered his voice, and whispered to me: 'He's *texano*, Sofía.' And I smiled at him in return. It made sense, because I remembered that accent from when I slipped into the United States across the Arizona border, you know? Anyway, I haven't been there since. But those were pretty much the guests at the lavish dinner parties that Señora Gross-Wayne threw once or twice a month . . . along with her husband Larry, depending on the night. Sometimes, though, a new guest would appear: another older man, always an older man, never a young woman or wife. The youngest one there was always Señor Marco Aurelio Vasco-Osama, very shy, like I said, but also very polite. Have you met him, ma'am? He was the only one who ever paid attention to me, who ever said 'good night' to me and sometimes even offered me a tip when he thought of it, as a way of thanking me, of course . . . though I never asked for one. Señora Gaudencia would have killed me if she found out. She would have wrung my neck like a chicken right then and there. Well, Eusebio, the fact is that the strange smell was spreading everywhere, making the poor girl sick as she served the sumptuous dinner, beginning with appetizers and salad topped with Roquefort cheese before moving on to battered fish, lamb with almond sauce, marinated Provençal beef, French cheeses, frozen desserts, and everything else. According to what Sofía told me, when Larry disappeared for the night, the fetid smell in the dining room had already reached an unbearable point; similarly, the ambiance and sense of formality so apparent earlier in the night had been toned down to a much more casual degree, so much so that by the time the coffee, cognac, and anis were being served, they could hear each other doing it, one after another, as unstoppable as they were incorrigible: tiny creaks and squeaks here and there, brief little explosions or eruptions coming from under the wide, mahogany dining room table, from the chairs with the magenta upholstery, or even from the depths of the abyss, who knows. Nobody seemed to mind or even notice the agglutination of sounds and scents and toots and odors; the table chatter continued unchanged, with light, pleasant, even humorous equanimity, as if what were going on under the table wasn't even the least bit malodorous, noteworthy, or even noticeable to anybody. Sofía, the docile, helpful Honduran, came and went as she was needed, which the Gorgon woman signaled with a tiny bell, bringing additional courses from the kitchen or bottles of wine from one of the display cabinets located throughout the other, empty rooms of the mansion. Sofía says that she would have to take a big lungful of air and hold it every time she entered the dining room, where the stench had become all but unbearable, even though the guests appeared to be completely oblivious to what was going on. Even Gaudencia contributed a number of flatulent notes, shifting her gluteals from one side to the other on her magenta-upholstered chair. Sofía saw her, caught her more than once trying to cover up a little blast or report with a refined little Ecuadorian cough. She saw how the Gorgon never apologized, how she never got up from her aromatic chair to leave the room in order to make these horrendous little noises, never relieved herself of her peristaltic rumblings in the bathroom, in a ladylike manner. No. Quite the opposite, in fact. Apparently, it was all part of dinner, part of the big opiparous event for which they had all gathered, and that's what it was, Eusebio, that's what it was. But I'm afraid the worst is yet to come. You haven't seen anything yet! After several hours had passed and several servings of desserts, cheesecakes, quinces, fruits, and coffee had been consumed, Sofía was dismissed to her room, which was separate from the house and located in the backyard, so she could rest . . . but not before she had finished washing and drying the everlasting conglomeration of Dutch-made dinnerware. That's when, according to the girl, Marco Aurelio would casually slip her a little tip, as would Dean Whitehead. It was on one of those occasions, as she incessantly and tirelessly washed and dried plate after plate (despite the fact that there was a brand new dishwasher in the kitchen, something which proved to be of little use to her) when Sofía watched, confused and astonished, as the Gorgon got up from her seat at the table. In the blink of an eye, she disappeared down into the fathomless basement. Nevertheless, the guests still seated at the table didn't seem too concerned. On the contrary, it was as if they all knew ahead of time what was about to happen, as if they knew what was in store for them, the true reason that had brought the academic millionaires here for a long, orgiastic dinner. Suddenly, in response to a signal from Gaudencia, who had reappeared through the same door she'd taken down to the basement (where, by the way, nobody ever went, according to what Sofía told me, nobody other than herself, anyway, and that was only for cleaning and dusting), one of the dinner guests stood up from his chair, excused himself with an affected cough and a giggle, and made his way down the stairs, discreetly closing the door behind him. Gaudencia remained upstairs with the other guests in the dining room, and the conversation continued as if nothing at all had happened, amidst those flatulent sounds and smells, until, ten or fifteen minutes later, the whole process began to repeat itself: Gaudencia again descended into the basement while the elderly guest—the first—returned to the dining room and took his place at the ornate table while another guest waited for Gaudencia's signal to enter the basement himself. Understand? They were all taking turns, all the dinner guests were, in the basement, and every time the Gorgon would reemerge to signal the next guest, she would remain upstairs in the dining room to enliven and carry on the conversation over digestifs and Cuban cigars. Wynn, Bormann-Smythe,

Davis, Vasco-Osama, Whitehead . . . these were the invariable ones, the regular guests, the brotherhood, the conclave. There were others who came every two or three months, and then they would come even less frequently. But those five were always punctual and present at those strange dinner parties hosted by Gaudencia and Larry in their High-point home. So, realizing that something very odd was going on in the basement—with the guests disappearing and reappearing up and down the stairs, taking turns, laughing and excusing themselves while Señor Larry slept or feigned sleep in his upstairs bedroom—Sofía decided one night, after two or three years of suppressing her curiosity, to hide herself in one of the basement closets. In fact, according to what she told me, it wasn't a very difficult task, because the basement was connected to the ample garage via an access door. So one night, after completing her arduous task in the kitchen, Sofía left her hovel of a room across the backyard from the house and entered the garage. Once inside, she opened the access door that led into three empty bedrooms and a game room with a billiard table which nobody ever used, as I said, with the exception of one relative from Ecuador who spent three or four days there around Christmas one year. But such things virtually never happened, and Sofía's task of cleaning and keeping up that part of the house was (or appeared to be) a pointless task, almost absurd, really, although—as you will see, Eusebio—it wasn't completely absurd, because in the days that followed those professorial dinners, Sofía could sense that something strange had happened down there, something beyond unusual, but it wasn't something she recognized, something she could identify or pin down. But right then, on that night, she would find out once and for all, she would learn the lesson of her life, pass through a hundred years of innocence and arrive at the doorstep of universal putrefaction, the outer limits of madness and shameless filth. The fact is that before Gaudencia descended the stairs into the basement, Sofía was already hiding there, peering through the slats in the door of a linen closet, yes, just like in a horror movie, you know? I could see everything from in there, but I held my breath, I didn't move a muscle for fear that even the slightest sound would expose me, that I'd be found out or killed or who knows what! I was truly terrified, you know, ma'am? At that point I was sorry I'd done it, I was so very sorry I ever got to that point, and all because of some relentless sense of curiosity that I'd been harboring for years. But there was no turning back, you know? Because the lady of the house suddenly appeared in the game room, and without a moment's hesitation, she moved to the powder room where I saw her lift up her fine blue linen dress, pull down her panties, and squatted—yes, squatted—but not over the toilet, not over the porcelain bowl, Señor Eusebio, but over something else, something I couldn't quite make out from the closet at first, something that turned out to be—after I verified it for myself—a tiny chamber pot, a child's potty-trainer, fashioned out of Ecuadorian clay. And right there, with the door ajar and the ceiling light on, Professor Gross-Wayne hunkered down on her haunches and evacuated everything, scattering the pounds and pounds of food stored in her intestinal tract from that dinner or perhaps even from days before, who knows, but in either case it was a world of shit that filled the beautiful little artisan chamber pot to the brim. The smell was unbearable, Señor Eusebio, truly revolting, as it seeped out of the bathroom and into the game room, impregnating the empty guest rooms and finally reaching the slats of the linen closet where I was hiding, shivering with fright, so quiet I was barely even blinking. It was then that I understood the source of the surprising and unusually fetid smell of the basement on the mornings after the dinner parties, when I was required to clean and dust the rooms, despite the fact that, as I said, nobody had slept down there, and Señor Larry hadn't gone down there to shoot pool or read. Now then, once the small clay chamber pot had been filled, once that beautiful piece of Guayaquil pottery had been slathered in shit, Professor Gaudencia stood up, sat down on the actual toilet, quickly cleaned herself off, pulled the chain, and reached into the shower to produce a plastic garbage bag containing a stack of disposable soup bowls which she had clearly stowed there long beforehand, in that bathroom which hadn't been used in years. And then, Señor Eusebio, from my vantage point in the closet, sweating profusely, I was able to see her take out a plastic ladle she'd brought down from the kitchen, who knows, and scoop out a serving into one of the disposable soup bowls. Then, again using the ladle, she proceeded to smooth it out, like when you're serving hummus or a delicious baba ghanoush, Eusebio, and you want to make a good presentation despite the soft, lumpy, paste-like consistency that makes it difficult to spread. Yes, Professor Gross-Wayne stirred a spoonful of her own feces into a little plastic soup bowl. Then the Gorgon closed the bathroom door, though not before leaving all the hidden utensils in the shower: the clay chamber pot, the plastic bowls, the ladle, and the garbage bag containing napkins and plastic silverware, you know, the sort that you might use at a child's birthday party. Next, she set the excrement-filled bowl (along with a plastic fork and spoon) on one of the tables in the game room, just a few feet away from where poor little Sofía was hiding and watching all this happen, quite literally under her very nose. And then, the Gorgon went back upstairs, almost preening, very proper and vain, and one of the dinner guests descended the same stairs to replace her, after closing the door to the dining room behind him. Santiago, Marco Aurelio, Dean Whitehead, Davis, Wynn . . . they all took turns, as I said, sitting down there, alone in the basement, with delirious looks in their eyes, tipsy with emotion, joy, and enthusiasm, apparently still hungry, and I don't know how, but they began to spoon the warm, fresh fecal matter of your esteemed colleague's shit into their mouths. And they left nothing, not one bit of it. Every last bite was devoured. They even licked the plates. The only one who didn't, Sofía says with certainty, was Señor Marco Aurelio, ma'am, but apparently it wasn't enough for Señor Santiago Bormann-Smythe and the bearded man Davis, since after they finished their portions of exquisitely rendered and savory shit, they tiptoed over to the bathroom, opened the door, bent down, and furtively raided that beautiful little chamber pot, the Ecuadorian potty trainer, using the kitchen ladle to help themselves to another serving, which they spooned into their same disposable bowls. And I'll tell you this, Eusebio: Santiago was still crouched down there, licking the ladle over and over again, until Gaudencia began to get suspicious and—thinking something unusual might be going on—called down to him in a very authoritarian voice to say that the others were waiting, and that it was time for him to come back up. With Professor Jeffrey Davis, though, she wouldn't dare to interfere. He was allowed to remain until he sated himself, until he could eat no more, and the gray hairs of his goat's beard were dripping."

For Christmas and birthdays, my brother Roy was the one who would always see that my sister Ruth and I had a toy. Roy didn't have much money but, by gosh, he always saw we had a toy. Roy was one of the kindest fellows I've ever known in my life.

—WALT DISNEY

"Do you know something?" he added, pointing to the toilet.
   "What?"
   "I have produced green shit."
   "And why do you think that might be?" I asked him.
   "By chance, of course. If I had set out to do it, I never would have managed."

—FERNANDO DEL PASO

It is a happy talent to know how to play.

—RALPH WALDO EMERSON

Art is a toy.

—ANTONIO MACHADO

PART TWO
EROS

I

My dear Reader, I haven't forgotten about you. Not at all. In fact, that would be quite impossible, really. Without you (remember?) there would be no story, nor would I have anyone to keep me company. I'd be miserably lonely! So rest assured, I didn't abandon you there in your luxury car, just as you (I happen to know) haven't forgotten about me, because otherwise you wouldn't still be reading, am I right? Otherwise you wouldn't have made it to this infamous and rather treacherous bend in the road, to this lengthydarkandtenebroustypographicalthread. Do you see? I've kept you in my thoughts during my most ominous moments in Madisonburg, and we both know what those were like! Everything came together in the blink of an eye, as I'll be explaining to you! I'm well aware of the fact that you have yet to get out of your Mercedes E 2025, which you drove through the insufferably crowded streets of Mexico City, from Narvarte all the way to Las Águilas, although in the end (of course) you decided against getting out of your car, against going up to your apartment, and against confronting your new reality as a cuckold, a husband scorned, a banker humiliated by his wife. I know that you've been sitting there, hanging by a thread, crying, sniveling like a month-old baby, looking up from the tree-lined street at your home, your soon-to-be former apartment, and I also know that you've been asking yourself (enraged) why, why the hell did this happen to you, but you can't develop an answer out of your mind, still foggy or spinning from the surprise, the shock, the vertiginous descent into Erebus that it was to see what you saw live and in full-blown Technicolor: nothing less than your gorgeous young wife being screwed by your old friend, the love of your life fucking someone else, going at it like a couple of animals. You've confirmed with your very own eyes, dear furious Reader of frictions, everything that happened both before and after you arrived at Arturo's studio, the studio of your former friend, your enemy, the traitor. You watched (both of them sitting there on that colorful quilt, facing each other, her straddling his hips, her legs locked behind his hairy back) as Arturo took her on that sepia-colored afternoon shortly before your first anniversary, and you also already knew the trifling minutiae and details that cast in such stark relief the mortal embrace, that disgraceful encounter between the two of them, between Maty and that damn Agro painter. Now you know (quite clearly!) about what was going on during the series of Empedoclean interviews, the subtleties, the flirtatious remarks, the comings-and-goings within the workshop, the questions and answers, the calculated scheming that took place before they reached the eagerly desired climax, the coveted melding of bodies, the joyful treason of sacrificing you, the sacred hecatomb, which did not include you on this occasion and into which you were thrown like a repeat criminal offender. And though the truth be now spoken, there is still no justification for this load of shit. I'm speaking, of course, about the hand Maty has just dealt you without regard for the consequences, without any recollection of your first anniversary, your sworn love, your promises, your nocturnal panting and grunting, her excited gasps whenever you touch her olive-colored skin in the fading light of that Bécquerian alcove, though you could, of course, admit that her deceit did not come easily, as you've read how Arturo truly had to apply himself to the task of seducing and conquering your old lady, you saw how Arturo over-came her by applying the necessary pressures of desire, experience, and lust: the painter wanted to screw your handsome wife ever since they saw one another for the second time in the unventilated studio on that shitty roof there on Narvarte. You've seen, at least at the outset, how she wanted to resist; you confirmed that Maty's original intentions were strictly academic and sociopolitical when she first began making her visits to that plywood-and-asbestos studio on the fifth floor. Nothing more. Matilde simply wanted to gather some unpublished information about Roberto Soto Gariglietti and the Partido de la Naturaleza y el Fuego Mexicano. That was truly her one and only objective. Just to finish her thesis. She had no other motive, but Arturo, on the other hand, did indeed have other objectives in mind, concupiscent objectives, you might say, carnal objectives, those of flesh and desire . . . and worse still: the objective of slyly betraying a dear, longtime friend. But I don't know that for a fact. I exaggerated a bit with the sly betrayal thing. Just a bit of invention to keep the friction more consistent, you know? I can't be sure that he was motivated solely by a desire to betray you, no. I believe it, yes, for as I've often said behind Irene's back, we often find ourselves attracted to the wife of a friend . . . more so if she is as beautiful as your wife Matilde—excuse me, your ex-wife—with those lovely gray-green eyes, those smooth shoulders, those perfect collarbones. But that is neither here nor there . . . As the psychiatrist Aníbal Quevedo once said, we always desire the desires of another, and as for me, Cardoso, from my perspective here on the other side of reality, I can say to you in good faith that I have also stubbornly desired the desire of someone else, my fellow man; I have also desired the wife of my dear friend from Turin, I have betrayed his trust, his deep sense of confidence, and I still don't know for sure why I did such a godawful shitty thing, what incredible devil moved me or impelled me every time I went over to his house to give his magnificent wife, gilded by the sun-god Inti himself, those so-called "applications of muscular pressure" which I've already described down to the most infuriating, insignificant detail and which you surely don't want me to repeat, now more than ever, of course. And so, dear Reader, I am also a treacherous son of a bitch, just as much as Arturo is, and I don't take the slightest bit of pride in that fact, I take no sense of satisfaction in what I obtained during the short period of time when I had those furtive, delightful episodes with Stephany, which—I admit—led me to come in my pants as if I were some overheated, pubescent teenager, though never outside of my pants, never . . . Actually, it's quite the opposite, my dear Reader: today I feel uncomfortable, foolish, and clumsy. Yes, mainly clumsy . . . and this obtuse stupidity is what causes me the most anger and pain when I think about what has taken place, which is quite frankly next to nothing, since we didn't even kiss (let alone fuck), but it amounts to quite a bit if I think about what those visits revealed or put on display: my own personal character, my ruinous nature, my tenebrous side, my treachery, my shamelessness, or perhaps simply my own weakness when faced with the flesh of my own neighbor. It's like the old fable about the scorpion and the frog, do you remember that one? Of course, I'm not using all of this as an attempt to explain (that is, to justify) Arturo's sly desires, his incredibly bad intentions, even though these two stories are not one and the same. In fact, they're not even close. To begin with, one might argue that you, dear Reader, weren't as close a friend to Arturo as I am (or as I was) with Stefano Morini, Professor of Italian at MFU. And if you were that close to Arturo at one point, then—truth be told—you no longer were when you got back in touch, when you reacquainted yourselves, when you began buying his phantasmagoric paintings, and finally, when (knowing full well what type of man he is) you sent Matilde to his workshop to interview him not once but on several different afternoons . . . and shame on you for that! So, we can't compare the two betrayals . . . not completely, anyway, since although Arturo betrayed you, he did not betray a real, living breathing friendship; perhaps, if anything, the Agro painter betrayed the memory of that old bond, whatever it was that you had back when you were both teenagers, back in the years of your defiant youth. My story, you must admit, is quite different from yours. Stefano has been my very best friend ever since I first arrived at Millard Fillmore University some five years ago. If we weren't exactly old childhood friends (I was in Mexico and he was in Italy) we had become close—very close!—by the time I started surreptitiously visiting his house when he wasn't around, when Irene wasn't around, when our children weren't around, and became involved with his wife under the pretext of providing "applied muscular pressure" to her clitoris so that she could relax, the poor woman, as tense and throbbing as she was with her moist, delicious cunt. What I want, then, before I begin to relate the details of the explosion and subsequent, delayed shrapnel—the splinters that splintered the intractable skin of Irene, my wife—is to explain the obtuse, awkward reasoning behind my unbelievable actions, the genuine motivation behind my treachery. And you know what? The worst part is not knowing where to begin this damn confession or *auto-da-fé*, not knowing whether I really want to, or even if I have something concrete to say . . . but as I see it, as of now, I'm obliged to reveal that which I do not in fact know about myself, that which I would or should know if a gun were put to my head, that which I keep buried in my brain or in the secluded corners of my ragged heart. And all this imbecilic circumlocution is only because I cannot imagine, dear Reader, I truly cannot fathom how I became such a treasonous son of a bitch, even more so than Arturo. I just haven't been able to figure out how I could have committed the most appalling of actions: getting involved with the wife of a friend. You see! I still haven't been able to eradicate the thought, which is why I'm writing, writing like a madman, perhaps as some sort of disingenuous exorcism, as a primitive attempt at redeeming my sense of guilt, or simply an urgent necessity to confess the truth. I don't know. I would like to understand a bit more about myself, just a tiny little bit, at least. And in fact, at this moment, I believe (I'd like to believe) that if I could acheive that minimal amount of understanding—that partial or limited bit of it—then perhaps I wouldn't still feel so clumsy or uncomfortable or bothered, perhaps I wouldn't be the fatuous, feverish professor Cardoso expelled from Millard Fillmore University and the middle-class community in this valley where I currently find myself (now and forever) without my son and without my wife. Like the Tenth Muse or the Phoenix of Mexico, my dear Reader, I also beg your forgiveness for this unbearable digression, which the force of truth has dragged me into; yet if I am to confess everything, then this digression is also an attempt at evasion, an attempt to flee from difficult answers, and I've almost decided to leave the matter in silence; and while this might be viewed as something negative, silence also explains much by virtue of leaving it all unexplained, as it's necessary to put a quick little label on the silence in order to explain what the silence is trying to say; and if not, the silence will say nothing, because that's its primary objective: saying nothing . . . So in this way, regarding those things which cannot be spoken, it is necessary to at least say that they are impossible to say, so that it's understood that the silence is maintained not for want of things to say, but rather because all the many things to say simply cannot be conveyed in mere words. Now do you understand?

You know, when Emilio woke me up the next morning, I wasn't sure if what I heard over the phone the previous night was a coprophagic nightmare I'd had, which had left me exhausted and stretched out there on the dining room floor, or whether it was simply the delirium of a former colleague hell-bent on exacting revenge on the university that had disgraced and dismissed her. I even asked myself if it could be true, if it could be a factual description of a secret society of professors who gather together in order to conduct scatological rites in the exclusive and affluent Highpoint neighborhood of Madisonburg. So what, then, was to be made of all this? Or, as I should say, of all that? What happened on the phone last night, or perhaps all those previous years, right under my very nose and the noses of my innocent colleagues there in the department? Had Marion Siegel really called me and told me what Sofía, her Honduran housekeeper, had told her? Or did I (or perhaps the housekeeper) dream it all up? Evidently I did not: there were open bottles of beer everywhere, I had passed out in the dining room, I hadn't gone in to turn out the light in my son's bedroom as Irene had asked me to, and—in case this all wasn't evidence enough—the cordless phone was lying there, its batteries dead. Therefore, I did not dream up the call. That left three and only three remaining options: either Siegel had gone crazy, or Sofía, her housekeeper, had tricked her with that extraordinary tale, or it was all bizarrely true. Needless to say, I quickly favored the latter of the three possibilities (of course!), and that very same morning, after eating breakfast and dropping Emilio off at the day care center, I called up my three colleagues to relate the story to them and listen to their objective, rational opinions. Tino, Javis, and Stefano arrived at the Barnes & Noble café at eleven o'clock sharp. As soon as I arrived at the bookstore, I noticed something strange and unusual, something entirely different in the olive-colored countenance of my friend Stefano, which I ignored owing to my hangover from the night before, my wariness at being the bearer of Marion's news, or simply because of the vehemence and necessity of spilling the gossip about the group of influential, shit-eating members of our distinguished university. So, with the four of us seated in soft armchairs in a calm corner of the bookstore, with our steaming cups of Starbucks coffee in hand, surrounded by immense bookcases stacked high with classic works of literature and portraits of famous authors, I set about relating the story of Sofía, the Honduran maid, which in turn became the story of Marion Siegel before finally being transformed (by the Fate of destiny) into my incredible and delirious tale of coprophagia. I'm afraid to say, however, that suddenly, in the midst of my narration or harangue on that memorable morning, I discovered with horror that I, myself, hadn't even come to terms with what I was saying between swills of Guatemalan coffee, and for that reason, and that reason alone, I suddenly stopped, almost at the end of the tale, and looked at them, disconcerted, as if I had just realized that I was sitting with a group of strangers, as if I were seeing these people for the first time, and I embarrassedly asked them if we weren't simply dreaming this whole meeting, or better yet: if I weren't dreaming of them right there in the middle of Barnes & Noble. Tino, the taciturn Galician, nevertheless said (whether to calm me down or not, I do not know) that how could a poor, humble, uneducated girl invent a story as disturbing and fantastic as this? It was so fantastic, in fact, that it wasn't improbable at all, concluded the man from the northwestern Spanish town of Vigo, convinced that every word he'd heard was the pure and simple truth, and that she was a trustworthy and reliable source. This latest rationalization calmed me down a bit, since, as you know, verisimilitude has always been the backbone, the axis on which this humble professor of the revolutionary novel has turned.

So as not to draw this out any further, I'll say that during the whole time we were sitting there in the soft, cushy armchairs with coffee in hand, Stefano didn't say as much as a single word, nor did he give any physical signs of approval or disproval. He was more silent than he had ever been during one of our encounters. He nursed his Guatemalan coffee and he prolonged each and every sip, evidently not even wanting to open his mouth. So, once Tino the Taciturn had concluded with his Aristotelian logic, Javis observed, with a serious yet contrite look on his face, that something had always smelled a bit strange to him in the air surrounding Whitehead, Davis, Gaudencia, and the other members of the tribe, which (of course) produced an explosion of hearty laughter in all of us, save the Italian, who was steadfastly unmoved by the brown-nosing Galician's filthy joke. It was then—yes, at that very instant, in the midst of the laughter that had overcome us—that I realized Stefano must have already known (or at least suspected) that something had happened between his wife and I during the past few weeks. And I admit that I realized it too late, that I had stupidly realized it too late, on that supremely important occasion during which I should have been more suspicious, during which, if I had known that he knew, I wouldn't have been recounting that fantastic and demented story of university coprophilia, since the very next thing that happened was what I feared most in this world: I heard his voice, his accusation and his terrible verbal irascibility, the revelation of pristine truth on the livid, purplish lips of Stefano, my old friend and my current archenemy:[2]

"I just can't believe how shameless you are, Eusebio. You son of a bitch. You're a real piece of shit. How naïve of me to think that you brought me here to apologize, to explain yourself to me, to beg forgiveness for what you've done behind my back, and instead I find out that you also invited Javis and Tino so you can tell us your degrading and dishonest tale about shit . . . and just to fuck with Davis and the Dean, right? I know—we all know—how much you hate them." Stefano's eyes were glassy, filled with a malice I'd never seen before that day. "Look, Eusebio, Stephany told me everything . . . every last detail. So there's no reason for you to hide it anymore. *Stronzo, fottuto, stronzo.* How could you do that to her? How could you get involved with your friend's wife, and take advantage of her sweet naïveté and goodwill, her intransigent, blind Christian faith? And abuse her when she was feeling down, the poor thing, thinking you only went over there to listen to her, but really it was quite the opposite, wasn't it? You went there for the sole purpose of seeing if *se potevi fartela.* But *che razza de amico sei?* What sort of cowardly rat bastard would do that? A *fottuto codardo,* that's who. She told me everything: *te la sei fatta* that you wanted to sleep with her, and that she had to say no not once but several times. She told me that you tried to get up into her virginal ass and grab her breasts and take her just like that, but she was steadfast and resisted . . . like a saint. *Lo neghi?* Am I lying? Tell me, you *cazzo marica.* See? You don't have the words or the balls to respond, to defend yourself, *cazzone di merda.* In fact, you know what? I'm glad that Tino and Javis came. I'm glad you invited them. Now they have firsthand knowledge

---

2   Here I will attempt to put his Italianized Spanish into something more legible, because it is exceedingly difficult to transcribe that mixture of languages that our colleague from Turin uses to express himself around us, not to mention the sense of fury that clouded his speech, causing him to commit a number of errors with verb tenses, nouns, and above all with the adjectives he used to insult me on that memorable morning there at the Madisonburg Barnes & Noble.

of the kind of a person you are, of what a low-down, dirty, good-for-nothing rat you are . . ."

In the face of that unstoppable defenestration of which I was the object, I decided (wisely?) not to say a single word: no explaining, no justifying, no defending myself like some John Doe who isn't exactly innocent. And why would I? What good would it do if, no matter what I said, Stefano was going to believe her, his perfect wife, the mother of his little girl anyway? Thinking practically—even pragmatically—about it, what good would it do him to believe me, his former Mexican friend, the *cazzone di merda*, the back-biting, yellow-bellied rat bastard? Nothing. Not one damn bit! On the contrary, if he were to believe my side of the story (even a sliver of it), it would have been a big nuisance for him, a tremendous moral dilemma, assuming that what he desired above all else was to care for and preserve his nuclear family (of course that's what he'd want, as would I . . . why deny it?) like any sensible father and husband who isn't a womanizer or polygamist would want deep down in his heart (perhaps not so deep down). Between his wife (however flirtatious she might be) and his immoral former friend, the choice is clear, isn't it? First, though, he would have to convince himself that Stephany was in no way a flirtatious or coquettish woman, and secondly, he would have to sacrifice me, Cardoso, who of course didn't provide any positive benefits or even consolation to him, and was instead a headache for not mentioning that damn outrage which, upon further examination, I had precipitated by my actions. By sacrificing me, he was consequently able to convince himself that Stephany was right, yes, that what Stephany had said was the absolute, clear-as-crystal truth, and that I, therefore, had lied . . . when actually I hadn't so much as opened my mouth to refute his accusations during the Spanitalian tirade to which I was subjected on that unfortunate morning.

It was clear. Clear to me, at least. Anything I might have said there, in front of them, would have fallen on deaf ears, and would do me more harm than good in the long term because—even if we assume I could have shed a little more light on the truth—my words would invariably have sounded cowardly and defensive. I had to stay silent, and I did. I had to weather stoically (which I did) that onslaught of insults and partial truths, half-truths and cunning, female lies, that litany of filth that Stephany had fed to her credulous cuckold, and all this without me having the slightest idea as to her motive, her reasons. Yes, I admit, I still can't fathom what had really taken place in Stephany's soul (if the whore actually has a soul): Why did she tell him? Did he drag it out of her? Or had some bug bitten that simple country rube? I would learn the answer to that question one hour later. In that (and only in that) the agony was over quickly. So, in the midst of that large cloud of invading killer locusts spewing from his mouth, I was only able to catch one more fragment of Turinese wrath, because I was no longer listening to most of it, since it was just the loud, demented ravings of a madman sitting right in front of me, sometimes half out of his seat, his fury waxing at times while at other times it seems to wane, which, of course, only happened when Tino (less taciturn now) managed to calm him down a bit, and finally when the manager of the bookstore came over to ask us (to ask Stefano) to lower his voice. Well, so as not to drag this out any further and instead cut right to the chase, here was the lone fragment that I managed to grasp out of that nebulous cloud of killer locusts:

"So right now, you miserable wretch, Stephany is speaking with Irene. That's right, she's telling her everything. And I mean everything . . ."

Yes, I was able to gather that much. I repeat: I fully understood that little snippet, which turned my stomach, made my hairs stand on end, and made me feel as if my entire life was suddenly hanging by a very thin thread . . . that is, if I hadn't already fallen into the Stygian waters of Hades. Even so, in truth, I still couldn't figure out the thing I wanted to know most, although it didn't much matter at that point: what had moved Stephany to fuck up my life like that? And in doing so, fuck up the lives of Irene and Emilio as well, not to mention the close friend-ship between the four of us (or between the six of us, if you include our respective children)? What the hell could have driven her to this point of insanity? These questions would plague me for (as I said) less than an hour, when I finally returned home, when I finally saw my exhausted, enervated wife, when I could finally stop worrying about Stefano and his barrage of insults, about Stefano and his infinite rage, about the frightened, incredulous faces of the two Galicians who didn't know what to say, who had no idea how to ameliorate or alleviate that horrific massacre . . . and when I finally confirmed with my own eyes that yes, Irene was crying hysterically, her face blotchy, completely overcome by emotion as she stood there in the bedroom packing a suitcase just as scorned women have done in every movie I've ever seen in my life:

". . . Stephany says that she told her pastor because she was so deeply afflicted by what's been going on, Eusebio. She just couldn't take it anymore. The poor girl couldn't bring herself to kick you out of her house, since the four of us are such good friends. She says that you took advantage of that friendship, of her innocent intentions. Her intentions, of course. Not yours. She says that she tried to explain time and time again that what you were doing wasn't right, that those untimely visits to her house were inappropriate; she says that she tried turning you down politely at first, and that she rejected your advances not once but several times, but that you kept pushing and pushing and pushing . . . you kept insisting, you were angry, and you wanted to do it right there in her home, while I was in Mexico with Emilio and my mother . . . and her pastor told her she did the right thing by not allowing herself to be besmirched, despite it all; that she had acted righteously in not succumbing to your devilish, unfaithful, vile sickness, and that Christ would fix things, and yes, she told me that she had to speak up, to bring it all to light, that's what the pastor told her to do, that she needed to tell her husband about everything, and that she also needed to tell me, the wife of the illustrious sinner, which is you, you filthy pig, you, in order to save our five-year relationship, but what does that even mean now, our relationship? Do you think Stephany wants to save our relationship, our friendship, when there isn't so much as a spark of affection between the two of us, Eusebio, now that everything is gone forever . . . ? Because— listen to me now—today I realized that I do not love you, that I no longer want to be with you, that you betrayed me in a way that I never—do you hear me?—in a way that I never, ever could have imagined . . ."

I cut her off:

"But it's already over, Irene. It has been for a long time. I swear it. Ever since we decided [right, kemo sabe?] to put an end to our games, to my visits, which were no more than four or five at the most, nothing else has happened. I swear, I swear to you, my love. Never again will I so much as set a foot in that house. And besides . . ."

"Shut up. Don't say another word, and don't you dare call me 'my love.' I don't want to hear it. You disgust me, Eusebio. You're a pig."

"It's just that . . . things didn't exactly happen the way she said they did, Irene. They didn't. They really, truly didn't."

"So what the hell did happen then?" Irene had finally taken the bait: she wanted—she was dying—to hear my version of events. I had touched something deep in that woman's dementia. "Or are you too much of a coward to tell me?"

"Well . . ." Now I was trapped, of course, for no sooner had I opened my mouth than I realized that it might not be such a good thing to tell her the truth. Couldn't it make things even worse? Would it be an act of suicide to provide her with a vivid description of what actually happened . . . ? I'm quite good with descriptions, and you, my dear Reader, know that better than anyone!

"So . . . ?" She turned to me, sobbing yet determined, obsessed, and offended. "I'm waiting. Are you going to tell me how everything happened or not, Eusebio?"

"Look, why don't you sit down. Let's just talk . . ."

"I'm not sitting down," she said vociferously. "I'd prefer to remain standing as I listen to you. And do me a favor, don't touch me. Don't you dare."

"Okay," I said, searching for time, hoping for divine inspiration from Nestis or Hera or whomever, just as Empedocles had when he was preparing to make his formal exordium to his beloved disciple Pausanias. "Would you mind if I sat?"

"Whatever you want. I'm listening."

There was nowhere else for me to go. No place into which I could escape. So I sat down on the edge of the unmade bed, took a deep breath, and pondered something, deep down, although I sincerely wasn't quite sure what that something was. Finally, I murmured a few words, taking greater care in choosing them than I ever had before in my life:

"First I want to say forgive me. I've done something wrong—very wrong—and there is nothing I can say to justify myself or my actions. Nothing . . . do you hear me?" I asked in a full, deeply serious tone of voice. Then I paused, took another deep breath (it couldn't hurt, right?) and continued . . . yes, delivering the low blow that I've wanted to deliver for so long now, my dear Reader: "But the one thing—just this one thing—that I want you to know is that there is no justifying her, either . . . she's a grown woman, an adult [and adulteress], and Stephany permitted each and every one of those visits to take place. She encouraged them, Irene. She caused them. I swear it."

"I don't understand . . ."

"Look: she opened the door of her home to me. I never forced her to do it, and there was no trickery or deceit involved . . . we were both completely in agreement. That's all. She would lay down on the sofa, and I would give her a back massage . . . nothing more. That's it, Irene. I swear."

". . . A back massage?"

"The first thing she said was that she was feeling very tense . . ." I'm not sure why I said that, dear Reader, because it was patently untrue. ". . . and things just went from there . . . little by little, not intentionally, but spontaneously."

"And what is all this supposed to mean, Eusebio?"

"Exactly what I said to you: it was all just a game, fiddling and fondling . . ."

"So you two never slept together?"

"No, of course we didn't. I only touched her, like I said, and she let me touch her . . . clothed . . . fully clothed, on the four or five occasions when I went to her house. And that's it. But . . ." I hesitated for a moment, teetering on the question, trembling and reflecting on things before continuing: "Did that crazy woman say that we slept together?"

"I'm not saying another word. I don't even know why I'm listening to you, Eusebio, because I'm gone. I'm leaving. It disgusts me. You disgust me. I'm going to pick up Emilio at school and then I'm out of here."

"But, Irene . . ." I tried to reason with her, to talk to her, to calm her down, and calm myself down in the process. "Where are you going? My God . . ."

"To my mother's . . . where else?"

I was about to ask her which of her two mothers, but fortunately Nestis, once again, the beautiful personification of serenity and composure, reached out with her long fingers and covered up my toothless mouth, so that no more toads or snakes could escape my lips.

Honestly I didn't know what to do or what I could have done to keep her there: I was on tenterhooks, desperately watching (in slow motion) as Irene packed her bags in preparation for leaving me, preparing to march right out of there without a second thought, without any desire to try and fix things, without so much as an inkling of mercy with which to forgive me. That was her nature, and I knew it only too well. In circumstances such as those, it was literally impossible to deal with her, to reason with her. As I sat there, crestfallen, I began to feel more frustrated and dejected than ever. But was it simply pain that I felt, or was it also remorse, perhaps it was even pure and simple incompetence that I felt at not being able to vindicate myself as I had so hopelessly wished? Or was it my impotence in not being able to explain myself better, not being able to relate something that I myself cannot understand, something that obviously is beyond me and continues to be so to this very day? Whatever it was, the fact is that all of a sudden, and without knowing what drove me to say it (perhaps it was the accumulating sense of frustration that had been weighing down on me since that morning when I was forced to listen to Stephany's partialized version delivered by both her husband and my own wife), I asked Irene out of the clear blue sky:

"Will you come with me?"

"Are you insane?" she replied without turning around, too busy packing her second or third bag to bother. "Where do you want me to go with you?"

"To Stephany's house."

"What are you saying?"

"If you're going to leave me and take Emilio with you, then I should at least have a right to ask you to listen to something, just so you know a little bit more . . ."

"A little bit more about what?"

"Just come with me and you'll see."

Irene remained pensive, and did not respond. Instead, she continued packing her things for a few minutes, as if she hadn't heard me. I left the bedroom and waited for her outside. I knew she would come. Her lack of a response was an all-but-irrefutable sign. I was right. She came. After wiping away her tears and making herself up a little bit, she emerged from the bedroom and went straight for the door. I followed her like a sleepwalker, dreaming my steps, dreaming everything that would come. We got in the car. I started the engine and headed off for the Morini house, which was not very far from where we lived. In fact, it was quite close by.

Much to our dismay, Madisonburg is a rather small city, half-rural and half-urban, as I've said, and that is why everything is fairly close to everything else: after a five or ten minute drive, you can find yourself in the middle of nowhere, with nothing save cows, horses, donkeys, hogs, pastures, fields, the countryside, the bucolic, pastoral landscape, and miles and miles of highways crisscrossing the dark, inviting meadow . . .

We arrived.

Just as we were getting out of the car, I saw Stephany explode out from the front door: she had seen us pull up to the house. She ran straight for Irene, and—with tears in her eyes and no questions asked—she burst into a peal of sobbing and embraced her tightly. Irene, as surprised as she was perplexed, was still standing there on the sidewalk next to the car, not knowing what to do or how to respond to that effusive display, which I immediately understood (upon hearing her speak) as nothing but a disturbing Christian paradox, a frightfully charismatic enthusiasm: that of the penitent sinner, the lost soul returning to the flock or something like that, but in any case it left me disarmed, of course, unsteady, and wholly out of place because I, on the contrary, hadn't managed to obtain that sort of inspiration, that sense of divine grace, and therefore my own sin (unlike Stephany's) had yet to be forgiven.

More angry than ever, I interrupted this lovely scene that might well have been taken out of *Quo Vadis?* to tell Morini's wife:

"We're here because I've got something to say to you, Stephany, not so you can hug my wife."

"I do too, Eusebio . . ." She interrupted me; her eyes were like those of a mangy old bitch or a repentant vestal virgin, and without letting me continue, she broke out into the following litany of screwed up Spanglish, which I will translate here: "I want you to know that I love you both, I love you both so much, we've been such good friends, and that we can continue to be so. I'm sure of it. I already told this to Irene this morning, right? I truly believe it. My pastor told me that with the love and forgiveness of Christ, everything can be resolved. All of the marital problems the two of you have can be worked out by accepting the Holy Spirit . . . I know it, I've felt it within me . . . all you need is to have faith . . . a strong sense of faith . . . and that's why I want to invite you to come with the rest of the Quakers and us to Sunday services. It's a lovely little church, near Highpoint. I promise you'll be welcomed with open arms. They'll pray for you, for your horrible sins, Eusebio, and they'll lay their hands on you both. They'll heal you, you'll see . . ."

"How the hell can you talk to us about marital problems, you fucking gringa, when your own husband has been humping his way all over town for years, and when you—yes you, you crazy gringa—lay down on the sofa of your own free will so that I could console you about your own marital problems?" I interrupted my own non-Christian paroxysm, which was on the verge of madness, bordering on anti-Christian hatred, which was roiling under my skin, beneath the very fibers of my epidermis. "Why are you only just now talking about Christ's forgiveness when it was you who let yourself be touched, when you—knowing full well that I was coming to your house to massage your ass—opened the door for me and invited me in so very kindly? Did I push you, did I force you, did I order you to lie down on the sofa so I could get on top of you? Or did you lie down, willingly and appreciatively, so that I could rub down your body because you were feeling so depressed?"

"So you could rub down my body?"

"Yes, Stephany, so I could apply a little friction to your legs and ass, remember?" I was emphatic, I was focused on the details of our encounter in a way that I had never focused on them before, with Irene. And then, in the blink of an eye, I changed course and suddenly asked her: "Where did you ever get the idea that we made love? Why would you say that to Irene when you know it's not true? We never did it, we didn't even attempt to do it . . ."

"She never said that to me, Eusebio," Irene cut in quickly. Her tears and sobbing were getting worse.

"No?" I replied.

"But you're saying that Stefano has cheated on me and you didn't say anything about it?" Stephany interjected angrily.

"Yes, he cheated on you with two different women that I know of, and he has been for a long time now."

"You're just saying that because you're angry, Eusebio," Morini's wife replied, trying to convince herself of her own argument, I suppose.

"I don't want to listen to this anymore," interrupted my wife, standing there between us: pallid, haggard, probably disgusted, blotting her tears and eye shadow. "I want to get out of here. I've had it with the both of you. And Stephany, thanks for the invitation to your church, but you and I can no longer be friends. Good-bye."

I'll summarize what happened from that point on thusly, dear Reader, because it's not worth the pain, as they say, to go picking at unhealed scabs . . . and mine have certainly not healed yet, not in the least! Half an hour later, Stefano would find out that I had gotten into it with his wife, and that—unwilling to submit myself to such a sacrosanct woman—I went to his house one more time and confirmed for Stephany that he had been unfaithful with two other women. Right away—that same afternoon, to be precise—Stefano went straight to Davis's office, the interim Dean of MFU, and, brimming with anger, he proceeded to repeat for him everything I'd told him that morning at Barnes & Noble. But he wasn't merely satisfied with that, because he also told him what he, Morini, and nobody else, knew, which was, as I said before, an extremely delicate secret: that I had previously sent a letter to the Office of Affirmative Action accusing him, Jeffrey Davis, and Whitehead (who was no longer with MFU) of nepotism and corruption with regard to the removal of Marion Siegel in order to offer her position to Katrina, the toad-daughter of the Gorgon Gross-Wayne. He came straight out and said that it was clear to him, to Stefano Morini, the honorable Italian, that Siegel had simply acted out of resentment and revenge, and that evidently Siegel and I had planted that emetic rumor with the intent of propagating it all over campus, thereby fucking with the careers of both of them, Davis and Gaudencia, not to mention the other honorable and respectable professors whom I'd accused. In conclusion, he assured the Dean that he had no reason to be concerned, because under no circumstances would he ever corroborate that nefarious conspiracy, because on its face it was a complete farce, a scatological fraud.

Oh, dear Reader! I can't even begin to tell you how many times he and I—Stefano and I, that is—got together over beers and laughter and swearing to complain about Gaudencia and her toadish daughter, how many times we ruthlessly ridiculed Whitehead's obesity and Davis's doglike behavior, and now, all of a sudden, with great vengeance and a desire to inflict the most amount of damage upon me as possible, he was going to spill his guts and expose this mound of injustice and obscenities . . . all of which are true, of course, despite what anyone else might say. Davis, as far as I know, listened patiently, with the wisdom of a skillful strategist who has persevered long enough to become exactly what he always wanted to be: the dean of a respectable college, a powerful administrator who controlled the future of a handful of average professors. He listened, he considered, he took note (of course!) without ever saying a word, encouraging him to continue, allowing Morini's imbecilic tongue to run, taking full advantage of his irate verbosity and his patently obvious feelings of pain. From that moment on, once Stefano had excused himself and left the dean's office, after unloading his Turinese antipathy towards me, as of that afternoon, I submit, everything came down with the resounding force of an exploding bomb, and shrapnel flew through the air, cutting into everyone, the entire city in fact, starting with me before moving on to Irene, who, as I said, was the first one to turn her back on me, the first person to leave Madisonburg disappointed, disillusioned, hurt, and angry. I barely even had time on that warm afternoon to say good-bye to my son Emilio, who didn't understand one whit of what was going on between his parents. Confused and a bit scared, he gave me a hug and a kiss, and said, "Don't worry, *papá*, we'll see you soon. I promise."

Davis called Ritter, made an *ipso facto* appointment to meet in their little lair, and without any further deliberation or consideration, he laid out what he had to do as head of the Department of Foreign Languages for the good of the meritorious university itself: retract my imminent promotion and tenure, drum up some excuse for the administration, and then simply toss me overboard and let me sink down into ignominy. The fact was (and this I learned from Phillip Ritter three days later) that the tenure committee had already voted in my favor, approving my promotion and ensuring the permanence of my position. All that notwithstanding, however, the official announcement wouldn't be made until after the upcoming academic year had begun, in September, which meant that the decision wasn't yet finalized, and therefore there was still time for a single stroke of the pen to change everything and allege that Professor Eusebio Cardoso did not deserve tenure, that he had been an incompetent educator during his five years here at the university, that accusations had been reported by some attractive female student . . . anything they wanted, any pretext, no matter how excessive, could be used to eliminate me and send me packing, the sooner the better. Obviously, I was in a very precarious position, between a rock and a hard place, at least from Dean Davis's point of view. My ego should have been flying high at the time, of course, but that wasn't the case at all.

According to what Ritter explained to me three days later, when I was having dinner with him at his house, he didn't accept the abominable accusations against me. In other words, he opposed the orders given by the boss, the all-powerful interim Dean, and ultimately that proved to be a very costly decision for the good and decent Germanist, because during that same three-day period (which led up to our dinner together) he was relieved of his position; or rather, he received a very amiable letter which specifically stated that, given his enormous contributions to MFU and the Department of Foreign Languages over the previous five years, it was past time for him to take some well-earned time off—a sabbatical—which, of course, he had little alternative but to accept grudgingly and with great difficulty.

That the autistic giraffe, a specialist in Benno von Archimboldi, would so completely disagree with the Dean of the College would certainly sound improbable, outlandish, and unheard of to anyone who understood the great suicidal act that this represented. No other human being would have acted in such a way; that much I'm sure of. Not many, anyway. But knowing Ritter as I did, it wasn't quite that odd; on the contrary, it was almost to be expected. His stubborn faith in rectitude and neutrality, in individual rights, respect, and justice, combined with his strict Protestant ethics, made him a truly unique individual in the history of the Pocket Book: a sort of untimely Kant, or some kind of evangelized Socrates.

At noon, three days later, as we were eating turkey sandwiches alone at his house, he said to me, almost ashamed, that he'd already heard the rumor about my unscrupulous and clandestine visits to Professor Morini's wife at home, and that he was of course disappointed in me, surprised even . . . but that was none of his business, and not his problem. He made it clear that, at least for him, nothing that happened between my colleague's wife and me, Cardoso, had anything to do, *sensu stricto*, with my formal performance as a professor in the department for the past five years, which has *clearly* been quite good (I stress this last point here, because he made it quite clear to me). Let me emphasize that this was the one and only reason that impelled him to contradict the Dean's dogged injustice. As we finished our sandwiches, he brought up another punctilious subject: I shouldn't confuse what he considered to be his duty, as boss, with things that might nevertheless lend themselves to misinterpretation; for example, any semblance of approval, consensus, or solidarity with my very serious lack of judgment with regard to Stefano's wife. And I repeat, as Ritter repeated to me, that he was sorry but this had nothing to do with the good work I had done there at MFU . . . and then there was, like corroborating evidence, the unanimous vote of the administration and the senior members of the department, including—surprise, surprise!—Bormann-Smythe. I listened to him for a long time without once attempting to justify myself in that respect, without trying to define what had actually happened with Morini's wife. Why would I? It would be totally pointless. That fact notwithstanding, I waited until we had finished eating those succulent turkey sandwiches he had carefully prepared for lunch that afternoon at his home before I ventured to tell him that which (obviously) he did not know and which was (in my opinion) the eye of this hurricane, the true heart of the matter: first, my letter to the Office of Affirmative Action following the unwarranted dismissal of Marion Siegel, and second, the story Siegel had told me about the coprophagous sect involving Davis, Gaudencia, Wynn, the two little bald guys, and fat old Whitehead. Those were the two true reasons why Davis was throwing me out of Millard Fillmore. At first, the giraffe was overwhelmed by my exhaustive narration (could it be his latent autism acting up again?); then he was overcome by waves of nausea, which he wasn't able to repress in time, and he ended up expelling the sandwich from his stomach, into which he had only recently finished cramming it. Bits of turkey and other, unidentifiable objects splattered across the tablecloth and even onto my hands, pants, and shoes.

But . . . leaving behind the detailed description of the turkey and getting back to the chain of events that were set in motion after Morini's unannounced visit to the Dean—according to what I later learned and even what I was able to find out—Porzia Fazzion phoned Davis or Davis phoned Porzia (who called whom doesn't much matter, really) regarding Ritter's position as the new chair of the Department of Foreign Languages, even though it wasn't technically available yet. If it was Porzia Fazzion who called Jeff Davis, it was because (as I said) Stefano sought her out after first having spoken to him; in other words, that same afternoon, or the next morning at the latest. If, however, it was Davis who called Porzia, it was also because (and this is more likely) Stefano had told him something about her or about both of them, or because Davis knew of the friendship between Porzia and Morini (after all, they were the only two Italians at the university). And so I repeat: those bits of barfed-up turkey—and the network of human secretions—are not entirely irrelevant, considering that Madisonburg (being what it is) is both a very small town and a very deep circle of hell.

In any case, once she was named interim chair, my very dear friend Porzia was easily able to stomach the decision to retract my tenure and my promotion to Associate Professor, both of which I clearly deserved, as I've said, and if someone disagreed with that . . . there was the unanimous vote of the administration! Fazzion was truly appalled by what had happened, by my shamelessness and cynicism, and by my betrayal of a friend who (to make matters worse) happened to be an Italian from Turin, one of her very own *paisanos*. She simply couldn't believe her ears: first, the chilling version Stefano had given her, and then, of course, the version that Stephany could have provided, which, as was to be expected, would have been redacted and distorted down to the last detail.

If I'm describing all that has happened here in one fell stroke of my pen, it's because—as I previously warned you, which I'll repeat here—it's because I don't want to reopen old wounds, and mine still have yet to heal, dear Reader. The events that befell us were a source of agony (and they continue to be agonizing) and, by definition, they have been protracted, prolonged, and slow to go away; however, they took place in such an unexpectedly precipitous manner that I'm no longer sure whether it all occurred in slow motion or if it all happened much too fast. Of course, I could have waited a bit longer before giving up the last juicy details for the sake of cruel exacerbation, just as my academic lynching was delayed, but then again I prefer to settle the score, to put an end to things, to *zanjar*, as beautiful Arabicism has it.

The Hiroshima bomb fell, then, directly on top of my home, and many things blew up along with it: I've lost Irene (I don't know if it's forever), I haven't seen Emilio again despite the departing promise he made to me, his father, the one who should have been making the promise, and now (to make matters worse) I found myself with no children, no wife, no tenure, no promotion, no job, no friends . . . well, that last one isn't quite true, dear Reader: there was the taciturn Tino and the brown-nosing Javis, who—just like you, dear Reader—listened attentively to me, despite all the weariness and fatigue, listening time and again to my version of the facts, reconstructing a history of errors and manifold backstabbings with traces of what I say and fragments of what Stefano and Stephany likely said to the two Galicians when they had them over for drinks. Fortunately, I've seen Tino and Javis several times since then, and they represent just about my only support in this splintered little town. In fact, we never stopped getting together after that nefarious (and very recent) day on which the three of us gathered at Barnes & Noble with Stefano. But that doesn't necessarily mean, though, that Tino and Javis have broken off contact with the Morinis. As far as I know, they are still as friendly with Stefano and Stephany as I am with them.

In conclusion, bringing an end to this long-winded and rather annoying discourse, I will add that just yesterday I received a backhandedly cruel letter of dismissal advising me that, although the distinguished and never presumptuous committee approved my promotion and tenure, the brilliant new interim chair, Porzia Fazzion, and the superb new interim dean, Professor Jeffrey Davis, by common consent, considering the lack of conviction and spirit that characterizes my teaching ability and my own lack of dedication to the university, decided (or preferred) to take everything—absolutely everything!—away from me, as if at gunpoint. The letter concludes by stating that as of this summer—once my intensive course on the Novel of the Mexican Revolution is over—my employment with MFU will be terminated and my current salary and benefits will continue (contractually and legally) for one year while I seek employment at another university. All that notwithstanding, both of them, Porzia and Davis, wished me luck in my new search for work here in the United States, and they were sure that I would be able to find a place more in tune with my professional plans and academic interests. Just as they'd done with Phillip Ritter—can you believe it?—they'd presented me with a sabbatical, dear Reader, yes, you heard me, a sabbatical! The one difference was that the autistic giraffe could return to Millard Fillmore University, whereas I was shoving off, setting sail, never to see these shores again . . . but with no wife and no son, the question was: where the hell was I going to go?

2
(TUESDAY, MAY 23RD)

On the Tuesday that Maty visited the painter, the afternoon sky was crystal clear, which doesn't often happen in the capital in late May. The sun was shining tepidly, but it wasn't cold, though there was just a hint of a chill in the air. It was five o'clock on the dot. The clouds seemed to have vanished from the sky; all that remained was the sun, hanging there like a flower basket, as yellow and brown as a rotting apple.

From Arturo's roof in the Narvarte neighborhood, the *Distrito Federal* appeared in bas-relief, an ornate inlay of plazas, buildings, and homes with balconies stained with blotches of stale light and crisscrossed by cars, motorcycles, and taxicabs, mothers with children in tow, carpenters and construction workers, teenagers and attorneys, housekeepers and panhandlers: a human ant farm five stories below. Up top, Maty and Arturo were wordlessly contemplating the teeming multitudes after having shared a kiss. Their bodies brushed together as they were swayed by the north winds, their silhouettes standing out against the ocher, amber background: the horizon looked neither cold nor ardent but rather stony and unyielding, as was their certainty that Tamara would not be there, not that afternoon or the next, and, above all, their certainty that you, dear Reader, wouldn't suddenly appear there either, because after all, you have a lot of work to do, and perhaps—who knows—a lot of reading to do as well . . .

The wake left by the initial enthusiasm at the victorious Partido de la Naturaleza y el Fuego Mexicano earlier the previous year had faded, though it hadn't completely vanished: it was still commemorated with public celebrations and fireworks, especially in the more remote places like Chiapas, Chihuahua, Sinaloa, Tampico, and Oaxaca. It was the first green party in history to have won an election without forming any alliances and in an undisputed manner, with over fifty percent of the popular vote. It was, without a doubt, an incomparable landmark, not only for

Mexico, but also for the entire world. Ever since the PAN left office with Calderón in 2012 and were supplanted first by the PRD and then by the PRI (one failure after another), nobody in their right mind would have predicted that in August of 2024, just a few months ago, a much-lampooned environmental candidate would nevertheless become Presidente de la República Mexicana. It was all quite unexpected. Needless to say, the respective candidates fielded by the PAN, the PVEM, the PRI, and the PRD were deeply disheartened, incredulous, and in some cases even reluctant to accept the fact that a fifth—yes a fifth—party candidate had been able to win and force them out of power. But today it was a verifiable fact, and beginning on December 1, 2024, a sixty-six-year-old attorney by the name of Gilberto Rendón had assumed the office of the presidency. It could be argued, though, that this old politician had little or nothing to do with the intellectual Roberto Soto Gariglietti, who founded the PNFM in the late twentieth century. Rendón, if you will, looked more like a traditional member of the PRI from the 1970s or '80s than he did any other sort of Mexican statesman: he was an environmentalist in name and (of course) in color only, after the "green party" designation caused a significant uproar in the PVEM, which was the other false environmental party. His past, his education, and his political trajectory were consistent with those of your average hack lawyer, the sort of two-bit attorney with delusions of grandeur: not for money, fame, or women, but simply for power, quintessential power, ubiquitous power and glory. Along with the environment, indigenous people, and endangered species, Rendón had inherited the worst possible characteristic of Mexican politicians during the previous half-century: a hollow, haggard, irritating, and insincere-sounding speech he gave every time he had the opportunity to bring up these three issues, though of course it was quite clear that he either didn't care about them at all, or that he simply didn't understand them. In fact, when it came to ecology or a respect for Nature in the most spiritual sense (that is, not in the scientific or technological one), only

Gariglietti himself had a genuine grasp of it at the time: a sort of *nous* or premonition that urged him to pursue the salvation of the country by exploring the origins of its people, and that drove him even deeper still: to exhume the gods, the mythologies, and the symbols of pre-Hispanic civilizations. His search, then, led him towards what he passionately termed Mexico's Chthonian Force—its telluric energy—which, he believed, would have to be recovered in order to restore the lost respect for Nature, the equilibrium of the *kosmos*, and the consubstantiation and love of the original elements, the four indestructible roots or *archai*: Zeus, Hera, Nestis, and Aidoneus, who of course had corresponding representations among the four primary Aztec gods and also with the four cardinal directions. Everything in Mexico was, according to him, inverted, turned back upon itself, returning to a disaster that dated back to the days of the Spanish conquest. Like a meteor from the heavens, he wrote, this country has fallen into *miasma* or *mysos*, a plague that has devastated Mexico for more than five hundred years: in submitting to Christianity we had forsaken that which united us with the Earth and those tutelary gods, which, he argued, had also happened in Egypt and Greece, and later in Rome. But above all in ancient Greece, the old world that he venerated more than any other. For him, like many romantic types, Nature was a fundamental, primordial thing, and do you know why? Because my father believed that men are derived from Nature and are part of its continuum, yes, derived from plants and animals, from stones and gods . . . that everything was integrated in a sort of infinite, harmonious scale along which each of us ascended and descended according to our stigmas, our virtues, our knowledge, our sins or ignorance, our respect for life and the gods and rituals. He called all of this metempsychosis . . .

"Metem . . . what?" Matilde repeated without understanding, though also without taking her eyes off of him, listening, enthralled, to the words of the painter who was still standing there next to her, solemn and inscrutable, continuing his lengthy speech.

"The transmigration of the soul. Reincarnation." Arturo sighed, embracing her though still looking out into the distance at the cluster of buildings pierced by rays of light. "That's why the church detests my father . . ."

"To this very day," Maty affirmed. "Just recently, monsignor Cabrales said that we were much better off with a secular state, separated from the church, like the one we've had for two hundred years, than with a party that favors the abnormal and dangerous idea of reincarnation, of metemp . . ."

"Metempsychosis."

"Yes. That."

"But Gilberto Rendón doesn't really believe in reincarnation or the transmigration of souls, Matilde. He's an opportunist, a cagy old strategist who amuses himself by shuffling cards and changing colors whenever it suits him the most. He doesn't believe in anything other than himself and his unyielding desire to succeed. It's clear, at least to me, after knowing him for more than twenty years, that his ideological creed has nothing to do with what my father wrote and thought some thirty or forty years ago. To begin with, there's one thing you have to know, Matilde: the PNFM victory had nothing to do with Roberto Soto, his memory, and his books. Rendón and his followers simply used it all to their advantage. His name, his memory, his achievements as the founder . . . but in no way—listen to me now—in no way does the actual ideology of the PNFM correspond with the ideology that Soto Gariglietti had for Mexico! I want to make that perfectly clear to you. I'm saying this—I'm telling you this—so that you and you alone will know the truth, so you can put it in your thesis or do whatever it is you want to do with this information."

As this heated discourse on the roof came to a conclusion, they entered the studio. Matilde sat down. Arturo stepped out for a moment before returning almost immediately with an uncorked bottle of wine, along with the same two tin cups that they used every Tuesday and Thursday.

Apparently, they were the only ones. The painter then sat down on the dilapidated sofa, filled each cup halfway, and they drank. After savoring the taste for a moment, Matilde switched on her mini tape recorder and said to Arturo in a journalistic tone of voice, ready to get down to the business of investigative reporting and leave the business of sex and passion for some other time:

"So tell me more about this belief in reincarnation. What did your father think about all of that?"

"First, let me ask you something, Maty: do you remember me telling you how my great-grandfather Enzo, from Sicily, was very nearly poisoned, along with Pancho Villa, by two Japanese cooks along with Pancho Villa back in 1917?"

"Of course, but what does that have to do with all of this?"

"Look . . ." Arturo began, deeply stirred by what he apparently considered to be a priceless secret: one that cut to the bone of the historical question. Before proceeding, he took another sip from his cup, swished it around in his mouth, taking an excessive amount of time to savor the tannins that the wine left on his taste buds, took another sip, and spent a few more seconds putting on airs before he finally said, lowering his voice and exaggerating the need to speak in whispers: "Apparently that discovery was very late in coming, because he was already an old man by the time he uncovered those FBI archives at the University of Texas at Austin. But nevertheless, that discovery led him to believe that he, Enzo Gariglietti, was himself a demigod, and that that was the reason he survived the poison. Yes, you heard me. Don't look at me like that, Maty. It's true."

"What are you trying to say?"

"I'll explain. Maybe I should have warned you first, to avoid any surprises," Arturo said, settling down into the worn-out sofa, uncrossing his legs and taking Matilde's hand—the same hand with which she was holding her recorder—drawing it a little closer to him, perhaps just to make sure that his words would be clearly preserved. "The ancient

Greeks believed that some men could be gods and that some gods could coexist with men and even look a bit like men without losing their spirit of immortality. It sounds confusing, but that's what they formally believed, from Homer to Hesiod, and perhaps even before that. At least, that's what they believed until the arrival of Xenophanes of Colophon, history's first atheist, and after him, Socrates, its first great ethicist; the two of them dismantled many ideas, or superstitions. Not all of them, of course, because Plato appeared shortly thereafter to return many of the old beliefs or conjectures (*doxa* and *dokeō*) to the places they previously occupied. Both the Eleatics and the Atomists believed in this sort of coexistence: that the celestial and terrestrial worlds could mix together, be confounded, a bit like imagination and reality can be mixed or superimposed from time to time. Things in ancient Greece weren't as clearly defined as they are today, Matilde. Some individuals—those who had reached a certain, superior level of virtue or knowledge—could be considered demigods. It was assumed or understood that these extraordinary people would have been reincarnated several times over in order to have reached the realm of the, shall we say, semi-divine. Are you following me? The *psychēs* or *daimones* of these people would come, then, to coexist with the immortal gods in all their glory. In fact, in his later years, Empedocles was convinced that he was no longer mortal and that he had been transformed—while still alive, right there in Agrigento—into a divine man who should be loved and revered by his people. And in fact, he was . . ."

"And what does this have to do with what you've told me about your great-grandfather?"

"Well, as astonishing as it may seem to you, Maty, Enzo thought, being the good Sicilian that he was, that he was a demigod, and for that one, simple reason, he believed he was able to survive that morning when he drank poisoned coffee with Pancho Villa. That's what I've been trying to explain . . ."

"That's crazy. It's like a fairy tale."

"Yes, but I'm only telling you what I know, the information I've received, what my father told me when I was very young."

"How do you know he didn't just make up those stories he told you, Arturo? How can you be so sure that you didn't simply construct this all out of old childhood memories?"

Arturo laughed and simply replied with a resounding boast:

"Because I also read it, Matilde."

"What?"

"There was a letter—a letter which today cannot be located—that my mother and I both read, and in it Enzo himself spoke about his discovery, his revelation or whatever you want to call it, after discovering those documents in Austin when he was already an old man, as I've said. You could argue, if you want, that my great-grandfather was senile by that time, sure, and maybe that's true, but that does nothing to change the fact that, one, Enzo was sitting at that table with Villa that morning and drank the poisoned coffee, and two, that it was, above all, a common belief in Agrigento, home of the philosopher whom he read and admired."

"Yes, but that's not nearly enough to transform yourself into a god or demigod, Arturo."

"Of course, nothing is enough for godly status . . . but everything is enough," the Agro painter said, contradicting himself with ruthless sarcasm as he lay his wine cup down on the quilt, spilling a few drops. "What I mean is that everything is relative, Matilde; it all depends on what you believe, on what you want to believe. Whether you're a rationalist through and through, or a skeptic or a materialist or a Cartesian, then everything I'm telling you amounts to a lovely fable or a tale of madness, but if you're not, you can ask yourself what the hell was going on in my great-grandfather's mind, or in the minds of other people—people like Hölderlin, Pessoa, and Nietzsche, among many others—who also believed in such things. You see? It all depends . . ."

"And so . . ." Matilde was determined to see this through to the end, ignoring the painter's harsh, taxing voice. "What did Empedocles have to say about reincarnation?"

244

"Towards the end of his life, before his death at the age of sixty, he wrote a book or treatise, *Katharmoi*, which is tangentially opposed to its predecessor, the one I've been telling you about: *On Nature*. But, for many students, the second work isn't so much an opposition to the first work, but rather a continuation of it, a sort of spiritualization of the ideas proposed in the first." Here Arturo paused to take another sip of wine from his tin cup, delighting in either the wine or his own words, and pouring a little more for his lover, who hadn't yet finished her half a cup. "If, for example, in *On Nature*, Empedocles was trying to be more or less scientific, or looking for scientific bases (better yet: empirical bases) for his discoveries, then in *Katharmoi*, the philosopher had already fully immersed himself in the theological, mystical substratum, as we say. Imbued with Orphism and many Pythagorean ideas—all of which, of course, came before him—Empedocles believed in an eclectic system that combined his earlier findings about the order of Nature and the Cosmos (which I've been explaining to you) with his more recent religious principles. To begin with, Maty, he was convinced, as I said, that Nature is a system of gradations, a universal scale for the successive reincarnations of all *psychēs* or *daimones*, and this is so because, in *On Nature*, he had already discovered that matter does not disappear, but rather is transformed, it reshapes itself like the particles of color on a painter's palate. And therefore, he adduced that human beings would also be transformed into other things, resulting in souls being reincarnated into something else. Are you following me? This time, though, in *Katharmoi*, Eris and Eros, the main protagonists of his philosophy and the engines that turn the gears of the universe, play a part, yes, but they do not influence physical things; rather, they influence morality. In other words, they have a moral effect on the union or division of nations and men. Since the phase through which the world is currently passing has been devastated by war, violence, destruction, and other human vices, we need to cooperate with Kypris—that is, with Aphrodite—in order to reinstate the lost unity, to return to the perfect sphere, to the mixture of the four elements that combine in differing ratios to form everything that exists in our cosmos."

"And how is all this achieved?" Maty still hadn't shaken the notion that perhaps that afternoon in Narvarte wasn't simply part of some grand dream that included everything, even her questions. "How is that consistent with Aphrodite, or is it even possible to know?"

"Though *teletai*. In other words, through the ancient rituals . . ."

"What rituals, Arturo?"

"A series of practical rituals of purification that are called *Katharmoi* and which were more or less common among some mystical sects. Empedocles collected a number of them, and invented other ones. With *Katharmoi*, he made it so that the *miasma* or *mysos* that were sent by Zeus as punishment for man's disobedience disappeared, and that the city became purified."

"Yes, of course, but what are those rituals, Arturo?" Matilde was beginning to feel a bit hopeless, rudderless, like she was losing control of the interview. What did all this nonsense, this absurdity, have to do with Mexican politics or Soto Gariglietti or her master's thesis?

"First and foremost, they were to maintain the Hellenic spirit of proper proportions: the sense of form, symmetry, order, and good taste in everything we do and the way we live. But along with that, and contrary to how it might seem, it is also necessary to achieve the opposite: you need to acquire *enthousiasmos*. In other words, the exultation of being possessed by the divine, the intoxicating joy of turning into gods."

"The Apollonian and Dionysian . . ."

"More or less, but it's more than just that, Matilde. It's also necessary to lead a pure life. For example, you must abstain from eating any meat or beans; you have to sustain yourself mainly on grains and vegetables. There is no slaughtering of any animals, because—remember!—either we were animals before this life, or we will be after it, so it's possible that we might be butchering a son or even our own father instead of a bull or a hog . . ."

"That's horrible!"

"And that's exactly what Empedocles himself said in a fragment of text," Arturo remarked, and then immediately—as if inspired by some god to continue his interminable lesson that day—continued: "But that's not all. Each and every day you have to cultivate the spirit of Kypris in your soul, Maty, just as we Agro painters used to do during our pilgrimages with the Yaqui Indians . . . You have to purify your body every so often in the waters of a river and make libations, which is another thing we did. You must never, under any circumstances, approach the laurel because it is the most sacred tree of them all. But the most important, most difficult, or most impossible thing of all: you must not sleep with any woman. You must remain chaste . . . even if you're already married."

Matilde couldn't help but flash, almost against her will, a broad, white smile of delight when she heard those final, ridiculous-sounding words come out of her lover's mouth. It was almost immediately followed by an outburst of laughter:

"You're not telling me that your great-grandfather carried out all those rituals, since you, my love, obviously do not . . ."

"No, my great-grandfather Enzo didn't participate in those rituals, but my father did," Arturo responded seriously, matter-of-factly, his dark eyes still focused on Matilde's green ones. "And that's why my mother left him."

III

But where do we go? Where do we go from here, dear Reader?

Let me get right to the point: why keep running circles around the idea that's come to me, making its rounds in my mind like a Bengal tiger in its cage ever since this Virginia circus began, ever since Irene and Emilio left me, ever since I finished my intensive course on Martín Luis Guzmán and his *Memorias de Pancho Villa*, ever since they threw me out of Millard Fillmore without my tenure and promotion, with my closely guarded secret about influential shiteaters, but without any idea about what to do with such information?

Well, there is a town, a small village, really, that I've wanted to visit for months, though for whatever reason I never did. It's called Las Rémoras. Perhaps you've heard of it? Does it sound familiar? Yes, near La Paz, in Baja California Sur. No more than twenty thousand people, with just one perpendicular avenue cutting through the middle of this little town and descending straight to the sea, or better put: Libertad runs perpendicular to the sea, where it hits a beach that would resemble (when seen from the sky) a perfectly formed shell, if not for a rugged, craggy outcropping on the left-hand side, an enormous stone or meteorite wedged between the sand and sea. Look: let me explain to you how I learned of this place, how I happened upon this lovely little hamlet of fishermen, murderers, prostitutes, hunchbacks, and madmen . . . Not long ago, four or five months at the most, during a lightning-quick visit to Mexico City, a strange book fell into my hands which is entitled *The Obstacles* and largely set in the town of Las Rémoras itself. I read it all in one sitting, on the flight back to Virginia. The author . . . well, I don't remember who it was, but that's not important anyway. As Borges said, the issue of authorship is an exaggerated one, since all of us may be the authors of any given book, we are all its writers, we are all its accomplices, which ends up being a dangerous Leibnizian and Parmenidean liaison since (when seen clearly) it suddenly denies the individuality of the souls, the distinction between you, my dear Reader, and me, Cardoso, who is relating this friction to you. Ultimately (and so I don't get mired down in abstractions), what matters is that there, in that little town of tourists and idlers, a number of notable events took place, which, in my opinion, have yet to be resolved. Open cases, you know? There was one horrible crime in particular that nobody was able to clear up, and with which I, shortly after reading about it, became obsessed, obsessed with exposing it. But in order to do so—to continue my investigation and ascertain the truth—I would have to visit Las Rémoras and verify something, a fundamental key, which you, dear Reader, will learn about in due course. However, before I was able to get the okay for a trip from Irene and Ritter,

I was hit with a series of new and debilitating responsibilities, including a couple of dull, departmental committees and the internal squabbling, which I've already mentioned, so between one thing or another, the last five months have passed so precipitously that I haven't been able to do much of anything, let alone continue my investigations into that unusual coastal labyrinth, that *terra ignota* in the northwest corner of Mexico. I say *ignota* because, to confound things even more, there has been more than one occasion where I've bumped into someone who hails from La Paz and were caught off guard when I asked them about Las Rémoras. The man or woman in question invariably answers—with the composed arrogance of a Baja native who surely must know their beloved region better than me—that they don't have the slightest idea what I'm talking about. When I produce the book and the little map that is included within it, they hesitate for a moment, searching within their own memories, but in the end they always tell me that they don't know the place or that the town in question doesn't exist, that it must be a work of friction. At that point, I'm disappointed enough to simply drop the matter. But I will admit that, after the third or fourth time this happened, I finally overcame the typical laziness or inertia that takes hold over me from time to time, and I got my hands on one of those gigantic world atlases that include every known place on the planet, and I immediately set about searching for the town in question. I never found it. I never found the town, and that, I suppose, planted the unhealthy itch that bugged me day and night for no good reason at all. As I said, I needed to shed some light on a key element of the crime that's described in the book regarding Inés, a favorite of the lawyer Rosales and madam of the brothel where the heartbreakingly beautiful Roberta worked, whose eyes were so intensely green, by the way, that they reminded me of Maty, your wife.

Now then, during these past few days (again, suffering from my own sort of personal inertia) a rather monstrous—or macabre, if you prefer—idea has occurred to me: why don't you, my dear Reader, come with me to that little, one-horse town? To Las Rémoras? Yes, that's

right . . . you heard me! Look, at this point in your life, you don't have much to lose. Maybe your Mercedes, and of course your job . . . but honestly that's not all that much, if you consider the fact that you no longer have anybody or anything to work for, and that for the first time in your life you have no reason to work like crazy to make enough money to pay for a mountain of luxuries that you never really wanted or needed, not even in the beginning. As for me, I don't have anything to add that you don't already know full well: I have no woman (women), no child (children), and twelve months to do whatever my heart desires, but mainly I now find myself in command of my own given desire, the first of which is to get to know you, dear Reader, and secondly to leave Madisonburg as soon as possible and head down to Baja California Sur with you. Neither Javis nor Tino could accompany me, even if they wanted to, which I'm sure they don't, knowing the Galicians as I do. So that leaves you. What do you think? Sound good? If you're not interested, if you don't agree . . . then shut this book, put it down, and forget I ever mentioned it. I'm serious; all joking aside, as of now, from this moment onward, things are going to take a ninety (or even a one hundred and eighty) degree turn, and for that I need your complete willingness, desire, and cooperation . . . .
. . . .
. . . .
. . . .
. . . .
. . . .
. . . .
. . . .
. . . .
. . . .
. . . .
. . . .
. . . .

Okay! Wonderful! Perfect! Apparently you've decided to continue, and to go ahead with the adventure. Everything seems to indicate that if you're reading these lines—if you're still following along, stultified by and engrossed in this indecent book—then you've chosen to press onward with me. As for myself, dear Reader, I can only promise you one thing: that you will not end up like K, the poor old Surveyor who never reached that fucking castle in the snow-covered mountains even though it was sitting there right under his very nose. Yes, we'll get there, I assure you. If the young Ricardo Urrutia (a character from *The Obstacles*) can make it, then surely we will be able to as well . . . But first, I suppose, I assume, we should meet each other and get acquainted, don't you think? Look, I took the liberty of moving ahead just a little bit, and I've already booked my flight to Mexico City today . . . yes, today, Thursday, you heard me! I get in at 3:15 P.M. Please don't be upset. This in no way implies that I had any advance knowledge or that I presumed that your answer would be yes. I couldn't have known that. How could I, if I don't believe in predestination? You could easily have tossed this book in the trash, and then our entire collaboration would have gone to shit, right? So, dear Reader, please don't get upset . . . just wait for me at Benito Juárez International Airport. From there, if you like, we can leave together for La Paz, the capital of the state of Baja California Sur. Also, I bought two tickets on a Mexicana Airlines flight that departs tonight at 7:00 P.M. Yeah, sure, you can pay me back later, or if you prefer, simply consider it my treat, and you can throw in a few cents here and there for expenses . . . Anyway, figure out what you're going to do with your car, but before you do that—yes, first of all—you have to get over that paralyzing fear that's kept you sitting there for some time now in your Mercedes under the shade trees only a block from your apartment in Las Águilas, waiting for God knows what, maybe a solar eclipse? I have no idea . . . evidently, you're still undecided about going in to get your clothes and personal things; perhaps you'd rather not, perhaps you'd prefer not to set one foot in that apartment, since after all, Maty inherited it from her parents, your in-laws . . . But go in, just go in there one final time, Matilde isn't home, you've already seen her screwing Arturo, I've described it so meticulously for you, or are you such a fool that you'd forgotten already? Go pack a suitcase—don't forget swimming trunks!— but most importantly, don't bother leaving a note. You're not that limp-wristed, so try and maintain a bit of dignity, of pride, at least. Understand? Do you promise? Have you read my instructions carefully? Don't write a thing, nothing, not one word. Let her worry, let her celebrate your upcoming anniversary (hers and yours) with the Agro painter instead of you. It won't be pleasant—quite bitter, in fact, I can promise you that—but we can talk about that and many other things later this afternoon when we meet at the airport . . . ahhhhhhhh . . . and don't you worry: I'll recognize you as soon as I see you, and the differing dates that currently separate us will be completely annulled and erased, for they are, of course, nothing more than the perks of the trade, the advantages that come with writing any friction. You know, that's actually why I took this job, even if I'm known more as a professor.

4
(THURSDAY, MAY 25TH)

"Arturo . . ."

"Yes? Talk to me . . ." The painter embraced his lover, pulling her against his taut, bronzed skin, which barely seemed able to cover his ribs on that new, rainless Thursday evening. It had cleared up not twenty minutes before to reveal a sky somewhere between cobalt blue and azure in color that poured into the studio like a heavenly light. Arturo and Matilde lay there, exhausted and sticky, on the same old mat on top of which they'd added a quilt and a few old cotton sheets that Maty had smuggled over the second time they met to make love/fuck like rabbits.

"I had a dream . . . and I wanted to tell you about it. In fact, I've had it twice now, on consecutive nights. But the strangest thing is, I remember it all quite clearly, even after I wake up."

"You remember it clearly?" Arturo asked, stretching to reach the small pack of cigarettes before lighting one with extreme languidness or lethargy. He didn't appear to be interested in Matilde's dream at all . . . but he positioned himself to listen, prepared to display a level of attention that he evidently did not feel.

"Well, as clearly as one can remember a dream, you know."

"No, I don't know, but that doesn't matter. Go on, Maty. I'm listening." The painter took a drag on his cigarette, almost content, good-natured, even, as he waited for his lover's story.

Matilde sat up and hesitated for a moment, not entirely sure how to begin.

"All of a sudden, I'm in bed with someone. But it's not my husband. It's someone else."

"Was it me?"

"No, it wasn't you either. But wait, wait . . ." Maty paused for a second, placing her still sweaty hand over the Agro painter's mouth before continuing, a bit nervous and hesitant: "It was night, but not all that late. There were a few candles burning in the room, and everything smelled really good, you know? Like musk, or orange blossoms, yes, that was it, I think it smelled like orange blossom water. My grandmother used to float little votive candles in orange blossom water in the foyer of her house when we went to visit her . . ."

"Don't change the subject, Maty."

"I'm sorry," she rectified immediately. "I knew there was someone in the room; first I heard a sigh, then I sensed a body lying there next to me, and finally I felt very smooth skin touching my own, or perhaps I brushed up against it myself without intending to, without wanting to actually turn over and see his face."

"And?" Arturo said without removing the cigarette from his mouth, sounding kinder by the moment . . . almost involuntarily, tenaciously holding the hostile smoke in his lungs.

"Well, I pulled back the sheets and all of a sudden there was another woman lying there next to me. Yes, you heard me: another woman, naked

254

like me, sleepy and intrigued. She watches me, we watch each other in amazement, intently curious, and then suddenly she smiles at me as if she just now remembers me and knows exactly who I am. She's gorgeous, but I have no idea who the hell she is. I feel like I'm on the verge of recognizing her, but no matter how hard I try, I just can't seem to remember, I just can't . . .''

Upon seeing her so pensive, so hung up on the edge of her ponderings, Arturo gently urged her on:

"Yes, I'm listening, Maty. What happened next?"

"Well she starts touching my shoulders, my neck, my back, my collarbones, my cheeks, and suddenly I start doing the same to her, without smiling, without any shame, you know, without any sense of modesty, and that's when I discover that her nipples have darkened at my touch, her nipples have darkened, yes, they've darkened quite a bit and grown as sharp and pointed as a lance . . .'' Maty paused and meditated for a moment before proceeding (almost melancholically) with her detailed, dreamlike description: "A few seconds later, much to my embarrassment, I discover that my own nipples are erect and that I'm horny as a goat, on the verge of coming right there with her, can you believe it? I'm so incredibly happy with this stranger lying there next to me in bed, surrounded by the smell of orange blossoms and candles . . . until, all of a sudden, I'm wide awake and everything vanishes in a puff of smoke like in a goddamn fairy tale."

"And that's where it ends?"

"Yes," Maty said, still pensive, still mourning the sweetness of that memory, perhaps recalling some specific fragment from the recurring dream, perhaps longing for its tenderness and happiness, feelings which were (she was now learning) perhaps greater than what she felt during her (furtive?) visits to Arturo's workshop every Tuesday and Thursday evening. Finally, with no small amount of effort, Maty awoke from her lethargy and—languidly turning up the corners of her lips—asked her lover: "What do you think? About what I just told you? Crazy, right?"

Arturo didn't speak for a long while, continuing to ponder without removing the cigarette (or what was left of it) from his mouth. Finally, he asked:

"Tell me this: are you certain that this other woman had darkened nipples?"

"Yes, of course. Huge, pointed, darkened nipples. Why do you ask?"

Arturo continued his deliberations, turning ideas over and over in his head, until suddenly he sat up straight on the quilt and said to Matilde in a very serious voice:

"Do you know what this could mean?"

Maty didn't seem able to intuit the meaning of the look in his eyes or what he was hinting at with that question. What the hell was her husband's friend talking about? She sat there, watching him for a while, trying to discern her lover's winding thoughts, to see if perhaps she might understand the intricacies of what Arturo was conjecturing without explanation.

"Think, Matilde . . . think for a moment," the Agro painter insisted, his voice different now, thicker and more guttural.

Finally, after some time, Maty thought she understood, thought that she finally comprehended what was, apparently, the revelation of a mystery . . . but she found it impossible to accept, to believe. Of course it was impossible: she was sterile. At least, that's what she thought. Nevertheless, in a strong, defiant tone, she said to Arturo, as if refuting one of Zeno of Elea's aporias.

"But in my dream, I don't have darkened nipples. It's her . . ."

"That's because you don't see them, Maty," the son of Soto Gariglietti answered, full of conviction, understanding that Matilde has also understood in turn. "It's because you don't actually look at them . . . it's natural, but—believe me—yours are just as dark and swollen. That's why, if you stop and focus for a moment, you'll see that you noted in your dream that your own nipples were sharp and pointed as a lance. You can feel them, Matilde, of course you can feel them, but what you don't see yet is that the other woman is you."

"Don't be ridiculous!" Maty fussed, smiling, trying to add (a bit too late) a dash of irony to her exclamation.

"I'm being serious. Like I said, it means that you've connected with yourself, with the darker side or your deep-rooted identity. But above all, it means exactly what you think it means . . ."

"Don't even say it. Don't you dare . . ."

"Yes, Matilde, I think you're pregnant." By then, of course, Arturo's fingers were burning: in one swift, extinguishing motion, he threw his cigarette butt into a corner. "That's how dreams work; they tend to appear before the facts do. Dreams know what's incubating."

V

Reader was standing there waiting for Cardoso. He did not know him—he hadn't even seen him before—but he had read him attentively, with a keenness and perhaps even a great calmness of mind, and, ultimately, he had indeed gotten out of his Mercedes, overcoming his bitterness and impotence. The very next thing he did, after ratcheting up his courage, was to enter his apartment there in Las Águilas: he packed his bags in a flash (including a pair of trunks), left no note or message for his wife, and—last but not least—he set out to meet the ill-fated professor at Benito Juárez International Airport in Mexico City, which is exactly what he was doing at this very moment, standing amongst the nomadic multitude, dying of curiosity, in a mental state not unlike vertigo, from which he had yet to completely emerge. What could he lose in all of this? At this point, as Cardoso had written, absolutely nothing. Reader, as depressed as he was, knew it deep down to be true, which is why he called his office to say that he wouldn't be in for the next two or three weeks under the pretext of needing to take a very important trip: a trip involving a life or death situation, which is how he described it to his astonished and clearly overwhelmed secretary. Cardoso, tired from the trip but excited nonetheless, immediately recognized him as he exited the international terminal: he looked, needless to say, exactly as he had imagined him to look this whole time. Yes, there was no mistaking it: his suit and gray tie had given him away. It was him. Not too tall and not too short. Neither ugly nor handsome, neither fat nor thin . . . with that ridiculous comb-over covering his balding crown. Meanwhile, you—the scorned husband—saw me in the distance, saw the one and only Author of this scatological friction that you've been reading. Eusebio (meaning me), resolved that there be no beating around the bush, strode right up to him (meaning you) with his leather satchel in hand, and said, very amiably:

"I believe you're waiting for me. I am Eusebio Cardoso." He extended a warm, supportive, almost fraternal hand.

The other dropped his suitcase, taken a bit by surprise (though not too much, of course), and extended his own hand to Cardoso and responded, fascinated:

"Very pleased to meet you."

"I see you're all packed up and ready to go . . ."

"Well, yes . . ." said the other, smiling, before he continued on, almost apologetically: "Like you said, at this point, there's nothing left to lose." With that said, he changed the subject; after all, he didn't want to dive right into an intimate conversation about Matilde: "What I still don't quite understand, though, is whether we're in your year or mine . . ."

"It's whichever you prefer. Honestly, in terms of the friction that I'm writing, it doesn't matter. At least, not from here on," Eusebio replied. Next (with Reader still incredulous, and Cardoso rather incredulous as well), they slowly began to make their way through the intolerable masses that were congregating around the International Arrivals gate. Suddenly, without stopping their forward progression, the professor added, "What you do need to know is that from this point forward, you will no longer be reading about what is happening to you in the second person, as you have been. Nor will you read what's happening to me

258

in the first person. It would be a real mess—utter confusion, really—to continue on like that, right? I think it would be much more convenient and much more in accordance with the plotline we've set out before us if we simply move into the third person . . . don't you think?"

"Absolutely," answered Reader, not quite sure he knew what Cardoso was explaining, but he wasn't worried about it anyway: literary minutiae, he supposed, without paying too much attention to the odd, Cardosian slang. There were other, more pressing things on his mind at the moment.

"I'm hungry," Eusebio blurted out. "Would you like to grab a bite? All they give you to eat on these international flights is a packet of peanuts," he said, before adding; "Besides, if I'm not mistaken, we still have a couple of hours before our next flight leaves . . ."

"Yes, I checked the schedule and the flight to La Paz is on time. Seven on the dot, just like you said."

"Perfect, let's get something to eat and chat for a bit, if you like."

Calmly, they both kept walking down the long, lustrous, well-lit corridor until they found, at a bend in the illuminated walkway, a restaurant that, at first glance, didn't seem to be a half-bad spot. They went in. *Luckily the wait won't be too long,* thought Reader: *there's barely anybody here.* A woman a bit larger than what you would call "plump" approached them and, a few seconds later, led them to just the table they wanted: a corner booth, free of noise, music, and customers with children, with soft lighting and a vase of azaleas and violets decorating one side of it. They laid their respective luggage on the ground next to their chairs, and Eusebio requested menus. He asked Reader if he'd like a glass of wine, to which the other agreed without a moment's hesitation, asking himself what the hell he was doing there, sitting at a table with a complete stranger, about to embark on a journey to an unlocatable place. They asked for the wine list and the hefty woman disappeared: vanishing in a puff of smoke forever more. Eusebio took the opportunity to ask a pointed question:

"For what it's worth, what name do you go by?"

"If you like, you can keep calling me what you've already been calling me . . ." Reader laughed, perhaps for the first time since he happened upon his unfaithful wife in the arms of the Agro painter the previous day at his plywood-and-asbestos studio in Narvarte.

"Reader?"

"That's what I am, right? At least, that's what I have been . . ."

"That's true," Cardoso conceded, though he was slightly surprised or resistant. Needless to say, he had taken quite a slap to the face.

"Or, if you'd rather, you can call me Anagnostes," pressed Reader, dying of laughter at this particular issue. "Characters in novels always seem to have two or three different names . . ."

"Yes," his unnerved dinner companion agreed. "I suppose they do that to lend some credibility to the characters, to make them more flesh-and-bone, as it were."

"And, so you're not always repeating yourself," Anagnostes added knowingly. "It's a question of style, I suppose."

"Yes, of course . . . but, why Anagnostes?"

"You're a Hellenist. See if you can figure it out."

"I have no idea."

"It means Reader in Greek," Anagnostes fired back impetuously, with no small amount of humility.

Another lady, younger and much more attractive than the first, appeared with the menus and two glasses of ice water. They both took a cursory look at the offerings, and ordered the first thing that sounded good to them (steak tartare for Anagnostes, and pepper-crusted filet mignon for the Professor) and dispatched the young waitress, though not before ordering a bottle of Côtes du Rhône, dated the year before whatever the previous year actually was.

"So," Reader asked Eusebio, hoping to break the ice a bit, "How is everything with you? How do you feel?"

"Well, no better than you, of course. Considering everything that's happened . . ."

"I can imagine," Anagnostes answered, lowering his eyelids in a sign of solidarity and understanding, before adding, almost in a whisper, really, as if he were telling a secret: "And what about Irene and your son?"

"Honestly, I haven't heard a thing from them. I assume they're with my wife's mother," Eusebio said, pensive, almost grieving as he was once again forced to remember the ultimately disastrous events in Madisonburg. Every time he found himself recalling his recent and involuntary bachelorhood, he felt (of course) the absence of his beloved Irene, whom he missed every minute of every hour of every day, just as he missed his son.

Quite carelessly, Anagnostes was about to ask him which of her two mothers his wife was with, but fortunately the lovely appearance of Nestis (also known as the waitress) holding their bottle of red wine in her fine, lithe fingers was enough of a distraction to dissuade him from saying another word. Instead, both men simultaneously caught notice of the name tag affixed to the girl's shirt: not because they were trying to read her divine name, but in fact because their eyes were drawn to the young woman's enormous tits. Nestis uncorked the bottle of wine (of unknowable vintage) and decanted a bit into a glass; they took in its aroma and scrutinized the liquid before taking the first, parsimonious sip, like a couple of champion French vintners. They did not clink their glasses together in a toast; this was not an occasion for such things. To do so would have been an excess of fanfare. Finally, lacking any further intercessions from Nestis, who had suddenly vanished—thus fracturing the majestic sense of circumspection the goddess had provided a few moments before—Reader took a daring shot at the author of *Friction*:

"Would you mind telling me what motivated you to get involved with Morini's wife in the first place? You never quite finished explaining that part. If memory serves, you half-addressed it as an apparent *auto-da-fé*. Then you went off on a tangent, with your insightful quote from Sor Juana, which left me wondering . . ."

Faced with the unexpected question, the Professor of the Novel of the Mexican Revolution dropped his chin for a few seconds and stared down into his glorious glass of Côtes du Rhône, submerged in a sort of reddish, iridescent oblivion. Given that he stayed silent for at least a little while longer (perhaps thinking about how he was going to respond), combined with the fact that Anagnostes didn't think to drop the subject at this in/opportune occasion, Eusebio was forced to listen to Reader's question once again:

"The truth is, I'm asking you because for the life of me I can't understand how that son of a bitch Arturo could do what he did to me. You understand? How could someone do that to his friend's wife? There are so many fish in the sea . . ."

The desire to cry was not lost on Reader-Inquisitor, no, but he contained himself; he held strong, as they say about macho men from Jalisco. He took a prolonged sip from his glass, and as he did, he heard the unmistakable voice of the former MFU professor:

"I believe I was motivated . . . precisely . . . by the desire to feel that flesh, yes, that illicit skin because . . . after all, it didn't belong to me; because, in the end, it wasn't mine to touch. It was—how can I say it?—foreign flesh, forbidden flesh . . ." He hesitated, not very sure of whether he'd started off correctly, weighing his words with the same caution and care that a sommelier from the fertile valleys surrounding the Rhône River, with his renowned and well-seasoned gustatory papillae, would take as he assays, savors, and absorbs the acidulous secretions of . . . but this is all really rather obscene, yes, obscene, unbecoming, and vulgar.[3]

"Yes, the desire to feel, the unstoppable, goddamn need to touch that which is prohibited, hidden, taboo . . . that is, that which isn't yours, and never will be. Do you mean to tell me it's never happened to you, Reader? As stupid and paradoxical as it may seem, I can come up with no other answer to offer you, for I have exceeded my grasp of words and explanations. It might be argued that nobody's skin belongs to us, but least of all the skin of your friend's wife . . ."

---

3   Please delete from final proofs (editorial note to the printer in bright red ink).

Eusebio suddenly stopped there, before completing his final thought, which he was just about to drag out from deep in his guts, from the sewer of his own soul, if you will.

"And . . . ?" Anagnostes gently urged him on.

"Listen: I never expected Stefano to find out, I never thought that Irene would find out, and I certainly didn't think everything was going to go to shit in the end. But I do know that neither of those reasons is a response to your question: why the hell did I do it? The truth is, I have but one answer . . . and unfortunately, it's not my own; it's an alternative explanation, if you like, one that my former colleague at Millard Fillmore, Tino (of course), gave me yesterday or the day before."

"I really don't see what your colleague has to do with this whole funeral of sorts."

"Look, it all happened because of a dream I've had on a number of occasions since Irene left me. And let me tell you this: It's the most horrifying dream I've ever had in my life."

"And what dream is that?" Tino asked me, *ipso facto*, eager to investigate, for the interpretation of dreams has been one of his favorite hobbies ever since his distant, boring childhood in Vigo, where it often rained cats and dogs all day long.

"In the middle of the night, I get out of bed where—like always—I'm sleeping with Irene. Some strange noise has woken me up. I leave the bedroom expecting something bad, something very bad. I walk down the darkened hallway and, finally, I'm standing in front of the sliding glass door that separates the dining room from the deck and backyard. There's a man standing out there, about my height, and his face is obscured, though it's because of the darkness and not because he's wearing some sort of mask. All of a sudden, this man bursts out laughing at me, guffawing like a madman, and he doesn't stop. And I still can't see his damn face. But what I can see is that one hand is tightly holding onto the hand of my daughter Dulce, as if he were about to escape with her, about to run off into the night. Then, suddenly, another peal of laughter breaks out, one that takes my breath away and sends shivers up and down my spine, just a few feet away from where they're standing. Then, mockingly, he cries out, "I raped her, I raped her," referring of course to my daughter, and the next thing I know, he leaps from the deck down into the yard and takes off, disappearing into the darkness. I run out to Dulce and embrace her, crying uncontrollably, terrified. That's when I wake up, crying just as compulsively . . . and when I open my eyes, I can see that Irene isn't there with me, because—and this is not part of my fucking dream—she has left me. The first time I had the nightmare, Reader, I was home alone, when the worst of the storm had blown over, or almost had, and when the pain and solitude were wreaking havoc on me . . . in other words, just recently; I mean, just yesterday and the day before that and three days ago and right this very moment, as I'm telling you about my misfortune so that perhaps you will be consoled in yours, Reader. But what does that dream mean? Who is that faceless man who came to my house to rape my little girl?"

Tino, with the same taciturn frown so common to the Galician, neither slowly nor sluggishly but rather intrepidly, in fact, beat Reader to the point, with tact and composure, and without a seed of doubt thanks to the experience he'd gained from interpreting hundreds of such dreams back in his native, rainy Vigo:

"It's you, Eusebio. How is it that you haven't figured that out? You are the man who entered the house and violated your little girl . . . symbolically, of course, since that girl wasn't actually a girl but rather your son Emilio. Do you understand? In your nightmare, you've interchanged your children by way of a verisimilar urge, because you've symbolically violated Emilio through your involvement with his best friend's mother, and this brings us back to what you already know: that ultimately, Emilio will never see Alessandra again, he'll never have a chance to play with his little friend, because the relationship between the two families has been shattered by your imbecility, and there's no way to go back and repair things after they've happened."

"But why me? Why the hell would you say that man is me . . . how could you possibly know?" Cardoso demanded, upset, his eyes inflamed, staring down the Galician without so much as a blink.

"I guess it's because you're inflicting this fucking punishment on your-self, Eusebio. Because you're deeply sorry, because you never would have imagined that this whole mess would come to pass, and because you're begging—begging as loud as you can—for redemption. In a way, you're begging Emilio to forgive you for taking away his little playmate, the one friend he grew up with all these years, ever since he was born, in fact, if memory serves."

Faced with this Freudian interpretation (which didn't allow for even the tiniest of rebuttal given the categorical tone of voice he used), the two of them fell silent . . . the three of them, in fact, Anagnostes in-cluded. Tino's words were harsh; almost as harsh and violent, in fact, as the recurring dream of the Professor of the Novel of the Mexican Revo-lution. In fact, Eusebio was covered in goose bumps, and the hairs on his forearms were standing on end like a hedgehog's spines or some sort of fuzzy caterpillar. He was suffering, alright. The poor guy was fucking suffering. But, at that very moment, the beautiful Nestis appeared again, this time with a pair overflowing dishes carried chest-high, which is to say, just at the level of her ample, luxurious, silicone breasts. She refilled their glasses (with wine, not milk) and floated off again, weightlessly, as if walking on air. No longer hungry, Eusebio started grudgingly cutting into his steak. He'd lost his appetite when he recalled (or relived) the nightmare, and during the Galician's twisted (though quite sensible and intuitive) interpretation. Anagnostes, however, dove right in to his steak tartare along with his salad, fries, and spicy Dijon mustard. It was then that Cardoso heard Tino's voice ring out from across the table:

"You know that I'm no moralist—less so than anybody, really—but why the hell would you get involved with the one woman on Earth whom you should have avoided? Fuck! Alessandra's mother and Irene's friend, but worse still, the wife of your friend and colleague Stefano, who also happened to be good friends with Porzia Fazzion, Chair of our Department. I really don't understand. I'm sorry, but you're a damn fool, Eusebio."

Waking up from his stupor or pit of despair, and lacking any desire to take a bite of his pepper-crusted filet mignon, the Mexican professor responded in a weak, wounded tone:

"You know, not long ago I read Coetzee's novel *Disgrace*. Are you familiar with it?"

"I read it a long time ago, yes."

"For me, it's one of the best works of friction of the entire twentieth century. As you'll recall, it involves David, a professor, who's found himself jobless after having an affair with a student. They gave him the opportunity to apologize for his actions, and therefore retain his position, but nevertheless, he chooses not to do so. He won't even make an attempt at contrition: he either can't or won't or something inexplicable is preventing him from doing it. Later, when a departmental committee (like the one those assholes at Millard Fillmore formed) asks him what motivated him to sleep with a student, David simply replies that it was Eros and nothing more. Just that. He says it plainly, without any added conditions or justifications, and he only offered that much because his colleagues and the committee that was going to decide his academic future had been hounding him for an answer—any answer—I suppose (and you probably know) because they were dying of curiosity to understand something that Ritter, a Germanophile through and through, once wisely dubbed the abyss of every human being."

"You're right. If I recall correctly, David attributes it to Eros," the Galician added from the other side of the table.

"Yes, that and only that. He had nothing else to add. I don't know whether it's because he didn't know what else to say, or because he definitively believed it was Eros that had pushed him to it. I really don't know. Coetzee has nothing to say about it; he offers no further clarifications."

"You know," interjected the man from Vigo after calmly considering David's enigmatic answer and Eusebio's words (while Anagnostes

266

gobbled down his steak tartare and French fries without coming up for air), ready to make a fundamental point, as if he were Empedocles or Xenophon himself. "David erred in his answer. He had it backwards. It wasn't Eros; it was Eris. Strife is what moved you, just as it moved David; discord, your infinite ability to boycott life. Discord, the thing that both you and Coetzee's character have carefully crafted with the skill of an artisan and a terrorist. And you know what else? I think it's about time you put a goddamn end to this drawn-out process of destruction. I'm serious. I'm telling you this because you're my fucking friend. And you can achieve that end without the need to punish yourself with that nightmare, which (from what you've told me) you've inflicted on yourself ever since Irene left you. *Disgrace*, like *Crime and Punishment* before it, is friction about redemption *par excellence*. You know that, right? Both tell a story about the sense of forgiveness or forgetfulness a man grants himself when he needs it most, when he's in it deeper than ever."

"But in both books, the protagonist pays a huge price in terms of merciless agony, remember?" Cardoso cut in before immediately falling silent again, considering the implications of his words, his own agony, his own personal cross. Quite honestly, he was exhausted. He took another drink. After a couple of minutes of silent camaraderie, he spoke up again, changing the subject and directing it this time at his revered dinner companion: "But you, Reader, do you honestly believe that Arturo betrayed you because Eros drove him to it, or was Eris pulling the strings there?"

Taken by surprise—and with a bite of raw, bloody beef halfway down his throat—Anagnostes responded as best he could:

"You should be answering that question instead of asking it, Eusebio. You're the one who wrote it."

"You know," he said, looking at his watch, his untouched plate of pepper-crusted steak in front of him. "We should get the check. We don't want to miss our flight . . ."

"Aren't you going to eat? I thought you were starving!"

"You know, I've lost my appetite." He suddenly turned to face Tino and said, disdainful and offended: "Look, Spaniard, if you're so hungry, why don't you help yourself to my steak . . . from that hangdog look on your face, a few bites might do you some good, *cabrón*."

"Look who's talking," replied the quiet man from Vigo. "When was the last time you looked in the mirror?"

Reader, meanwhile, had signaled to Nestis, who immediately floated, like Dumbo through the *aether* (though not by virtue of her two ears), over to the table where the three of them sat, plenty fed up. Without any elegant theatricality, Reader paid the check with his American Express card (don't leave home without it) and then he and Cardoso stood up, grasped their respective leather luggage, and bid a kind farewell to the Freudian Galician or his *daimon* before heading off down the concourse to their gate. It was six in the afternoon. Any moment now, they would be boarding.

6
(TUESDAY, MAY 30TH)

She was already one week late.

But it can't be, Matilde said to herself over and over as she squeezed her belly during that long weekend of unbearably stressful sleepless nights: *I can't be pregnant; it must be a tumor, or something else. I always assumed I was sterile. We'd been trying for six months . . . and nothing. Absolutely nothing.* Which is why, sick and tired of being exhausted, irritated, and anxious, she decided that first thing Monday morning she would call Doctor Lascurain, her gynecologist, having opted not to use those home pregnancy tests, with their dubious results. The secretary (or whomever it was who answered the phone on that tense morning) said that the doctor was on vacation and wouldn't be back for another three weeks. *How fucking convenient! Right when I need an answer the most!*

But there's nothing else you can do, the contrarian Maty said to herself, picking her way around the issue like a cat on a tightrope. And she was right: she wasn't about to trust any more home pregnancy tests. In order to be certain, she would have to wait and undergo a new test, because the last few she'd tried—for over a month now—hadn't clarified a damn thing. Yes, that's what she would do: as soon as she saw Dr. Lascurain, she would demand a sonogram and a definitive exam so she could learn once and for all whether or not she was fertile, whether or not she was pregnant, or whatever the hell it was that was going on inside her . . . that is, if there was even anything going on, because if there wasn't, she could happily denounce the Agro painter and his interpretation of her dream. Yes, she would wait for Lascurain. At least, that's what she planned to do on that Monday morning (the sixth day past her usual menstrual cycle) after saying good-bye to her husband with a kiss on the cheek, but in the end either curiosity or uneasiness won out (she was exhausted and bleary-eyed) and that Tuesday she decided not to go Arturo's studio, breaking their ritual date, the agonic friction of their hot, salivating bodies. Something (her feminine intuition, her paranoia, perhaps?) also told her that you, dear Reader, were suspicious, or that you were starting to get some sort of inkling: a scent, a stench, a tic, a moan, an attitude. Who knows? Something diaphanous and elusive . . . She preferred instead to stay home, fix a cup of Turkish coffee, and finally read the Vincenzo Herrasti biography of Empedocles that Arturo had loaned her, which she had put off time and again, never even imagining that the exact dates of Empedocles' birth and death were uncertain because Apollodorus of Athens situated his *floruit* in the 84th Olympiad (that is, between 444 and 440 B.C.) even though this period happens to coincide (just to be clear) with the founding of Turii, the resplendent city which, according to Glaucus of Reggio, the great philosopher himself visited during his life . . . Up to this point, frankly, she hadn't understood anything, and then, to make matters worse, according to Eusebius's chronology (which, of course, was relatively dubious) Empedocles first became known along with Parmenides in the 81st Olympiad (in other words, between 456 and 452 B.C.) and then, his prominence grew with Democritus in the 86th Olympiad (between 436 and 432 B.C.), at which point she finally took her first sip of sweetened coffee, hoping that it would help clarify the relationship between the years of the Olympiads and the philosopher from Agrigento, since according to the authority Neanthes of Cyzicus, Diogenes wrote that when signs of tyranny began to emerge in the tiny mountain town of Acragas, Empedocles persuaded his people to put aside their rivalries and instead adopt a democratic form of government, a move that soon won him a number of enemies, including the very same aristocrats who would end up ostracizing him at the end of his life. According to Diodorus, this had to have happened shortly after the overthrow of Thrasydaeus, son of Theron and the last tyrant of Acragas, during the year 472 B.C.; therefore, we cannot reach any conclusions beyond the fact that Empedocles' work took place between 477 and 434 B.C. Matilde was getting annoyed, but nevertheless she pressed on and read a little bit more about how, according to Theophrastus, Empedocles was an admirer of Parmenides and even imitated his poetry, though this doesn't necessarily imply that they were well known for their poetry, save for the fact that they both wrote in hexameter. *Hexameter? Theophrastus?* Empedocles paid special attention to Parmenides' work, and his later theory is, ultimately, a simple retort to his Eleatic master. According to Alcamenes, Empedocles was Parmenides' disciple at the same time as Zeno, and the *Souda* confirms that Melissus, Empedocles, and the perplexing Zeno were contemporaries. She yawned. The dates of Parmenides and Zeno could more or less be calculated from Plato's *Parmenides* dialogue, which establishes that the former was sixty-five years old and the latter was forty when they both met the young Socrates in Athens. She felt lost, overwhelmed, with a sort of incipient, acidic aftertaste in the back of her palate, but nevertheless she continued on, obstinately, since the majority of Hellenists are in agreement that the death of Socrates took place in 399 B.C., and if we factor in the fact that he was twenty years old at the time of their encounter, then Parmenides' birth would have been in 515 B.C. and Zeno's birth would have been in 490 B.C., which in turn supports the hypothesis that Empedocles was born some time between 495 and 490 B.C., and—above all—the claim by Aristotle who, according to Apollodorus, believed that Empedocles died at sixty years of age. *Enough, enough, I can't take it anymore,* she cried, feeling weary and beaten down. Her head was throbbing; she could save the rest for later, but . . . instead, the reliability of old Alcamenes, according to the established Diogenes, is called into question because once Empedocles leant an ear to Parmenides, the first thing he did was become a disciple of Anaxagoras and Pythagoras, imitating the former in terms of his psychology and the latter when it came to his refined manner of living, but above all, in his subsequent theory of the transmigration of the soul. She took another sip of her Turkish coffee. The panache—the outlandish accoutrements, ostentatious displays, and affected personality that Empedocles adopted—is in and of itself a tribute to the Anaxagorean influence, and then Maty really couldn't take it anymore and was temporarily overcome by a dizzy spell or a bit of gas, and meanwhile it's been said that Gorgias, the long-lived rhetorician, could have been a disciple of the philosopher from Acragas, and she rubbed her eyes bewilderedly. After finally concluding that Empedocles lived between 494 and 434 B.C., she tossed Herrasti's biography off to one side and, almost immediately, exasperated and tense, she opened her copy of *What to Expect When You're Expecting* and read the entire first chapter there, in one sitting. She'd just bought it the past Sunday at a used bookstore, and she was able to hide it quite well at the bottom of her crocodile skin Louis Vuitton bag. Of course, Matilde wouldn't want anybody to see her dragging around that extra weight, whether it was a tumor or some rare condition, some gastric problem that had already delayed her period for seven days. But be that as it may, the fact remains that you, illustrious Reader, still had no idea what was going on inside your wife; the fact remains that you still hadn't felt the little horns that were beginning to sprout like vine shoots at an alarming rate just above your temples, and all because of your lies, dear Reader, because you're a fucking liar and a son of a bitch to boot . . .

VII

Just as they were arriving at their gate, at the other end of the airport, they heard the voice of a ticket agent blaring on the public-address system, calling for one *Doctor Lascurain, Doctor Humberto Lascurain*, repeated the tired, irritated voice, *please check in at the counter, Doctor Lascurain* . . . Anagnostes and the professor watched as a tall and gangly man (who looked exactly like you'd expect a gynecologist to look) got up from his seat and approached the counter under the lighted display where the irritated ticket agent was standing. Eusebio, stupefied, turned to Anagnostes and said:

"Do you know who that is?"

"I have no idea."

"That's Humberto Lascurain."

"Of course it's Humberto Lascurain. I heard them call his name three times. I'm not deaf, you know."

"What I mean is that it's the same doctor who appears in *The Obstacles*."

"The obstacles to what?"

"No, not literal obstacles. I mean *The Obstacles*, the book I was telling you about. That friction where I learned about the existence of the secret little town we're headed to."

"I'm completely lost."

"At the beginning of that piece of friction, when Ricardo Urrutia is sick, a doctor named Lascurain shows up and prescribes him something to heal his ulcer. Lascurain's teeth were covered in a disgusting plaque, and his breath smelled like an onion. After that, he just disappears. He never appears in the book again."

"I still don't understand."

"That's got to be the same doctor. That's what I'm trying to explain," Eusebio said just as Humberto Lascurain happened to be passing by them on his way back from the counter toward a row of seats.

"The one from the book, you mean?"

"Yes, who else could it be? There can't be that many Humberto Lascurains in the world, especially one flying to La Paz, and a doctor to boot. Doesn't that seem just a little bit strange to you?"

"Well yes, a bit," Anagnostes nodded. "Why don't we go over there and ask him? That's the only way to know for sure . . ."

"Let's go."

They made their way, luggage in hand, over to the corner where Lascurain was sitting, reading a newspaper, and waiting for boarding to begin.

"Excuse me," Cardoso said as he leaned in a bit. "I couldn't help but hear that you are Doctor Humberto Lascurain."

"At your service," he replied, somehow managing to hide his disgust at being distracted from his paper for the second time.

"The thing is, well, it's just that my friend here and I . . ." explained Cardoso, a bit nervous, suddenly finding himself a little confused. "You see, we're not exactly going to La Paz."

"Ah, no?" the now-curious doctor replied. "Then you're at the wrong gate. This flight is going to La Paz. The woman at the counter just told me so."

"What my friend here is trying to say," Reader intervened, clarifying the situation, "is that La Paz isn't our final destination. It's somewhere else. A place called Las Rémoras, to be precise. I understand it's a little town on the coast not far from the state capital, right?"

At that, Lascurain's jaw dropped. He rolled up his paper and looked at the two men, stupefied. They now had his full attention.

"Yes, I happen to be heading there myself . . ."

"The problem is," Cardoso explained, "that, unless I'm mistaken, it doesn't actually appear anywhere . . ."

"That's true, it's not listed on any map." As Lascurain spoke, an odorous wave of the smell of fried onions escaped from his mouth. The same onions, perhaps, as in the previous friction? Good God . . .

"Just a slight problem, right?" Reader said, a malevolent smile on his face.

"May I ask why you're traveling to such a remote place, doctor?" the professor cut in.

"It's a bit complicated . . ."

"Don't worry, you don't need to explain anything to us," said Anagnostes, not wanting to bury the good doctor under a mountain of ridiculous questions, and eager to go back to his own chair. But nevertheless, the doctor continued:

"No, it's not a problem at all. I'd be happy to explain, but please, have a seat. It looks like we're going to have a bit of a delay, anyway, from what the young lady at the counter told me."

He didn't have to ask them twice. Eusebio and Anagnostes sat down next to him, apparently unconcerned with the inconvenience of a delay. Then, Lascurain ventured a question of his own:

"So, what are your names?"

"Eusebio Cardoso, at your service," said the professor, offering a firm handshake.

"Anagnostes," Reader said, in Greek, also extending his hand.

"What a strange name," Lascurain said, though he immediately apologized. "Forgive me; it's just that I've never heard it before."

"It's quite alright," he replied, in English.

"Anagnostes what?"

"Anagnostes Leser," Reader replied, this time in German. "But I just go by Anagnostes."

"Pleased to meet you," said the gynecologist, and—not wanting to delay the issue with further introductions—he then moved on to his explanation: "Well, it all began when the son of a good friend of mine ran away from home some nine or ten months ago, without warning and without any indication of when he might return. Apparently the death of his father (whom I also knew quite well) had affected him so deeply that he ended up in bed with a very high fever. That was the last time I saw the boy: when Helena, his mother, desperately called me one August night (if memory serves) and begged me to come visit him."

"And . . . ?" said Eusebio, who was on the verge of adding, *I already know all that, doctor, I read the book, so please, just get to the point. I know that friction like the back of my hand.*

"The fact is that, a few days after I saw him, the boy took off without a trace, without telling anyone where he was going . . . Since then, nobody has heard anything from him, not even his neighbor, Laila, a very beautiful young girl who was quite taken with him."

"If you don't mind me asking, what does Ricardo's disappearance have to do with this trip you're taking?" interrupted Reader, who evidently wasn't following the intricate threads that Eusebio, the experienced connoisseur of *The Obstacles*, was weaving together in his head as he listened to Lascurain's story. The doctor's response made it clear to Cardoso that he himself didn't have all the facts, no matter how many times he had read about that odd, ornate little town. The doctor continued:

"This is where everything gets complicated, my friend, because just a few days ago—yes, five or six days ago, and by pure, random chance—I learned that Ricardo, my friend Helena's son, either was or is, in Baja California Sur . . . and, as it just so happens, in the very same town that the three of us are headed to now."

"How did you find out?" Cardoso asked, truly fascinated.

"You see, among my many responsibilities, I happen to make regular visits to a half dozen quality brothels . . ." The doctor emphasized the word "quality" while simultaneously flashing a broad, wolfish smile that reeked of moldy onions. "As I'm sure you both can imagine, it's important to verify that the girls offering their services aren't—how can I put it?—carrying a disease they could pass on to their clients. Are you following me?"

"Of course," Reader replied.

"So, like I said, it was only by chance that—while making my standard rounds through the city's red light district—I met a beautiful young woman who also knew Ricardo. Her name is Roberta, and the poor girl's got a young son she has to carry everywhere she goes. She told me that she met Helena's son in La Paz some months back, and according to what she said, he was heading to Las Rémoras, the very same town in Baja California Sur from which she had fled. Yes, that's what she said, she'd fled from some boyfriend who simply wouldn't leave her alone and who seemed to have gone completely insane."

"Was it Elías?" Eusebio asked.

"Why yes, how did you happen to know?"

"That, too, is a bit complicated, doctor," replied Eusebio. "But, don't let me interrupt you. Please continue. This is all quite fascinating. More than you might imagine."

Without pressing more for details about how he knew this, the doctor continued telling his story and spewing forth his horrible, fried onion breath:

"Well, during my visit to the brothel, I discovered that the girl . . ."

"Roberta?" asked Reader, confused.

"Yes, Roberta . . . she had a very uncommon venereal disease; in fact, it's extremely rare. Hers is only the third case I've come across in twenty-five years of practicing medicine. It's a form of syphilis commonly known as 'lover's rage,' and it occasionally—though not always—manifests itself in a sort of frenzy or impassioned delirium that drives lovers to commit acts that are truly *in extremis*."

"I understand," Eusebio said, tying it all together, holding his breath in anticipation of the invaluable news Humberto Lascurain was about to provide.

"Of course, there was no way for Roberta to have known this, and therefore she never even considered the possibility that she, the poor girl, had actually been the cause of the 'lover's rage' afflicting her boyfriend."

"You mean Elías?" Reader asked, still confused, though only because he hadn't already read *The Obstacles* himself.

"Yes, Elías," Cardoso said curtly, irritated with Reader. Then he turned back to Humberto Lascurain. "And . . . ?"

"And that's it. That's all there is," he replied through his all-too-visibly incrusted teeth. "I just told Ricardo's mother Helena, and that's why I'm here now, trying to be of some help to my old friend, trying to discover the whereabouts of her only child, her missing son. You see, she's a widow, and doesn't have anyone else."

"How are you going to go about finding this town?" asked Anagnostes.

"Honestly, I have no idea," was his categorical reply. "I'm caught up in the middle of all this mess, and right now I need to figure out a way to resolve it."

"Clearly."

"In fact, it's a bit encouraging to learn that I'm not the only one headed for Las Rémoras today."

"I suppose you're not . . ." Anagnostes said, right when the same tiresome, irritating voice of that disgruntled ticket agent came blaring over the P.A. system, advising the passengers to line up in such-and-such a way at the gate, because boarding was about to begin. The three travelers checked their boarding passes and got in line, luggage in hand, ready to embark on their journey. Just before heading down the jetway, Eusebio gently tugged at Reader's coat, pulled him off to the side of the line, and said, suddenly, carelessly, with a touch of treachery or slander in his voice:

"I think it's better that I tell you this now, rather than later."

"Tell me what?" Reader asked, taken aback, still standing there alongside the line of passengers boarding the plane.

"Apparently Matilde is pregnant."

Staggering and trying to recover from the blow, which had clearly rung a resounding bell deep inside of him, Anagnostes could barely whisper, whimpering like a girl:

"Who's the father?"

"I don't know."

"How could you not know?" he exclaimed, now irate. "You wrote it, Cardoso. You're the one writing all this shit. How could you possibly not know?"

Feeling insulted and offended by the implications of Reader's questions, Eusebio angrily replied:

"Hey, if it's all just shit, then why are you still reading it?"

8

(THURSDAY, JUNE 1ST)

"When my father arrived in England in the summer of 1969, ready to matriculate at the London School of Economics and begin his first semester studying philosophy, logic, and the scientific method with his beloved professor, he was struck with an incredibly bitter and painful surprise: that very year, just a month before he arrived, in fact, the renowned Karl Popper—the man for whom he had traveled to the other side of the Atlantic, to that wasteland of incessant rain—had retired, never again to teach philosophy. While initially this was a slap in the face and a serious inconvenience for Roberto Soto Gariglietti, who had gone to England excited and hungry for knowledge, in the end it wasn't quite so bad, for—as luck would have it—he did get to meet the man and eventually became one of his dearest friends and protégés, one of the select few companions who was invited to his apartment on Abbey Road for tea and ginger biscuits on Thursday afternoons, and sometimes even on Monday and Tuesday as well, just the two of them, debating matters of Greek philosophy in that *lingua franca* (English, that is), which wasn't the native language of either of them. In fact—did you know this, Maty?—they became quite good friends, despite their difference in age. Popper would have been in his late sixties, while my father was about to turn thirty. By time Popper had departed from the subjects of his early works—especially the one that first garnered him fame, *The Open Society and Its Enemies*—and was devoting all his time to the study of his true passion: pre-Socratic philosophy. Apart from Xenophanes and Heraclitus, about whom he wrote a thing here and there, his true idol and primary subject of study until the end of his life was Parmenides of Elea, whom he saw as the first great rationalist thinker in Western History, the first great logician, and the kind of man he himself was (or wanted to be) throughout his entire life: a critic of the idea, someone who fought against the current. To better understand the attitude or mentality that my father was developing during the five or six years he spent at the professor's side, you should remember one very important point, Matilde: without Parmenides and his theory of the universe, the Atomists never would have existed, nor would their opponents, who were devoted to refuting them, and without them, modern physics wouldn't exist, or at least physics as it was understood up until the days of Newton and Kepler . . ." Arturo paused here for just a moment before continuing excitedly: "In any case, the bridge—the transition between Parmenides and his disciple Zeno on the one hand, and between Democritus and Leucippus, the Atomists, on the other—is none other than the very man I've been telling you about all this time: Empedocles of Agrigento, who was, of course, a bit younger than Parmenides, about the same age as Zeno, the aphorist and prominent defender of his Eleatic master. Can you see how all these threads come together? Do you see the close relationship, the concentration of facts which, bit by bit and almost unconsciously, formed the framework in my father's young mind when he arrived in London at the height of Beatlemania and Vietnam?"

"I think so," Matilde stammered, feeling crushed under the sheer weight of all that information, unsure whether she could support it. "I don't know. I'm still a bit confused. There are just so many names . . ."

Without paying her even a modicum of attention, the Agro painter hopped on his high horse and continued his afternoon lecture at full gallop:

"In the famous poem where Parmenides describes his irreverent theory of the cosmos, the goddess Dikē reveals herself to the philosopher and informs him that she will tell him the whole truth about all that exists: about the world of reality and about the nature of things in and of themselves. The first part of the poem's revelation is known as the *Way of Truth* because it's the truth and nothing but the truth that's being narrated, that's in play. In the second part of the poem, the goddess speaks about the world of appearances, about the deceptive, false world of mortals. Nevertheless, at the beginning of the second part, Dikē warns Parmenides that from that moment onward, his words—although true—will no longer be true and will instead be fraudulent, pure conjectures, *doxa*. From that point on is the second part, which is known today as the *Way of Opinion*. As you might have guessed, this strange division creates, in and of itself, an unsolvable problem. In other words, the first question that jumps out at us is why the hell do we need to offer a true explanation of the universe if a false definition is subsequently offered? What's the sense of it, if we already have the true explanation? Why even offer a false explanation when the true one is already out there?"

"Exactly," Roberto replied, animated, stroking his thin Mexican moustache with one hand while holding a ginger biscuit in the cold, tumescent fingers of his other hand. "That's the question that's been bothering me, Karl, ever since I first read the poem many years ago."

"Let's take it one step at a time, Roberto. The goddess has promised to tell him the truth, and she did so in the first part, yes? Now, the very next thing she does is advise him that her subsequent explanation of the world, the one that arises from error and consists of illusions, will be very deceptive and appear quite similar to the truth, because it will become apparent how it arose almost logically from what was a simple, fundamental error. To begin with, Parmenides understands the difficult task of refuting the question of change—Heraclitus's problem of inherited change—and applies his own predecessor's argument, which states in quite a definitive manner (as you know) that 'all things are one.'"

"Yes, I remember. That sort of refutation is known as a *reductio ad absurdum.*"

"Correct," Karl replied, without touching the tiny cup of hot tea that the Jamaican maid had just served him. "In other words, Parmenides argues that if, as Heraclitus asserts, a) the universe truly exists, and b) if this is a reality, then change is essentially a paradox. There can be no change. You see? Reality is one, as Heraclitus has already determined."

"No," Maty said, her mini tape recorder still in hand. "I don't see. I don't understand."

"Look at it this way: how is change possible? How is it logically possible? How can something change without losing its identity? If it continues being the same, then it is not the thing that has changed."

"That happens, Karl, and you know it does, because for Heraclitus there is only change," interrupted Arturo's father, still holding his tiny cup of tea while the London rain outside prolonged the discussion that gray, early-April afternoon. "For Heraclitus, there are no things, only processes, transformations, like fire, like flames . . ."

"Exactly, Roberto. For Parmenides, the Heraclitus solution was logically inadmissible. For the Eleatics, there is no change, because it is patently and necessarily paradoxical. Change is an illusion of the senses: things may appear to have changed, yes, but in truth they haven't. To move from that logical premise or *reductio ad absurdum* to his later concept of the universe as a sort of inalterable, immobile, and eternal block takes only a small step, one which I think you're already beginning to glimpse, no? Look, Parmenides' deductive proof can be summed up more or less thusly: if only that which is can be true (as Heraclitus states), then that which does not exist cannot be. In other words, the 'nonexistent' is impossible; nothingness cannot, by definition, exist . . . we can agree on that, at least, correct?"

"That much is clear; at least, I think so," Maty mused, uncertain, though engrossed and intrigued. "That which is, is, and that which is not, isn't."

"Exactly. So everything is composed of what exists. Everything is continuous and is One. Everything that is exists everywhere, in perfect contact with everything else that exists. There are no pores, there is no discontinuity, no space, no emptiness. Ultimately, the universe is an eternal block, an undifferentiated unity, a *plenum*: it is One, it is the same (*homoiconic*), and it is indivisible. As you well know, this takes us to an irrefutable conclusion: if that which exists—the cosmos—is perfectly immobile, comprised entirely of itself, then movement is also impossible, since there is no direction to turn, no space to extend into, no place for change to occur. Everything is full. Everything is complete."

"But we now know that isn't true, Karl. We know that there are pores, there is emptiness between one space and another."

"Of course we know that, thanks in part to Leucippus and Democritus, and, of course, thanks to twenty-four centuries of scientific advances, but remember that they, the Atomists, were refuting a genius, Parmenides, and they only did so based on their experience. They were not logical, they weren't empirical; their method was axiomatic, and they operated with unproven suppositions. Leucippus and Democritus were guided by the one thing that Parmenides said we should never hold up as our guide: our senses. For this reason—as paradoxical as it may seem—without the scandalous cosmology of Parmenides, the Atomists would never have existed, and without the obstinate Atomists, physics as a science wouldn't have evolved until the arrival of Newton and Kepler, and without them (and Galileo and Copernicus, of course) we wouldn't have modern physics, quantum physics . . . we would be stuck in prehistory. Basically, Democritus adduced that the impossibility of movement was itself false, since motion does indeed exist; therefore, it is likewise false that the world consists of one single, invariable, immovable block. As such, it must instead consist of many things, many small corporeal blocks that are or must be invisible; in other words, an eternity of atoms. If the existence of the self-filled, self-complete *plenum* is false, *ergo* emptiness must exist through the force of pores, even if we cannot see them."

"So in conclusion, the nonexistent emptiness does indeed exist . . ." interrupted Maty, who was beginning to grasp the essence of the explanation.

"Right. Of course emptiness exists. But the Atomists couldn't know that; they could only suppose it. Nevertheless, this supposition would go on to revolutionize physics and the natural sciences, even in modern times, you know? Without Parmenides and his innovative theory of the universe, there would be no Einstein, no Schrödinger, no Planck, no Niels Böhr, no nothing."

"Excuse me, Arturo, but I'm getting a little queasy . . ."

". . . Maybe it's because you're pregnant," added the painter, pulling her towards him in an embrace, who knows whether he was being playful or maybe even getting angry at having been suddenly interrupted by your wife.

"I already told you that I'm not pregnant, so you can stop making jokes about it."

Popper crossed his legs and said to Matilde:

"In any case, I told you as soon as you got here that for me, ultimately, Parmenides felt and even admitted the need to justify himself, remember? And that's exactly what he did with the second part of his great poem, the *Way of Opinion*, even though it was patently unnecessary to do so once the goddess had revealed the truth to him. I believe that psychologically, and after turning the matter over and over in his head, Parmenides ultimately felt a sort of burning, implacable need to justify himself, you know? He intuited that, despite everything, there was an infinitesimal but extant weakness in his *Way of Truth*, despite the fact that it was perfectly irrefutable and incontrovertible (at least, logically incontrovertible). I can see no other motive that would have driven him to draw up that second part, other than the fact that, by explaining the conjectural and false universe, he would be eliminating it. Something like that, like the titanic creation of a cosmos, when fundamentally he was only trying to demonstrate the deceptive nature of that cosmos, the illusory nature of the world that we accept, out of habit, as reality."

"Sort of like what happens in 'The Aleph,' where a man called Carlos Argentino Daneri sets about writing a long, meticulous poem that contains the entire history and geography of the world."

"And who wrote 'The Aleph'?"

"Borges."

"Borges?"

"Yes, Karl . . . Jorge Luis Borges, who more or less did the same thing as Parmenides with a number of his stories, by which I mean that he strives to create logical worlds which he nevertheless knows do not exist . . . At one point, he even calls them 'false consolations' because he insists on divesting them of time, movement, and sometimes even of space and the *ego*, as if none of these actually existed. But if that's the case, then why go ahead and demonstrate that it does exist? Why endeavor to recreate the impossible in such painstaking detail?"

"Exactly: it's a paradox, an effort that appears to be in vain," Karl replied, quite intrigued, taking a sip from his tea, which was now almost ice-cold. "I've never heard of that book, but I would like to read it."

"I'll bring you his book on Tuesday when we see each other again, Maty."

"Thanks. Anyway, getting back to the point," said Popper, "what I've been wanting to tell you since the beginning is that this great intellectual failure ultimately shines an immense amount of light on the genius of Parmenides and his poem, a light that no historian or critic I'm aware of has paid much attention to."

"What are you referring to?"

"To the fact that *Way of Opinion*—as unnecessary and ineffective as it may seem—demonstrates that Parmenides was less dogmatic and much more self-critical than we've been led to believe. That's why, for me, this Eleatic is the first great Western rationalist. He was the first to believe in the use of critical reason, logical argumentation, and above all, most importantly, he was the first realist in history."

"A realist? That's completely ridiculous, Karl. How can you sit there and tell me that Parmenides was a realist?"

"He was, like me, a recalcitrant realist inasmuch as neither of us is interested in ideas per se (though we do adore them, for they inspire us to continue formulating theories of the universe); what really moves us is the desire to learn something about the world, something unprecedented in the cosmos and nature. No matter how much knowledge we've gained and how many theories we've produced, it's always conjectural, and no matter how much we know in advance, we will never actually reach the truth."

"Maybe you're just a skeptic, Karl."

"No, I don't think so, Roberto. Otherwise, I wouldn't seek out answers, I wouldn't investigate. Skeptics give up. I don't," Popper said firmly, though without changing his inalterable tone of voice. "Rather, I'm on the side of Xenophanes, who was convinced that we will never be able to achieve truth . . . as he said, some 2500 years ago: 'as for certain truth, no man has known it, nor will he know it; neither of the gods, nor yet of all the things of which I speak. And even if by chance he were to utter the final truth, he would himself not know it; for all is but a woven web of guesses.'"

Matilde was struck silent for a long, thoughtful moment as she brooded over that apothegm. Arturo asked her to move to one side a little, so he could light up another cigarette.

"Look . . . it doesn't matter that ultimately we never discover truth. What's important is the intellectual exercise, the critical exercise, the exploration of the boundaries of science, the rebuttal of all theory, and debating without compromise. And perhaps, one day, we will unwittingly approach the solution . . . if there is one, or ever was."

"And Empedocles?" Matide cut in suddenly, still unsure about the supposed relationship between the two thinkers, despite having gathered (or so she believed) the importance Parmenides holds for the philosophical development of science. "What does Empedocles have to do with all this you're telling me?"

"It has to do with the fact that Empedocles was not a rationalist, Roberto. Empedocles was not a typical thinker for his day. A *démodé* thinker, you might say. Something of a romantic in a time of Enlightenment."

"If he wasn't a rationalist, Karl, then he certainly was a realist. That being, of course, according to your own notion of realism."

"That much we can agree on, Roberto, but for me Empedocles was, above all, a mystagogue, a mystic, like my great old friend Ludwig Wittgenstein."

"What are you talking about?" stammered the Mexican, impatiently plucking at his black moustache. "A mystagogue . . . the champion of democracy in ancient Greece? A magician . . . the same aristocrat who turned down the crown after having abolished the oligarchical Assembly of the Thousand? A poor old mystic who maintained, throughout his life, an ideal of political fairness unlike any other in history?" Roberto exclaimed, leaping from his rather uncomfortable chair, a bit irritated with his mentor's sarcastic commentary. "A magician? Really? The founder of Sicilian medicine and the man whom Galen, Philistion, and Hippocrates revered as their master, their precursor?"

"Empedocles, a doctor? Don't try to sell me that line. He was more of a healer . . ." Popper laughed, looking out the window of his flat. The rain was getting worse outside, which meant he couldn't throw out his young disciple, and instead would have to see this dull discussion to its completion. "Reviving the dead, channeling and controlling the wind, proffering funds to the poor citizens of Agrigento . . . is that what you're talking about, Roberto? A champion of democracy while at the same time being anointed as the Savior of Agrigento? Excuse me, but no, it's a huge leap—an abyss, even—from being a pure-and-simple rationalist like Parmenides managed to be and the pseudo-Orphean religious puppet that Empedocles became at the end of his life, especially when he wrote that nonsensical collection of rituals that make up his Pythagorean *Purifications* . . ."

Roberto had clenched his jaw, irate at the sarcasm: certainly Popper had no idea about how important it was to him and his grandfather Enzo—not to mention all the people of Italy, Sicily, Mexico—to hold up the majestic, illustrious figure of Empedocles, the brilliant philosopher of cosmic cycles, the Leonardo da Vinci of antiquity, the man whom Renan called the Newton of his day, whom Matthew Arnold, Eliot, Hölderlin, Nietzsche, Romain Rolland, Brecht, Juan Gil-Albert, and Carroll admired with true *ekstasis*. He took a deep breath and responded to the Austrian with a vast and ferocious knowledge of the subject:

"A mystagogue, a puppet, a healer, you say? When he was the only man to describe the circulation of blood and the invisible respiration through pores two thousand years before such things were discovered? Empedocles was the first person in the history of biology to identify similar organs in different species of animals. He was the true founder of what's called comparative morphology. Perhaps you knew that? He was the first person to deduce, via an autopsy of a pregnant woman, that the embryo takes on a different form after the forty-ninth day, which isn't far from the truth. He also deduced that children take their resemblances from the dominant qualities of the father's sperm or the mother's ovum. He maintained that plants sustain themselves as much through the leaves in the air as with their roots in the soil. Theophrastus and Aristotle, who came after him and between them had only half his genius, ridiculed him whenever they could, adducing that it was absurd to believe in such things, Karl, when today—quite to the contrary—any six-year-old kid walking down the street knows he was right, and that that's how plants really function. And to make matters worse, as Lambridis says, every time Aristotle diminishes his predecessor, he's simply compounding his error, because those unpopular theories have now been vindicated by modern science. And if that weren't enough, getting back to the issue incumbent upon us—the question of philosophy— Empedocles was the first to refute the principle of immobility; it was he who intuited the transformation of matter; nobody else at the time understood that the universe was constantly changing, and changing in an infinite number of ways through the *archē*, and it was his brilliant intuition that there are four universal roots, not to mention the two forces that drive the expansion and contraction of the universe, Eris and Eros . . ."

"Of course, Roberto, but those are pure intuitions, *noesis*, that you're talking about. Not logical deductions . . ."

"Empedocles anticipated that porosity, Karl, and beyond that, he intuited that every thing—every corporeal object—had a different, specific porosity, a sort of emptiness, and although he was never able to divine the atom, Leucippus and Democritus did just that shortly after him. Still, though, we should consider it significant that he discovered divisibility and verified movement, which your crazy idol Parmenides had denied. Those aren't the accomplishments of a mystagogue or a puppet . . ." Roberto paused here, setting up an emphatic, conclusive blow: "And if all that isn't enough to convince you, he also discovered the fact that like attracts like . . ."

"I know, I know."

"You know or you understand?"

"Of course I understand . . ."

"And that's why we're here, lying down, naked, and alike, Matilde . . ." Artuo said, cigarette still in hand, excited by the blue smoke and once again mad with desire for the dark-skinned body of that beautiful woman, the young and (probably) pregnant wife of his friend, Reader, your lovely bride, don't forget it, learn it and repeat it to yourself. "That's why we're together: because like attracts like, happiness attracts happiness, and flesh attracts the flesh, yes, through the exquisite symmetry of our pores."

"Fine, fine . . ." Matilde interrupted, a bit exasperated, before asking, "And after all this, where is Tamara? Does she even exist?"

"Yes, that's why we're here, Roberto, taking our tea and ginger biscuits, debating, sharing our ideas, our points of view, a beloved young Mexican and a tired old Austrian. Otherwise . . ."

"Roberto, my father, wasn't listening anymore. He didn't want to listen anymore, Maty. He spun around, bumping into the Jamaican housekeeper, and blew out of there like a sad and angry storm. He was thirty-some years old, and on that torrential afternoon, he chose his path. Disconcerted, Popper could only watch through the window as his young friend walked away under the London rain without having said good-bye, never to return, never quite sure as to why his dear disciple, the young Mexican philosopher, had suddenly flown into such a rage and left, snorting like an angry goat." Arturo stopped short and simply said, almost sullen, sunk in his own thoughts, "Tamara, you say? She's on a trip, Maty. A long trip . . . and you know what? I've never shared the symmetry of the pores with her. So don't you worry."

IX

"Reader, if you don't mind, I'd like to recite a poem I wrote for Irene a few days ago."

Emerging from his daze or what almost seemed like a cloudy, aerial stupor—perhaps due to the monotonous drone of the gigantic engine turbines—Reader wearily replied, without much interest:

"Go ahead."

Anagnostes immediately drew the shade on the window, blocking out the harsh clamor of blinding light, and indulgently added, out of pure courtesy:

"What's the poem called, if you don't mind my asking?"

"'The Custom,' Eusebio replied, a bit ashamed. He wasn't the type of person who enjoyed reading his own poetry, but this one in particular had been gnawing at him ever since he wrote it. According to him, he was drawing on his sense of pain, loss, and above all, he was trying to address the eternal question of love . . . but what fucking poem ever written didn't attempt to do that?

"'The Custom,' eh?" Anagnostes repeated. "Please, read it."

Cardoso cleared his throat, unfolded the small scrap of paper on which he'd written the poem, and began to recite it right there, in the seat next to Anagnostes, his voice low and discreet, not wanting the other passengers to hear him:

> *As if something were being built . . .*
> *Without my even realizing it,*
> *Since the day I saw you,*
> *The custom of your skin was also built,*
> *The routine of my veins mingling,*
> *Melding with your veins, your flesh,*
> *Alongside your soul,*
> *And the blind habit for your waist.*
> *But perhaps love is a habit as well?*
> *Perhaps what we go in search of every day*
> *Is not just the memory of the skin,*
> *The omen of the skin's satin color,*
> *The custom of my arms extending*
> *And trying*
> *Incomprehensibly*
> *To take hold of you or your fecund being,*
> *For a moment or two or three or four*
> *Which then convert*
> *Into what*
> *We customarily call*
> *"Forever?"*

When he finished, and before Reader could express his admiration, they heard the childlike voice of the flight attendant announcing their descent into La Paz International Airport. At the end of this announcement, the bitchy, in-flight maid casually added, as if an afterthought:

"Those passengers looking to make the connecting flight to Las Rémoras, please proceed to Gate 64D, and thank you for flying Baja Airlines, the airline that's always taking you higher . . ."

A moment later, after noting the oxymoronic comment made by the poor flight attendant, Anagnostes remarked:

"I didn't know you were also a poet, Eusebio. I thought you were a professor who taught the Novel of the Mexican Revolution and *ce tout*. In fact, I must confess that I enjoy your poetry more than your truculent stories of sex and coprophilia."

"Are you talking about the sect back in Highpoint?"

"Of course, what else would I be referring to?"

"How the hell do you know about that?"

"Because of *Friction*. I haven't been able to put it down."

At that moment, the plane began its slow descent into La Paz, and the divine light of Apollo entered into both their *psychēs* as if it were lightning falling from the heavens.

10
(TUESDAY, JUNE 6TH)

"So what happened next? What became of your father after he walked out on Popper and the London School of Economics?" Matilde asked, continuing her interview with the painter, in earnest, now desperate to pick up the threads, eager to get back into the time and place inhabited by Soto Gariglietti, the subject of her thesis, of course, and her reason for being there . . . stretched out with the Agro painter, betraying her husband, and probably pregnant besides (Pregnant? Fuck!), but how was she supposed to find out now? That worthless doctor, Lascurain, wouldn't be back for another two weeks, and the blood—the goddamn blood—still hadn't appeared. Fourteen days, and no blood, not even a drop.

"Well, there were a number of gaps and complications that came up after that, and I don't always try to fill them in for fear of getting something wrong. But if you want, I'll try. I can fill in what pieces I know . . . more or less."

"What are you talking about?" said Maty, as she stopped caviling about becoming a mother for a moment and held out her recorder towards the painter's lips.

"Nobody knows—not even my mother, who was still with him at the time—exactly what had become of him, or why he joined Greenpeace in 1983."

"Greenpeace? Really?" Maty exclaimed.

"Yes," Arturo confirmed, evidently not joking. He brushed off an unfinished canvas (still fresh, as evidenced by the colors it left on his hands) and placed it between his long, hairy legs. "I'll try to summarize it for you. After he retuned to Mexico in '74 or '75, there was something different about him, a restlessness that never left him in peace, an irritation that prevented him from living and kept him in a permanent state of uneasiness, both day and night. I know he started writing at that time, and he even published a number of essays in various magazines, some of which you're already familiar with. Reading Rawls, Weber, Popper, Wittgenstein, Spinoza, Marcuse, Camus, Bobbio, Keynes, Vargas Llosa, and Eliade, among others, transformed him. But above all, it was the pre-Socratic philosophers and studies on them, as I've already mentioned. Still nothing on politics; at least, not in an active, committed manner, like he would in the late 1980s and beyond. So, a few months after returning to Mexico City, having spent the past five years in the world of objective logic and epistemological problems, he had some of the craziest ideas you can imagine floating around in his head . . ."

"Greenpeace?"

"No, that was seven years later, Maty. In '83."

"What, then?"

"Look, in order for you to believe me and to understand his madness—his newly acquired madness—you have to keep two very important things in mind. First, there's his money; well, his parents' money, the millions of dollars and the level of comfort that fortune had always afforded him. They were extremely wealthy. He was always very well provided for, and never lacked any amenities. He could do whatever he wanted. He could study or not study, change careers, work or not work, travel, squander his money, or simply just sit around at home. It made no difference. His family's fortune allowed him to do whatever his heart desired . . ."

"Yes, you already told me that, Arturo. You already explained how wealthy they were, and how you and your mother would later spend what money remained from that fortune . . . so what's the other thing?" Matilde insisted, spurring him on like a determined, diligent student. "You said there were two things I had to be aware of before we got down to the matter at hand. So . . . ?"

The Agro painter answered with a question of his own:

"Do you remember the first couple times you came to see me? One of those first interviews?"

"I don't know specifically which one you're referring to, Arturo. There were a lot."

"When I told you about my first memory . . ."

"Ah, yes . . . with the other children in the San Nicolás neighborhood, right?"

"Yes, all of us piled into that truck . . ."

"Heading to the store to buy toys for everyone . . ."

"Yes . . ." Arturo confirmed as he slid his hand through your wife's dark hair, Reader, turning her around on the sofa just slightly so he could touch her more easily, stroke her more gently, this beautiful woman of yours, as fragile and vulnerable as all women are in their first or second month of pregnancy, when the bump in the belly is still barely even perceptible.

"And?" Matilde pressed, serious and tremulous, allowing herself to be caressed, letting herself be taken over by history, by the central figure of her thesis.

"Well, as you've probably guessed by now, Soto Gariglietti was clearly tremendously interested in the future of Mexican children: in impoverished children, those disinherited from the Earth, the abused, the orphans, those who never had nor ever would have any opportunities whatsoever. He believed those children were the source of everything else, the source of this shitty country's past and future: its prosperity or perdition, its strength or stagnancy, its development or degradation. So it all had to begin somewhere, and he always believed it was there, with the children (especially indigenous children), that it would happen. But how? That he didn't know. He had to find out, of course; he had to figure out how to take that first definitive step, and the opportunity came (almost by chance) when he took a five-month trip to Oaxaca, Tabasco, and Chiapas with his friend, Jack, a millionaire from California. In fact, it was originally supposed to be something of a vacation: you know, one of those anthropological tours to see the pyramids along the Mayan Riviera: Palenque, Monte Albán, Chichén Itzá, Bonampak, Yaxchilán . . . all those remote places in the jungles of the Mexican Southeast. But the trip was extended beyond their original itinerary. They were both fascinated by the pre-Columbian rituals, which my father would later hybridize with other rituals and include in his political rallies . . . a true spectacle and a sight to behold, if ever there was one. There, in the Southeast, he learned the techniques of Mayan witchcraft, the celebrated cleansings with eggs and branches, the curative powers of herbs, rites performed with copal or *pom*, the oration performed in any alveolus of the Earth that he found: cracks, caves, ditches, cenotes, wells, hollows in the trees; the ritualistic dances, saluting the four cardinal points—which, according to him, corresponded to the four *archai*: Zeus, Hera, Nestis, and Aidoneus were Quetzalcóatl, Tezcatlipoca, Huitzilopochtli and Chalchiuhtlicue (or Tláloc) respectively—with the conch shell he always carried with him; the releasing of iguanas and quetzals, along with many other customs of the Nahuas, Zapotecs, Chontals, Lacondons, Tzotzils, and Mayas, all of them interwoven. Oaxaca is also where he became a vegetarian, began fasting, engaged in Empedoclean rituals of purification and abstruse sexual abstinence . . . although this last one,

I must say, he didn't exactly fulfill, because if he had, he wouldn't have married my mother and I would never have been born."

Arturo could only laugh as he related this last little bit of his father's outlandish story. He couldn't help but laugh—even when the words came from his own mouth—whenever someone described the adventures and vicissitudes of his father, especially the ones regarding his sexual abstinence. Nevertheless, when he turned ever so slightly, Maty jammed her mini tape recorder back towards his mouth, urging him to continue.

"And what happened next?"

The Agro painter recomposed himself and continued, absorbed, spellbound, entranced:

"Look, just to make it clear to you once and for all: my father was not one of those retrograde leftists and so-called liberals who do nothing more than gripe and complain about everything without offering any sort of remedy; leftists are, at their heart, whether they know it or not, more dogmatic and orthodox than a rabbi, and they label everyone who thinks differently from them a conservative. But listen, my father wasn't a right-wing reactionary either. He never affiliated himself with the PAN or the PRI or least of all the PRD. His message or philosophy, if you want to call it that, was essentially anti-demagoguery and anti-ideological, which was quite the contrary to what seemed to be the trend in Mexican politics at the time. He was both anti-populist and anti-government. In economic matters, for example, he followed Keynes's theory of effective demand where the essential point of departure (whether we like it or not) is consumption; in other words, the level of demand controls the level of production, which in turn determines the level of employment. Keynes believes that the state should limit itself to fomenting this demand, this consumption, so that things work, so that countries can grow and develop."

"But how is this attained, then?"

"By increasing social services and increasing the minimum wage, which therefore increases the spending power of the population. In short,

Maty, it's not taking from the rich to make the poor less poor, but quite the opposite: it's producing wealth, which creates more wealth and more jobs and greater well-being for all."

They both paused for a breath, although Arturo started back up almost immediately:

"Roberto Soto Gariglietti believed in democracy despite the fact that, like Ortega y Gasset, he thought that an educated, free-thinking, and progressive class should take over the reins of the country . . . he believed this, as long as there was a balance—a counterweight—that would eliminate the ill-fated *presidencialismo* that Mexicans had grown accustomed to over the previous century. Like Popper, his teacher, Roberto was an enemy of all totalitarianism, be it left or right; what he believed in, then, was an open society, in the fact that men can transform their society from within by repairing dysfunctional social anomalies, without sacrificing the rational (I repeat, rational) criteria that enable and orient those changes. He detested the Trotskyites, the Maoists, the neo-Fascists, the supporters of Chávez, Castro, and Franco, the followers of the PRD and PAN, the right-wing Catholic thinkers and even some on the left, above all the so-called liberation theology; he repudiated the neo-Hegel crowd, and the only Freudian-Marxist he admired was his dear Marcuse . . . and even that was with some reservation. In his writings, as you know, he argued on behalf of a free press and a market-based economy; he also came out in favor of private ownership of the means of production and the right of inheritance; he fought for genuine political liberalism, not the frictional liberalism that is referred to today without any rhyme or reason by people who don't even know what true liberalism means . . ."

"And what does political liberalism mean, *papá*?"

"It means individual freedom throughout all aspects of life, Arturo. Listen: I mean all aspects of life, without restrictions, the sort of freedom born in France when the people revolted against the monarchic absolutism, against the enlightened despots of the seventeenth and eighteenth centuries. That is the exact reason Soto Gariglietti was in favor of a nonpaternalistic state that could still compensate for the shortcomings of a market-based economy; in other words, a state that only intervenes in creating justice and social security programs, public assistance, and free health and education; a state whose primary purpose is guaranteeing the rights and freedoms of the individual, freedom of the press, freedom to worship, a woman's freedom to have an abortion; a state that oversees and regulates prostitution, that legalizes the selling and consumption of drugs; a surefire way (as he said) of dismantling the multimillion-dollar corporate cartels and their conspiring politicians. So with all that in mind, let me ask you: is that what it means to be conservative? Reactionary? Is that the definition of 'right wing,' Matilde? It's all just arbitrary fucking nomenclature! Nobody on earth was less right wing (or what people consider to be right wing) than my father, and nobody was less of a leftist (or what people have snobbishly dubbed the 'new left') than my father. He couldn't be constrained by some hollow terminology, and he simply believed in and defended the things I've told you here. That was him, to be taken at face value, without any additional labels or definitions." He stopped for a second before continuing feverishly: "For Soto Gariglietti, the task was then to begin privatizing the management of services (like electricity and water) and not the network. For example, energy management, including PEMEX, should pass into the hands of competent, modern, private companies, not obsolete, corrupt, ineffective companies. Also, according to my father (and in this he was in line with Keynes), the state should invest in public works projects, which would create more jobs and also greater demand. So yes, Maty, employment (although it is an inalienable right) must be achieved by competition; it's impossible to officially authorize or guarantee that, of course, otherwise the system would become sclerotic and the country would fall behind, as happened with France in 2018."

"What happened in France?"

"When then-President Phillip Durand wanted to establish a work contract for young people under the age of twenty-five that would allow employers to more easily fire them—as is the case in the United States or any other part of the world—hundreds of thousands of students, fearing for their future, left their homes and went out into the streets to protest the move and call for reform . . . reform that, in the long run, my father (who was an old friend of Durand) thought would prove beneficial to the country despite the fact that it had failed in 2006 when Chirac wanted to bring it about. Nevertheless, the French leftists, as wise as they are spiteful, urged on the young people and almost overnight France turned into a powder keg of police barricades, protesters, fasting, and even deaths. Look, Maty: in France the left has traditionally prevented the kind of internal reforms that Popper was always talking about, referencing (when convenient) the social conquests that were made in the wake of the French Revolution and in the nineteenth century. Still, though, the ineffectiveness and pent-up frustrations finally erupted, as I said, in 2018. The people, that is, the bourgeoisie—which basically means nearly all of France—were not willing to change at that point; the Gauls tried to continue enjoying the same guarantees that they'd grown accustomed to, although, yes, they were up to their necks in perpetual and incongruous hypocrisy: I'm a leftist because it works to my own benefit, it's chic and intellectual, but at the same time, I want guarantees—yes, guarantees— that I can live the life of a capitalist citizen, a citizen emancipated from the state . . . and of course, I want to live in the First World. I want my wine, my cheese, my books, my walks with my dog, I want low prices for stamps, gas, and phone service, I want vacations to the beach and all the freedom in the world, and if I don't get them, then I'm going out into the streets to fight for them. On the one hand, I demand that the state give me everything and guarantee it to me because I'm French, and that the state participate in everything that suits me even though I am a complete and total imbecile, I have no job, no degree, but at the same time I don't want the state to mess with things that don't matter to it; in other words, I don't want the state to mess with things that benefit me. For example: not paying much in the way of taxes. I, for my part, say what my father said, you can't have your cake and eat it too. Look, Maty, the leftists, the French and Italian *bien pensants*, have bastardized the term whenever and wherever it suits them. It's very similar to what the so-called Latin American left has done. The *ñeñés* try to lump everyone together under the mantra of being a conservative piece of shit, a lapsed Catholic, a depraved Yankee, or a greedy, unscrupulous capitalist whenever you don't think exactly as they do, if you don't defend and praise the son of Hugo Chávez and the tyrant in Cuba, the young heir to Raúl Castro, who (according to the farcical theologians) are the ultimate heroes in the battle against the Great Satan, or if, for example, you don't take to the streets to strike and protest at least twice a month against transportation, schools, services, roads, or whatever. And just so you're not confused, my father was profoundly liberal, as I've said; he wasn't Catholic, he wasn't conservative, he wasn't reactionary; he was die-hard anti-Yankee, anti-imperialism, anti-nationalism, and anti-xenophobe; he believed in the free market, yes, and at the same time he embraced ethnic and cultural diversity and fought oppression, especially of indigenous peoples, but mainly he was much more conscientious than any of those overly pious members of the Latin American left who lived, you know, like capitalist kings dedicated to the highly profitable sport of tossing industrialists and capitalist investors out the window, yes, throwing out the people who work and create wealth for themselves, of course, but also for everybody else, and without thumping their chest like the leftist saints are wont to do."

"I understand. The businesses can't commit suicide; they can't act like Robin Hood or like nuns running an orphanage."

"Exactly. As I've said, Roberto Soto didn't believe in a protectionist state like, for example, America and its infamous double-edged political sword. Let me give you an example, Maty: for decades now they've been looking the other way while thousands of illegal immigrants enter the country every day, but then they bitch and moan and make their lives miserable once they're there. And then, to placate the myopic radicals, they send ten people home while another hundred are allowed in through the back door. Then again, he believed in a free market economy, in which the state's involvement was limited. He thought that capitalism was, unfortunately, the lesser of the two evils known by man, and the only system that stimulated individual work, although—of course—there is the harsh price of inequity. This inequity (which is not the same as inequality, since for him—as it was for Nietzsche—the idea that two people are equal is a lie) had to be attacked or regulated, he said, by other means . . ."

"What means are those, *papá*?"

"Endeavoring, for example, to make the public schools superior to the private schools, as has happened in many European countries. That way, the poorest children can have a relatively even playing field with the children of the rich." Here he paused for a moment to light a cigarette and smoke. "What cannot be permitted under any circumstances is to cut the head off capitalism under the pretext of the aforementioned economic and social inequality. On the contrary, my son, it's important to encourage private initiatives, the small and micro industries; to not leave anything (or as little as possible) up to bureaucrats and other functionaries of the state. Any other starting point is an aberration, a political maneuver designed to deceive and oppress those who have already been beaten down the most, something which, as we know, enables the controlling class in Mexico to keep the workers and farmers under its thumb. You didn't have long to wait in order to see the sudden transformation of China after Mao and the Tiananmen Square massacre, nor did you have to wait until the end of the Cold War and the fall of the Berlin Wall, wrote my father in one of his books, in order to recognize the stagnation of the Soviet Union and discover its faults and deficiencies. You didn't have to be clairvoyant in order to see that the United States had been winning this game for quite some time; or rather, if the game wasn't won by capitalism, it was definitely lost by the Soviets. You had to act, Maty. Unlike Echeverría and his partisans, unlike

300

López Portillo, my father believed in action, in immediate execution, that's what he did, or at least what he tried to do in his own very peculiar and eccentric way."

"A school? Is that it? Did he open up a school?" interrupted Maty.

"There were already plenty of schools out there, and there still are," said the painter, his hand stroking his lover's hair as he smoked. "They were awful, but at least they existed. What they lacked—what Mexico has always lacked—were teachers, rural teachers, Maty. The teaching vocation has been in decline since the days of President Miguel Alemán, in the 1950s, if not before . . ."

"An orphanage, then?"

"No, nothing like that," Arturo said, not moving from his spot on the dilapidated old sofa in his studio while he continued to run his fingers through Matilde's hair, who had now almost completely turned her back to him. "Just hold your horses. Look, he knew he wouldn't be able to change things overnight. In fact, he knew that he wouldn't be able to change anything on his own; at least, nothing of a social or judicial nature, much less of a mental or moral one. He understood that, at least at the time, he couldn't take on the giant, corrupt machine, couldn't fight our sclerotic, inattentive government, which has been that way since time immemorial. Not when there was so very much he could do—and this is something he understood full well—by using his money to make children happy. Do you understand? He couldn't offer them lifelong happiness (because that is the task for all of us; that is to say, every child, every human being), but at the very least he could bring them some joy for a week, a day, even a few hours, at least; he could give them a bit of respite they would never, ever forget, a bit of time which would hopefully motivate them, encourage them to grow and study and move on to bigger and better things . . . and that they could (if they wanted to) achieve what my father believed to be one of life's most important things: wellness, happiness and wellness, a mixture of the two, you know? Because for him, Maty, happiness is almost always achieved through wellness.

On the contrary, it's much more difficult, if not impossible, to be happy if you live surrounded by misery, sickness, and ignorance."

"But there are people who live well and yet aren't happy, Arturo."

"Of course. That's why I used the word wellness. Think about it: wellness. Happiness is a completely distinct thing, and it's incumbent upon the individual, his nature, his spirituality, his intelligence, his character, or his ethics; in other words, the passion of his tears or the passion of his joy, as Spinoza believed," clarified Roberto Soto, a bit annoyed by his son's inopportune interruption, just as Arturo was irritated at the need to correct your wife, Reader. "Wellness, on the other hand, is incumbent upon the state, for it's the state that must guarantee it no matter the cost . . . except, of course, at the cost of freedom. Wellness is not, as Hegel taught us, something that comes at the end of history, Arturo. It's not an exogenous force or an abstract idea; it's not an impossible conquest, but—unlike happiness—it should be a more or less enduring good, one guaranteed to the public . . ."

"Fine, so, what the hell did he decide to do? You've left me hanging here, Arturo. I'm lost. So just lay it down for me . . ."

"Along with his millionaire friend Jack, he opened a small amusement park in Chiapas, near Tapachula, where those immense landfills are piling up . . ."

"What?" Matilde swung around, stupefied.

"Look, almost nobody knows about that. Maybe nobody knows, even, but he brought that park into being, he put it on the map, he . . ."

"Are you talking about the Parque Rosario Castellanos?"

"That's it, yes."

"I can't believe it. I heard all about that place when I was a kid."

"Well, believe it, Matilde," Arturo said, lighting his second cigarette of the afternoon, just as his father was doing. "Everything pretty much began when this American and him ran into a group of children, seven or eight years old, from as far as Honduras and Guatemala, and as nearby as San Juan Chamula, who spent ten or eleven hours a day, seven days a week, scavenging for bottles and cans, like beasts of burden. They earned fifty *centavos* for every ten kilos of rubbish they collected, hoping to eventually save up the ten thousand *pesos* they needed to pay a coyote to smuggle them into the United States. During the few brief moments of free time that they had, they played with bottle caps on the ground. Of course, these children didn't need anything else in order to be happy, because they simply hadn't known that there was anything else out there . . . although they did have a sense of intuition, because they saved their *centavos* desperately hoping to one day be able to flee that miserable hellhole. Schools, hospitals, electricity, sewers, clean water, health care, effective elections, social justice . . . these were all tasks that belonged to the state, not to Soto Gariglietti and the *gringo*. They, for their part, were businessmen and had to behave like businessmen, and as such, offer up an example of investment and capitalism. So that's what they did, shortly after my father went to visit Jack in Los Angeles and saw, for the first time, at thirty-seven or thirty-eight years of age, Disneyland. After that, of course, he took my mother and I to see it on a number of occasions. Needless to say, he detested those anti-Yankee intellectualoids who use their rejection of American foreign policy as an excuse to renounce Santa Claus and to refuse to take their children to McDonald's even though they clearly have the money to do so. They were the sort of parental buffoons who (as he said) would rather take their children to El Prado because it was interesting to them, but not to a seven-year-old kid, you see? He considered that problematic, weed-like Puritanism and dogmatism to be a sort of revered stupidity, typical of a backward, reactionary, communistically closed mind, like what you might find in a village priest, for example. What does a child's illusion have to do, he said, with an empire's foreign policy? But that's a whole other story, one we won't be getting into . . ."

"But Disneyland?" Maty repeated, as if it were a spell, some formula that could never be solved once it had been spoken. "Soto Gariglietti? You might as well be reading to me from *Alice in Wonderland* . . ."

"Exactly. That's what he wanted to bring to the children of Chiapas and Oaxaca: Wonderland, the one toy they would otherwise never have been able to play with in their lives . . . at least, not while it's still worthwhile to have such a toy, which is during childhood, of course. Amusement parks can only be one hundred percent appreciated by children. Nobody else comes close."

"On that we can agree."

"So anyway, he and Jack spoke with the Disney executives, and spent the next two years traveling, talking, and negotiating in an attempt to convince them of their vision's worth, but in the end, of course, it fell apart: they didn't want to invest in another such park, much less one in Tapachula. It's one thing to have good intentions, said the Gringo businessmen, and it's quite another thing to invest in a patently nonfunctional business model, a financial black hole. In other words, to be an irresponsible ass. Business is business."

"And they were right," Maty affirmed, completely captivated by the story.

"Of course they were right, but my father (and Jack as well) were dedicated idealists, and in the end, through their own methods, they achieved their goal: they opened a small amusement park that lasted for two decades until, as you well know, the Zapatista National Liberation Army used it as a bunker during their war with the federal army in 1995, which left it completely destroyed. Still, though, they had managed to do what they always wanted: to take the most expensive toy in the world and hand it over to the poorest children of Mexico for almost twenty years. No small thing, if you think about it . . ."

"That's the most ridiculous folly I've ever heard in my life, Arturo, and I swear I had no idea that he was the one behind it."

"Almost nobody does."

"It must have been a complete loss."

"Yes, it was foolish, dysfunctional, and absurd, but . . . like almost everything else my father did, he had a very deep, almost indiscernible heartfelt sense about it. If it hadn't been overrun by the soldiers, it would have been dismantled by the governor, who was colluding with the park director at the time. After all, both of them were from Chiapas . . ." Arturo took one long drag off what remained of his second cigarette, and pulled Matilde tightly against him. They both fell silent. The Agro painter then tossed the butt into a corner of the studio and finally, after some time had passed, he asked his lover a question: "You know what happened next?"

"There's more?" Maty asked, stretching and releasing herself from his hairy arm.

"What I'm about to tell you was a less foolish project, I think, and my father and Jack embarked on it almost immediately after they opened Parque Rosario Castellanos."

"What are you talking about?"

"A chain of toy stores throughout the Southeast called Chimera. Over a hundred and fifty of them, scattered throughout small cities, remote towns, and places like the sierra Mihi and the Lacondon jungle, where there were no paved roads, no electricity, no potable water or any other damn thing except for dogs and chickens and hogs running around. Can you believe it?"

"But that's even more foolish, Arturo. Where were the kids going to get the money they'd need to buy those toys, when their parents barely had enough to spend on beans and tortillas? It's like a cruel joke."

"No, Maty, the toys were free, or very nearly so . . . Let me explain. To go along with the Chimera toy stores, Jack and my father designed a payment system in which poor children would receive colorful faux money in exchange for good grades in school or community service like cutting the grass, sweeping the plaza, painting a fence, who knows. With that Monopoly money, the children could go and buy the toys they wanted to buy. It was that simple. On one hand, they were completely free to choose (a freedom they'd never before had in their lives), and on the other, they had in their hands the money to pay for whatever they wanted. But above all, my father once told me when I was still a child myself, this exercise would serve as a stimulus for study or work. Of course, they have to carry out a simple task in accordance with their age, a symbolic matter, if you like, Maty. But in any case, all those indigenous children living in the poorest, most remote areas of the Southeast were provided with a gift, a trivial little object, an 'inutensil,' as my father called them. Do you see? Do you see the genius? It was like putting a new twist on the old proverb about how it's better to teach a poor man to fish than it is to give him a fish . . . which my father considered the worst of insults."

"An insult? But why? On the contrary . . ."

"Because it's the state that should guarantee and provide fishing poles, not average citizens, no matter how wealthy or philanthropic they might be. Do you see? Remember, for example, how my father would often stop suddenly and buy a popsicle for a homeless kid on the street. What he didn't do was take the kid to the dentist to have his cavities filled or give money to his parents so they could buy him clothes. My father was no fool, Maty. He understood that any act of charity or philanthropy has no purpose (whether we know it or not) other than to alleviate our own conscience, to make us feel less guilty or more satisfied with ourselves. Nevertheless, using this same principle to justify not giving a popsicle to a poor child, since it's better to take him to the dentist, seemed the worst possible insult, a perverse aberration, and one made even more perverse if, in the end, you don't take the kid to the dentist. Understand?"

"I think so . . ."

"Now, for the first time in their lives, these forgotten little youngsters could take their fake money and go buy whatever their hearts desired, they could actually own something, they could at the very least feel free to choose a toy."

Once again, Maty could only stammer, still lost in her sense of astonishment:

"Incredible. Listening to this anecdote sent chills up my spine. Honestly, I don't know what to think about all this. It's truly strange; eccentric, even."

Emerging from her reflections, still with her back to the painter, Maty heard the son of Soto Gariglietti, surrounded by the thick cloud of cigarette smoke, suddenly say something apparently irrelevant:

"You know, I've been wanting to ask you, is this a period in hell, or a period from hell?"

"What are you talking about?"

"I mean, have you had your period?" Arturo added, laughing at his own joke.

"Oh, very funny!" Maty muttered angrily, coming out of her thoughts. "No, it hasn't happened yet. And it's been a week."

"So you probably really are pregnant."

"I don't know," Maty replied, shutting off her mini tape recorder and stowing it back inside the Louis Vuitton bag that you gave her, for there was no reason to be recording this intimate, unpleasant part of the conversation. "What I do know, Arturo, is that if I don't have my period soon, then it means that my son of a bitch husband has been lying to me ever since we got married."

"I don't understand . . ."

"I'm not supposed to be fertile, Arturo. At least, that's what he told me. He said it was my fault that we couldn't have children, and that's why I underwent a bunch of uncomfortable tests with Doctor Lascurain, the gynecologist . . . My husband, your trusted little friend, asked me to start them, because he assured me that it was me, and not him, who was infertile. Can you believe it?"

"So . . . ? What did Doctor Lascurain say? What were the results?"

"Nothing, still nothing . . . but if I don't get my period soon, then he's the one who's sterile. That son of a bitch. It's always been him. Now do you understand?"

"I think so," the painter said, hesitantly, before continuing: "Don't tell me it's my baby then . . ."

"I'm not telling you anything, Arturo, because I don't know myself. I'm not even sure that I'm pregnant. Just leave me alone. I have a lot to do back at the house."

"But don't you want to have a little naked time before you go?" asked the painter as he leaned over and kissed her on the neck, perhaps feigning a lack of concern with an issue whose gravity, all things considered, was truly weighing on him.

"Of course not. Especially not today," Maty said, pulling away from him and heading for the studio door in the blink of an eye. "I'm leaving. See you on Thursday, okay? I need to finish my thesis, and I want you to tell me what happened next with your father. When he got involved with Greenpeace."

XI

At La Paz International Airport's tiny Gate 64D, the three assembled characters (Lascurain, Cardoso, and Reader) were waiting for the charter which any moment now would be taking them to Las Rémoras, when they heard a shrill voice break out over the loudspeaker asking for a last-minute volunteer because unfortunately the flight had been overbooked and there weren't enough seats on the tiny little regional aircraft. The next available flight, advised the same, high-pitched voice, would be departing in approximately two and a half hours. In exchange for giving up their seat on the earlier flight, Baja Airlines would offer travelers a complimentary dinner at the airport's famous Restaurante Esmeralda.

Needless to say, neither the doctor nor the professor (much less Anagnostes) thought, even for a moment, about giving up their seats; their desire to reach Las Rémoras at that point couldn't be bought off. Reader, for example, was already running low on patience and very much on edge: after 308 pages, he still hadn't arrived at the aforementioned coastal town. Cardoso, too: five months had passed since he read that old used copy of *The Obstacles* back at Millard Fillmore University, which is why he was so eager to arrive and finally get to know the town that Elías, the aspiring writer, had called home. Humberto

Lascurain had a similar need: he had patients to care for, pregnant women and women about to go into labor, and thus he didn't have the luxury of giving up his seat for some fucking airport food. So who, then, would trade their seat for a disgusting wrap or perhaps a fried taco with chicken and guacamole? Sitting there at Gate 64D, the three characters silently counted the rather limited number of passengers: besides themselves, there were only five others. A total of eight, plus the in-flight bitch and the two pilots. This would indeed be a small plane. A puddle jumper.

At long last, they saw a more or less young but enormous, obese, in-credibly fat woman, like a character out of a fairy tale, who was barely able to get up from her seat: the poor woman pitched and swayed her way across the concourse like an unmoored ship on the verge of sink-ing in the Atlantic. Her flesh heaved to and fro, and it felt like the entire room was being swamped with each of her tiny steps. The three of them watched as she shambled over to the counter and spoke with the airline representative with greasy, slicked-back hair. After a couple of minutes with him, having reached an understanding despite an evident linguistic difficulty, he broadcast yet another announcement over the P.A. system with his unbearably childlike timbre:

"Ladies and gentlemen, we have a volunteer: Mademoiselle Boule de Suif. A warm round of applause for her, if you please. A well-deserved round of applause for this handsome French lady who has come so far to visit us here and who nevertheless is willing to sacrifice her own travel plans for our benefit—excuse me, for your benefit, ladies and gentle-men—hardened travelers who would never give up your seats for fear of delaying the time of your final arrival. But what a terrible mistake you've made!" he added, playing the jester. "Mademoiselle Boule de Suif will be enjoying a Mexican-style buffet at the exquisite Restaurante Esmeralda here at La Paz International Airport. There, she may stuff herself with all the *chiles rellenos* she desires, for they come breaded or not breaded, and with a delicious tomato sauce glaze; they also offer an exquisite Oaxacan *mole* (and yes, it comes with golden-brown sesame seeds and refried beans); green or red enchiladas topped with melted cheese or our house cream sauce, pork loin with wilted collard greens, or, if you prefer, succulent shrimp *a la diabla*, with just a touch of spicy heat; langoustines sautéed in garlic sauce, or a chilled fish ceviche with avocado and lime; and if there's still room to cram down a few more bites, we offer our world famous yet locally harvested chocolate clams on the half shell with a side of vegetables, or a succulent grilled filet of freshly caught mahi-mahi, if you prefer; you may also enjoy our Tampico-style steak, which comes with spicy *rajas con queso*, Mexican rice topped with your choice of a fried egg or a sliced, deep-fried plantain, all of which comes—as you'd expect—with fresh, handmade tortillas . . . and this is only the beginning, ladies and gentlemen . . . because this feast includes a tall, refreshing glass of *horchata* with a cinnamon swizzle stick, or instead of that, a shot of tequila Herradura and a bottle of ice-cold Corona . . . not to mention our French pastries, but I've said too much already. Why go on? Why should I continue when I can already see you all just drooling at the thought . . . So you see, this is what happens to the impatient traveler who wants nothing more than to arrive early. The Bible says that those who enter first will leave the last . . . No! Wait! Forgive me! It says that the last shall be first . . . But I'm wrong again, good heavens, and babbling too . . . it must be the hunger, my appetite, that's got my mouth going on with all these culinary descriptions. Yes, I know: he who laughs last laughs best, and that is why Mademoiselle Boule de Suif, corpulent yet benevolent, gelatinous yet generous, is laughing out loud; rather, she would be, if only she spoke a lick of Spanish, and had any idea about the grand banquet that we've reserved for her at our legendary Restaurante Esmeralda . . ."

Disconcerted, awash in the waves of euphoric applause from the other passengers there in the meager waiting area, the gynecologist, Eusebio, and Anagnostes began to applaud as well, like a trio of raving lunatics . . . annoyed raving lunatics, because they'd just realized that they themselves (and especially Cardoso) were feeling hungry as well: the sharp, spruce, fastidious airline employee had whetted their appetites, and now there was nothing they could do save hunker down, wait it out, and join in cheering the tubby French lady along with the rest of the anonymous travelers.

With huge, contrite, pearl gray tears rolling down over her kind, chubby cheeks, Mademoiselle Boule de Suif could only blubber, emotional and overwhelmed by such a resounding public display of honor and rejoicing:

"*Merci, merci bien. J'aime le Mexique et les mexicains.*"

12
(THURSDAY, JUNE 8TH)

The paintings were scattered across every inch of the asbestos-and-plywood studio: unfinished oils, broken, dusty frames, empty tubes of paint, dirty rags reeking of colophony and turpentine, canvasses covered in charcoal sketches, young models drawn or outlined in positions that conjure up (clearly intentional) images of Bonnard, Kokoschka, or a young Egon Schiele. Two portraits of Maty were laid out, finished works but for the frame, in one corner of the workshop, next to a busted easel, one not far from the other. The first was destined for Arturo himself, and right now it was bathed in a tenuous ray of light that shone in through a window looking out over Narvarte: it depicted a nude Matilde with a miniature Popocatépetl volcano between her legs, a pensive look on her face, with her chartreuse green eyes looking slightly off towards the edge of the canvas, with a deep Prussian blue sky in the background containing only a few wisps of clouds. That was how he had imagined her the very first time he saw her there in his workshop, and that's how he'd painted her. The second portrait, however, was for you: a smooth cerulean blue background, a slight (minimal) hint of disdain in the light-colored eyes and a sense of haughtiness in her profile, two qualities that were exemplified by your iniquitous lover, Reader. Arturo had managed to capture that beautiful, obscene facial expression, incipiently aquiline and unique to Matilde: tender, but always tinged with scorn, with an unconscious feminine cruelty. You, unaware that the photo you provided had ended up being all but useless (since she, the model herself, had been there in the flesh every Tuesday and Thursday with your friend the painter), would be coming to pick up the portrait in a few days, ready to flatter your beloved wife with it on your first wedding anniversary after dining at one of Mexico City's finest restaurants. All that was going to happen, but first . . . there were still a couple of lingering, unanswered questions, and it was important to fill in the gaps with names and dates and anecdotes. First and foremost, there is the question of what Matilde learned about the final years of the missing Roberto Soto Gariglietti, the iconoclastic founder of the Partido de la Naturaleza y el Fuego Mexicano, the famed grandson of Enzo the Sicilian, friend and loyal servant to General Pancho Villa.

What had happened after the destruction of the Rosario Castellanos amusement park and the Chimera toy stores in the Mexican Southeast? What new venture had the politician endeavored upon in the 1980s and 1990s, before his final apotheosis?

"Greenpeace," Arturo said. "But his involvement with them was brief, Maty, two short years which ultimately did nothing but leave him disillusioned about the institution he devoted so much effort to and idealized so much, just as so many others have. But despite all that, this disillusionment would soon spur him to create—as contradictory as it might seem—his own ecological strategy, one more directly attached, let's say, to the realities of Mexico's indigenous population." Here, he paused to light up a cigarette, his first of the afternoon. "You see, it all started with the famous Central Park rally on June 12, 1982, in which my father participated alongside dozens of ecological groups after having left London and his complicated relationship with the old rationalist

Karl Popper behind him, as you know. He was joined at this massive demonstration by his friend Jack, who I told you about earlier, remember? The rich philanthropist. He knew a Canadian businessman from New Zealand named David McTaggart, the chairman of Greenpeace who, in 1980, had converted the organization into an international network able to mobilize demonstrators in any part of the world. Greenpeace owned a fishing vessel, the mythical Rainbow Warrior, which carried out a number of famous missions, blockades, sabotages, and even terrorist acts, all widely reported and controversial at the time. Once he had joined Greenpeace, around 1983, I think, and was onboard the Rainbow Warrior, he met a group of volunteers that included a young Dutch photographer of Portuguese descent named Fernando Pereira, who became a great friend, and he also reunited with a young American rebel, Allison Moore, the daughter of a Republican senator, whom he'd first met in New York during that historic 1982 gathering, which—in part, at least—had motivated him to join Greenpeace in the first place. That's where, from what I understand, my father fell in love with Allison, and where Allison—bit by bit and without even realizing it—fell in love with Fernando . . ."

". . . and I suppose Fernando, then, fell in love with your father," Matilde added, smiling, toying with him.

"How do you know that?"

"I read it."

"You read that?" the Agro painter demanded, throwing the trembling, ash-laden cigarette butt to the ground. "Where?"

"Well, I read it in *The Gift*, by Nabokov. It tells a similar tale. But don't let me distract you, Arturo. Please, continue," Maty said, still holding her mini tape recorder, still half-naked, sitting cross-legged on the quilt, using her knees to caress the protruding ribs of her hairy lover.

"Well, the great adventures of the Rainbow Warrior and the ecological dreams of Dad and his friends ended in October of 1984 when the French government succeeded in infiltrating the volunteer group with

313

a couple of young spies. These supposed scuba divers were given the mission to sink the ship, and they were successful."

"Why would they want to do that?"

"Greenpeace wanted to prevent a nuclear test that France was preparing to run in Moruroa. And believe me, McTaggart and his followers would stop at nothing or nobody. They were reckless; or rather, they were proud and reckless. Pereira drowned that tragic night, and with him, of course, the love triangle was broken."

Maty was struck silent for a long while after listening to this sad tale of love and woe. She seemed to reflect on that distant event, which, truth be told, she'd never even known about, before finally emerging from her Moruroan dream to ask:

"So what happened then?"

"Well, owing to the double blows absorbed by my father—the Greenpeace tragedy and his unrequited love with the young Allison Moore, who by the way never entered into his life—he decided to return to Mexico, and so, from 1985 to 1988 he organized housewives in upper-middle class neighborhoods and lobbied the government to require curbside recycling, and, later, he established the 'A Day Without a Car' program which was designed to improve the smog conditions and air quality in Mexico City. Although the first effort wasn't successful and today, in the middle of 2025, there are no recycling laws, the 'A Day Without a Car' program was finally implemented . . ."

"Except it doesn't do a goddamn thing. It's never worked. All it does is make the auto industry richer. We live in a carbon monoxide haze; our children are born with respiratory problems . . ."

"Yes, that's true, Matilde. But be that as it may, remember that Roberto Soto managed to inform thousands of women and families about the urgent necessity of recycling and how to separate biodegradable objects from the rest of the trash. It was an ant's work, titanic and apparently futile, but my father always believed in those sorts of fights, you know? So, along with thousands of housewives, he launched an effort—among many other projects during those gray years—to rescue some parks that were in danger of being rezoned for residential communities, churches, and factories. For Soto Gariglietti, these green spaces were the lungs of the city, and they had to fight tooth and nail to preserve them, utilizing every resource and ounce of energy. He followed the tactics of Gandhi, one of his most admired models: the peaceful struggle, the constant, unwavering use of nonviolent pressure. Look, in Mexico, you know as well as I do that everything usually begins with a good bribe: City Hall gives permits to developers and construction companies to put up a skyscraper or condo where there's no electricity or potable water—an ecologically untouchable area, like a park, a beach, a lake, a forest, or river—and eventually, on some unannounced and clandestine night, the heavy equipment shows up. However, my father's followers always had their ears pricked, and—just as construction was about to begin on one of those projects—they appeared as if by some magic: there they were, a hundred or so wealthy women, very well dressed, some even bringing their drivers along with them, lying down on the ground in front of the bulldozers and preventing the workers from demolishing trees or plowing over a footpath or whatever else might lay in their path. It was a sight to see, and completely insane: you didn't know whether to laugh or burst into tears, said my mother, who happened to be there that day, which was how she met and fell in love with my father. I think it was after one of those skirmishes that—according to my sources—my mother got knocked up with yours truly, before she was even married . . ." Here Arturo broke out laughing and wiped away a few drops of sweat that were forming at his temples before adding: "I wasn't around to see any of these ecological melodramas, of course, but there is amateur video footage and news reports filmed about these hysterically funny events, these scenes that you can hardly believe took place because of their heroic or pathetic ridiculousness. I think in the end they saved a fair number of greenways, nature preserves, beaches, and waterways, but unfortunately many others perished. You know as well as I do that in an urban area like Mexico City, it was and always will be impossible to be everywhere and to stop every fucking abuse of authority. There are no superheroes ubiquitous or powerful enough to manage that. There are just too many shameless assholes out there. This place is teeming with them; they're like sewer rats. You can kill one, but one after another will just come out to take its place. It would take the Pied Piper of Hamelin to get rid of them all . . ." He paused here after mentioning this youthful allegory to light up another cigarette, before proudly announcing: "Still, though, this small civil movement—which was first comprised entirely of women, followed by students, and finally encompassing all groups of people—was growing, little by little, until 1988 when it reached the height of its political importance in a united front of hundreds of thousands of people protesting against the aberrant failure of the system . . ."

"The failure of the system?"

"Well, that's what they called the electoral fraud that carried Carlos Salinas de Gortari to the presidency, even though Cuauhtémoc Cárdenas had been the clear winner of the popular elections. It took twelve years—two presidential terms—before Mexico would finally come to know democracy and the crimes and abuses of the Salinas administration would be brought to light, in a sort of *glasnost*, so that this fucked up country could be done with them once and for all."

"And so what happened when the system failed?"

"Were you absent the day they taught political science, Matilde? Do I have to explain everything to you? What are you studying there at the university, Chinese history?" Arturo snorted, somewhat annoyed; however, he continued almost immediately: "Anyway, in the end, Salinas and his supporters got their way and managed—as only the geniuses can do—to corrupt and eviscerate Mexico in the space of six short years. It was a complete and total success. Nobody had been able to do that until then; not my grandfather's enemy from Veracruz, the oligarch Miguel Alemán and his cronies, not Echeverría and his thugs, not López Portillo with that whore of his, Carmen, and his infinite hordes of assholes. Look, with his catchphrases of 'modernizing the country' and 'entering into the global reality,' Salinas cheated the middle class, ignored Chiapas and the indigenous population, turned his back on the workers and farmers, and—to make matters worse—he saturated the government with technocrats and wealthy kids much like your husband, guys totally out of touch with the reality and the profound inequality that exists in our nation today. Well then, all that exploded in late '94 with Subcomandante Marcos and the EZLN . . ." Here, Arturo paused briefly in the middle of his boring, pedagogical litany. "But that doesn't really matter, since you can read up on it in just about any old history book. The fact is that between 1989 and 1993, my father was able to create his own green party, the first in Mexico's history, and he managed to obtain I don't know how many hundreds of thousands of signatures needed for the Federal Electoral Institute to register him. That's how it all began, and that's how the elections—the famous Comitia of 1994—which I think I told you about at some point . . ."

"Yes. You were nine years old then, right?"

"Exactly, which is why I only have a few, vague memories . . ."

"Like the boy with the harelip and that pre-Columbian style rally in the San Nicolás neighborhood, and then the visit to the toy store," Matilde recalled. "Was it part of the Chimera chain?"

"No, the Chimera toy stores were only located in the southeastern part of Mexico, but fundamentally, the actions were the same. They had the same heartfelt intentions . . ."

"Of course."

The two of them fell silent. They were sweating. Matilde leaned back, resting on Arturo's chest as she usually did after a debilitating bout of lovemaking or one of their marathon question-and-answer sessions. She watched him smoke, listening to his slow, deliberate, raspy breathing, feeling his chest rise and fall like a hairy wave beneath her ear, which was probably somewhat similar, Maty thought, to what it would sound like if she held up to her ear the conch shell that Gariglietti used during his pseudo-Orphean political rallies: the founder of the PNFM letting it resound clearly, in each cardinal direction, among prayers in Náhuatl and Greek, amidst the copal incense and animals set free in an act of mercy and consubstantiation with Mother Earth, while a number of indigenous peoples danced around a fire in the middle of the plaza in full view of the municipal authorities and the outraged local priest. The scrolls of blue smoke in the wood-and-asbestos workshop then brought Matilde back to the reality at hand, and a second later covered her skin in an orange-violet nicotine tinge. Then, without warning, still sprawled out there on the quilt, the Agro painter told your wife, Reader, in a calm yet firm tone:

"I suppose by this point in the story you fully understand that my father believed he was Empedocles of Agrigento."

"I think so . . ." she murmured.

"After his years at the London School of Economics, and after befriending and subsequently breaking with Popper and his Parmenidean ideas, he looked into himself and believed that he saw, more clearly than ever, many of the irrational attitudes and ideas that had characterized the Sicilian philosopher and were unfortunately being repeated in him. But everything seems to have begun with the trip he took to Agrigento when he was eighteen years old where he discovered, according to him, his vocation as a doctor. After that came the ill-fated summer of '68 and the murder of his friend Pablo in Tlatelolco, and that was where he made a complete and total turn towards pre-Socratic philosophy. Lastly, there was his burning political commitment to Mexico and the lives of the dispossessed. Starting more or less with the 1980s, he became the champion of democracy that you know—or are coming to know—just like his father, Pedro, and my great-grandfather Enzo Gariglietti, a true tradition of insanity, of marginalized fighters, if ever there was one. Look, my father felt that he was the confluence of everything, and that if—as Empedocles wrote in his *Katharmoi*—the reincarnation or transmigration of souls was true, if everything was in an eternal state of flux, then the ancient philosopher from Akragas had, twenty-four centuries later, been reborn as him. And once that highly unusual idea had taken root in his head, there was nothing anybody could do to rip it out. In fact—and much to the contrary—he convinced many people it was true. Although he never went out and publicly declared that I, Roberto Soto, am Empedocles, his heteroclite books, his political and philosophical opinions, his extravagant clothes, his dietary and even conjugal habits, as I've said, clearly indicated his belief that he and Empedocles were one and the same, and therefore he had to repeat or continue his original political program, his fantastic, incredible, and bizarre feats of *Iatromantis* . . ."

"Iatro . . . what?"

"*Iatromantis*. A sort of doctor-seer, a healing oracle, a mystagogue, a wizard," clarified the painter. "My father felt that he should pursue the same political agenda, the same ancient fight against oligarchs, and—above all—the search for *Philia* within the cosmic sphere. Everything was the same, yes, even the aristocratic style and ostentation, but this time in Mexico, at the end of the twentieth century, and openly in favor of indigenous people, whom he loved and respected above anything else. That's why, ever since you first came here, I've been tirelessly and incessantly repeating the importance of reading up on the pre-Socratic philosophers, but mainly the need for you to study the multifaceted writings of Empedocles, the greatest of them all, the indirect predecessor of Democritus and Plato, among many others. But all that notwithstanding, you should tell me now whether or not you believe in everything I'm telling you, whether or not you think my father was or was not who he thought he was . . ."

"Why don't you tell me what you think, Arturo?"

Her lover hesitated; he wasn't expecting the question to be shot back at him. But he still had to answer it. Maty had astutely replied to his initial question with one of her own: he could not, then, return to the original question. He was cornered. He inhaled one more lung-clogging puff of smoke, tossed out the unfinished cigarette, and finally said, nervous and flushed:

"I don't know. I really don't. Sometimes I think he was, and sometimes—like my mother—I think he was completely insane. Anyway,
Roberto Soto is the man I admire and miss more than anyone else, you
know? And the truth is, after reviewing time and time again what he did
and what he wrote—after going over the arc of his life and all the signs
along the way—I see that everything about him had an odd, recondite
feel to it, a little contradictory or confused at times, but that's always true
of great men. They're contradictory and complicated, right?"

"Yes." That was the only thing that Matilde could say from her vantage
point amidst all that human flesh: the painter's ribs, his ample torso, his
nipples ringed with dark hair, and the thick smoke emanating from the
still-smoldering cigarette that was lying there in a stagnant corner of the
fifth-floor studio.

XIII

Waiting for them at the arrivals gate of the Las Rémoras airport, under a blistering night sky that waylaid the newly arrived travelers with
a noonday heat, was a man dressed in his Sunday best: the town mayor
Fernando Sigüenza, and alongside him was his secretary Rosinda, the
same lovely Rosinda who formerly worked for the deceased Raimundo
Rosales, that little man who died of a broken heart when he was accused of strangling Inés, the well-renowned madam of the local brothel.
Just behind Sigüenza, and overshadowing him a bit, was Iginio Jasso,
the bald architect and old friend of the lawyer Rosales, and, like him,
a freethinker, Freemason, and failed ladies' man. Next to Jasso was the
unmistakable Doctor Díaz Gross, *older than ever, or at least older than I
could have imagined,* thought Cardoso when he saw him standing there
(anachronistically) in his invariable checkered attire, typical of a doctor from the provinces. In third place, standing further back still, was
the old black woman Santa—who worked as a maid for Rosales and the

late priest Roldán—and her husband Joaquín, the fisherman she'd separated from many years ago and with whom, much to Eusebio's surprise, she was now lovingly holding hands. *Well, that's life for you!* the professor said, almost melancholically, since from what he could remember from having read *The Obstacles*, Santa had raised a heap of children with Joaquín (none of which were hers), and had subsequently separated; and now here they were again, as if nothing had happened. Then, suddenly, as if returning from his involuntary impasse—or his literary ponderings—Eusebio saw what he could only define as a true apparition: the two brothers Cecilio and Solón: it was absolutely, unequivocally them, so affected and mellifluous, only now they were thirty years older and even more vain than before, both tangential characters from *The Abominable Tale of Solón and Zolaida's Love*. Finally, Cardoso discovered, just to the left of the lawyer Sigüenza, perhaps forming part of the welcome wagon or whatever you want to call the group of people gathered there at the airport, two singular, odd, unique sorts, judging by their clothes and their stern, quarrelsome faces: one was wearing a broad sombrero, cowboy boots, and two pistols hanging from a thick, low-slung leather belt, and the other was draped in a purple toga bound by a golden sash and wearing bronze sandals, with a tangled Delphic garland atop his head. *Who are those crazy guys?* Lascurain whispered to Anagnostes, exchanging a confused look with him, while the heat kept intensifying as the night wore on. As they were wondering this and gathering up their bags from the tarmac, they saw Sigüenza walk past everyone else and go straight up to the four passengers who had accompanied them on the barely thirty-minute flight from La Paz to Las Rémoras. The town mayor raised his hand, signaling to the others, but not (of course) to the three. That notwithstanding, Reader read how Sigüenza, heir to Rosales, said, in the pompous, bombastic voice so typical of young, rural politicians:

"Mr. Yuri Mikhaylovich Chernishevski, my friend and writer, it is truly a pleasure to have you with us, as it is with you as well, Mr. Marcelo

Chiriboga, legendary author of the Latin American Boom. You've both come so far to be here for the unveiling and the tribute. It's an honor to my fellow councilmen as well as to the entire town of Las Ré-moras." After exchanging firm handshakes with the Russian and the Ecuadorian, Fernando turned towards the two other passengers who had accompanied them, and added, effusively, as if they were lifelong friends: "Ah, the esteemed educator Eladio Villagrá, distinguished Secretary of Culture for the state of Puebla, my friend and brother, it is such an immense honor for us to have you here with . . ." and before repeating "us," stumbling on account of his ridiculous redundancy, he opted out of the jam by asking, "And who, my dear Secretary, has accompanied you?"

"Allow me to present my good friend, the illustrious Sergio Pitol," Villagrá answered, who really seemed to be the Secretary of Culture, judging by Sigüenza's words and the tie spotted with tiny green polka dots, the old-fashioned frock coat, the fake patent leather shoes, and his extraordinarily smarmy countenance.

"Pitol, Chiriboga, and Chernishevski! What a trio!" Cardoso repeated, stunned, after having overheard the long and treacle exchange of greet-ings and salutations while he still stood there, a little ways back from the action, along with Lascurain and Reader, who were absorbing and/or digesting all these surprises. "How did I not recognize them?"

While Sigüenza greeted Pitol and Rosinda greeted the distinguished Russian, who was sporting an impressive pair of broad boots, Anagnos-tes and Lascurain were received by the architect Iginio Jasso and Doctor Díaz Gross, respectively, who of course had never seen them before in their lives. *They probably have us confused with someone else,* Anagnostes thought to himself, *or perhaps they think we're also here to attend the un-veiling or whatever it is that's taking place here in this tiny, forgotten ham-let, cast away by the hand of Apollo.* In the end, though, almost everyone ended up greeting everyone else, exchanging effusive praise and even a few individual embraces despite the unbearably hot summer night, which had left them all drenched with sweat. All that was lacking was for Anagnostes, Cardoso, and the gynecologist to meet the two people to whom they hadn't yet been introduced, and who were keeping a bit of distance, smiling majestically, as if they were carved in stone. Rosinda came to their rescue (that is, she came to everybody's rescue) and offered a simple introduction:

"Gentlemen, I'd like to present to you the great pre-Socratic philosopher, Empedocles of Agrigento, and General Pancho Villa, who live here in Las Rémoras, and who have been distinguished members of our community for many years."

Stunned, blinded by the heat, or perhaps drunk without so much as a drop of alcohol in their veins, Reader, Lascurain, and Cardoso followed Chiriboga, Villagrá, Chernyshevsky, and Pitol as they exchanged firm handshakes (and even a couple of claps on the shoulder) with the characters in question. Only Eusebio spoke up, in a tiny, falsetto voice, perhaps not having anything else to say, or simply to break the ice:

"Mr. Empedocles, could I ask whether you speak any Spanish?"

"*Sí, por supuesto*," he replied.

"I just wanted to say that it's a true honor to meet you. You have no idea how much I've read and studied you . . ." he said, in Spanish.

"The only one here who doesn't speak Spanish," interjected Eladio Villagrá, "is the acclaimed author of *In Search of Kaminski*, Mr. Yuri Mikhaylovich. That is why, Fernando, I've taken the liberty of also inviting our good friend Sergio, who knows everything when it comes to languages . . ."

"Pardon me, sir, but do you mean to tell me you speak Russian?" asked Reader, innocently, of the novelist from Puebla.

"I speak it and translate from it," Pitol replied. "And please, there's no need to call me sir. We're friends now, Reader."

"Didn't you know that Sergio has translated works by several Slavic writers?" Chiriboga asked Anagnostes with a certain pomposity in his voice, which evidently hadn't emerged until that moment.

"Well, just a few, really . . ." Pitol excused himself, his face turning a bit red, though it was hard to tell whether it was from the heat or his own, innate sense of modesty when speaking about literature.

"You even lived in Moscow for a few years, didn't you?" inquired Cardoso, who had read some of his books and travelogues.

At that moment, however, Rosinda interrupted the chat to repeat what she was supposed to have memorized that morning, at express orders of the head honcho himself:

"Gentlemen, Fernando Sigüenza, notary, mayor, and renowned author of idyllic poems about our dear city, has asked me to inform you all that a great banquet is awaiting us, a succulent feast featuring the best of the cuisine of Las Rémoras, to commemorate tomorrow's unveiling at the plaza in front of Town Hall, to which you all are invited as honorable and illusory—excuse me—illustrious guests . . ."

"Dinner sounds absolutely wonderful," exclaimed the gynecologist, coming out of his stupor, though still oblivious to the secretary's momentary lapse.

"I agree," affirmed Cecilio, wiping beads of sweat from his forehead with the sleeve of his shirt.

"And don't worry about your luggage," added Rosinda with a beautiful smile, formed by her luscious and tempting red lips. "Joaquín will be kind enough to take them all in his car. He will drop them off at your respective places of lodging, where you can find them after what will no doubt be an opipriapic dinner . . ."

"Wait a minute . . . does she mean opiparous or priapic?" Reader exclaimed.

"Alright then, let's get going," said the mayor, taking Marcelo Chiriboga with one arm and Mikhaylovich Chernishevski with the other, both of whom were bestselling writers of the highest order in their respective countries. Despite the fact that the language barrier presented an absolute obstacle to communicating with the famous author from Azerbaijan, Sigüenza began to speak as he walked with the two characters flanking him on both sides: "You may well have the chance to read some of my poetry, gentlemen. Perhaps an ode or a short madrigal, who knows . . ." Then he excused himself, saying "But we can talk about that later. It's not important right now. What matters is that Tony, owner of the best *lonchería* in town, is waiting for us with an opipriapic dinner. To be honest, that fag is one hell of a cook. But wait a minute . . ." With that he stopped suddenly and turned to face the Secretary of Culture, who was a few steps behind, walking alongside Lascurain and Pitol, who seemed to be feeling a bit claustrophobic with so much going on. "What happened to Mademoiselle Boule de Suif? I didn't see her get off the plane with you, and I completely forgot about her . . ."

The esteemed Eladio Villagrá, who was walking with the others in exaggerated strides along Avenida Libertad, calmly replied:

"The poor woman was delayed in La Paz, and I believe she won't arrive until well after dinner. But don't you worry, sir. Everything seems to indicate that she'll be here in plenty of time for tomorrow's unveiling."

"Perfect," Sigüenza said, still without letting go of his guests. But, as soon as he said "perfect," poor old Chernishevski, of the enormous footwear, suddenly jumped with a start, like some sort of Siberian kangaroo: he had stepped on a small, sleeping lizard with one his broad feet. There were hundreds of the poor little things in the town, and they liked to come out to bask on the warm, paved streets. The mayor tried to comfort him: "Don't worry, Yuri. Soon enough you'll get used to squashing lizards in this town. They're like dog shit in France, only worse."

"Have you ever been to France?" asked Marcelo Chiriboga.

"Only Provence. Arles, to be specific," the mayor said without slowing his gait, just as hungry as all the guests were. "And much to my dismay, I found there to be dog shit everywhere."

"*Oui, c'est vrai! Il y a beaucoup de crottes de chien dans les rues d'Arles,*" intervened Chernishevski, who had evidently overheard the discussion while trying to scrape the smudge off his shoe against the edge of the curb.

"*¿Comprende español, Yuri?*"

"*Un peu, mais je ne le parle pas.*"

"And why were you there, Sigüenza?" Chiriboga asked. "I've also been to Arles, traipsing around in the footsteps of Van Gogh . . ."

But before the young mayor could answer him, Reader cried out from behind them, as if seeing it for the first time:

"The sea! The sea!"

From where they stood on Avenida Libertad, which ran down a slight hill perpendicular to the beach, they caught a glimpse of a swath of dense blueness, although at this time of day it was more like a patch of black foliage flecked with iridescent silver specks, and that smelled strongly of iodized salt.

"You can smell it," Empedocles said. "Even from here, you can still smell the sea. It's like Eolo in Sicily, you know? There, no matter where you set foot, you can smell and see the golden Akragas River and the Mediterranean . . . both so majestic, indeed, yet so different from the Pacific, with its depressing darkness."

"What are you trying to insinuate, Empedocles?" Villa demanded as he marched on down the street. "That our Gulf of California is a piece of shit?"

"Forgive me for getting involved in something I don't care much about, Pancho," Villagrá said reproachfully, with an extra layer of familiarity added on top, "but what do you know of the sea, being a man of the desert, where there's nothing but cacti and coyotes?"

"And from what I understand, you, sir, are a Puebla man, born and raised, no?" replied the brave general, bristling a bit at the Secretary of Culture's comment. "All they have there are churches and priests, one on every corner, which explains why the Mexican people are so oppressed and ignorant . . ."

"All right, all right . . . now's not the time to get into a debate about the church and the state, General," cautioned Solón, who was still walking in lockstep with his brother Cecilio. "Today all that matters is having a good time, enjoying dinner and drinks to our hearts' content, don't you think?"

"The General won't be doing much drinking," Rosinda said, knowingly. "He's become something of a teetotaler since his revolutionary days."

"I'll also be abstaining," added Empedocles, patting his good friend Pancho on the shoulder. "I stopped drinking a long time ago . . . when I began following Orpheus."

"When it comes to drinking, I have to admit, I'll be partaking . . . and in quantities worthy of the character we'll be commemorating tomorrow," Chiriboga chimed in festively.

"*Moi aussi!*" chuckled Yuri of the expansive shoes, his feet slick with lizard innards.

"*Et moi aussi!*" chortled the architect Jasso as the sweat rolled down off his bald head. He had absolutely no idea what the novelist from Azerbaijan was saying.

Through that parade of laughter and chatter they could barely make out Tony—or at least the silhouette of Tony—outlined against the blackness of the night and the blueness of the distant sea, standing there in the distance, on the median that divides Libertad into two lanes of traffic: one that runs up along the waterfront, and another that runs down . . . although, to be honest, there aren't very many cars on the streets of Las Rémoras, which leaves the roadways free to the pedestrians who, now that the sun has gone down, take advantage of the night to emerge from their homes, like thirsty vampires searching for blood.

"Welcome! We've been waiting for you for quite some time," said the owner of the *lonchería*, a tall and incredibly gay man, just as he was described, Eusebio thought, in that story he'd read: even his well-groomed yet out-of-place little moustache was just as he'd expected, and not at all long and thick like Villa's, which looked like it might have been embroidered right there on his lip from the moment he left his mother's womb. "But I see we have a few other guests . . . several others, in fact. But that's no problem at all; we have space for everyone. It's such a pleasure to have you here! Come in, sit down, make yourselves at home, please."

"Actually," Dr. Díaz Gross whispered to Tony, so nobody else could hear, "Mademoiselle Boule de Suif won't be with us tonight, who you know counts as three or four average diners, so we should be just fine . . ."

"On the contrary," he countered, giving his old friend an amiable punch and directing him to a metal folding chair on the sidewalk overlooking Libertad where a number of matching tables had been set up and piled high with shrimp, steamed clams, stuffed crabs, and giant oysters on the half shell. "We have enough here to feed an entire regiment. After all, it's on the town, right, mayor?"

"It certainly is," he said, quite proud of that fact, as he sat down between Chernishevski and Chiriboga. "It's on the town, of course."

And with that, everyone sat down, relaxed, some loosening their ties or rolling up their shirtsleeves, others unbuttoning their collar buttons, while still others—including Eusebio—undid their belts so they could ingest more food or simply to let their guts hang out. Chiriboga and Jasso also participated in this odd habit, but not the General of the Northern Division, who—despite his slight paunch—remained firm and erect in his iron chair. His broad *sombrero*, however, had to be removed, after he inadvertently struck Lascurain in the temple with it as he tried to sit down next to him. In the blink of an eye, scarcely giving the guests time to catch their breath, a crew of servers specifically hired for the occasion brought out ice-cold beers, two bottles of tequila blanco, shot glasses, limes, guacamole, fresh tortilla chips, sopes, salsa picante, fried corn tlacoyos, and bite-sized fried shrimp and fish tacos to start things off . . . and tall glasses brimming with barley water for those who didn't drink alcohol. Empedocles handed one to his friend, the General of the Division of the North, but just as he was about to offer one—gallant and accommodating as always—to Sigüenza's attractive secretary, she stopped him short and said that first she would raise a glass of tequila in honor of the invited guests,

Which Professor Cardoso,
Thinking quickly rather than slow,
Might interpret, correct or no,
This affectionate wink that she shows.

"The idea is to unveil the monument tomorrow morning around eleven o'clock, so that we can all sleep in a bit," said the mayor in one long breath. "It just seemed like such an inconvenience to ask you all to get up early and be in place at eight or nine after such a long and complicated trip."

"That's an excellent plan," said Reader, who had already wolfed down a couple of tlacoyos with beans and salsa borracha.

"So, what line of work are you in?" Solón suddenly asked Reader, still chewing on a golden prawn sautéed with a bit of lime juice.

"Well, I may be a banker, but I've taken a vacation or two in my time . . ."

"A banker, a stockbroker, and—most recently—a cuckold," added Eusebio, trying to make a tasteless joke.

"*Cornutto-lui?*" Yuri Mikhaylovich asked, not quite one hundred percent sure that he'd heard the epithet correctly, and looking to Anagnostes for corroboration.

"Don't tell me . . ." inquired the sympathetic Chiriboga, passing the bowl of shrimp tails to the architect Iginio, who had been eyeing them ever since he first sat down, but hadn't yet tried one.

"Well, yes," Reader replied, taking a bite of something so as to avoid offering up any further unnecessary explanations. In fact, he felt rather ashamed by the revelation of his new marital status, made public thanks to the former professor and current asshole.

Then, the Russian writer said something which Sergio translated as follows:

"Yuri, being the novelist and psychologist that he is, would like to know if you've had any thoughts of forgiving her, if you've thought about taking her back even with the knowledge that she betrayed you . . ."

"I don't know. For now I just want to put it behind me, you know? To just keep reading and figure it out later."

"Good idea," Lascurain offered as he spooned a gigantic helping of guacamole with coriander onto his plate. "Just forget about it . . ."

"Pardon me for asking," Cardoso remarked, turning to the author of *In Search of Kaminski*, "but didn't you once find yourself in jail after a complicated matter involving a skirt?"

Pitol translated the question a bit nervously, not quite sure of how Chernishevski would react; still, though, he tried to smooth over the harsh, uncouth tone of the requisition, or at least Chiriboga thought he did. Yuri, though, replied in his mother tongue—with a surprising level of tranquility—and immediately after he finished speaking, Sergio translated his words in the first person, although clearly without the same measure of calmness maintained by the celebrated author from Baku:

"Yes, I should be in prison right now, as a matter of fact, but I escaped a few months ago. The KGB has been on my tail ever since, but I doubt they'll ever find me again. Putin's pawns and partisans have no idea. In fact, it was quite a stroke of luck that I got the invitation to tomorrow's unveiling; otherwise, I'd still be sneaking around Europe right now . . . and to be honest, I was already fed up with Arles and its endless piles of dog shit. Plus, I can't live my life jumping around like a grasshopper from place to place. So I was thinking that perhaps—with a little luck—I could settle down here, in Las Rémoras, for a spell. That is, of course, if Señor Sigüenza and the rest of you wouldn't mind and wouldn't be too inconvenienced . . ."

Everyone was struck silent, overwhelmed by the astonishing confession made by the Azerbaijani author, as if he had just described the plot of a spy thriller, breaking it down into something like a simple, Slavic recipe. Nevertheless, the mayor recovered quickly and said, with a jaw-droppingly boundless sense of complete and total hospitality:

"Don't you worry, my friend. You can stay here for as long as you need. We don't give a shit about Putin, to be honest. Rosinda will see to it that you have something to occupy your time, other than writing, and she'll set you up with a place to stay in the meantime. In fact . . ." Here he paused, apparently reflecting for a moment before realizing something important: "If I'm not mistaken, our library is still closed and empty. It used to serve as a sort of house for that second-rate hack Elías. I think you could set up quite nicely there, don't you, Rosinda?"

"Certainly, mayor," replied the lovely and (why deny it?) servile secretary. "I'll see that it's cleaned and ready to move into tomorrow."

"He could even take over the job of librarian, which has been vacant ever since the writer left," added Dr. Díaz Gross, taking a quick sip from his Corona and adjusting his light-blue vest and checkered bow tie.

Pitol quickly translated everything that was said, and then Empedocles of Agrigento added, with solidarity:

"I also came here after being exiled from my own country by a bunch of goddamn oligarchs. In fact, nobody even knows I'm here. Just like you, Yuri. We are refugees, fugitives, defectors, deserters, outcasts, political exiles."

"As am I," Villa seconded, taking a long, delicious drink of his barley water. "After I spent all those months in the Coscomate caverns while that son of a bitch Pershing was trying to hunt me down with that Punitive Expedition of his. But I gave that fucking bastard the slip, and he never managed to catch me."

"The same goes for President Carranza, my General," exclaimed Cardoso, raising his beer in praise of the Attila of the North.

"That poor bastard was something else," Pancho laughed merrily, uproariously even, evidently enjoying the memory of those hard, revolutionary days. "How come you know so much?"

"He's a professor who studies the Novel of the Mexican Revolution," Reader explained.

"You're kidding me," Villa replied, once again dipping his moustache in his glass of barley water.

"Among other books, I teach your *Memorias*, General, which you dictated and left unpublished until they were rewritten by the novelist Martín Luis Guzmán."

"Ah, I've read them, and they're all false," bellowed Villa. "That guy Guzmán is a traitor and a coward, and if he weren't already dead, I'd shoot him myself."

"In fact, my General," Anagnostes added, more interested in screwing with him than in making an incisive comment, "Professor Cardoso is a bit of a traitor himself, just like that novelist Guzmán."

"How could that be?" said Empedocles, veritably leaping out of his chair, and almost falling over backwards, although Cecilio caught him in time.

"A traitor in the motherland?" Villagrá exclaimed, as astonished as he was greasy.

"No, no, nothing like that," Eusebio hurried to explain, not eager to be shot by Villa. "What happened is that I kind of *half*-cheated on my wife and she was pissed off enough to leave me not too long ago when—just my luck—she found out about it . . ."

"What do you mean, you *half*-cheated on her?" demanded the architect.

"It's true," Reader insisted, teetering on madness. "And the worst part about it is that he never actually slept with the other woman. He was just trying to, shall we say, cheer her up a little bit."

"Really?" Pitol asked, scrutinizing him with true Socratic skepticism.

"Yes, we were just playing around with each other," Cardoso explained, almost against his own will, but the fact was that he was already facing a firing squad and didn't have much of a choice.

"You were playing around with each other?" the philosopher from Agrigento asked, apparently not understanding the magnitude of the verb, or perhaps trying to dig down into the heart of the matter.

"Pardon me, *señorita*," Reader said to Rosinda, "but what Professor Cardoso wants to say—but is afraid to—is that all he did was to provide 'applied muscular pressure' to the clitoris of the wife of his best friend,

Stefano Morini from Turin, when he wasn't home and she opened the door and invited him in."

"Well goddamn!" exclaimed Chiriboga, trying to stifle a burst of laughter. "That's a whole other matter."

"Applying muscular pressure to the clitoris?" Cecilio repeated, not quite understanding the technique he was referring to. "Is that some sort of chiropractic therapy? Or acupuncture, maybe?"

"In fact," Anagnostes mocked, pressing the advantage, "Eusebio even thought about opening a sort of clinic or spa for bored, depressed house-wives who want their clits massaged. Can you believe it? Tell me that's not the most shameless thing you've ever heard . . ."

"Well, to me that doesn't sound like such a preposterous idea," Lascu-rain chimed in, displaying a mouth filled with drossy, scaly, rust-colored teeth caked in a plaque-like layer of *caepulla*.

"It's true," confirmed Díaz Gross. "There's a client for every service. You have to admit it. The customer is always right. And I say that as a doctor."

"Supply and demand, eh?" added Villagrá, jokingly.

"In any case," Pancho Villa said, hurrying things along with an impetu-ous slap on poor Cardoso's shoulder, "truth is overrated, *amigo*. Don't get discouraged. Your wife is exaggerating the facts. I, for example, fucked a ton of girls while I was married, and Luz, my old lady, never said a thing."

"But those were different times," cautioned Rosinda, growing a bit annoyed with the Northern Mexican *machismo* being displayed by the General.

"Wrong. It's the women who've changed. They can't stomach anything now. They'd rather just throw in the towel," replied Chiriboga, growing more and more emboldened.

Almost immediately, looking to get the bad taste out of his mouth, the Ecuadorian reached for a *callo de hacha* cocktail, which nobody had touched and was still sitting there in the middle of the table, surrounded by empty plates.

"I totally agree with you," insisted the architect Jasso. "This feminism is really striking a blow against the true, dyed-in-the-wool womanizers like us."

"I'm with Rosinda," said Solón, eager to join in the battle of the sexes. "Men have become too clever by half, and now is the time for us ladies . . ."

But then he changed his mind and decided to keep quiet. Cecilio, his brother, had shot him one of those knowing looks that anyone with even a modicum of sense could understand. Almost immediately, the voice of Cardoso wafted in, asking Villa if by any chance he had ever heard of someone by the name of Lucas Gleeson, a bugler with the 5th Infantry Division, who swears he served with you, General, a claim which the Attila of the North took quite seriously: "Lucas . . . what?" "Lucas Gleeson, a fat bugler from Scotland," Eusebio insisted timidly. "Frankly," replied Villa, "I don't have a fucking clue what you're talking about, *señor*. I shot the only bugler I had among my troops for being a traitor and a nitpicker. His name was Dominguito Cristóforo." Humberto Lascurain and Chernishevski were following the thread of the conversation while, at the same time, continuing to help themselves to crab legs and chocolate clams stuffed with vegetables that were being brought to the table. They ate, they listened, and they drank, completely enchanted with life. They cracked open the crab legs and sucked out the meat to their hearts' content before discarding the hollow, gutted shells. Continuing their difficult task, the servers brought over platters of majestic butterflied fish marinated in garlic and lime juice and grilled to perfection. They sat them down on the table, piping hot and very aromatic; nevertheless, in the blink of an eye, the fillets, the refried kidney beans, and fresh tortillas had vanished, leaving behind only remnants of what had been there a second before: several rows of fish spines and a few fragments of tortilla chips *et ce tout*. But more glasses of beer, barley water, and tequila blanco were served up, emptied, and returned to the three-waiter team, while bite-sized fried shrimp and fish tacos, sopes and tlacoyos with beans and shredded cheese, guacamole, various salsas, abalone cocktails, and ceviche followed, one after the other and without interruption, along with sliced avocado, pico de gallo, and lemon wedges. It was quite literally a finger-licking feast.

After a period of foamy silence, during which each of the dinner guests was consuming his own delicious victuals without coming up to breathe, and under the bituminous tropical night, which enveloped them in a warm embrace, like that of a fertile mother, content to be gathered there, filling their bellies for free, Cecilio asked Reader out of the blue whether he was the same Reader who appears in *Friction*, a book that he'd started not long ago, since that character was also a banker, stockbroker, cuckold, and traveling companion of one Professor Cardoso, an expert on the Novel of the Mexican Revolution, which was quite a coincidence, don't you think? Plus, Anagnostes appeared to be the same guy who, on the eve of his first wedding anniversary, found his wife getting hot and heavy with his best friend, a renowned painter and member of the Agro movement who maintained a small studio in the Narvarte neighborhood in Mexico City in the year 2025.

But was there animosity, equivocation, ingenuousness, naïveté, foolishness, good judgment, cruelty, or compassion in the question Cecilio had fired at Reader without warning? Had he thought about what he was saying? That was impossible to know; it was impossible to understand why the hell he had spouted off on that torrid, opipriapic evening. Judging by the look in the eyes and on the face of Cecilio, it was nothing more than curiosity, plain and simple, the same healthy sense of inquisitiveness that any reader might feel when he finds himself (by chance) face to face with his favorite character, something which (as we know) doesn't happen very often.

With a piece of marinated fish still stuck between his teeth, Anagnostes' countenance was changing colors in a precipitous and very obvious way: it shifted from scarlet to fuchsia and mulberry before transitioning into, first, a methylene blue and then something that can only be described as a sort of livid, lazulite blue before culminating in a pallid, ashen white . . . until, finally getting him out of that tight spot, or that tight range of colors, Marcelo Chiriboga, that master of colors and landscapes, suddenly said:

"What the hell . . . I thought that the Reader you're referring to was me. Myself. I swear, that's what I assumed when I was reading *Friction*."

"Me too," confirmed the architect Jasso, "although I'm not a banker or stockbroker. I'm just a simple, trusting reader of frictions."

"The same with me," confessed the Secretary of Culture for the state of Puebla. "And I have to admit, I often found myself getting quite upset at reading about myself."

"Well, shit! It sounds like everyone here is reading *Friction*," Cardoso murmured, feeling at once astonished and taken aback, caught in an indiscernible mixture of the two, and that was because he honestly didn't know whether to feel honored or beg forgiveness for the entanglement he'd created. Nevertheless, at that precise moment, he came to understand that it was ultimately nothing but a horribly dense narrative contradiction: how could all these people have read his book if he was very much in the process of writing it? How could they, if he still had yet to finish *Friction*? He was still pondering this abstruse and bizarre situation when he heard Chiriboga chime in, in a rather annoying tone of voice:

"Therefore, I must insist that we assign names to the characters, Eusebio, so as to avoid any further confusion."

"*Je suis d'accord*," nodded Yuri from his seat, following the conversation as closely as a native speaker would, even though he was only tangentially participating in it.

"It's just that I was trying to write the first work of virtual, interactive friction in the history of world literature," Cardoso explained, rather carelessly.

"Don't be so smug," snapped an ill-tempered Iginio.

"Yuri and I agree with Chiriboga," Pitol translated, "and we know what we're talking about. So don't try and explain yourself. Here, all of us (or almost all of us) are frictionists . . . just in case you hadn't figured that out by now."

"While you, on the other hand, are an insignificant and excommunicated professor with writerly pretentions," accused Reader, piling on to the avalanche of attacks that was quickly burying his traveling companion, the only one to blame for his cruel romantic destiny. In other words, he was the lone individual responsible for his own current state of pain and humiliation.

"You think you're a frictionist, Cardoso! Admit it!" Doctor Lascurain said, crossing and uncrossing his legs . . . as if it were some fucking nervous tic.

"Yes, why don't you just mind your own business!" agreed his colleague Díaz Gross, elegant and old-fashioned, the same way he'd been the year before and the year before that.

Everybody had stopped eating; nobody was even drinking anymore. All of a sudden, for some mysterious and nefarious reason (*Tyche*? *Ananke*?), all of the criticisms and insults had—deservedly or not—been piled on poor old Eusebio Cardoso, former professor at Millard Fillmore University, and simply for authoring the infamous *Friction* and for having used you, Reader, as the main character in his coprophilic story about sex and feminine malice, about human betrayal and disloyalty.

Cardoso responded, this time speaking directly to you:

"The fact that your wife cheated on you is not my fault. It never has been, and it never will be . . . And it's even less my fault that you, yes you, Reader, were reading *Friction* while your lovely wife was off sleeping with your best friend . . ."

"But he's not even my best friend . . . you know that as well as anybody," countered Reader, mad as a bull now, standing up from his seat as if readying himself to charge Eusebio, who, despite it all, remained calm and seated in his chair, surrounded by a growing mountain of plates, oyster shells, and empty bottles. Just to be safe, though, Villa and Villagrá managed to stop you, raging Reader, and directed you back to your seat, which you vehemently protested at first, until the Commander of the Northern Division himself had to suddenly restrain you by twisting your arm behind your back, a move that had you shrieking like a hog in a slaughterhouse.

"And to make matters worse, everything seems to indicate that she's pregnant," Cardoso countered, showing no mercy as he sat there in his folding chair, not even turning to look at you when you, unprepared Reader, had sat back down again, humbly rubbing your left wrist. "And it's not yours, as you know. I just barely told you that back at the airport . . ."

"Pregnant?" stammered Rosinda, who evidently had not been reading *Friction*, nor had she heard anything about that salacious little toy or the awful rumor mill it had produced, which was now running full throttle in the Las Rémoras night.

"Yes. It's the painter's," Cecilio, Iginio, Chiriboga, Pitol, and Villagrá all replied, almost in unison, like a very well-informed chorale, all of them lowering their eyes in a sort of facial contraction, which perhaps was intended to show you just a hint of sympathy or compassion or even (who knows?) to cast the tenuous light of mourning upon you.

"It's because you're infertile, and you lied to her about it," Chiriboga suggested, turning to face you, Reader, and pointing a fiery finger in your direction. "Isn't that it? You were fully aware of the fact that you couldn't have children, but you sent her to see Doctor Lascurain anyway . . ."

"You sent her to see me?" Bits of onion spewed from his mouth.

"Yes, doctor, he sent her to you," affirmed Pitol, who seemed scarcely able to contain his elation at being abreast of each and every detail. "Reader was playing the fool . . ."

"Well," Sigüenza chimed in, "We don't need to keep poor Anagnostes turning on the spit any longer. I think this roast is just about done . . ."

"Or, as they say on my ranch," added the Attila of the North, "there's a time to cut bait, and there's a time to fish . . ."

"Gentlemen, there's no need to come to blows here," said the Secretary of Culture with his greasy demeanor and fake patent leather shoes.

"Exactly," agreed the mayor. "As you know, we're gathered here to celebrate a great monster—a happy ogre, if you will—and in honor of the occasion our sister city of Chinon will be presenting us a magnificent statue which we will be unveiling tomorrow morning in the plaza." And with that, the mayor got up from his seat, adjusted his tie, and with a decidedly proud gesture, he added: "Rosinda, I ask that you go and find Tony. Tell him that we're ready to go, that it's time for us to bid each other good-night."

Excusing herself, either solicitous or servile, the secretary got up from her chair and, in four long strides, had crossed the avenue in search of the lean, lanky owner of the *lonchería* who, with so much going on in his kitchen, hadn't been able to escape for even a second to come out and visit with his guests at that opipriapic dinner. And no sooner had the lovely Rosinda disappeared into the darkness than Sigüenza extended the following invitation to the men gathered there:

"I expect that many of you are tired from travel, but if anyone is up for continuing the festivities for a bit, then we can go for drinks with Josefina, the new madam of the house."

"Of the house?" inquired Eladio Villagrá, not quite sure of whether he'd understood the rather ambiguous reference.

"Yes, of the house," repeated Iginio, fastening his belt and exploding out of his chair as if he were sitting in a catapult: he wasn't about to let an opportunity like this pass him by.

"Is she the one who took over after Inés?" asked Doctor Lascurain, picking at the sour sediment encrusted around his gums.

"Exactly," confirmed Cecilio, getting to his feet. "She's been expecting you all; she knows you're here on official business, and the girls have promised to treat you like kings."

"And of course, gentlemen, all expenses are being paid by the city council," Fernando Sigüenza said, excusing himself with a ceremonious bow and calling for Rosinda to return.

Cardoso couldn't help but watch, jealously, each and every movement, hint, wink, or word that the mayor directed at his attractive secretary: despite the embarrassing and rather unpleasant quarrel with you, Reader (which, you should know, he feels deeply sorry about), he hasn't for a single moment taken his eyes off those ruby-red lips, that jet-black hair, and of course the infundiblular ass belonging to that young woman. *But are they lovers?* the professor wondered silently. *Was Sigüenza really that lascivious?* He was hoping—he had been hoping all night, in fact—for the tiniest indication, some sort of hint to help clarify their situation (and his possibilities, whether real or frictitious, with the girl) or one that would at least help him decide whether or not to follow the ridiculous retinue on to the famous Las Rémoras brothel. *What should I do?* he asked himself, growing less and less certain as he watched the other invited guests draw themselves heavily up and out of their seats, stretch out their legs, adjust their belts, blot the sweat from their necks with a napkin, and button up the cuffs of their sleeves. Villa belched and Empedocles cinched up his toga. *Whatever the case may be,* thought Eusebio, *paying a visit to the whorehouse isn't such a bad idea,* since there, in the murdered woman's own house, he might be able to find a clue, a key bit of evidence related to the horrible crime that had been bothering him for some time now, ever since his Barthesian reading of *The Obstacles*. But before heading off towards the brothel, and after bidding good-night to Tony, his three servers, Rosinda, and the mayor, still standing there in the middle of Avenida Libertad under the waning though still oppressive tropical heat, Sergio Pitol said, as if in a sudden stroke of enlightenment:

"But herein lies a blatant contradiction, gentlemen, and most of us haven't even realized it yet. It's the same contradiction that Professor Cardoso, the budding frictionist, has incurred. The problem is this: there would be no way for us to know what we know about your marital problems, Reader, if we hadn't already read *Friction* . . . but if we've already read it, then why are we living it right now?" mumbled the man from Veracruz, his revelation somewhat hindered by the fact that he was smacking his lips and scratching his incipient little moustache. "And to make matters worse, a number of us who claim to have read it somehow don't seem to know what we should know by now. Doesn't that seem just a bit strange?"

The majority, though, couldn't understand Pitol's gibberish. They would have to reread it.

"Exactly," Marcelo Chiriboga affirmed. "How the hell could we have read *Friction* if, as Sergio says, everything that's happened tonight already exists within *Friction* itself and forms part of your goddamn virtual book, Eusebio? Would you care to explain that to us, because in all honesty, this is quite a tangled web you're weaving . . ."

Just as he was about to say that there was no need for him to respond to such accusations or to explain either himself, the tangled web, or anything else, it was you, illustrious Reader, who came to Eusebio's aid, apparently harboring no resentment towards your traveling companion:

"Why don't we leave all that until after we spend some time at the Casa de Inés? I'm ready for another drink, and it would be quite uncouth to keep the lovely ladies there waiting any longer . . ."

"*Moi aussi,*" said Chernishevski, who hadn't understood either Pitol or Chirigoba, although he'd clearly understood you, having finally offered up a decent idea.

"I'm with Yuri. I say we go," decided Iginio, who could intuit French even if he couldn't speak it. But it wasn't the heat of the night that was driving his decision; it was a fever of a different sort. "And by the way, it's no longer the Casa de Inés. Now it's called the Casa de Josefina. Ever since Roberta left town and Inés was found strangled we changed the name. Or rather, La Gringa changed the name."

"She even had the living room and the suites reupholstered," added Doctor Díaz Gross.

"Well then, let's go," suggested Lascurain. "Maybe someone there can give me a clue as to the whereabouts of Ricardo Urrutia."

"Ricardo Urrutia?" Cecilio asked as he started heading down the avenue in the direction of Atuneros, towards the trashy outskirts of town.

"Yes, Ricardo Urrutia."

"That's a name we know around here. He's the one who took off with Elías, the writer, and Pili, Sigüenza's fiancée, in my blue Ford. They've been gone for months now."

"Really?" Lascurain asked without slowing his step. "Where were they going?"

"We don't know," Solón replied, with a hint of something—either annoyance or sadness—upon being reminded about that vehicle, which was a wonderful machine in its day.

"At the end of *The Obstacles*, it says they were heading for Los Angeles and after that, who knows, San Francisco, maybe, or some place like Seattle or Vancouver . . . even as far as Alaska."

"I highly doubt that old Ford would get them that far," clarified Cecilio. "It was already quite old when they took it; well on its way to the scrap yard. It belonged to my father. It was a '64."

While this dialogue was being bantered back and forth, the group continued along its slow path, moving away from downtown Las Rémoras, from the plaza that faced the sea, the town hall, and an old, forgotten basketball court. The newly arrived visitors wouldn't even have a chance to catch a glimpse of the ocean (as they had hoped) nor of the virulent way in which the stars imprint themselves upon the water's black metallic back. Instead, they were all heading down Avenida Libertad and away from the shell-shaped beach with its famous rocky crag. Once that Baja Californian boulevard had come to a rather abrupt end, the retinue pressed forward along a series of uninhabited and unpaved streets that marked the outskirts of the little coastal hamlet: a few apple trees and empty lots, thickets and ravines, poorly constructed fences, unfinished entelechial housing developments, and a few asbestos hovels scattered throughout the desert built by migrant paragliders who quite literally drop in and out of the area on the whims of the wind. Electric lights began to disappear or at least became scarcer as they got further from the center of town: the light posts were set fewer and farther between, but they continued to stand, devoted (like God's cypresses) to the very end. Starving dogs nosed around an old bag, an empty tin can, even another dog's shit, but there was nothing, absolutely nothing there but sharp stones and nettles . . . how long had it been since a kind soul had tossed the poor beasts a crust of bread or a bone to chew on? The dinner companions continued to make their way through the night until—just before reaching Pescadores, half a block from the brothel, across the intersection with Atuneros—Cecilio and the architect Jasso announced that they were getting close. *But where are we?* wondered Villagrá, who was unable to see past the tip of his own nose and felt completely helpless in the Las Rémoras night. *Look,* cried the Secretary of Culture, but there was nothing there save the scurrying lizards and swarming flies. A few steps later, though, under the feeble light of a leaning lamppost, they found a house—a big, dingy, almost ocher house—right in the middle of that sad and half-deserted neighborhood. *This must be it,* Reader thought correctly, as did Eusebio, who more or less recognized the place he'd read so much about.

No sooner had they all gathered on the threshold in front of the building than they heard the clear tones of a familiar old bolero cleaving the virginal night air:

> *Because I'm just so tired of loving*
> *Someone who doesn't love me . . .*

He couldn't help it: Cardoso was instantly reminded (in a fit of déjà vu) of the moment when Raimundo Rosales, the poor little man with green, oval-shaped, Coke-bottle glasses, came here to visit his beloved Inés on that final, bitter evening, that dark and distant night, which nobody, not even Cardoso, would ever forget. *But that's a horse of another color entirely,* Eusebio thought to himself. *An old, tired, spent horse that's been put out to pasture in a whole other work of friction.* Now he was caught up in this one, with new fellow travelers, and the only thing that mattered here was to solve the mystery that had been consuming him: the death of Inés. Empedocles rapped on the knocker and almost immediately they could hear someone (a body) turn off a record player, stumble into a piece of furniture (a small table in the foyer) and finally appear, hurried and harried and fixing loose strands of black hair, at the door: it was Josefina, the same young girl who had opened the door to Rosales on the night of his nefarious arrival, the final night of his love. Standing there with her, half-hidden by the doorjamb, was Ruth, at once curious and engrossed. They both ushered in the guests, quite amiable and flattering, greeting each of the travelers with a coquettish kiss on the corner of his lips. Once inside, they passed through an entryway adorned with mirrors and a candelabrum, and found themselves in a grand, rococo, eighteenth-century sitting room, although—as the good local doctor had said—the upholstery was brand new. It wasn't nearly as hot as it was outside, although they could feel the heavy effects of cigarette and candle smoke rarefying the air, along with the scents of musk, lavender, and lemon. Standing there among the sofas, divans, and ottomans set back in the dim corners of the room were seven or eight girls between the ages of twenty and twenty-five. A ruddy light, coming from some indefinable place in the room, softened their corseted waists, their long legs and languid arms, their true height, their rouge-powdered faces. Of course, for those who were regular guests at the old brothel, like Díaz Gross, Iginio, and Cecilio, the absence of Roberta and Inés lent a distinctly different feeling to the place, and that lacuna delivered a painful jab, an undeniable sorrow, a feeling of irreparable loss despite the fact that—no matter how you look at it—they were still just a couple of whores.

After turning the phonograph back on, Josefina went about the task of introducing each of her young ladies by their names and nationalities . . . almost as if she were hosting an international beauty contest. Among them was a mahogany-haired girl Bonifacia who went by the name of Selvática, apparently because she was descended from the native people of Iquitos, a remote, sylvan place in the middle of the Peruvian Amazon. Next was a spectacular, copper-skinned Brazilian mulatta, a seasoned, sensual, and courageous woman just home from the wars, known throughout the world of working girls as Teresa Batista. With them were four other girls: two Hungarian sisters, Nina and Nana, and two milky-white Russians, all

344

of whom had one day simply shown up unannounced, speaking nothing but Hungarian and Russian, respectively, which is why it didn't take long at all before the two inveterate Slavists, Pitol and Chernishevski, found themselves strongly attracted to the two young ladies from Moscow while you, Reader, were engaged with one of the Hungarian beauties, and Cardoso with the other, who might even be twins judging by their hair (which was long and blond) hanging loose and free down to the middle of their backs, their clear, cold aqua-blue eyes, their long, lithe, sleek, exposed arms and legs, qualities that, of course, in no way reminded them of the voluptuousness and dark-toned plumpness of Irene, Eusebio's ex-wife, and were even less like Matilde's more or less Mediterranean look (olive, chestnut). You sat down with the first of the young Magyarian women (Nana?), who absolutely had to be the sister of the one (Nina?) with whom the Professor had settled down, possibly already aroused, judging by—and based solely on—the bulk in his pants, which wasn't exactly due to the folds of the pleats. They conversed with the two sisters in Spangarian, after having sat down in a calm corner of the room next to a bottle of tequila blanco that Josefina brought out on a little gold service tray, along with four shot glasses, lemon slices, and salt. For Yuri and Pitol, who were getting acquainted with the two milky Russians in another corner of the room, she brought a bottle of Stolichnaya vodka, and for the architect Iginio and the teacher Villagrá, who were getting to know Selvática and the jubilant mulatta Batista, respectively, she had a bottle of Jamaican rum with bottles of Coke, a bowl of ice, and slices of lime. Meanwhile, Cecilio and Lascurain were having an animated conversation with Ruth about the disappearance of Roberta and her little boy, and about the reasons (or lack thereof) for their sudden departure from Las Rémoras and the scornful, disdainful way she treated Elías up until the last day they were both seen there in the brothel. The gynecologist was telling them—between sip after sip of whiskey—about his completely random first encounter with the aforementioned Roberta (a very beautiful woman, of course) on one of his routine, professional visits to the brothels of Mexico City. He was also telling them how, by fate of destiny, the amorous tale of Roberta and the writer had come up during conversation between the two of them (between doctor and patient) after he, Lascurain, had diagnosed her with a very rare venereal disease. It was, he said to Ruth and Cecilio in confidence, a form of syphilis commonly known as "lover's rage," and the primary symptom exhibited by the infected person is a sort of impassioned madness, a strange form of *enthousiasmos* that manifests itself in truly imprudent, careless, and uncalled-for acts. Humberto continued on, whiskey in hand, with his emotional tale, describing how dumbstruck Roberta was to learn, from the good doctor's own mouth, about the diagnosis of dementia in Elías, her former lover, and how the poor woman was unable to hold back the brackish, crocodile tears that rolled precipitously down and over her glossy, polished cheeks while she demurely covered up her cunt, which Lascurain had only just recently auscultated while wearing his special gynecological gloves during one of those routine visits. Needless to say, Cecilio and Ruth, who had been friends for a very long time, were also quite shocked and saddened by the hair-raisingly lurid anecdote: until that very moment, they'd had no idea whatsoever about the all-consuming obsession that Elías, the town's native son, held for his green-eyed whore, the beautiful Roberta, legendary heartbreaker of Las Rémoras and neighboring towns. They fell silent for an incalculable moment, not knowing what else to say, for the final, unwritten words in the history of *The Obstacles* had finally been spoken.

While this revelation was taking place, Villa and Empedocles had gone off, smug, self-satisfied, and talkative, to sit (each with his respective glass of mineral water) in a couple of big green armchairs located on the threshold that divided the entryway from the reupholstered main sitting room. It should be said that ever since they left Tony's *lonchería*, the two of them had been caught up in their favorite debate, the one subject that had been a continuous point of discussion for years: how Eros and Eris influence the complicated yet subtle machinery of the

Mexican Six-Year Plan, how the four phases of the cosmic cycle affected Mexico's internal history, and—above all—how the Revolution and the Agrarian Reformation were ultimately betrayed by a group of shameless fucking bastards, as the General of the North said, never at a loss for colorful language when it came to describing the Mexican political class. The two of them spent their entire friendship in this particular political maze without ever reaching any sort of consensus: one constantly comparing the incipient Mexican democracy with the incipient Sicilian democracy from the fifth century before Christ, while the other always (without exception) came out on top despite any interruptions or clamor to the contrary. It's just that, truth be told, Pancho Villa wasn't what you'd call a man of democratic principles or ideas. He never had been. The rugged life and cruel realities of the countryside had taught him something which he repeated *ad nauseam* to whomever would listen to him: like it or not, it takes a strong, hard, commanding hand to take the reins of a nation. It was an assertion that old Empedocles—who had been offered the crown by his own people after liberating them from the oligarchs—simply could not accept. Despite the fact that he himself was an ancient, unabashed aristocrat, anything resembling a tyranny or dictatorship ran completely contrary to his deeply ingrained liberal, democratic principles. But in the end, as you know, said Villa between sips of mineral water: the very same people that were lauding and praising you were the same ones who threw you out of Sicily. But the same thing happened to you, Pancho, refuted the philosopher with plenty of knowledge of the subject, or have you already forgotten? What, exactly, are you talking about, thinker? I'm talking about the fact that you could have become president of Mexico in 1915 when you and Zapata entered the Capital, but you turned it down. We're the same in that regard; we were both put up on pedestals, but in the end we decided to walk away. No, it's different, replied the Attila of the North: I wasn't cut out to be the president, I didn't have the background, the education, so I couldn't possibly have accepted such a position; I believed then—and

347

I still believe now—that there were others better equipped to fulfill that position than me. Ah, but let's think about that for a moment, cautioned Empedocles of Agrigento, brandishing his fiery sword: you were once the governor of Chihuahua, right? Yes, and I wasn't too bad at it either, scolded the Robin Hood of the Frontier, remembering that year or so of governance. My task was and always has been to destroy oligarchs, landowning families like the Terrazas-Creel family, the powerful groups that control the country as if it were theirs for the taking, and that's exactly what I did: I kicked their fucking asses while I was governor, and did the exact same thing afterwards, too. Nobody's saying that you didn't run them ragged, acknowledged the pre-Socratic philosopher, but they didn't exactly thank you for it either, let's say . . . For me, the shortcomings of Madero and Abraham González, continued the General, ignoring his companion's response, made me realize once and for all that I had to continue fighting, because all the Porfirian structures had done was change the proprietor's name on the signs, while leaving all the fundamental roots in place. On that I'm in agreement, said the philosopher: there is no more noble thing in life than to fight ceaselessly, to struggle without respite; nevertheless, let me say to you frankly, Doroteo: Mexico, like any other country, has been hijacked by the wealthy, those who own and control the means of production. Like it or not, it's the price of living in a system where everything can be bought by or sold to the highest bidder, and . . . Here Villa interrupted, a bit annoyed by the libertine views of his dear friend: . . . and where, of course, the most despicable spirit of competition—the law of the craftiest, most underhanded people—prevails, isn't that right? Exactly, replied the man from Agrigento, but that system, as asinine as it might seem, eventually (yes, with time) does offer benefits to those who are the most downtrodden. It's much more preferable, I tell you, to a completely proprietary state that owns the individuals and their souls, their land and their family property. No, when it comes to that, you're mistaken, Empe: the state must make sure that the land—yes the land, first and foremost—belongs to the people who work it, to the farmers, the laborers, and nobody else. But in that sort of state, as paternalistic, gluttonous, and bureaucratic as the one you're painting, there is no freedom, no stimulus, and no competition, the philosopher pointed out as he took another small sip of mineral water. At least with Capitalism, as savage and ruinous as it might seem to you, it allows (however grudgingly) for a certain amount of freedom and creates the incentive to have just a little bit more than the next guy . . . and without it—believe you me—everything will grind to a sclerotic halt. That's exactly where I differ with you, Attila grumbled: how can you talk to me about freedom and Capitalism when here in Mexico so many people are illiterate and those who can read aren't able to pick up a book because they don't have the money to buy one, or because they simply don't have the time to read because they're out there in the fields doing backbreaking labor from sunup to sundown? To be free and truly democratic, my friend, as you're suggesting, first you have to have equality, followed shortly by education, and Mexico is sorely lacking in both of those things, lacking in both education and equality . . . instead, it's pure, blatant inequality and the most pathetic state of social injustice. That's for sure, agreed Empedocles. At the very least, Villa continued, his harangue now unstoppable, there should be the opportunity to prepare yourself for equality, to cultivate the spirit of equality, which would therefore require a grassroots change, and along with that, time—centuries, perhaps—to let the new tendrils take root . . . And *kinēsis*, volition, said the philosopher. Voli . . . what? Desire, added the man from Agrigento. Desire? Villa asked, surprised. Yes, the desire to be better than the next guy, the will to leave mediocrity behind you, the need to not only keep up with, but surpass the Joneses, Empedocles specified. The Mexican people are spineless, envious, and conformists . . . and that's because of their inherent Catholicism, their irredeemable Guadalupeanism, and their history so rife with defeat. On that we can agree, Philosopher, consented Villa. Desire should be the moral of a man, stated Empedocles; the will is, in the end, what makes us all different, for better or for worse, knowing or ignorant, great or small. But how dare you say that we are all different if we are all equal under the law, and the Constitution is applied equally to all of us without exception? We are not equal, Doroteo, no matter how much you may want to think so; the Constitution is something else entirely and has no bearing, no relevance to what I'm saying here. Nevertheless, the imperturbable General responded in a resounding tone: If we are not equal, then we would have to become so. If not, then how can we speak of freedom, competition, or democracy when opportunities aren't the same for all? I'm adamant about this: in Mexico, the only thing we've ever had is a gang of rich men exploiting the poor, and another gang of politicians operating at the expense of the downtrodden bastards. That is exactly why, attacked the Philosopher of the Four Elements, the politicians exploit and humiliate the poor with rigged, populist, messianic measures, which amount to pure, dirty tricks which in the long run are going to do nothing but mire them in inaction, ignorance, and misery . . . Don't talk to me about messianisms, when you, of all people, put so much faith in the gods back in your day. Well that's what we are, Pancho: gods. Each of us is a god, or at least we can become one if we observe the precepts of my *Purifications*, the three *manias* or divine possessions: prophecy, medicine, and poetry. Look, *cabrón*, every time you go there, I have no fucking idea what the hell you're talking about, interrupted the Scourge of the Frontier. To me, there are only powerful men. No gods, no manias, none of that shit. You don't understand, Pancho, because you're not listening to me . . . and it is only through learning that wisdom is increased. As Felipe Ángeles, your own Chief of Artillery, has said, you're blinded by your own willing stubbornness. Once something takes root in that thick head of yours, there's no getting it out; I can see why you got into it with the Carnivore of Cajeme in Celaya . . . and not just once, but on several occasions. Look, I'm not going to get into the whole Manco thing and all the fucking battles he lost, and I'm certainly not going to argue about my dear Felipe, may he rest in peace: that's a whole other kettle of fish, and I don't want to get distracted. I just want to make one thing clear, philosopher: the political measures you're speaking so scornfully about are not Populist. Far from it. Public services are social guarantees that the state must provide equally for everyone, because they protect the people I fight on behalf of: farmers and miners, railroad engineers and craftsmen, indigenous people and shopkeepers, the old colonial settlers who are down on their luck . . . all those who've had neither voice nor vote since the Conquest, run over and beaten down by those who have more, by those in positions of power, who sit in the captain's chair of society, unmindful and unheeding of the underdogs . . . Listen to me, everyone they've humiliated deserve fair wages, eight-hour workdays, free education, justice, health, social services, decent pensions, wellness, freedom, and—above all—land, land, land. Empedocles was growing a little tired of all this, and opted not to reply to this broadside volley from the General from Durango. He simply took one last sip of mineral water and closed his eyes in a heavy, sorrowful manner: they would never really understand each other, despite the fact the two of them were, deep down, so very close indeed. He could feel that. After a good bit of silence broken only by the music wafting over from the record player on the other side of the room, Villa remarked: What I don't understand is that, according to you, we are all made equal by Eros, right? The force that supposedly unifies and amalgamates all the distinct elements into a single, compact mass. But then you go and say that we are not, in fact, equals, that desire and will differentiate us, emancipate us. I honestly don't understand you, Empe. Look, Pancho: to begin with, it was Parmenides who came up with the concept of the One, not me, replied the man from Agrigento, emerging from his silence. He's the monist, not me. In fact, I'm the first pluralist in history. Listen, Leucippus ended up copying my ideas. Now then, although Eros does tend, yes, toward unifying the diverse, you have to bear in mind the fact that now, at this very moment, we are in the opposite phase, Eris, Discord, Strife. Everything, then, is currently being divided up into millions of sets and subsets and sub-subsets. Only like attracts like, and in this way the nucleus forms itself, forms its own microscopic unity, its set of similarities, its element. That's why, or how, we aren't all equal, Pancho. And we won't be, because as soon as soon as we attain the aforementioned sphere, which unites the contrary and amalgamates all the innumerable diversities of the cosmos, the eddying force, the *dyne*, the engine that moves Discord, or Strife, will disintegrate everything all over again. It will separate the dissimilar, remove the wheat from the chaff, if you will. Honestly, you always confuse me, Pancho concluded, lacking the necessary desire to prolong the night's political-philosophical carousal. He added, as he adjusted his broad sombrero, do you want a little more water, Philosopher? My throat's getting dry from all this talk . . .

In response, Empedocles got to his feet, sulking, perhaps just a bit frustrated, gathered up the folds of his purple toga with wounded majesty, and set about locating Cardoso amidst the mass of smoke and divans there in the reupholstered eighteenth-century sitting room. As he began to wander about, the great Philosopher of Agrigento could see how, amidst such noise and activity, Morpheus was able to vanish *déjà* from the house of Kypris without bothering to say whether or not he'd be back; the drowsiness and dreams drifting down upon every member of the opipriapic dinner party was transforming the effects of the feast at Tony's *lonchería* into a sort of Orphean fucking apotheosis: coexisting there, right under their very noses, was an eruption of carnal hunger melded with a centuries-long thirst and an unspeakable desire to start singing or dancing, to laugh, to fart, to belch, or to pepper with kisses the young women who were as scantily clad as the maenads running, frenzied, through the forests. Even the girls themselves, unaccustomed to receiving more than one or two parishioners a week, and sometimes none at all, suddenly found themselves content, relaxed, their tongues loose, eager to enjoy themselves with the recently arrived regiment. Only Solón seemed a bit tense, sitting there at the bar, talking with Josefina and Díaz Gross about the whereabouts of La Gringa Jenny, the true proprietor of the rebaptized brothel.

The new madam offered them each a cigarette, saying:

"What surprised us all the most was the demise of the poor old priest Roldán. Remember him?"

"Of course," replied the doctor, graciously lighting Josefina's cigarette while declining the one offered to him. "The look on the face of my good man Augusto, may he rest in peace, when he saw the gringa show up there in the middle of the funeral service he was conducting at the cemetery by the sea, was enough to set your hair on end. He must have thought she was an angel . . ."

"But not a guardian angel," Josefina added, patting him on the side of his face.

"Not at all," said Solón, stifling a slight chuckle, although—to be honest—Roldán's descent into the grave and its ultimate consequences were quite a serious matter indeed.

"It's nothing to joke about," said Josefina, quite rightly scolding him. "The town has gone without a priest ever since. And although we're prostitutes, we still believe in God, the Virgin Mary, and in Divine Providence."

"In that, you are all exactly the same," said Solón. "You all love God and you believe in Mary Magdalene."

"Speaking of guardian angels," interrupted Díaz Gross, just now emerging from his self-absorption, "I recently had the chance to read Roldán's confessional tale, *A Convert's Chronicle*, and in it he talks about how he met Jenny, your boss, in La Paz, when they were both young, back in the '70s, I think . . ."

"You did?" exclaimed Josefina, astonished, because she had never heard him speak of that manuscript.

"Roldán does indeed call her his guardian angel. Can you believe it? And together they gave birth to our Elías, the town's native son."

"We know that, we're familiar with that story, Doc," said Josefina, reminiscing about the priest's final, agonizing moments at the colonnade that the locals call the Altozano when he revealed—on his deathbed— the consanguinity of Ricardo and Elías, who were half brothers.

"But if it were Abaddon the Destroyer who appeared at the funeral," suggested Solón, remembering the moment and the terrified face of the poor priest when, on the verge of bidding farewell to the lawyer Rosales on his voyage into the Great Beyond, La Gringa appeared, unannounced.

"It wouldn't have mattered. She was the mother of his son," said Díaz Gross.

"And that whole thing about not wanting to bury Inés alongside the lawyer just seemed so shameful to me, like a breach of trust, an act of cowardice," added Josefina, growing ever more irate as she recalled that unfortunate day. "Is that what awaits us in the next life? We're going to get spit upon?"

"I couldn't agree with you more," said the doctor in his dated, blue, three-piece suit and his out-of-style checkered bow tie. "It was a fucking disgrace, Jose, but it wasn't Roldán's fault. If it had been up to him, I'm sure Augusto would have buried Raimundo and Inés next to each other."

"It was the local recalcitrant Catholics, the supplicants, the league of mothers," added Solón, who had lost his faith (and his mother) many years before. "The way I see it, what harm could it do to bury them next to each other if that was their wish? How could that bother anybody? I'm sure that the lawyer Rosales was just waiting, every afternoon, for the right moment to pay a visit to the Bermuda Triangle."

"The Bermuda Triangle?" asked Díaz Gross, startled.

"Yes, that was the nickname Iginio and Rosales had for the brothel owner. Didn't you know that, Doc?"

"But how did you manage to get a copy of *A Convert's Chronicle*?" interrupted Josefina, drawing in a puff of smoke as she tried to get the bitter taste out of her mouth, which cropped up every time someone recalled the inhumane manner in which poor Inés had been laid to rest.

"Santa lent her copy to me. She's been taking care of the Altozano until the new priest arrives."

"Do you know anything about him?" asked Solón, fanning away the swirls of sour smoke that were gathering in front of his face.

"About the new priest? Not much. Just that he's an honorary member of Opus Dei and that any day now he's supposed to appear here in Las Rémoras with his gold crucifix on his chest. I think his name is Urbano."

"What kind of a name is that?" cried Josefina, horrified. "We've gone from bad to worse."

"Indeed." Solón and Díaz Gross nodded in unison, feeling somewhat taciturn about the news.

And that put to rest the lamentable matter of the priest Roldán and La Gringa and, by extension, the fateful end of the lawyer Rosales and the former madam of the brothel. Nevertheless, Josefina remained thoughtful, pensive, taking long drags on her second cigarette, while Solón hummed along to a new bolero by Lolita, and Díaz Gross took canary-like sips from his glass of whiskey on the rocks. The heat was beginning to fade; either a silent air conditioner had been switched on inside, or—more likely—the alcohol was helping them all to forget what the dog days of summer were really like. Whatever it was, some people had already made their way onto the smallish dance floor at the center of the room and were sashaying their bodies in time with the beat of the *bolero*. And there you were, risqué Reader, right in the middle of it all, with Nana, who was a bit taller than you, and much less ungainly; big-footed Chernishevski was also there, with one of the milky-white Russians, as was Ruth, dancing with Doctor Humberto Lascurain, who looked more like a father and daughter sharing a tender dance on the day of the young prostitute's wedding. The others watched, impassive, wan, vapid from their seats on the various sofas and divans scattered throughout the room: they sipped from their drinks or tapped their feet in time with Lolita's *bolero*, or—of course—they amused themselves with their respective partners under the furtive light that sheltered and obscured them in the corners of the cavernous space. Cardoso, who hadn't gotten up to dance, opting instead to sit there and sweetly embrace Nina, thinking of nothing else save for nibbling at her alabastrine neck in between shots of tequila, suddenly realized that he hadn't seen the novelist Marcelo Chiriboga since they first arrived at the brothel some time ago. *Shit! Where had the Ecuadorian gone?* He had simply disappeared. Alarmed, he suddenly jumped to his feet and, without offering any explanation to his lovely Nina, he strode across the room over to Pitol, who was also comfortably reclining, enjoying life with his Moscovite companion. But Eusebio was met with a fusillade of scorn and insults as the sole response to his genuine curiosity,

"That's what happens when you insert so many characters into a single chapter, Eusebio. Let this be a lesson to you. It's just too hard to keep track of everything. While you're focusing the plot on one or two of the characters, three or four others go off to the bathroom, to bed, to get drunk, or what have you. Which is why I strongly suggest that you cut it down to no more than three or four. Your style is madness. It lacks symmetry. That's why *Friction* doesn't work; that's why not even your own friends read you anymore. Do the math: how many of us are milling about in here? You'll see that I'm quite right."

Unnerved by the lecture (or rather: the Pitolean beating), Cardoso began counting, on trembling fingers, as if he were a frightened, six-year-old schoolboy, each of the characters, listing their names . . . including the names of the appetizingly tangible prostitutes. However, truth be told, no matter how hard he tried, he just couldn't add up the total number of characters he'd brought with him to the brothel that night. It was impossible. The more he tried to concentrate, the more the poor old professor seemed to lose count, forcing him to start all over again, like a student about to fail basic mathematics. In the end, he could only offer the following excuse to his admired Pitol:

"Look, to be honest, I'm a bit worn out, Sergio, but I think you're right. There are too many characters, and I've left myself with a colossal task . . ."

"A colossal task or a colossal mistake?"

"Hey, what can you do? That's how the frictions come out of me. My pals, on the other hand, are very organized and take careful notes, they plan everything in advance, down to the last detail, they fit everything into a structure or scheme, and—like Stendhal—they even sketch out the psychology of four or five characters . . ."

"And to cap it all off, look who's here . . ." interrupted Sergio, a bit fed up with Professor Cardoso. He was pointing to the carpeted staircase that led to the rooms on the second floor. "Speak of the devil! Marcelo Chiriboga, live and in the flesh. You see, Eusebio, the slightest oversight is enough to cause you to lose track of your characters. They're weak, fragile little things that can up and evaporate in the blink of an eye. Next time, don't assume you're such a craftsman. Now, please, leave me alone . . . the Russian is falling asleep on me!"

It was true. Marcelo was coming down the stairs arm in arm with a diminutive Japanese woman whom nobody had seen when they first arrived at the house on Atuneros . . . at least, he didn't remember having seen her. *How had that son of a bitch Chiriboga managed to contrive such a thing?* Cardoso muttered to himself, feeling a bit woozy. *When did he find time to sneak upstairs without so much as a word, without telling anyone where he was going? This Ecuadorian bastard doesn't waste any time . . . he looks radiant, rejuvenated, as if this Japanese girl decided to give him some sort of head-to-toe Eastern massage instead of fucking him,* thought the professor as he dragged himself dejectedly back to his soft green sofa and his girl . . . Nina? Nana? Whichever one she was, it honestly didn't matter much, since they were virtually identical, and he didn't give two shits about trying to distinguish a freckle, a face, or even the sour smell of an armpit, since everything is One and the Same at this point in the night, a great mixture integrated by the powerful force of Love, the compelling, centripetal energy of Kypris the Beautiful. Eusebio was feeling a bit dizzy, not exactly drunk but, yes, in a state of *ekstasis*, existing outside of himself, in a sort of cosmic eddy and with open affection for every human being, in complete harmony with every object adorning the great hall there in the eighteenth-century brothel on the Baja California coast, wandering (like the poet) through the forest of symbols; he suddenly imagined himself in love with these amiable whores and the aroma of their benzoin perfume; he felt as if he had already lived (for centuries now) that sordid, noctivagant life, as if he knew long ago about the infinite transformations of the concupiscent flesh; he saw himself happily submerged in that deep, tenebrous unity, reincarnated or revived, who knows, as if he'd experienced all this before, only in the form of a bat, or as Baudelaire; everything was a vague or false memory, the shimmering mirage or hallucination of an abandoned drunk, but how surprised would he be to find, on his way back to his seat, the great Philosopher of Agrigento cozying up to his beautiful Nina on the exact same sofa he had just vacated in order to go speak to Sergio Pitol? But this little detail didn't seem to bother the former professor very much. On the contrary, in his delirium or intoxication, he was even happier now that he had him there (finally), and had him to himself (somewhat), because there were so many things he'd been wanting to ask him ever since they first met at the Las Rémoras airport: cosmological doubts that had been tormenting him ever since he first read, over five hundred nights ago (during his unfortunate time in Madisonburg), his fragmentary poem "On Nature" and his *Katharmoi.*

Plastered but lucid, Eusebio sat down on the opposite end of the sofa from Empedocles, so that the lovely Hungarian was situated between them. The philosopher said, with his arm still wrapped around his Eastern European whore:

"I've been looking for you. Do you remember you said you wanted to speak with me, or have you forgotten?"

"I didn't want to interrupt you," he lied. "I saw you were busy with the battle-hardened general."

"And you with Pitol . . . and before that, with the young Magyar girl," he said, winking at Nina, who was still sitting there between them, smiling sagaciously, like a sphinx.

"But we're here now, my dear Philosopher, and the truth is that I do have a couple of questions that have been keeping me up at night ever since I read your two great poems."

"I'm all ears, my friend."

"Everything in your wise and sensible writings seems to indicate that Love, the universal engine, prevails over Strife."

"One does not prevail over the other. They are equal. They have equivalent forces."

"Okay, but nevertheless, Eros is something . . ." He hesitated for a moment before continuing on. "Something positive, let's say, while Eris clearly is not. At least, that's what I've gathered from my readings."

"Exactly. Obviously."

"But here's where I differ, Empe, because although I share your theory of the cosmic cycle and the four *archai*, I nevertheless see the force of Discord, of Strife, as something quite positive, at least from a certain point of view, because it foments the joining of the similar, the parallel, and on the other hand it is able to separate the unlike. These latter elements in turn create (happily, sympathetically) other groups of likenesses, and so, in the end, all things seem to be more content, living peacefully in their little subsets side by side with their respective equals and without the need to bump shoulders with their contrarian others. If what I'm saying is true, then I don't understand why it's so important to you that everything be mixed, be united, if ultimately, as you say, only the symmetry of the pores, the attraction between like and like, is what's going to make us better, make us more happy."

Almost excited by his own (abstruse) defense of Discord, Cardoso took a moment to catch his breath before continuing on, undeterred, intent on overcoming the intoxication that was slowly but inexorably beginning to dull his mind:

"If memory serves, it was Theophrastus, your doxographical writer, who quoted you as saying that 'one must enjoy the similar, according to its mixture of components, and on the contrary, find disgust in the dissimilar.' He went on, adding that 'knowledge is produced by likeness, while ignorance, on the other hand, is caused by difference.'"

"It's true, I said that, I wrote that . . . and then, unfortunately, it was lost."

"Then explain to me how the hell you attribute harmony to dissimilarity? Why do you worship Eros if doing so is a virtual contradiction, if it ultimately produces ignorance and misfortune?"

"It's not about attributing one thing to another, Eusebio. It's just the way it is. It's all part of a cosmic cycle."

Cardoso, however, was no longer listening (not completely, anyway) because he was focused so intently on his own little soliloquy. The half-empty bottle of tequila and the bite marks on Nina's shoulders had fazed him, plunged him into a vortex of shining, shimmering colors and smells. But even in the midst of all that, a certain lucidity remained . . . which is why he pressed on:

"And not only that, but it's clear to me that, according to your theory, if Eris is subject to *Ananke* (and therefore there is no remedy, no means for changing this), then I pose to you that the wars, arguments, conflicts, complaints, crimes, disputes, and differences . . . all of them have their own reason for being, their hidden, umbral sense, their unfailing cosmic necessity. It's basically a reaffirmation of that old, popular Mexican expression, 'it's an ill wind that blows no good,' since ultimately all things evil or odious are necessary and everything wicked or iniquitous will inevitably, inescapably lead to a distant, ulterior good, with the sphere and Love at the center of it all."

"I can see that you've studied my theories quite extensively; nevertheless, thanks to your obtuse and limited thoughts, I can't help but be reminded of poor old Pausanias, my young disciple, may he rest in peace. Yes, the two of you are very much alike. But I'm not going to rake you over the coals, because clearly you've got a handle on some very complicated questions. The only problem with giving prevalence to Discord, as you say (in spite of its Necessity), and if we take the old proverb at face value, is that we become dangerously teleological, do you see? In this way, we—like the Marquis de Sade—might justify any aberration, any crime or atrocity, any human corruption, by means of its aim, and this simply cannot be, Eusebio. You know this better than I . . . aren't you a humanist?"

"Yes . . ." Cardoso replied, overwhelmed, after a few moments of arduous reflection interrupted by unbearable bouts of alcohol-induced hiccups and belches. "I hadn't thought about that particular detail, you know? I just don't want you to think that I'm one of those worthless pseudo-Hegelian utopians, who believe in or worship Aristotle like a god . . . his myopic teleological vision doesn't allow for the in-depth insight of your other intuitions."

"What are you referring to?" asked Empedocles, a bit vain, and perhaps even a bit fed up with the pestilential fumes of tequila and beer emanating from the distinguished Professor of the Novel of the Mexican Revolution.

"To your theory of *Tyche* and *Ananke*, which, as you know, seemed to Aristotle to be the height of impudence, a last-minute addition, a philosophical footnote which loses its significance when placed alongside your theory of the twin engines of Eris and Eros." Here, Eusebio paused for a moment to caress one of the naked legs of the young Magyar girl, who was following the conversation as if it were a game of ping-pong, some sort of plaything which she couldn't even remotely understand, owing to the fact that she didn't speak a lick of Spanish, other than certain, cute little dirty words like *métela, sácala*, and *ay, papi, qué rico, qué grande está*, and a handful of others that come in handy in her particular trade.

"Look, Eusebio . . ." The philosopher again took over the reins. "If Eris were a positive force like you say, then we would have to recognize the fact that your cunning bit of betrayal and its ulterior consequences were also benign . . . and the fact is that they're not. Just look at the results."

"My cunning bit of betrayal?"

361

"Your betrayal of Stefano Morini, my Italian compatriot, by getting involved with his wife. Don't play dumb with me," said the man from Agrigento, shooting him a stern look. "Yes, Eusebio, the betrayal of Irene, your beloved wife, and by extension your son Emilio, suddenly snatching him away from his sweet little playmate Alessandra. Tino, you know, was completely right about all this. It wasn't Eros, like Coetzee's character argues; it was Eris that drove you to do it."

"Did you say Tino? You mean the quiet, melancholy Galician?" Eusebio was mired in bewilderment.

"Yes, Tino, your *daimon*, what difference does it make?"

"How is it that you know so many details about that story . . . I mean, my story?"

"Do you take me for a complete imbecile? Like Reader, I am also reading *Friction*."

"But I still haven't finished it yet!" said Cardoso, unnerved, whining and whimpering like a wounded dog.

"Who said I was done? We're all still working our way through it, my friend."

"But how . . . ?" Eusebio stammered. *Am I dreaming?* But before he could answer his own question, he heard the philosopher's parsimonious voice yet again:

"In any case, that's a separate question . . . a metafrictional question, if you like. Up to now, we've managed to stay on track. But answer me this: do you still believe that Eris, Hate, Strife, Discord, is ultimately a kind, beneficent, positive force . . . and merely because it creates small pockets or redoubts of similarities and millions of subsets? Or do you understand that Eros, with its mixing and unifying force, is what brings us happiness, joy, peace, and love?"

"Honestly, I really don't know. I think I'm a bit dizzy, a bit confused . . ."

"Or are you just drunk?" Empedocles smiled, giving him an amiable slap.

In response, the professor from MFU smiled for a second, crossing his eyes, and then nibbled at Nina's naked, snow-white shoulder before

moving up to kiss her long, lithe, swan-like neck; however, right before he was about to put lips to flesh, he let loose a belch worthy of the
prodigious herald Stentor himself. Eusebio blushed and immediately
apologized in Spangarian, and—after taking a moment to recompose
himself—he turned to the wise Philosopher of the Four Elements:

"There's just one more thing . . . Something that leaves me completely
restless and uneasy, unable to sleep, and incapable of moving forward
with the friction I'm writing . . ."

"What's that?"

"The whole issue of transmigration and reincarnation that you ex-
pound upon in your *Purifications* . . ."

"Yes?" pressed the ancient Philosopher from Akragas, who suddenly
looked a bit anxious, his face unable to belie his evident feeling of malaise.

"Are you or are you not Soto Gariglietti, founder of Partido de la Naturaleza y el Fuego Mexicano? Did you throw yourself into the crater of
Popocatépetl?"

Despite and because of his tragic misfortune (in other words, his recent and unstoppable string of bad decisions), at that precise or precious
moment of asking him whether he was or was not the famous Mexican
politician—or, more accurately, whether Empedocles had been reincarnated as Soto Gariglietti twenty-four centuries after his own death—and
still hoping for a definitive, concrete answer, Eusebio suddenly excused
himself from Nina and the philosopher as best he could because an im-
mensely powerful wave of ethylic gastrointestinal contractions had come
upon him from some otherworldly place, doubling him over in pain and
threatening to explode out of his wrenching guts in a spume of seafood
and shellfish. He staggered up off the broad sofa, groped his way through
the mass of clutching bodies slowly swaying in time with a new Lolita
ballad, and somehow managed to stumble up the same set of stairs that
Chiriboga had just descended as if he were a feral mountain goat scal-
ing a sheer escarpment. When he reached the long, upstairs hallway, he
opened the door to the first chamber he came to (and please forgive the

antiquated jargon here) and found a blessed water closet from which a surprisingly ammoniac effluvium was emanating. He instantly entered, closed the door behind him, got down on his knees like Holy Child of Atocha, and proceeded in one fell swoop to expel everything that was bottled up inside him (and then some), vomiting out an endless sea of marine debris (note the rhyme) and then, exhausted, he closed his eyes without knowing what had happened.

14
(TUESDAY, JUNE 13TH)

As the old superstition goes, Reader, Tuesday the 13th is neither a day to get married or embark on a journey, and on this particular Tuesday, June 13th, your lovely, half-naked wife with the green, feline eyes admitted to your friend, the painter:

"You know what? I'm starting to think that I might actually be pregnant."

"Why would you say that?"

"Well, Lascurain still isn't back, and I'm already three weeks late. So I decided to go to the pharmacy and buy a home test . . ."

"A test?"

"A home pregnancy test, you idiot."

"How does it work?"

"You pee on it, and it tells you whether you're pregnant or not."

"And so yours was positive?"

"I think so. But they're not a hundred percent accurate."

"So who's child is it?"

" . . ."

"Who's the father, Maty?"

"I think you are . . ." Your wife's voice sounded like it was about to falter, Reader. "It has to be you, if my husband is infertile, like we think."

" . . ."

"An infertile liar."

"An infertile liar, and a son of a bitch to boot," added the Agro painter, deeply upset.

"Well, aren't you the pot calling the kettle black," said Maty, and who knows whether she said it seriously or in jest. Perhaps, even, it was an insoluble mixture of the two.

"So are you," Arturo replied, stretched out naked on the quilt.

After that, neither of them spoke. A rustic silence descended upon them. For several minutes, neither of them made a sound, unsure whether to insult or defy one another, perhaps aware of the fact that there was nothing more they could do for now (on that lenitive afternoon) except to try and draw out that immeasurable width that comes into existence when one must wait, the *aeon*: waiting, yes, waiting and seeing how this plot, this friction of their bodies or *daimones*, would develop. Aeolus was blowing just enough to dry their naked torsos on that hot afternoon there in the studio. Finally, emerging from her state of muteness and shaking the Agro painter out of his, perhaps snatched up by the *ekstasis* of a sudden recollection, Matilde asked:

"Arturo, what happened in Sicily?"

Caught off guard, he replied:

"What are you talking about?"

"The very first time I came here to see you—or maybe it was the second—you said that something strange happened in Sicily. Something very strange."

"Are you talking about the trip my father made with his friend Pablo?"

"Yes, what other trip could it be?" she said, meanwhile grabbing her portable tape recorder from her Louis Vuitton bag and switching it on.

"Are you sure you really want to know, Maty? I thought you'd forgotten all about it . . ."

"Absolutely," she answered, sitting down like a lotus flower on the same old quilt. "Just the other day I was going over some of the first interviews we did, you know? And much to my surprise, I discovered that you never actually answered that question. You never told me what the hell happened in Italy. I don't know if you just let it slide, or if it's really not all that important after all. But then, yesterday, I was thinking about it again, and I realized that if it weren't so significant—if nothing really happened in Sicily after all—then you wouldn't have told me that this trip to Agrigento marked a turning point in his life, right? Or am I wrong here?"

"No, you're not wrong."

"So how, then, did it change his life? And why?"

"Look, if I didn't explain it at first, it's just because you never would have believed it at the time. First you needed to hear things in order; I mean, first you had to understand his life, his achievements and failures, before you could fully appreciate this period of his youth."

"Alright, alright, enough already . . . You've left me hanging yet again," Maty insisted, leaning up against her lover. "But now that I understand that your father believed he was Empedocles, what more could there be to surprise me?"

"Look: Roberto Soto Gariglietti was eighteen or nineteen years old. This was, if I'm not mistaken, the summer of 1963 . . . though it could have been in '62. Who knows. Anyway, his father (and my grandfather) Pedro Soto, gave him a trip to Europe as a reward for having graduated with honors from Lasallista Prep. So he and his best friend Pablo threw backpacks over their shoulders and set off to spend that torrid summer crisscrossing Europe. From what he told me, it wasn't easy to get to Sicily, and even less so to Agrigento, but my father had his mind set on getting to know the land of his maternal ancestors—the so-called *Magna Græcia*—and for that reason he hauled his old prep school buddy along with him. But once they reached the philosopher's island, they set about the task of exploring every street and corner of the city: there was the beautiful church of San Nicola and the gothic cathedral in the historic district, they visited Luigi Pirandello's house in the oddly named Agrigento suburb of Kaos and the awful beaches around Porto Empedocle, until finally, exhausted, a bit sunburned, and lacking anything else to do, they returned to the only hostel in the city, where they had left their backpacks and other belongings. They slept like a couple of babies. The next morning, after debating whether to leave for Salerno or stay for one more day, they opted for the latter, and headed off to the Valley of the Temples, on the outskirts of the city; they wandered around, by themselves, strolling about like a couple of vagabonds, among dwarf evergreen chaparrals and almond trees in full bloom, unmolested by tourists as they explored the paleo-Christian necropolis and the Temple of Hercules; they passed by a small amphitheater and visited the Temple of Juno, followed by the unfinished Temple of Jupiter, and finally the marvelous Temple of Concord, the best-preserved in all of Sicily. Later in the afternoon, they took up a position on the jagged cliffs not far from the valley with a splendid, majestic view of the sea. From that point, the terrain fell off abruptly until it met with a long, low, rocky ridge. There, in the midst of an agitated discussion with his friend Pablo, a woman of fifty-some years of age suddenly appeared (as if emerging out of the Earth itself). She was obviously a very humble woman, a *ciociara* judging by her ragged clothing. She sat down not far from where the two of them had settled and began to cry, yes Maty, softly at first but soon bawling, uncontrollably and inconsolably. She just couldn't stop. She probably chose those solitary confines facing the sea because she wasn't expecting anybody else to be there, but there they were: two young, confused Mexican boys looking out at the Mediterranean under the crepuscular summer sky. I'm telling you, the woman just sat down there and kept sobbing and staring out into the distance. Pablo and my father watched out of the corner of their eyes without saying a word. The heat at that time of day was beginning to wane. At first, of course, they didn't want to approach her, but then they either overcame their cowardice or gave in to their own curiosity, whichever you prefer, and walked over to her, asking what happened and if there was anything they could do to help. At first, the peasant woman couldn't even bear to look at them, and she didn't even seem to understand my father's rickety Italian, but then, a minute later, she stood up, dusted off her dress, and took them by the hands, one on each side, like two children, and wordlessly led them away. Pablo and my father simply didn't know how to react. At first they were somewhat fearful—*what if she tries to throw us off the cliff?* they both thought—because the three of them were indeed winding their way along the edge of the precipice; nevertheless, my father says that they allowed themselves to be led, peacefully, by that strange woman with disheveled hair and vacant eyes. They picked their way down the cliffs as night was beginning to fall, they passed the six great Doric temples, walked another mile or so, crossing through some thickets and walking across fallow fields, until they suddenly found themselves on a cobblestone cart path that led into a sort of narrow valley spotted with funnel-shaped fig trees. There, according to my father, they merged into single file and made their way up a long and terraced garden path constructed *ex professo* by the *ciociari* themselves, paths they called *macere*, because after plowing the ground and removing the weeds and stones from the soil, they cultivated wheat, flax, herbs, vegetables, and the like. Finally, Maty, weak and exhausted, they arrived at the woman's humble home there on the plateau, which according to my father looked more like a wolf's den or a thief's hideaway. They crouched down and passed by the two vertical stones that marked the entrance; the walls inside were black with soot, and there, in the very back of the room, they could just make out the profile of a man squatting on the ground and crying softly. Then she let go of their hands and went over to kneel down next to this lost soul, his eyes puffy with tears. Pablo and my father gradually began to notice that all along the walls and in the corners of this habitation were sacks of flour, lentils, and vetchlings, tins of lard, and strings of mortadella and salami hanging from the rafters. But there was something inscrutable there in the middle of that hovel, that darkened hollow, that horrible, windowless cave which only they—the woman and her husband—seemed able to discern . . . but what was it? Pablo and my father were still growing accustomed to the darkness despite a brightly colored valence and a cast-iron trivet that shed a meager bit of light; it took them another three or four minutes before they were able to finally perceive what was there in the room with them besides the unbearable heat: it was scantily furnished with two beds, two chairs, a wooden basin with handles, a virgin and a crucifix, a hanging demijohn of wine, an empty basket, two empty bottles, a gas stove on top of a table, a few half-melted candles and, yes, the smell of wax, which had gotten into everything, overwhelming the place. But it was only then, my father says, that they saw the girl. She was lying there, almost right at their feet, on a ragged mat set directly on the packed-earth floor, curled up like a fetus, clothed though shoeless, exposing her small, dingy feet. She was clearly dead. My father felt like an idiot, the biggest idiot in the world, he said. How did he not realize it? How did they not see the body there when he and Pablo entered the little hovel? Why didn't they just follow the eyes of the man and woman hunkered down there against the wall? If he had, he would have seen the body there right away. But he hadn't, and that didn't matter anymore. There they were, my father and his friend, not knowing what to say, not knowing what to do, in the middle of Agrigento, one of the most remote (and possibly one of the most primitive) locations in all of meridional Italy. *How long has this child been lying here in this house?* My father had just finished asking himself this question, awkwardly or intelligently, he wasn't sure, when he saw the *ciociara* pick herself up off the floor and approach him, looking him directly in the eye like nobody else on earth has ever looked at me before, Arturo: her eye had an intensity that cut to the bone and burned itself into my soul. I don't know what that woman wanted or sought in me, but she continued to scrutinize me, boring into my eyes and searching my face for something, trying, perhaps, to recognize someone—anyone—in me, to recover the face of some remote, long-lost acquaintance. I was scared, my son. Why say otherwise? Much more scared than I was when we were navigating the sheer, craggy escarpments, you know?

More afraid than I'd ever been in all my life. Did this rustic woman believe we had something to do with the death of her daughter or whoever that young girl lying there on the floor of the hut was? Did she have me confused with somebody else? I wanted to leave, to offer my condolences and leave as soon as possible, but the *ciociara* took me firmly by the arm and pulled me down towards the body of the dead girl. Yes, she was a girl about twelve or thirteen years old. Once again, she made me sit down next to her and explained to me, in her difficult dialect, that her daughter had been dead for four days. Yes, Arturo, that much I could understand. She placed her rough, callused hand upon the corpse and began to caress it as she began sobbing softly again. Then, suddenly, she grabbed my own hand and placed it directly on the dead girl's face . . . *What does this grief-stricken, powerless woman want from me?* I had no idea, but still I allowed her to guide my hand. I was terrified, of course, but I also felt an incredible sense of compassion. I don't know how else to describe it, Arturo, other than to say it was some sort of cosmic sympathy, a sense of pious mercy unlike any I had ever felt before in my life, but one which I would, indeed, feel many times later in life, as I grew older. I turned my head to look at the man; he was still sitting there, his back up against the wall, broken and crestfallen. Then I turned back around the other way to look for Pablo, searching with my eyes for help or a way out, and discovered, to my absolute horror, that he was no longer there. He had left me without warning. From that moment on, I don't know how much time passed, my son, how many sleepless hours I spent staring at the dead girl, but the next thing I knew dawn was breaking, my body was aching and exhausted, and I got up and exited the cave arm-in-arm—listen to me now—with that same young girl. That's right Maty, yes, you heard me Arturo: we were standing together like old friends, like siblings, while the distant hills began to reveal themselves in the blue morning air, with the Akragas River not far off. The girl hadn't been dead at all. Her breathing was so subtle and shallow that she seemed dead, but she was definitely alive. She had experienced a cataleptic attack, but of course neither I nor her parents knew what the hell catalepsy was. All I felt were the rough arms of the woman upon me, embracing me, crying and thanking me, while the strong arms of the father wrapped around my legs as he kissed my feet, his sobs mixing with words of gratefulness spoken in his Sicilian dialect. The young girl didn't seem to understand anything about what had happened: she didn't know who I was, why her parents were in tears, or what the hell had happened that night and during the past four days she'd spent completely rigid and catatonic. I swear, I still don't quite know myself. To this day, I'm still not sure what happened that night, Arturo. At first, being an eighteen-year-old kid, yes, I believed that the young girl had been resurrected. You heard me, Maty. I thought she'd been brought back from the dead. But don't be alarmed: what other conclusion could I have made when Pablo and I came upon her deathly pallid face, her still, lifeless body, not breathing, and with no discernible pulse? Months later, once I had returned to Mexico, I decided to study medicine, I read every article and book I could get my hands on, and—much to my astonishment—I discovered a number of fairly well-documented cases of catalepsy like the one suffered by the young girl in Sicily. What most likely happened that night was that she experienced an attack of catatonic schizophrenia, though it's also possible that she was under the effects of a drug known as haloperidol, which was used to treat a number of manic conditions in those days, despite the fact that it had significant effects on the brain by blocking neurotransmitters. Her pallor and rigidity were caused by vascular constriction of the capillaries, but of course I had no way of knowing or even suspecting that at the time. As you know, that episode is what led me into medicine, my son. But my father, Maty, found himself changing positions, changing theories . . . Yes, as surprising as it might seem to you, he made a hundred and eighty degree turn, very *ad hoc*, of course, with regard to his rather unorthodox vision of the universe. I'm talking about the fact that first, when he was studying medicine in Mexico from 1963 to 1968, he believed that the young Sicilian girl had suffered from catalepsy; but then, after Pablo was murdered in the summer of '68 and he had his dramatic shift towards Pythagorean philosophy, which I've already told you about, he began to think that what had really happened there—what he had witnessed that night in Agrigento—was a genuine case of metensomatosis."

"Meten . . . what?"

"Metensomatosis, Maty. It's similar to metempsychosis, remember? Only the difference is that, in these cases, a somatic change can also occur. In other words, it's not just the *psyche* that transmigrates from one being to another, but also the body itself, or some aspect of it."

"Sounds complicated."

"It really is. Very. I don't blame you for being skeptical, but cases do exist."

"You don't say," replied Maty, halfway between sarcasm and fear, no longer quite so sure about wanting to delve into all this.

"Abaris the Hyperborean, for example, who appears in one of Herodotus's books. And Epimenides and Hermotimus, who were well-known by both Plato and Aristotle. Or Aristeas the Jew. But above all, the most famous is the one documented by Plato, which has been preserved in its entirety."

"But all these cases of metensomatosis you've mentioned took place in ancient times."

"Of course, Maty. These days nobody believes in such things."

"Except your father . . ."

"Yes."

"So, what is the case documented by Plato, if I may ask?"

"The case of Er of Pamphilia, which appears near the end of his *Republic*," replied the painter. "Look, I'm not about to tell you one of those old fables that Odysseus told to Alcinous, but rather the true history of the hero Er, son of Armenius, a Pamphylian by birth. He was slain in battle, and ten days afterwards, when the bodies of the dead were taken up—already in a state of corruption—his body was found unaffected by decay, and carried home to be buried. And on the twelfth day, as he was lying on the funeral pyre, he returned to life and told them what he had seen in the other world. He said that when his soul left the body he went on a journey with a great company, and that they came to a mysterious place at which there were two openings in the earth; they were near together, and right above them were two other openings in the heavens."

"But that's completely ridiculous, Arturo."

"Just hold on and listen a little more . . ." Arturo paused here to embrace her, drawing her gently towards him, enveloping her in the vapor of his voice. "Now you'll better understand what metensomatosis truly is. According to what Er described in his report from the other world, he traveled with spirits to a place where Lachesis, the Daughter of Necessity, addressed them: 'Mortal souls, behold a new cycle of life and mortality. Your genius will not be allotted to you, but you choose your genius; and let him who draws the first lot have the first choice, and the life he chooses shall be his destiny. Virtue is free, and as a man honours or dishonours her he will have more or less of her; the responsibility belongs to the chooser. Even for the last comer, if he chooses wisely and will live diligently, there is appointed a happy and not undesirable existence. Let not him who chooses first be careless, and let not the last despair.' She cast lots randomly at their feet, and every soul took the one that landed closest to them, all except for Er himself, who was there only to bear witness. Er was fascinated to watch the different souls chose their new lives. Most curious, he said, was the spectacle: sad and laughable and strange; for the choice of the souls was in most cases based on their experience of a previous life . . . Animals were there too, and not only did men pass into animals, but there were also animals tame and wild who changed into one another and into corresponding human natures: the good into the gentle and the evil into the savage, in all sorts of combinations." Here Arturo paused briefly to catch his breath, panting like a beast, then continued in an almost apodictical manner. "Before Plato, Democritus also liked to document these supposed cases of resurrection, but only as a means of proving his own atomic theories; for example, his theory that the *psyche* (being made up of small, round, heated particles) cannot transmigrate into a new body once the original has begun to decompose, which is a clear contradiction of Empedocles and the Pythagoreans and Orpheans, who believed just the opposite to be true: that the *psyche* can indeed transmigrate after the body has entered the decomposition phase. Democritus wanted to establish two things: first, that there was no reason to worry about any sort of subterranean life, and that we shouldn't suffer foolishly for fear of postmortem punishments, and second, that death doesn't occur in an instantaneous manner, but rather in a gradual one, just as the body decomposes slowly instead of being instantaneously destroyed, which makes it very difficult (both then and now) to determine the precise moment at which death truly occurs. When considering this question, it's important to recognize that the Abderite is correct, just as he was when he opined, for example, that some dead bodies still respond to stimuli. If not, then why do their hair and fingernails continue to grow, my son? But I insist that the most important part of all is that this disciple of Leucippus was more than two thousand years ahead of his time when he declared that there are no established scientific methods that doctors can agree on for determining the exact moment of life's termination . . . Anyway, that was more or less what happened that night in Agrigento."

"I'm completely lost."

"What I'm saying is that my father had no way of knowing with any degree of certainty whether or not the girl in question was dead," said the son of Soto Gariglietti. He immediately followed his statement by asking his lover, in a somewhat harsh tone of voice, "Had the soul left her body or not, Matilde? Was she or was she not resurrected after four days of being entombed there, barefoot and dirty? And, above all, the most difficult question: who could conclusively make that determination? A doctor? No, of course not."

"I'm confused," interrupted your wife, before adding immediately: "Or is it that your father recognized, like Democritus did, that the young girl he helped wasn't really dead at all, but instead just appeared to be dead, plain and simple?"

"No, Maty. You're wrong. Empedocles didn't think, as Democritus or Epicurus did, that the soul is mortal. Not at all. They, Democritus and Epicurus, were staunch materialists when it came to this subject, make no mistake about it. *Psyche*, to them and their followers, carried a specific weight, and—with the onset of death—their spherical atoms dissolved into the *aether* and that was it . . . Everything was finished: organic life, *psyche*, everything, understand? But my father didn't see it like that. He believed in the immortality of the soul . . . and, in a certain, roundabout way (difficult to describe, I admit) in the immortality of the body."

"You've already lost me . . . Please, stop, Arturo. Just tell me what you're getting at with all of this."

"Haven't you figured that out yet?"

"No, of course not. Well, maybe I have . . ." stammered Matilde, putting her hand to her stomach, feeling for the first time a slight flutter, like that of a tiny snake. She continued, not very sure of her own words: "It's that your father was convinced—despite everything he knew to the contrary—that he had resurrected that young woman in Sicily."

"Yes, just as Empedocles resurrected, according to legend, a poor young woman from Agrigento whose name was, believe it or not, exactly the same as the young girl my father encountered."

"What name was that?"

"Both women were named Panteia."

"So your father honestly believed himself to be a reincarnated Empedocles, and that the young cataleptic girl he met in 1962 was the same person from antiquity?" Matilde laughed, shocked, before adding: "In other words, the soul of Empedocles (and that of Er of Pamphilia and all those other resurrected souls) chose to inhabit his own body over two thousand years later?"

"That's pretty much it, Maty. It's all just metensomatosis . . ."

When he woke up, all Eusebio could manage to do was paw at the black-ish, sticky air surrounding him. A throbbing headache prevented him from moving. He struggled mightily to raise his hand, waving it around like some sort of undeveloped, squid-like fetus swimming around in an emetic, meconium-filled uterus. Immediately he noticed a tingling sen-sation in that hand, which ran past his elbow all the way up his arm; the same sensation extended down his left leg. *Fuck, they're cramping*, he thought to himself, unable to move his leg without feeling a sharp pain jabbing or tugging at his tendons. Laid up, feeling revived by the warm, liquid penumbra, he tried three times to get to his feet (or at least in a squatting position) but he failed: the tingling and burning in his limbs prevented it. He fell back, staggering like a baby. His body felt dull, as if he'd been greased up with fried butter and tossed out there on the floor. He recalled the crude, cruel night before, and the sudden, pressing need to find a bathroom; he remembered bounding up the stairs like some crazy goat and vomiting everything up: the gallons of alcohol-steeped seafood that all started with that gluttonous dinner at Tony's *lonchería* back on Avenida Libertad . . . Suddenly, though, he put a stop to all those reflections to ask himself an important question: *where were all the dinner guests? Where were the twins Nina and Nana, where was Empe-docles of Agrigento, Chiriboga, and Pitol, Theophrastus and Democritus, Josefa and Josefina, the Gorgon Gross-Wayne, Ruth and Er of Pamphilia, Whitehead, Selvática, and Chernishevski, Isabel and Gilberto Rendón, Matilde and General Pancho Villa, Inés and Fedra, my ex-wives, the taci-turn Galician or his daimon, Lascurain and his colleague Díaz Gross, Par-menides and Jeffrey Davis, the autistic giraffe, Captain Reed and Stefano Morini, the Japanese assassins Dyo and Fusita, the architect Jasso and Rosinda, you, Reader, and all the other insane characters from* Friction? *Where had they been left? And what's happened to them in the mean-time?* His head was a mess and everything around him was spinning;

nevertheless, he needed to find out what had happened during that brief lapse in consciousness. *Is the evening over? Did I miss the orgy?* He had to get up, wash the vomit from his mouth, get out of that unsanitary cubicle, figure out what time it was, and—most importantly—find out if the celebration was past its apogee. But he didn't hear a sound: not a single voice, not a single tune, not a single snore. *Was everyone asleep, scattered throughout the eighteenth-century sitting room, or had they paired off randomly (naked and sweaty) into the various bedrooms? Fuck, I can't think, can't concentrate, with this headache, and the cramp in my leg has crippled me . . .* He dragged himself painfully—*a little further, yes, just a little more*—until finally, overcoming his aching, throbbing hangover, he was able to sit up straight, using the toilet for support, and unsuccessfully feel around for the light switch. *Where the hell is it? Where's the door?* Finally, after a long minute sunk in darkness, he found the switch and flipped it on . . . but the unleashed photons made things worse, blinding him, causing him to lose his balance and tumble over, his cramping arm ending up submerged in the turbid water in the toilet. He said a hundred curses, wiped himself off with a towel, and walked out of the bathroom in a daze.

Once he was out in the long, narrow hallway, Cardoso pricked up his ears: still nothing. Total silence . . . almost. Just the vibrating blades of a ceiling fan off in the distance. He went downstairs, but still didn't see anyone. He made his way down a second hallway and found himself in what must have been the brothel's kitchen; again, there wasn't a soul to be found, not even a mouse. He made his way back to the antique sitting room. The same, spinning fan: its humming blades were the only sign of life, the only reminder of the recent activity there. He rubbed his eyelids and scanned the room: cigarette butts, empty glasses, half-full bottles, leftover food, even a pair of glasses, a necktie, and a woman's hat. That was it. He decided to peek into the upstairs rooms: he stealthily made his way back up to the second floor so as not to wake anybody up. Once he reached the long hallway, he carefully grasped the doorknob of the first room he came to, turned it, and slowly opened the door. To his complete astonishment, the room was empty: just an unmade bed, rumpled sheets, women's clothing strewn about, stiletto heels lying on the ground, and even a whip. He closed the door and went directly to the next room down the hall. This time he took no precautions and threw open the door in a flash to discover . . . nobody. It was the same with the third and fourth rooms. *What's happening? Where could they all have gone?* Just then, a benign ray of sunlight, shot from the bow of Apollo himself, pierced a window, striking him right between the eyes, and—for the first time since he woke up—he remembered the morning's appointment: they were to congregate in the town plaza for the unveiling of a statue of that famous French monster. *Of course. What else could it be? But what time is it? Could it be eleven in the morning already? Am I that late? Did they forget about me, leave me here, believing that their beloved Professor Cardoso would be waiting for them at the plaza, bright eyed and bushy tailed and ready for the unveiling, next to the town mayor and his attractive, incredibly sexy assistant?* Unfortunately he wasn't wearing a watch, and he didn't see a clock on any of the walls around him. He decided to leave the brothel and run back to the plaza, not wanting them to start—or perhaps finish—the ceremony without him. *Shit, I'll miss it!* He went back in the bathroom, splashed some water on his face, washed his hands, tucked his sweat-stained shirt into his foul-smelling trousers, and descended the stairs. But just as he was about to open the door to the street, he was hit yet again by one of Apollo's rays of light: *The crime, yes, the murder of Inés, the previous madam of the brothel. How could I have forgotten?* This was his opportunity to go and investigate for himself the question he'd wanted to answer for so very long now, ever since he read *The Obstacles* for the first time. He retraced his steps, past the landing and the sitting room, went back upstairs, and headed straight for the fifth and final room at the end of the hall, the only one he hadn't looked in, but which he nevertheless recognized immediately from having read a cautionary description of it before: it was, of course, the old bedchamber of Roberta, the beautiful yet heartless whore with green eyes who had disappeared with her son into the hellish grottos of Mexico City. Following a reckless impulse and sensing what he had to do, he went straight to the bed, got down on the ground, lifted up the silk skirt, eased his entire body under the bed, and there—with scarcely enough light to confirm it—he found what he knew or intuited would be there: the last, melancholy words of a woman strangled by a young writer, the final scratchings of a dying madam, the only remaining mark which she made just before she was cruelly finished off by Roberta. There, engraved in the floorboards, were the words, "Elías killed me."

A piece of a fingernail, which still had polish on it, was stuck in the wood where Inés had recorded (or carved) her ultimate inscription.

Now Cardoso had his incontrovertible proof. It came a bit late, yes, because Raimundo Rosales had died of a broken heart in the local jail there in Las Rémoras, so now there was nothing left to do but free him from the indignity that had been hanging over his corpse: the suspicions of having killed his mistress, his beloved Bermuda Triangle, his beautiful Inés.

And he would have to inform Sigüenza of this discovery so that he could issue an arrest warrant for the eccentric writer who was, among other things, despised by the young mayor with all the energy his resentful little civil servant's heart could muster. The problem, of course, would be locating the three fugitives: Pili, Ricardo, and Elías, the writer, the murderer.

16
(THURSDAY, JUNE 15TH)

The same June 15th on which you, tame and trusting, began reading this devilish book, around four thirty or a quarter to five in the evening, your good friend Arturo—with the first cigarette of the day stuck between his

379

lips—was talking to Matilde (how ironic!) about gratitude and respect for life; in other words, he was talking about his father's posthumous book entitled *Ingratitude, Indifference, and Utter Apathy in the Mexican People* (are you familiar with it?), perhaps the most well-known and polemical of the many extravagant essays Roberto Soto Gariglietti wrote, in which he expressed (quite irascibly) his disdain for the Mexican people brought about by their (and his) own doing. What else can you call it, he wrote angrily, when a man can shit himself in his own house, defiling his own home, and feel no sense of remorse, modesty, or guilt? Mexicans lack self-respect; it's a tangible, irrefutable fact, he says. They trample all over everything that Nature has granted them: beaches, lakes, rivers, forests, fields, tourist regions, and yes, everything they touch, Reader, they desecrate. Mexicans are like a plague of locusts or termites . . . or worse still: like a horde of predators who are as foolish as they are puerile. Even the founder of the PNFM must admit (not lacking in harshness and carrying pacifist theory to its very limit) that Mexicans subconsciously hate themselves like no other population on the planet, and from that hatred stems their implacable, cosmological history full of defeats, fuck-ups, and troubles. And to cap it all off, he declares that, if it is true that *homo homini lupus*, then a Mexican is a wolf to his fellow Mexican.

Since I'm assuming that you're quite familiar with it, let's get off the well-worn subject of ingratitude and apathy and cut straight to the chase, yes, to the last years of the Mexican politician's life, when he was at his peak, his zenith, which is ultimately what your wife is dying to know about, what she's been longing to learn ever since her very first visit to your friend, the painter . . .

"After Empedocles dismantled the so-called Assembly of the Thousand, about which little is known, Maty, other than the fact that Thrasydaeus, son of the tyrant Theron, was overthrown, the people of Akragas wanted to crown him king. Instead, he encouraged them to form the first democratic party in the history of Sicily and one of the first in all of *Magna Græcia*, convinced that—although he considered himself a demigod possessing divine powers—monarchies and oligarchies weren't the right way to govern a populace," Arturo spat out in a single breath. "That's why, some time later, those same resentful tyrants or their offspring (there isn't a clear consensus on this) forced him into exile: the dates of his banishment and the tyrants' (or their offsprings') return to power are not exactly known. But in those days, love, you have to bear in mind that ostracism was much more common than you'd think. It didn't really signify public shame; all that happed was that the person in question would be confined (along with his property) to the outskirts of the city, within a hundred mile radius. And that's exactly what happened with the philosopher, but it's important to know that, according to Aristotle, my father went off to Peloponnese when he was around sixty years old, and he would pass away there a short time later. Still, though, considering all the known historical chronicles, it's safe to assume that, first, Empedocles could have gone to Olympia (where he'd garnered many honors and where Cleomenes the Rhapsodist recited his *Katharmoi* at the Olympic Games) at the age of sixty and that, after he was there, far from his native land, he was exiled in absentia by the descendents of the oligarchs. Are you following me? It's the same with the fucking members of the PRI, the PRD, the PAN, and the environmentalists who, united and growing in confidence, made a last-minute decision to deprive the genius from Agrigento of his rights and privileges, deciding months before the 2000 elections that a madman couldn't possibly be a viable candidate because, if he were actually to become President of the Republic, the country would be doomed to one of the worst setbacks in history and would become lost in an economic and social debacle. Thus, despite the polls being in his favor (and decisively so, Maty), Soto Gariglietti, the Philosopher of the Four Elements, couldn't ascend to the presidency on that memorable occasion, although, as you know, an opposition candidate would, for the first time in history, win a national election and topple the infamous PRI, known for seven decades as 'The Perfect Dictatorship.' In 2000, Empedocles was fifty-six years old, and I was fifteen. By the end of that same year, having accepted the mandate from Vicente Fox's administration, they made my father Mexico's ambassador to Italy, and of course I went with him, leaving my mother at home, abandoned and alone. Deep down, you know, the members of PAN were willing to do whatever it took to bring my father down, since his popularity in Mexico was on the rise. Much to their surprise, and the surprise of others, many of his political and cosmological meditations started to become a reality during that first presidential term at the beginning of the new millennium, so much so that millions of Mexicans who were disappointed with the new opposition president and millions of others who were even more fed up with the petulance shown by the leftist candidate began to look for a way to bring my father back home from exile in Italy. His enemies, then, either afraid or intimidated, who knows, took on the impossible task of keeping him there, which they, in fact, managed to do for just over four years, during which time I got to know Italy top to bottom and also discovered my vocation as a painter. But that's a whole other story, Maty . . ." Here the painter paused, staring at her with his opaque eyes, his black, opaque eyes, like those of an owl or a jackal. Then he hugged her tight and said, almost as if he were watching the scene being played out in the clear, crystalline eyes of his lover: "They were successful, yes, for almost a full lustrum, when—at sixty-odd years of age, and with his influence still intact—he retuned to his lofty, majestic Akragas, his beautiful native land, from which, on a clear day, you could just make out the coast of Africa. There, according to the remaining fragments of information left by later historians, four separate banquets were held in honor of his homecoming. There could have been more, of course, but there are only records of four, Maty, that took place after his return from exile . . . although I was (of course) not present at any of them. But there's no reason to describe what went on at each of the feasts, though, because it was the final one (the Last Supper, if you will) that gave rise to the legend of his disappearance. Among the many chroniclers who wrote about it, the one who stands out is

Heraclides Ponticus," Arturo said, taking the recorder for himself and lighting his second cigarette of the afternoon. "According to Ponticus, once my father returned to the place of his birth, after those trying years of political ostracism, a man named Peisianax, a native of Syracuse, organized yet another banquet at his farmhouse in Milo, near Catania, to pay homage to the revered scholar of biology and medicine, the unvanquished miracle worker, and leader of Hellenic democracy . . . all of which describe my *papá*. As I said, there were four such feasts, but this final feast is the one that's important to us because what happened there would end up unleashing the imagination of millions, all across the globe. Apparently, after the banquet had ended, the guests (as they often would do back in those days) spent the night camped out under the almond trees on the farm instead of inside the house, owing to the oppressive summer heat. But my father, though, remained in his seat at the table, leaning back pensively. Remember, Maty, that Empedocles had given up alcohol ever since his conversations with the Orpheans and Pythagoreans, when he wrote *Purifications*; the other guests, however, had been drinking tequila, mescal, and rum-and-Coke to their hearts' content. So, as rumor has it, they all went to sleep fairly drunk, and didn't find out what happened until the following morning."

"But what the hell happened, Arturo? I'm on the edge of my seat here . . ."

"Well, Empedocles left his friend's home there in Atlixco, near Puebla de los Ángeles, and walked a few miles until he reached the foothills of the famous volcano, the temple of Demeter and Kore, the primary goddesses and caretakers of the region. When he reached the foot of the mountain, around four or five in the morning, he found a young, well-equipped group of alpine climbers about to set out . . . Along with them, (fearless, invincible) he began to climb the steep slope. It was still dark, and the ascent, believe me, is far from an easy one, particularly the second half of it, after reaching Las Cruces, where you can stop and rest, have something to eat and drink, or smoke a cigarette before making the final push for the summit. Finally, after six debilitating hours, he reached the lower lip of Popocatépetl's crater, shivering in the frigid altitude despite the summer's heat; he stared down into the abyss, tiptoed along the snow-capped rim like a tightrope walker, and then—right in front of the climbers who had helped him reach the summit, he threw himself into the chasm without so much as a second thought. Yes, you heard me right, Matilde: Roberto Soto Gariglietti, my beloved father, leaped—alive—into Mount Etna's active crater." At this point the son stopped, sad, a bit nostalgic and deflated. A few moments later, after recomposing himself, he added, changing the subject just a bit: "In fact, they say it's one of the most active volcanoes on the planet. At least once a year there's an eruption on that island, and all those eruptions have produced over three hundred and fifty small craters, swellings, and vents all across the mountain's flanks. People will even bring their pots and brew hot tea on fresh lava slopes in the months after an eruption, can you believe it? Etna has destroyed nearby towns on several occasions, including the rustic farm owned by Peisianax . . ."

"But, wait a minute, Arturo . . . Why did your father—I mean Empedocles—do that?" Maty blurted out, as scared as she was stunned.

"Because he was a god, or a demigod, and because he wanted to demonstrate his supernatural powers to the world. In other words, because men like him never die . . . they're just plucked up by the greater gods and spirited away to the kingdom to which they truly belong. That's what Empedocles believed, and he carried out his actions without fear, without hesitation, and at exactly the right age. The Greeks, after all, felt a deep aversion for physical decay. It was better to die; that is, it was better to be reborn and transmigrate through time than to become old, bothersome, and useless. For example, in *On Nature*, the philosopher writes, 'Fools—for their meditations are not long-lasting—are those who expect that what previously was not comes to be or that anything dies and is utterly destroyed.' Then, in another fragment shortly thereafter, Empedocles says to his young disciple Pausanias: 'I shall tell you something else. There is no birth for any mortal being nor any abominable death, but only mixture and the interchange of what is mixed exist, and birth is the name given to it by men.'"

"Like the mixing of colors on a painter's palate," Maty added, quite observantly. "Everything is constantly being transformed, being combined . . ."

"Exactly. Now I see that you understand my father, and therefore a bit about the revelatory art of the Agro painters," said her naked lover, with his long, lean ribs and broad, ample smile. Then he added, "Popocatépetl is just a short distance from Atlixco, which is where the myth of Pluto is said to have arisen. Pluto, of course, is who took Kore-Persephone to Hades. Only later would Demeter go off in search of her, which is why the people of Atlixco claim to have originated the so-called Eleusinian Mysteries, and not Athens and Eleusis, who were always thought to have been the source."

"The Eleusinian Mysteries?"

"It's complicated. Let me just say that they have to do with agricultural rites based on the myth of Demeter, who neglected her duties as the goddess of fertility to go off in search of her daughter Persephone, and because of that, the world froze, there were no harvests, and the people were forced to endure extreme hunger."

"And what happened to Persephone?"

"Well, Hades-Pluto kidnapped her and took her to the underworld where they fed her pomegranate seeds. Eventually, though, her mother Demeter found her under the volcano, and she was able to reach an agreement with Hades-Pluto where Persephone would spend eight months with her on earth and four remaining months in the underworld with Hades."

"That's awful!" Maty exclaimed, bolting upright (terrified) and naked, her nipples exposed, erect, and accusational. "Why four months with Hades?"

"Because the Greeks only had three seasons, Maty, and because once you've eaten the seeds, you can never return to the world of the living:

385

your fate is one of revival, understand? So winter represents the season that Persephone spends under the volcano. Her resurrection or return with her mother marks the beginning of spring, and that's where the Eleusinian Mysteries came from, which were celebrated until the Holy church prohibited them." Here he paused for a moment, and took one final drag on his cigarette before continuing: "They were broken down into the Lesser Mysteries and the Greater Mysteries, the latter of which lasted for nine days and were conducted by the hierophants; in other words, priests who had been purified by the *myesis* of initiation, which I told you about before. After that the hierophants began a long processional towards Eleusis; when they arrived, they commemorated Demeter with a day of fasting, which was broken with the drinking of a special tonic of barley and pennyroyal called *kykeon*, similar to what the Agro painters prepare and imbibe on the sacred trips we take to Chihuahua, which I've also talked about before. The drink produces beautiful hallucinations, Maty; you have visions of the future, mysteries reveal their secrets, you can see further than you ever thought possible . . ."

"That's enough, Arturo, I believe you, I believe you . . ." interrupted Maty. "Enough with the Eleusinian Mysteries. Just tell me what happened the next morning when the dinner guests woke up and couldn't find your father anywhere. How did they figure out what happened? How did they learn that he had thrown himself into the volcano?"

"That morning, when everyone woke up on the farm and saw that the philosopher was nowhere to be found, they formed a search party and went out looking for him; even the housekeepers. One of them swore he'd seen a light shining on top of Popocatéptl, and then—off in the distance, yet still quite clear—he heard a voice calling out, *Empedocles, Empedocles* . . . It was shortly after that when they discovered the famous bronze *huarache* sandal."

"What *huarache*?"

"My father always wore *huarache* sandals, didn't you know that?"

"You never mentioned it before . . ."

"Apparently, Etna experienced a small eruption that morning, only instead of expelling lava or ash, it spat out one of my father's unmistakable *huaraches*."

The painter looked in his pack for another cigarette; finding it empty, he threw it into his clothes hamper.

"You know? I'm dying for another cigarette."

"Are you kidding? The whole studio is filled with smoke."

"I'm going to the bodega on the corner for another pack. I'll be back in five minutes."

"Just hurry up. I want to hear how it ends."

"How it ends?"

"Yes."

"But that is the end, Maty. What were you expecting?" Arturo veritably jumped up off the quilt. "Don't you think a divine, heroic death unlike any other in history is enough?" insisted the painter, angrily buttoning his shirt and zipping up his pants, ready to walk down the five flights of stairs and out into the street. "Isn't it clear to you by now? Empedocles of Agrigento threw himself into Popocatépetl and he threw himself into Mount Etna and everything is always happening simultaneously, constantly, infinitely . . . like you and I, sitting here talking about my father while your husband is reading, yes, reading all of this, over and over again, for centuries upon centuries . . . do you see? Everything is repeated, Maty; all that changes are the places, the dates, and a few of the names. Everything is combined, like the mixing of colors on a painter's palate, when you stir them, mix them, creating friction, and apply them to a canvas. Look, I really need a cigarette. When I get back, I'll try to explain it all a little better . . . Just stay here and relax, don't bother getting dressed, because when I come back I'm going to fuck you a thousand times, I promise you. Do you have any idea how gorgeous you are? Stunning, olive-toned, and unclothed . . ."

Your young ex-wife flashed him a smile, not really sure of how to respond; then she curled up in the quilt like an Angoran cat, contemplative or perhaps even a bit disturbed by the fusillade of information. Had she comprehended this story, this final apotheosis? Were her ears deceiving her, or was Arturo crazy? In any case, barely a minute later, she felt a small twinge in her belly and doubled over in pain, still alone there in the asbestos-laden studio. It was then that she remembered that her tape recorder was still running. She grabbed it and stowed it back in her Louis Vuitton crocodile purse, which you yourself had given her (remember that?) right after you got engaged, back when she was still betrothed to you, your virgin, your priestess, your vestal, your beloved hierophant.

It was then that Maty felt the first wave of nausea rising from her stomach.

XVII

When I finally left the brothel and stepped out onto Atuneros, the sun beat down on me like an iron yoke laid across my shoulders. Thanks to the damn hangover, I was feeling a little like El Pípila, the hero of Guanajuato, who famously turned the tide of a battle during the Mexican War of Independence when he wore a long, flat stone across his back to protect himself from the muskets of the Spanish troops. But despite that painful burden, I worked my way back along the unpaved streets I'd traversed just the night before with that eccentric group of visitors. First, Encaladores, lined with sad, empty lots filled with junk and trash; a bit further on, the first, uneven rows of houses and streetlights began to creep up like nettles and weeds popping up out of the desert land. As I neared the sea, more shacks appeared, and a fresh, burnishing breeze tempered the morning heat. Then, just as I stepped off a curb and onto Avenida Libertad, I squashed a small lizard; angry, I wiped off my shoe as best I could, and continued on, quickening my pace. There wasn't a sign of life be found anywhere; it was a veritable ghost town, populated only by the light howl coming from deep within the innards of the Sea of Cortez. *Of course*, I said to myself, *everyone must already be gathered at the plaza: the ceremony had begun, and without me. It must be almost noon by now* . . . I looked up at the sky, and good Tonatiuh, god of the poor, confirmed it for me by blinding my eyes.

When I finally arrived, I pushed and shoved my way through the mass of sweating bodies until I reached the center of the plaza where I found all my new friends and enemies gathered around the statue: Empedocles of Agrigento, General Pancho Villa, Pitol, and Villagrá; Yuri Mikhaylovich Chernishevski; Tony, owner of the *lonchería*; the abominable brothers Cecilio and Solón; lovely Rosinda, her pouty lips painted dark cherry red; Fernando Sigüenza, mayor, mellifluous poet, and former fiancée of Pilar, for those of you who've read *The Obstacles*; Mademoiselle Boule de Suif, fat and pretty, plucked straight out of a work of literary Naturalism; Santa and Joaquín; the anachronistic Doctor Díaz Gross, who was squished, shoulder-to-shoulder, up against his colleague and your wife's gynecologist, the man with the fuzzy teeth and rotten breath: Doctor Humberto Lascurain. Also gathered there, smiling silently, were the lovely ladies from the brothel, all made up and dressed to the nines, just as they were when they had attended mass with Padre Roldán, may he rest in peace. Off to one side, the eternal suppliants were draped in black and hunched over like bedbugs hunkering down in an old mattress. And standing right in the thick of things was you, Anagnostes, mopping the sweat from your brow with the cuff of the same shirt you were wearing yesterday, paying very close attention to the speech that the Ecuadorian Marcelo Chiriboga, microphone in hand, was giving, either to the general public, to the select group of guests, or to the extraordinary statue of the extraordinary Gargantua himself, which was standing there in the middle of the sunny, Baja Californian plaza:

"Ladies and gentlemen, we are here to celebrate, as my distinguished colleague Chernishevski has so accurately said, a great monster, the greatest, kindest, and most beneficent of all the giants that have set foot upon this Earth since God created it: Gargantua, father of Pantagruel and illustrious son of Grangousier, the three original inhabitants of the land of Chinon, in the heart of the Val de Loire, home of fine wines and majestic castles . . . Well then, from this memorable day forth, the beautiful, medieval city, located on the banks of the Vienne River, birthplace of Joan of Arc, will become the sister city to the splendid, picturesque Las Rémoras, renowned for her insane and suicidal citizens, *daimonic* possessions, fugitives from justice, devout pilgrims, pre-Socratic philosophers, absentminded writers, and even generals of the Mexican Revolution. I myself am Ecuadorian, ladies and gentlemen; to be more specific, I am from the humble town of Guayaquil, and not the more exalted capital city of Quito. I belong, justly and in my own right, to the so-called Latin American literary Boom, although there are an uneducated few who claim that I am simply an invention of the Chilean writer José Donoso. This is not true. In reality, Pepe simply used my name in one of his buffoonish frictions that narrates my various feats and failures at a university in the American South, the name of which I have no desire to recall. I only mention this because it was at that particular university that I met and came to know a legendary compatriot, a young student of Latin American literature, a diligent protégée of my dear departmental colleagues, Professors Avellaneda and Macpherson, who years later would write a doctoral dissertation on the role of primary colors (Or was it secondary colors? I can never remember . . .) in my narratives. That young student, who goes by the name of Gaudencia Gross-Wayne, is in fact none other than a direct descendant of the genial Gargantua and his venerable son Pantagruel. Of course, one has only to look at her to know that this is true, to recognize without a shadow of a doubt that she, Gaudencia, is the final depository of the Gargantuan seed. But all that notwithstanding, we mustn't forget that both Rabelaisian giants, as with Grangousier, Gargantua's father, were models of generosity and composure, true examples of justice and democracy, of humanity and respect for others, while Gaudencia, on the other hand, even at a young age, was completely the opposite: arrogant, vain, ill-tempered, unjust, racist, cruel, impudent, despotic, and afflicted with a severe inferiority complex—yes, you heard me, ladies and gentlemen, an inferiority complex—for, behind that staunch mask, she harbored a deep and ominous sense of puerility, fragility, insignificance, and insecurity. In other words, everything that the great French giants who preceded her were not . . . that is, if she is indeed a descendant of them, as she argued at the top of her lungs to anyone who would listen. Considering all that, could this young woman truly be a direct descendant of these medieval monsters? Yes, she could, at least in part . . . but then again, that means that in part she is not. I'll explain. If, for example, we rely on the established case of my colleague Avellaneda, who (and this has been confirmed by a reliable source) despised the sexual advances of his student Gaudencia so much that he preferred instead to amuse himself with a fugitive orangutan escaped from the county zoo, then we may easily infer the devastating repulsiveness of that young Ecuadorian woman, who is in no way, shape, or form representative of the other, quite lovely young women in my dear country. However, on the other hand, if we recall the sum total of the moral defects, anomalies, and vices of this female orangutan (I'm talking about Gaudencia here), then it is all but impossible to link her with the genealogy of the eminent monsters Gargantua and Pantagruel. These medieval ogres were, as I said, shining examples of virtue, models to be emulated, kind and generous and good-natured giants who are truly unique in the entire history of universal teratology. I should also say that, on more than one occasion, over coffee and cigarettes during the long, bitter winters we were forced to endure together, Gaudencia told me in great detail (and in private) about her perilous birth, her precocious childhood, her preposterous adolescence, and the general ups-and-downs of her Ecuadorian upbringing until she matriculated at that Southern American university which Donoso describes somewhat haphazardly in that friction of his in which I am the primary antagonist. But I don't want to get off track here, ladies and gentlemen, so let me now proceed to relating Gaudencia's own confessions . . . beginning of course, with the story of her father, old Shrek Gross, who was a good fellow in his time, and a notable jester; he loved to drink, as much as any man, and enjoyed salted meats. To that end he was ordinarily well furnished with gammons of bacon and plenty of links of *salchichones, chorizos, morcillas, butifarras, chistorras,* and *sobrasadas,* when they were in season. In the prime of his life, Shrek Gross married Gaudencia's mother, a well-mouthed wench by the name of Mostrenca, granddaughter of an old Ecuadorian dictator much despised by his people. Gaudencia spent eleven long months in Mostrenca's womb, for so long, and even longer, may a woman carry her great belly, especially when it is some monster of nature, a fact that the masters, the ancient Pantagruelists, have confirmed. So, then, on one afternoon, on the third of February, to be exact, after a great country buffet, Mostrenca's bum-gut, yes, her water broke after having eaten too many *jocobolos. Jocobolos,* so you know, are the fat tripes of beef cattle fattened at the cratch in llama stalls. Her good husband, Gaudencia's father, bade her eat sparingly, because she was near her due date, and because these tripes were not the healthiest of things to eat. Notwithstanding these admonitions, she did eat sixteen quarters, two bushels, three pecks and a pipkin full. The fecalphiliacs among you can surely imagine the excessive excrement swelling up inside of her, from the addition of such shitty stuff! So, while the others were on this discourse and pleasant tattle of drinking, Mostrenca began to feel a little unwell in her lower parts. At that point, Shrek Gross arose from off the grass, and fell to comfort her very honestly and kindly, suspecting that she was going into labor, and told her that it was best for her to sit down upon the grass under the willows, because she was likely very shortly to see tiny feet poking out, and that therefore she should pluck up her spirits and look forward to the fresh arrival of her baby.

"'Courage, courage,' he said. 'Don't you worry about a thing; just keep the horse before the cart. I'm off to have one more drink, and if anything happens in the meantime that might require my presence, I will be so near to you, that all you need is to call, and I'll be back here with you forthwith.'

"A short while later, she began to moan and cry. All of a sudden, the midwives rushed in from all around and began poking and prodding at her nether regions, where they found what they thought was a particular odorous case of meconium staining. But—lo and behold!—it was her fundament that slipped out there with the mollification of her intestinum crassum, her large intestine, or her ass-pipe, if you will, and instead of the baby, it contained the excess of tripes which, as you know, she had previously consumed. It was then that an ugly, elderly member of the group, who was rumored to be an expert in the gynecological sciences, gave her such an effective astringent that the full length of her colon dilated before the sphincters surrounding it compressed, slamming shut with all the force your teeth might apply to a piece of pork, which (I admit) is a terrible metaphor, if you think about it. This quite inconveniently caused the cotyledons of her matrix to loosen, through which the child sprang up and leaped, thus entering her vena cava and climbing up through the diaphragm towards the shoulders, where the vein divides itself into two, and from thence she made her way towards the left side, issuing forth through her mother's left ear. As soon as she was born, she cried not as other babes do—Waaah, waaah, waaah—but with a high, sturdy, and big voice shouted out for all to hear: *Crap! Crap! Crap!*

"I doubt very much that any of you will thoroughly believe the truth of this strange nativity. Whether you believe it or not matters little to me, but an honest man, and of good judgment, still believes what is told him, and that which he finds written. Well then, the good man Shrek Gross, drinking and making merry with the rest, heard the horrible noise which his daughter had made as she entered into the light of this world, when she cried out, *Crap! Crap! Crap!* At the sound of this, he said in Spanish, *¡Que garganta tan fuerte tienes!* That is to say, how great and nimble a throat you have. That, then, became the inspiration for the name, since the phonetics were almost too perfect to ignore: after gulping great gobs of grease down her gullet at a grand *gaudeamus*, the monstrous Mostrenca had given birth to a girl with a gargantuan *garganta*,

393

whom she would name 'Gaudencia,' instead of the more common name 'Carmenza,' because she was afraid that the other children would taunt her with chants of *Crappy Carmenza! Crappy Carmenza!*

"In order to provide the infant girl with her daily milk, seventeen thousand nine hundred and thirteen cows were commandeered, for it was impossible to find a nurse sufficient for her in all of Ecuador, considering the great quantity of milk required for her nourishment. Some specialists have affirmed, though, that her mother Mostrenca could safely pump from her breasts one thousand four hundred and two barrels and nine pails of milk at a time; which indeed is not probable, and has even been found duggishly scandalous and offensive to tender ears, for it smacked a little of heresy. But so it was that little Gaudencia was reared there in the blessed countryside until she was one year and ten months of age. Then, on the advice of the physicians, they built a fine little cart, drawn by burros, and carried her with great joy hither and thither, across hill and dale, to every corner of the land. She was worth the seeing, for she was a fine child with a burly physiognomy and eighteen chins. She cried very little, but shat herself every hour on the hour. Much like her mother, little Gaudencia was wonderfully phlegmatic in her posterior regions. So, from the ages of three until five, she was brought up and instructed in all relevant disciplines according to the dispositions of her father. And she spent that time like any other child of the wealthy in Ecuador; that is, eating, shitting, and sleeping, sleeping, shitting, and eating. She incessantly wallowed and rolled in the muck and mire of the pigsty, sullying her clothes and smudging her face with filth, wore down her shoes in the heel, gobbled up flies, and ran very heartily after the butterflies. She pissed in the groom's shoes, shit in her father's shirts, blew her nose in her mother's blouses, let her snot dribble into the governess's soup, dabbling and paddling and slobbering everywhere, she drank from her own chamber pot, scratched her belly with a comb, bushed her teeth with a clog, washed her hands with chicken broth, and combed her hair with a bowl. She would sit between two stools with her ass on the ground, would cover herself with a wet sack, and would drink *pisco* while she ate her soup. She licked the frosting off of cake, pissed on anthills in the garden, spit in the basin, and farted for fatness's sake. She would say the ape's paternoster, scratch where it did not itch, and tickled herself so she would laugh. She ate cabbage, shit beets, and when she found a fly in a dish of milk, she would tear off its legs. Her father's little dogs ate off of her dish, and she ate out of their bowls. She would bite their ears, and they would scratch her nose; she would blow in their asses, and they would lick her teats. Around her sixth birthday, old Gross returned home one afternoon, filled with joy, as any father might be at the sight of such a daughter. While offering drinks to his governesses, he asked them, among other things, whether they had been careful to keep her clean and sweet. To this, Gaudencia herself replied that she had taken care of that herself, and that a lovelier and daintier girl was not to be found in all of Ecuador.

" 'And how is that?' asked her adoring father.

" 'I have,' answered Gaudencia, 'by a long an curious investigation, found a way of wiping my ass, which is the most excellent, most convenient, and most ladylike the world has ever seen.'

" 'And what might that be?' said Shrek Gross.

" 'I'll tell you,' said Gaudencia. "First, I wiped myself with a governess's velvety scarf, and it was quite pleasing, for the softness of the silk was very comforting to my anus. Another time, I tried one of the maid's bonnets, and the result was the same. And, I admit, I once used one of your handkerchiefs. Then it was the crimson satin lapels of a lady's coat, but they were covered in golden studs and shitty little rhinestones that scraped my buttocks until they bled. May Saint Antony's fire burn the asses of the goldsmith who made them, and the woman who wore them! Fortunately, though, I was able to ease my pain by wiping a second time with a page's cap, which was adorned with a feather, as the Swiss are wont to do. Afterwards, I caught a March cat hiding behind a thicket, and I cleansed myself with him, but his claws scratched my perineum. I recovered from this the next morning by wiping myself with *mami* Mostrenca's gloves, which were perfumed with the beautiful scent of Arabian Benin. After that I cleaned myself with sage, fennel, dill, cilantro, marjoram, roses, calabash leaves, beets, colewort, vine-leaves, marshmallows, great mullein (which is a tail-scarlet), with lettuce and spinach leaves (which actually served me quite well). Then, with mercury, parsley, nettles, and comfrey, but that gave me a devilish case of dysentery, which I cured by wiping myself with the clasp of a corset, can you believe that? Later I cleaned myself with your bedsheets, blankets, curtains, seat cushions, the carpet, a Persian rug, a kitchen towel, a napkin, a handkerchief, and a currycomb. And I found it all to be quite pleasurable, *papi*, more pleasurable than do the mangy dogs when you rub them.'

" 'Yes, yes,' said Shrek Gross, quite surprised and a bit blown away by so much unexpected information, 'but which method did you find to be the best, sweetie pie?'

" 'I was coming to that,' said the not-quite-six-year-old Gaudencia. 'You'll find out soon enough, but I'm not quite done just yet. I wiped myself with hay, straw, flax, wool, and with paper, but as I like to say, *He whose foul ass with paper wipes / Shall find himself left with chocolate stripes.*'

" 'What?' Her father leapt to his feat, as proud as he was delighted. 'My little bean sprout is writing poetry already?'

" 'Of course,' Gaudencia replied. 'Here's one about what the toilet says to the person sitting on it:

> *Shitter,*
> *Pisser,*
> *Squirter,*
> *Turdus,*
> *Your bung*
> *Has flung*
> *Some dung*

Upon us;
Your sticky
And stinky
Eau de cologne
Hath splattered
And shattered
My porcelain throne.'

" 'Do you want me to keep going, *papi*?'

" 'Please do, my honey bun!'

" 'Listen to this little roundelay:

In shitting yesterday I had a realization
My ass was worthy of deification:
The smell which from my crack did slink,
Had legendary powers to bestink.
Hear me now, oh brave Ulysses:
I have the power to make things shitty!'

" 'Excellent, excellent,' old Shrek said impatiently, 'but let us return to our purpose.'

" 'And what purpose is that, *papi*? To shit?'

" 'No,' he replied. 'I'm talking about wiping your ass.'

" 'Ah, but there is no need to wipe your ass unless it is foul, and it can't be foul unless you've been shitting; in other words, you have to shit before you wipe.'

" 'Oh my goodness!' exclaimed Shrek Gross. 'What excellent wit and intelligence you have! One of these days you're going to become a professor of Latin American literature. My God! You are wise beyond your years. Now, please, go on with the possibilities for ass-wipage.'

" 'I wiped with a wig, a pillow, a pantoufle, a leather satchel, a basket, and a hat. But consider, *papi*, that some hats are made of felt, some of fur, while others still are made from taffeta or sateen. Without a doubt, the best hat for ass-wiping is a fur hat, because the hairs have a very abstergent effect on fecal matter. I've also wiped with a hen, a cock, a pullet, a calf's skin, a hare, a pigeon, a cormorant, a briefcase, a *montero*, a coif, and a falcon's lure. But, to conclude, I say and maintain that of all the many forms of all torcheculs, toilet paper, tail napkins, bunghole cleansers, and ass fodders, nothing compares with the neck of a well-downed goose, if you can hold its head between your legs. Believe me, *papi*, on my honor: your cornhole will experience a most wonderful pleasure, both in terms of the softness of said down and the temperate warmth of the goose itself, which is easily transferred to the rectum and colon and the rest of the digestive tract, and even as far as the heart and brain. And think not that the felicity of the heroes and demigods in the Elysian fields consists either in utilizing their asphodel, ambrosia, and nectar, as the philosophers used to say, for—in my opinion—they wipe their asses with the neck of a goose.'"

"That's certainly not my opinion," bellowed Empedocles, who suddenly found himself in the middle of the surprising plaza. "I don't know shit about goose down, but let me assure you that the beatitude of the Greek heroes and demigods like myself, Empedocles of Agrigento, often if not always employs asphodel, ambrosia, and nectar. That ill-bred and unmannerly girl doesn't know what she's talking about."

"Look, grandpa," Gaudencia replied. "I don't know shit about Greek demigods, but I know quite a bit about assholes and abstersion."

"Well you've certainly convinced me that you're a monster descended from monsters, and a spoiled brat to boot," said the old philosopher from Akragas, not mincing his words. "In fact, ladies and gentlemen, I can offer a very good explanation for the monstrosity that is this frightful young girl, this undignified descendant of Gargantua and Grangousier, a theory that predates Darwin and his theory of evolution by more than two thousand years. As some of you know, it is just at the end of the first stage of my intricate cosmic cycle, once the eventful confluence of Love has united the members and organs of the body, that cursed Hatred creeps in to cause the sudden formation of singular beasts, which signals the beginnings of the sad, second phase of our universe. In *On Nature*, I write, quite explicitly: 'Many creatures were born with faces and breasts on both sides, man-faced ox-progeny, while others again sprang forth as ox-headed offspring of man, creatures compounded partly of male, partly of female natures, and fitted with sterile parts.' It is, I insist, during the reign of Kypris that many species survive and assure (thanks to good coupling) their own conservation. For that reason, I wrote (and Simplicius soon rewrote) that 'the human head, when it meets a human body, ensures the preservation of the whole, but being inappropriate to the ox-body it leads to its disappearance. All that did not come together according to the proper formula, *logos*, perished.' Aristotle, as contrarian as ever, wanted to refute the fortuitousness of this cosmic process by adducing his own teleological concept of the universe in which, as you know, Mother Nature herself intervenes and gives everything an ultimate reason for being. But then old Charles had to come along and demonstrate the opposite to be true, and to clearly affirm that I was right all along in terms of describing how only those species who adapt, who adjust, who fit together suitably are able to survive. But . . . well then, we don't want to get off track here. All I want to do is remind you that the Minotaur, the Chimera, the Centaurs, Scylla and Charybdis, Hermaphroditos, even old Phanes himself, the Protogenos of procreation in Orphic cosmogony . . . all of them monsters from my homeland, and all of them examples of how, in spite of it all, some anomalous and defective beings have survived to the present day. There aren't many, but they exist . . . And let me also remind you of something I've been saying over and over again throughout my life: that we currently exist right at the height of Strife, of Discord, that the cosmos lives under its reign, and that ever since that second phase in which we lost the sovereignty of Love, we have been brooding over and longing for a happy and harmonious past, an impossible Arcadia. That is why I've come to the conclusion that we should not be so surprised that things are as they are, populating the nefarious world of Eris—our world—with wretched, garrulous giants, with arrogant and tyrannical monsters like the Ecuadorian professor Gaudencia Gross-Wayne."

"Your words are wise and well-reasoned, Empe," interjected Pitol. "However, we don't want to honor that shit-eating Gorgon woman with so many words; rather, we're here to celebrate Gargantua and also the renowned Rabelais himself, who deep down wanted nothing more than to relate to us, with unique skill, the very human experiences and feats of this singular French monster, victorious in battle over the evil king Picrochole and his sly partisans. Your extensive teratological vision has been, without a doubt, illuminating; nevertheless, we do not want to turn a tribute to a kind and celebrated character into an apology of a horrifying Ecuadorian Chimera. Which is why I would like to share with all of you, my dear people of Las Rémoras, the profound and solemn words of my good friend Kundera, who—during a recent visit to Arles with Chernishevski, Urrozkinski, and a servant—felt suddenly inspired to speak about François Rabelais and his famous giants:

"'*Pour Rabelais, la dichotomie des thèmes et des ponts, du premier et de l'arriere-plan est chose inconnue. Lestment, il passe d'un sujet grave à l'énumération des méthodes que le petit Gargantua inventa pour se torcher le cul, et pourtant, esthétiquement, tous ces passages, futiles ou graves, ont chez lui la même importance, me procurent le même plaisir. C'est ce qui m'enchantait chez lui et chez d'autres romanciers anciens: ils parlent de ce qu'ils trouvent fascinant et ils s'arrêtent quand la fascination s'arrête. Leur liberté de composition m'a fait rêver: écrire sans fabriquer un suspense, sans construire une histoire et simuler sa vraisemblance, écrire sans décrire une epoque, un milieu, une ville; abandonner tout cela et n'être au contact que de l'éssentiel ce qui veut dire: créer une composition où des ponts et des remplissages n'auraient aucune raison d'être et où le romancier ne serait pas obligé, pour satisfaire la forme et ses diktats, de s'éloigner, même d'une seule ligne, de ce qui lui tient à cœur, de ce qui le fascine.'"*

"Exactly. You've hit the nail on the head: total freedom of composition," exclaimed Urrozkinski, leaping out of his chair there at the French inn where the four of us were chatting away under a yellow, moribund lightbulb around a table adorned with empty bottles of wine and bread crumbs. "The intermingling of different eras, humor, identity, sentimentalism, betrayal, coprophagy . . . all of these things are elements of the freest of frictions, Milan. To hell with realism, rationalism, probability, and suspense! To hell with the distinction between the serious and the funny! It's better to equate them, to mix them. An orderly chaos, or better yet: a chaotic order . . . That's what I'd like to do, if only I had the genius to do so. Either that, or a Guggenheim fellowship . . ."

"*Je l'ai déjà fait*," Pitol interrupted, rather ungraciously, and without anybody having asked him.

"But why did you quote yourself in French, Sergio?" Eladio Villagrá exclaimed, suddenly returning to this world of frictional reality, snatching the conch away from him. "It just seems ridiculous to me, you know? I know you're just showing off for Urrozkinski and Kundera, but the rest of us are getting a little sick of putting up with your sarcastic remarks in other languages. How would you like it if I spoke to you in Otomi?"

"Actually, I'm quite fluent. As a matter of fact, I'm currently translating the greatest Otomi novelist of all time . . ."

"That's enough," intervened the Ecuadorian writer, before attempting yet again—after so many interruptions and digressions, in a much more conciliatory and *ad hoc* tone—to offer his own thoughts on the matter. He grabbed the public-address microphone and said: "As I was saying, bantering back and forth over coffee and cigarettes, trying to survive the inhospitable winters there in the American South, I was slowly learning (almost against my will) about the eccentricities and appetites of my Ecuadorian compatriot, an expert (as I said before) in how colors work and play in my sublime frictional novels of customs and manners. I was especially interested in issues related to her childhood and adolescence, which I've just now related, although I admit I forgot to mention the one experience which, according to her, came to have the greatest influence upon her life, the benchmark event that defined her flatulent youth. I'm talking about the fact that, while many of us were reading Dickens, Stevenson, or Emilio Salgari as nine- or ten-year-old children, Gaudencia once confessed to me that the work of literature that had the biggest impact on her life was a lovely little children's book that her mother Mostrenca gave her as a gift when she was very small . . . perhaps around the same time she began using feathered geese to wipe her pretty pink ass, being as they were quite aspergesent and alive. The book in question is called *Once Upon a Potty*. I'm sure many of you are familiar with it. It is beautifully illustrated and written in short sentences with big, friendly print for toddlers just beginning to read and spell their first words. Although we've already seen that little Gaudencia was writing quite lovely poems at quite a young age, it's still interesting to learn that her primary book of choice was not something by Sor Juana, Shakespeare, or Rabelais (she was, after all, a professor of literature at Millard Fillmore University in Madisonburg, Virginia). Quite the contrary. Even as recently as the time we spent together at the university under the tutelage of Professors Macpherson and Avellaneda, Gaudencia's preferred reading material was none other than *Once Upon a Potty*. Clearly, she was obsessed with it. An anal fixation, a mania . . . and please, Empe, do not interrupt or correct me here. I'm referring to the word's modern definition: that of an odd habit, a little fucking fascination and nothing else, okay? Something you engage in time and time again, ever since you were a kid. That being said, I'd like to read a few ingenuous yet candid passages from the book in question." Here, Chiriboga produced a slim, colorful, and beautifully illustrated children's book, and began to read it, almost euphorically, to the assembly in the plaza: "Hello. I am Prudence's mother. I'd like to tell you about Prudence and her new potty. This is Prudence. Prudence is a little girl." Here, Marcelo showed the people nearest to him the corresponding illustration: a mother and a one-year-old girl in diapers. He continued: "Just like you, Prudence has a body, and this body has many useful parts: A head for thinking. Eyes for seeing. Ears for hearing. A bottom for sitting, and in it a little hole for making Poo-Poo." Again, the corresponding illustration showed little Prudence with her backside up in the air like a dog, showing us her rosaceous little asshole. "Ever since Prudence was born, she's been making wee-wee and poo-poo into her diaper. And I, her mommy, have been changing her. Until, one day, Prudence's grandmother brought her a big present." Here, the illustration shows a kind, gray-haired grandma handing a box wrapped up in a bow to little Prudence, this time in diapers. "Prudence opened the box and found a strange something inside." Here, the lovely illustration shows the same gift . . . but now the bow had been torn off and Prudence was diving into the box, trying to find out what that mysterious object was. "Was it a hat?" Here we see Prudence trying to situate atop her head something which—while not obvious at first—was none other than a simple, green, burnished potty trainer. "Was it a bowl? A milk bowl for the kitty cat? No." Here, of course, was a picture of a ridiculous cat looking for drops of milk in the bone-dry bottom of the bowl. "Was it a flowerpot? Was it a birdbath? No, it wasn't a flowerpot or a birdbath." The corresponding illustrations showed, first, flowers placed in the potty trainer like a vase, and second, three small birds flying around that same, shiny pot as if it were a baptismal font. "It was a potty for sitting and peeing and pooping instead of using a diaper. How wonderful!" Here we see Prudence, in her birthday suit, touching her little anus. "Prudence sat on her new potty, she sat and sat and sat and sat and sat and nothing came out. Later, she peed and she pooped, but not exactly in the potty." The illustration corresponding to this page was important enough for Chiriboga to raise it up on high so that everyone in attendance could appreciate the colorful artistry: it showed the poor little naked girl observing—with a somewhat astonished look on her face—a smallish pile of fresh poop lying on the ground just off to one side of the potty trainer. "One day Prudence had a feeling that she was ready to poop and she ran to her potty and sat down." Here, you see Prudence sitting happily on her potty trainer with a big smile on her face, Reader. "She sat and sat and sat and sat and sat and sat and sat and sat . . ." Chiriboga was not exaggerating: as you can clearly see there on the page, the same verb is repeated *ad infinitum*. "And when she got up and looked at it, her poop was right in the potty!" Here, again, she was contemplating a small, baby-sized mound of poop, though this time it was squarely inside the potty trainer given to her by her handsome, gray-haired grandmother. "She was very happy and proud and came to show me her full potty and I was very happy and proud too." At this point in the story, nearing the end, we see the girl offering up her bowl full of shit to her lovely mother, who takes it in her hands with such pride that she might just be preparing to lift it up above her head as if she were Maradona lifting the World Cup trophy back in 1986. "And then the two of us emptied the potty into the toilet. *Good-bye, pee-pee! Good-bye poo-poo!* Prudence seemed to be saying, with tears in her eyes." The brief, educational tale concludes with a picture of the naked little girl touching her wee-wee and sadly bidding farewell to a fresh batch of feces as they wash away down an olive-colored, adult-sized toilet. "It was this conclusion, Gaudencia once confessed to me, choked up with tears, that moved her the most. Not even Anna Karenina, Silvana Forns Nakash, Emma Bovary, Tess of the d'Urbervilles, or La Regenta, she said, have been able to move me and affect me so deeply, Marcelo. *Once Upon a Potty* was a true watershed event in my life, she blubbered from behind a handkerchief as she blew her nose. She continued on, while I smoked a cigarette in stunned silence: Even to this day, whenever I reread this sage and scholarly children's book, I break down into tears—I break down into oceans and oceans of tears, Chiriboga—and I don't stop for days. It's just that, to me, the tragedy of Prudence and her potty is the great tragedy of my life, one that I never got over."

"It all makes sense. It all fits. Everything!" cried Eusebio, illuminated and ecstatic, forcing his way through the last few rows of people separating him from Marcelo on that radiant June day. Without waiting for Chiriboga or Sigüenza to hand over the microphone, Cardoso made his way front and center and continued the verbal frenzy: "The conclave of shiteating millionaires in Highpoint exists! It's a verifiable fact, just as I thought, and not an invention created by poor Sofía, the Honduran maid who worked for my former colleague Marion Siegel. Do you see? Do you understand? The complicated story about those scatological rituals held in the basement of the Gorgon's mansion were completely true. What you've heard here this morning, straight from the mouth of the master Chiriboga himself, confirms this, ladies and gentlemen. It's all so perfect. It all links together like a cheap bracelet. Ever since Gaudencia's fixation on everything from those poor little geese to fur, sateen, and velvet hats, to sheets, curtains, handkerchiefs, bonnets, and caps, to Mostrenca's Benin-scented gloves and a March cat (which, by the way, is one of the most belligerent of all the felines) to cilantro, dill, beets, cabbage leaves . . . everything on that lengthy list of putrid asswipes which were lorded over by that awful Ecuadorian girl—that ignoble heiress of Gargantua and Pantagruel—can be considered convincing proof that the lavish yet preposterous story of the coprophagous sect is an absolute certainty, and that everyone— from Marco Aurelio Vasco-Osama and Santiago Bormann-Smythe to the rustic Texan Wynn, obese Whitehead, and his ferocious little guard dog, the bearded Jeffrey Davis—every single one of them was a member of that execrable coprophilic cult in the American South. *Once Upon a Potty* was, for me, the last key bit of evidence confirming what I've said and believed all this time. That green, burnished little potty trainer you showed us in the storybook, Marcelo, is identical to the hand-crafted Ecuadorian clay chamber pot that Gross-Wayne had stashed away in the basement of her house in Highpoint. Now I see it all so clearly, as clear as the Las Rémoras sky, and as transparent as the waters of the Sea of Cortez itself . . . You all have no idea how truly happy all this makes me, after having been denigrated and expelled from Millard Fillmore University and, thus, from the pestilent town of Madisonburg. Really, I feel so much better. Now more than ever, ladies and gentlemen, I realize just how much danger I was actually in. I was unknowingly circling the bowl, you could say. And if I had stayed there any longer, the shit might have engulfed me as well. Who knows . . . the poor Galicians may already be up to their necks in it. Sooner or later, those zombie-like henchmen to the Gorgon herself would have found a way to get me to drink the feces of their dear leader, but . . . I was saved. I'm alive. By the hair of a March cat. Can you believe it? If it hadn't been for my grave mistake, that fault or failure which you're already well aware of, Reader, I wouldn't be here with you on this fine June day. If it weren't for Eros—I mean, if it weren't for Eris, and my unfortunate tendency to chase skirts—I might not be here with you today, chatting, sharing, and linking ill-fated past events together. Do you see? Or have I gone too far?"

"Yes, Eusebio, we follow you. We're following you quite well," replied the Secretary of Culture Eladio Villagrá, who, despite the burning Las Rémoras sun beating down upon them, was still dressed in the same greasy coat and tie from the previous night at the brothel. "Of course we see . . . at least, those of us who have been reading *Friction*. But you still haven't told us what the hell happened to Matilde, the attractive wife of Reader, who is here with us today, on that deplorable Thursday morning, the 15th of June, to be exact, when Arturo went out for cigarettes. Do you remember, or have you already forgotten all about her? Have you written it yet, or could you just tell us all right now? Yes, what happened to Matilde when Anagnostes showed up, quite unexpectedly, that afternoon? All of a sudden, for some reason, you interrupted the story of that love triangle and we watched as you and Anagnostes escaped from your respective familial tangles and ran here, to Las Rémoras, only yesterday . . ." Eladio paused here to catch his breath before delivering his decisive, powerful conclusion: "Tell us, Eusebio, what the hell happened?"

"Yes, yes, what happened?" cried Reader, as angry as he was desperate.

"But that's all part of the next chapter," replied Eusebio, his voice somewhere between conciliatory, slick, and evasive.

"Enough with the never-ending chapters, already! We've had it up to here; let's just put an end to this whole affair, once and for all," Reader demanded in front of the astonished multitude of people who, finally, made a sound, a collective gasp, which sounded like a whale surfacing for air or a choral *vibratum*, so morbidly enthralled they were with the story, as silent and expectant as a docile child.

"Fine, fine, if you insist, Reader," conceded the Mexican professor. And with that, he proceeded to bring his extraordinary *Friction* to its conclusion, relating to everyone gathered there (but especially to Reader) what amounted to the culminating Chapter 18 of his truculent and sordid story:

"After that first wave of nausea had passed, and after Arturo had left the bodega after buying his pack of cigarettes, Maty got up off the quilt, got dressed, and got ready to leave that plywood-and-asbestos studio, something which she almost never did, fearing (as she did) an encounter with the painter's wife. It was very hot that afternoon, do you remember? Your wife quickly made her way across the roof of that five-floor building in Narvarte, towards Tamara and Arturo's living quarters. To call it a house would have been a bit excessive, I think, although yes, in the strictest sense, it was their home, ever since they had to move in there, owing to the frugality required by a lack of funds, as you already know. In fact, I think I might have already mentioned the fact that the two-room shack there was actually built by the owners of the building for their servants, back when the Mexican economy still allowed for servants; that is, back in 2015, ten years before this bewildering mess you're reading actually occurred. Since it had gone unoccupied for so long, Arturo bought it for a very modest sum, since he and his mother had spent all of Roberto

Soto Gariglietti's money. Needless to say, the light provided certain artistic benefits; at least, that's what he always claimed. He loved living up there, out in the open, with its view of Mexico City infected with antennas and skyscrapers. It was quite bright and very hot on that afternoon when you arrived, either by chance or misfortune. At any rate, Reader, and putting an end to any more Balzacian descriptions, your wife decided to enter your friend's home for the first time since she had started coming to his building to interview him. Although she understood full well that Tamara had been out of town on a trip for some time now, she decided to knock: a patently useless act. Without waiting long (almost immediately, in fact) she entered the first of the two conjoining rooms. In the first, she found a couple of bookshelves placed back-to-back against one wall which (of course) were stacked with books, many of which pertained to photography or painting. There were a few pieces of old-fashioned furniture that tried to give the place a more cozy, more welcoming appearance; nevertheless, the disorder and a certain, indefinable, rotten smell made it a rather disagreeable and inhospitable place: carbonized, forgotten candles all over the place, overflowing ashtrays, stacks of old newspapers, empty bottles, and even—in one corner—a small sink piled high with dirty plates, some of which were covered with a gray, mossy, moldy substance. Whatever it was that was growing there in the sink, Maty felt a second wave of nausea welling up, much stronger than the first, and she began looking frantically for the bathroom. It had to be in the adjacent room, because she had seen no other internal doors. Panicking, she threw open the door to find an unmade bed and clothes scattered all over the floor. But she was able to locate the bathroom on the opposite side of the room, hidden behind a thin, multicolored, striped curtain. The smell there was even worse. *What the hell is that,* Matilde thought to herself as she bent down in front of the toilet, and whether it was from her pregnancy or the filth growing in the sink, she was no longer able to hold back any longer. Once she had ejected the undigested bits of chicken and vegetables that she'd eaten that afternoon without you, she flushed it down and washed her mouth and face in the basin. Mechanically, she drew back the plastic shower curtain hanging just an arm's length away from her, revealing the bathtub: floating on the dark, stagnant water were a few bits or pieces of some indefinable object which nevertheless smelled of rotting meat. She bolted out of there, through the thin fabric curtain separating the bathroom from the bedroom, rounded the mattress, and emerged once again in the main living chamber. Just as she was about to burst back out onto the illuminated roof, a fragment of a memory held her back. Was it even a memory? A vision? Conjecture, perhaps? Or was it a premonition, dear Reader? Whatever it was, Matilde stoked up her courage and turned around, retracing her steps, and made her way back towards the bedroom. She took a quick, nervous look around, trying not to breath through her mouth. Then, unexpectedly, she lay down on the conjugal bed. She remained there for a few moments, half a minute perhaps, pensive, and then, yes, only then did she take hold of the bed sheets and pull them towards her, revealing the mattress, and upon it the motionless body of a woman, a young woman. *It's Tamara*, she thought involuntarily. Yes, it was her, a fact which Maty couldn't comprehend until she reached out and touched the body with the tip of her index finger: yes, it was Tamara, perfectly embalmed, peaceful, frozen, eternal. A brown, sleeping, naked mummy. Your poor wife let loose with a frightful shout, Reader, which she immediately cut short for fear of being discovered. She shot out of there, ran across the burning plain of the roof, wanting only to get her Louis Vuitton purse and tape recorder and escape before her lover, your friend, returned. But, only a few seconds after she was back in the studio, she heard the unmistakable voice of Arturo shouting something about love or some such thing that Maty couldn't immediately process in her state of paralyzing fear which had frozen her there next to the ramshackle sofa and the colorful quilt. There was nothing she could do . . . *But yes, there is,* Maty thought to herself just as the painter was about to enter the studio. She could feign innocence. And that's exactly what she did while Arturo slowly undressed her once again, while he was kissing her alabastrine neck and shoulders, her erect nipples, her splendid arms, and even while he pulled off her panties and began to eagerly caress her curvaceous, silky gluteus . . ."

"Forget about the fucking details, damn it!" shouted Reader. "Not now, please!"

". . . Maty was able to act (and act quite well, as a matter of fact) when the Agro painter finally sat down on the quilt and made your naked, olive-skinned wife straddle him, staring her in the eyes while she wrapped her legs around him, exactly as they were when you found them there, remember? When you saw them, what . . . just two days ago? Thursday, to be exact. You watched her from behind as she romped up and down, and you also watched the hairy ass of your friend the painter, watched as he wrapped his hairy arms around her fragile back. The heat wouldn't allow you to concentrate; you were sweating like a hog, and for a second you actually thought that it wasn't Maty at all, because she was at the café in Polanco with her graduate student friends, gossiping, eating a slice of *pastel de tres leches*, discussing Latin American politics, all the changes, especially the big change that took place barely a year ago with the election of the new president, Gilberto Rendón, which had left the world totally dumbstruck, but no, you suddenly knew that that wasn't the case, that those clear green eyes belonged to Matilde, because they recognized you, Reader, they saw you there, just above the left shoulder of your friend Arturo, the artist, who had your magnificent and lovely wife there, on that afternoon (and many others) in his studio whether you were reading or not, since what does it really matter at this point anyway, what the hell could it possibly matter now that you're seeing this with your own eyes, crystal clear and real, the pain and the hurt burning through your corneas, you, the suffering voyeur, the little man, suddenly feeling as if an invisible object were drilling or boring into you, a hard, stabbing sensation, a stiff jab, a little chocolate-covered pepper that tastes sweet and then burns you from within, but it's not love that's doing it; rather, it's a lascivious burning, a burning sense of disgrace, a crushing, overwhelming sense of pain, like an eternity of hellfire, continuous, fluid, cutting, throbbing inside your head, refusing to let you breathe, refusing to let you blink in the face of what you're witnessing though sweat is running into your eyes, you're sweating like a hog on its way to the slaughterhouse, and man, you think, it's a good thing you left your tie back in your Mercedes, otherwise you might have hung yourself with that sopping wet thing!"

"Do I really have to hear you reading to me what I've already read one damn time myself?" stammered Reader, tense and trembling and burning with anger, feeling as if every curious eye there in Las Rémoras were focused on him.

Paying him no heed, insidious and frenetic, Cardoso continued:

"Then you heard Maty's voice, she was moaning or startled or saying something to you, something you couldn't make out, but you felt your stomach clenching up anyway, about to retch, but just as you doubled over in pain you saw there, along one of the walls and jumbled in with the other paintings, the portrait you ordered from Arturo two months ago, the portrait of your wife which, it appears, he's finishing after all, or at least he would be finishing it if he weren't fucking your wife—and then you vomited at the thought—who was right there fucking and fucking him on top of a patterned quilt, just fucking and moaning with delight there on top of that hairy artist, on top of the god of color, straddling that goddamn Agro artist's legs, clutched by his thick, powerful arms, her fingernails digging into his shoulder blades like she does to you when she's about to orgasm, although this time there was no way of knowing if the clawing was being caused by an orgasm or by the terrible scare that you gave the poor little thing by finding her in such a position, so pompous and blissful, sweetly tortured by the painter's primitive cock, his turgid penis running through her while you vomited and got the hell out of there, terrified, breathless, unable to say even one damn word, still tasting the coffee grounds stuck in your teeth, remember that? You were choked up, you'd gone numb, you'd lost your bearings, your compass, your mind; your sad eyes had glossed over, your soul felt overcast and dirty despite the intense sun, despite that rust-colored light that cleaved through the sky that Thursday afternoon in the capital city, that 15th of June, that day in which your whole life twisted and changed, my dear, amiable and distinguished Reader, my burgeoning friend, my traveling companion.

Harrisonburg 2003, Arles-Mexico-Charleston 2006, Nashville 2009

To the Editors of *Revuelta*:

Let me begin by saying that I take no joy whatsoever in writing this little note. Far from it. In fact, it's embarrassing, uncomfortable, and incredibly irritating for me even to have to do this (especially when I'm currently so occupied with my own divorce proceedings), but I do feel a moral obligation to send it to you, in order to edify the public that purchases this magnificent magazine. All that notwithstanding, I have already made the irrevocable decision to do this after having finally finished (with a great deal of effort and quite a bit of gastrointestinal distress) the newly published yet repulsive novel entitled *Friction*, authored by Professor Eusebio Cardoso, an expert on the Novel of the Mexican Revolution and incipient apprentice to the pre-Socratic philosophers, with whom he is evidently only tangentially acquainted. The reason for my letter is not to express the depths of my displeasure with the carminative and sulphureous pages of that unfortunate book, but rather to share with the demanding and cultured public the contradictions and vagaries incurred by the aforementioned Cardoso, who is an infantile novelist and a mediocre, third-world writer at best.

First of all, respected editors, I'd like to point to the out-and-out mishmash Cardoso makes, time and time again, with the names of the two Galician friends at Millard Fillmore University. He first labels Javis a brownnoser and then calls him taciturn, while Tino is taciturn first and then a brownnoser. Or it's the other way around. I don't know anymore. In either case, my point is to demonstrate the blatant carelessness inherent in his incredibly incoherent, possibly Pitolean and Del Pasoean prose. Whatever his goal was, he has failed to reach it, even in his own dreams.

Secondly, let me add that I've found, among the many other problems with *Friction*, an extraordinary incompetence regarding electronics, since Maty, my ex-wife, supposedly records her interviews with Arturo at his studio in Narvarte with a simple mini tape recorder . . . in the middle of 2025! Cardoso should be embarrassed by his technological naïveté because nowadays those antique things have been replaced by state-of-the-art Digital Voice Tracers which, aside from being tiny and elegantly designed, have several megabytes of memory and can automatically convert a recorded voice into text. In fact, Matilde has one of these (a Phillips 7675) that I gave her back when we were two turtledoves in love watching a documentary on the unjust and miserable conditions endured by the people living in the mountains of San Luis Potosí on our jumbo flat screen LCD which we have (or had) in our vaporous bedroom back in Las Águilas.

Third—and this delicate part of my note was very difficult for me to write—is the fact that it's highly improbable there was not even a simple bathroom or even a sink there in Arturo's workshop in which the two of them could wash up after those infamous fornications they (Maty and Arturo) conducted behind my back. I'm not as sure about Arturo, but my handsome ex-wife has always held cleanliness in high regard, just as your respectable wife certainly does, eminent Mister Editor. I can't imagine that Matilde (or your own lovely wife, for example) would have left that rooftop hovel crammed with paintings without having cleaned up her pudenda with a cloth or a moist towel before returning home (I mean: your wife to your house and my ex-wife to ours). What do you think of my observations? Are they accurate? Am I right, or am I way off base here? I say, they might be whores, but not filthy whores . . . and this fact, of course, was conveniently left out of *Friction* to further Eusebio's macabre and mischievous aims.

Fourth, Cardoso writes in some parts of *Friction* that I knew and encouraged my wife to go and interview that miserable wretch, and in other parts he contradicts himself, writing that I knew nothing, that I was completely oblivious, thinking instead that Matilde was having coffee with her friends at the café Polanco every Tuesday and Thursday afternoon while Arturo was painting her portrait from a photo I'd given him. Thus, it is clear that Eusebio has tied himself in knots, and because of his literary inexperience, the question remains: did I or did I not know? Evidently the poor little professor doesn't even know himself, which would explain the contradictions in *Friction*. But you, discerning Editor, and your readers will be asking yourselves (and therefore asking me) whether I knew about those "political-philosophical" interviews or not, and my reply is that I simply and resentfully prefer to leave everyone in doubt. You see, that's what happens when you buy lascivious and defective toys like this one. You end up paying the consequences . . .

Fifth, Cardoso makes yet another mistake and contradicts himself again when he has the promiscuous whore Josefina say that not wanting to bury poor Inés, the first madam of the Las Rémoras brothel, alongside the grave of Raimundo Rosales, the lawyer, town councilman, and her lover at the time of his death, was shameful, "like a breach of trust, an act of cowardice." However, if you consult pages 208–209 of *The Obstacles*, you'll see that Josefina was actually the one who objects, shouting at Padre Roldán, that "you can't bury that bastard here." I wonder if perhaps Josefina has had a change of heart, or if Cardoso simply doesn't know exactly what transpired there on the melancholy and fateful day of Rosales's funeral?

My dear Editor, I could continue *ad infinitum* delineating, as your elegant and perspicacious literary critics there at the magazine do, the aberrations that Cardoso incurs in his indecorous book which, instead of *Friction*, really ought to have been entitled *The Misadventures, Missteps, and Misfortune of a Mexican Loser in America*, but clearly this pathetic professor must have liked the sound of *Friction* more, after finding himself abandoned and remorseful, left to his own masturbatory thoughts of making love, making frictions, and making an ass of himself all the damn day while he ruminates and regurgitates his next literary belch.

ANAGNOSTES LESER

AUTHOR'S NOTE

There are beings who accompany us in life as if they actually existed, as if they were alive and walking among us. Such is the case for me with Empedocles of Agrigento, who—in an admittedly strange and inexplicable way—I feel like I know as if he were a friend with whom I've spent innumerable hours chatting in coffee shops each and every day for the past three or four years. I know him . . . but not completely. At least I think I do. I think I've come to intuit him better and better (but what does that really mean?) as we've chatted, as we've communed, and as I wrote this friction and it acquired its specific form, which I admit I never expected would end up being what (after all) it now is. And, what happened to me with Empedocles has also (I suppose) happened with a number of other characters who were not exactly plucked from history, completely imaginary ones like the architect Jasso, the painter Arturo, the prostitute Josefina or the Gorgon Gross-Wayne. Nevertheless, the fact is that you can occasionally coexist with them more than you expect . . . to the point where you begin to blur the distinctions (without even realizing it) between what is being lived and what is being written, between what isn't real and what we aren't quite sure whether it's real or not. It has to do

417

with a curious process that anyone who writes or tells stories knows very well; however, for some hidden reason, I felt the urgent need to repeat it (to justify it) here, as I bring this journey I made with them (the completely imaginary ones) to an end, now that my very close relationship with the rest (the not completely imaginary) has also come to an end: from Pancho Villa to François Rabelais, from Sergio Pitol to Milan Kundera, from Parmenides to Popper, from Coetzee to Donoso, geniuses all in their own peculiar ways, people I admire and to whom I would like to pay homage (extravagantly, outlandishly) in the pages of *Friction*.

My research consisted of a handful of books. Not very many at all, in fact. I wasn't trying to write a philosophical or historical novel, or even an analytic or interpretive one, but at times, of course, I felt bold enough to play around with genres. I simply couldn't have written a text of such a nature. Obvious limitations would have prevented me. Even in those passages where I may have been to some degree dense or petulant, what's notable, I think, is my lack of philosophical and historical (and perhaps frictional) skill and preparation. I have made up for it as Apollo has given me to understand, a lengthy process which involved much overtime, or what Hemingway called "ass hours." I beg your pardon, then, Reader, if I have burdened you unnecessarily and also if you haven't enjoyed yourself very much, which was my sole intention ever since I first started this damned, scatological, monster of a book. In my defense, I would only add that I believed it necessary to provide you with some important information which may make the theories and beliefs of Empedocles and his contemporaries more accessible and understandable . . . and in no way, shape, or form do I assume (or have any inklings) that you are uneducated. Far from it, in fact. The same can be said with respect to the political beliefs of General Villa and the rationalist theories of Popper, which overlap one another in ridiculous fashion in parts of the narrative. So, then, I will cite here those texts which have enabled me to write *Friction*, beginning with those related to Empedocles: the *Biographie d'Empédocle* by J. Bidez (published in 1849 and never reprinted),

the monumental *History of Greek Philosophy,* especially Volume 2, enti-
tled *The Presocratic Tradition from Parmenides to Democritus* by W.K.C.
Guthrie, *Empedocles: A Philosophical Investigation* by Helle Lambridis,
Empedocles: The Extant Fragments by M.R. Wright, the compilation *De
Tales a Demócrito: Fragmentos presocráticos* edited by Alberto Bernabé,
and, finally, the essay "The Unity of Empedocles' Thought" by Herbert S.
Long. When it comes to Parmenides, Guthrie's aforementioned volume
was again essential, as was *World of Parmenides: Essays on the Presocratic
Enlightenment* by Karl Popper. As far as General Villa goes, besides the
famous *Memorias* by Martín Luis Guzmán, there is the monumental biography *The Life and Times of Pancho Villa* by Friedrich Katz, which
was essential in terms of understanding that revolutionary character, the
man and the hero. In fact, Katz documents the story of the two Japanese men which also appears here, although I have allowed myself a few
slight alterations and variations. Sections of Chapter XVII of the second
part of *Friction* are a nearly line-by-line excerpt (again, though, with
some slight alterations and modifications) of certain chapters from *Five
Books of the Lives, Heroic Deeds and Sayings of Gargantua and His Son
Pantagruel,* according to Sir Thomas Urquhart's original 1653 translation, which is in the kind of English you just can't simulate. I have done
the same with the children's book *Once Upon a Potty* by Alona Frankel,
which I have allowed myself (for obvious reasons) to transcribe almost
literally in the nonexistent Chapter 18 of Part Two. I'll conclude here by
attributing the inserted commentary by Milan Kundera to his book *Les
testaments trahis.* All other plagiarisms, insertions, imitations, interpola-
tions, tributes, or parodies (whatever you want to call them) are yours to
discover, Reader. Otherwise, the game would be over . . . wouldn't it?

ELOY URROZ is the author of more than a dozen books of poetry, literary criticism, and prose. He was one of the authors of the "Crack Manifesto," a statement by five Mexican writers dedicated to breaking with the pervading Latin American literary tradition. He is a professor at The Citadel, South Carolina. *The Obstacles*, his first novel to be translated into English, was published by Dalkey Archive Press in 2006.

EZRA E. FITZ has translated Latin American novels such as Eloy Urroz's *The Obstacles* and Alberto Fuguet's *The Movies of My Life*.

SELECTED DALKEY ARCHIVE PAPERBACKS

PETROS ABATZOGLOU, *What Does Mrs. Freeman Want?*
MICHAL AJVAZ, *The Golden Age.*
The Other City.
PIERRE ALBERT-BIROT, *Grabinoulor.*
YUZ ALESHKOVSKY, *Kangaroo.*
FELIPE ALFAU, *Chromos.*
Locos.
IVAN ÂNGELO, *The Celebration.*
The Tower of Glass.
DAVID ANTIN, *Talking.*
ANTÓNIO LOBO ANTUNES, *Knowledge of Hell.*
ALAIN ARIAS-MISSON, *Theatre of Incest.*
IFTIKHAR ARIF AND WAQAS KHWAJA, EDS., *Modern Poetry of Pakistan.*
JOHN ASHBERY AND JAMES SCHUYLER, *A Nest of Ninnies.*
HEIMRAD BÄCKER, *transcript.*
DJUNA BARNES, *Ladies Almanack.*
Ryder.
JOHN BARTH, *LETTERS.*
Sabbatical.
DONALD BARTHELME, *The King.*
Paradise.
SVETISLAV BASARA, *Chinese Letter.*
RENÉ BELLETTO, *Dying.*
MARK BINELLI, *Sacco and Vanzetti Must Die!*
ANDREI BITOV, *Pushkin House.*
ANDREJ BLATNIK, *You Do Understand.*
LOUIS PAUL BOON, *Chapel Road.*
My Little War.
Summer in Termuren.
ROGER BOYLAN, *Killoyle.*
IGNÁCIO DE LOYOLA BRANDÃO, *Anonymous Celebrity.*
The Good-Bye Angel.
Teeth under the Sun.
Zero.
BONNIE BREMSER, *Troia: Mexican Memoirs.*
CHRISTINE BROOKE-ROSE, *Amalgamemnon.*
BRIGID BROPHY, *In Transit.*
MEREDITH BROSNAN, *Mr. Dynamite.*
GERALD L. BRUNS, *Modern Poetry and the Idea of Language.*
EVGENY BUNIMOVICH AND J. KATES, EDS., *Contemporary Russian Poetry: An Anthology.*
GABRIELLE BURTON, *Heartbreak Hotel.*
MICHEL BUTOR, *Degrees.*
Mobile.
Portrait of the Artist as a Young Ape.
G. CABRERA INFANTE, *Infante's Inferno.*
Three Trapped Tigers.
JULIETA CAMPOS, *The Fear of Losing Eurydice.*
ANNE CARSON, *Eros the Bittersweet.*
ORLY CASTEL-BLOOM, *Dolly City.*
CAMILO JOSÉ CELA, *Christ versus Arizona.*
The Family of Pascual Duarte.
The Hive.
LOUIS-FERDINAND CÉLINE, *Castle to Castle.*
Conversations with Professor Y.
London Bridge.

Normance.
North.
Rigadoon.
HUGO CHARTERIS, *The Tide Is Right.*
JEROME CHARYN, *The Tar Baby.*
MARC CHOLODENKO, *Mordechai Schamz.*
JOSHUA COHEN, *Witz.*
EMILY HOLMES COLEMAN, *The Shutter of Snow.*
ROBERT COOVER, *A Night at the Movies.*
STANLEY CRAWFORD, *Log of the S.S. The Mrs Unguentine.*
Some Instructions to My Wife.
ROBERT CREELEY, *Collected Prose.*
RENÉ CREVEL, *Putting My Foot in It.*
RALPH CUSACK, *Cadenza.*
SUSAN DAITCH, *L.C.*
Storytown.
NICHOLAS DELBANCO, *The Count of Concord.*
NIGEL DENNIS, *Cards of Identity.*
PETER DIMOCK, *A Short Rhetoric for Leaving the Family.*
ARIEL DORFMAN, *Konfidenz.*
COLEMAN DOWELL, *The Houses of Children.*
Island People.
Too Much Flesh and Jabez.
ARKADII DRAGOMOSHCHENKO, *Dust.*
RIKKI DUCORNET, *The Complete Butcher's Tales.*
The Fountains of Neptune.
The Jade Cabinet.
The One Marvelous Thing.
Phosphor in Dreamland.
The Stain.
The Word "Desire."
WILLIAM EASTLAKE, *The Bamboo Bed.*
Castle Keep.
Lyric of the Circle Heart.
JEAN ECHENOZ, *Chopin's Move.*
STANLEY ELKIN, *A Bad Man.*
Boswell: A Modern Comedy.
Criers and Kibitzers, Kibitzers and Criers.
The Dick Gibson Show.
The Franchiser.
George Mills.
The Living End.
The MacGuffin.
The Magic Kingdom.
Mrs. Ted Bliss.
The Rabbi of Lud.
Van Gogh's Room at Arles.
ANNIE ERNAUX, *Cleaned Out.*
LAUREN FAIRBANKS, *Muzzle Thyself.*
Sister Carrie.
LESLIE A. FIEDLER, *Love and Death in the American Novel.*
JUAN FILLOY, *Op Oloop.*
GUSTAVE FLAUBERT, *Bouvard and Pécuchet.*
KASS FLEISHER, *Talking out of School.*
FORD MADOX FORD, *The March of Literature.*
JON FOSSE, *Aliss at the Fire.*
Melancholy.

FOR A FULL LIST OF PUBLICATIONS, VISIT:
www.dalkeyarchive.com

MAX FRISCH, *I'm Not Stiller.*
  Man in the Holocene.
CARLOS FUENTES, *Christopher Unborn.*
  Distant Relations.
  Terra Nostra.
  Where the Air Is Clear.
JANICE GALLOWAY, *Foreign Parts.*
  The Trick Is to Keep Breathing.
WILLIAM H. GASS, *Cartesian Sonata*
  and Other Novellas.
  Finding a Form.
  A Temple of Texts.
  The Tunnel.
  Willie Masters' Lonesome Wife.
GÉRARD GAVARRY, *Hoppla! 1 2 3.*
ETIENNE GILSON,
  The Arts of the Beautiful.
  Forms and Substances in the Arts.
C. S. GISCOMBE, *Giscome Road.*
  Here.
  Prairie Style.
DOUGLAS GLOVER, *Bad News of the Heart.*
  The Enamoured Knight.
WITOLD GOMBROWICZ,
  A Kind of Testament.
KAREN ELIZABETH GORDON,
  The Red Shoes.
GEORGI GOSPODINOV, *Natural Novel.*
JUAN GOYTISOLO, *Count Julian.*
  Juan the Landless.
  Makbara.
  Marks of Identity.
PATRICK GRAINVILLE, *The Cave of Heaven.*
HENRY GREEN, *Back.*
  Blindness.
  Concluding.
  Doting.
  Nothing.
JIŘÍ GRUŠA, *The Questionnaire.*
GABRIEL GUDDING,
  Rhode Island Notebook.
MELA HARTWIG, *Am I a Redundant*
  Human Being?
JOHN HAWKES, *The Passion Artist.*
  Whistlejacket.
ALEKSANDAR HEMON, ED.,
  Best European Fiction.
AIDAN HIGGINS, *A Bestiary.*
  Balcony of Europe.
  Bornholm Night-Ferry.
  Darkling Plain: Texts for the Air.
  Flotsam and Jetsam.
  Langrishe, Go Down.
  Scenes from a Receding Past.
  Windy Arbours.
KEIZO HINO, *Isle of Dreams.*
ALDOUS HUXLEY, *Antic Hay.*
  Crome Yellow.
  Point Counter Point.
  Those Barren Leaves.
  Time Must Have a Stop.
MIKHAIL IOSSEL AND JEFF PARKER, EDS.,
  Amerika: Russian Writers View the
  United States.
GERT JONKE, *The Distant Sound.*
  Geometric Regional Novel.

Homage to Czerny.
  The System of Vienna.
JACQUES JOUET, *Mountain R.*
  Savage.
CHARLES JULIET, *Conversations with*
  Samuel Beckett and Bram van
  Velde.
MIEKO KANAI, *The Word Book.*
YORAM KANIUK, *Life on Sandpaper.*
HUGH KENNER, *The Counterfeiters.*
  Flaubert, Joyce and Beckett:
  The Stoic Comedians.
  Joyce's Voices.
DANILO KIŠ, *Garden, Ashes.*
  A Tomb for Boris Davidovich.
ANITA KONKKA, *A Fool's Paradise.*
GEORGE KONRÁD, *The City Builder.*
TADEUSZ KONWICKI, *A Minor Apocalypse.*
  The Polish Complex.
MENIS KOUMANDAREAS, *Koula.*
ELAINE KRAF, *The Princess of 72nd Street.*
JIM KRUSOE, *Iceland.*
EWA KURYLUK, *Century 21.*
EMILIO LASCANO TEGUI, *On Elegance*
  While Sleeping.
ERIC LAURRENT, *Do Not Touch.*
VIOLETTE LEDUC, *La Bâtarde.*
SUZANNE JILL LEVINE, *The Subversive*
  Scribe: Translating Latin
  American Fiction.
DEBORAH LEVY, *Billy and Girl.*
  Pillow Talk in Europe and Other
  Places.
JOSÉ LEZAMA LIMA, *Paradiso.*
ROSA LIKSOM, *Dark Paradise.*
OSMAN LINS, *Avalovara.*
  The Queen of the Prisons of Greece.
ALF MAC LOCHLAINN,
  The Corpus in the Library.
  Out of Focus.
RON LOEWINSOHN, *Magnetic Field(s).*
BRIAN LYNCH, *The Winner of Sorrow.*
D. KEITH MANO, *Take Five.*
MICHELINE AHARONIAN MARCOM,
  The Mirror in the Well.
BEN MARCUS,
  The Age of Wire and String.
WALLACE MARKFIELD,
  Teitlebaum's Window.
  To an Early Grave.
DAVID MARKSON, *Reader's Block.*
  Springer's Progress.
  Wittgenstein's Mistress.
CAROLE MASO, *AVA.*
LADISLAV MATEJKA AND KRYSTYNA
  POMORSKA, EDS.,
  Readings in Russian Poetics:
  Formalist and Structuralist Views.
HARRY MATHEWS,
  The Case of the Persevering Maltese:
  Collected Essays.
  Cigarettes.
  The Conversions.
  The Human Country: New and
  Collected Stories.
  The Journalist.

FOR A FULL LIST OF PUBLICATIONS, VISIT:
www.dalkeyarchive.com

My Life in CIA.
Singular Pleasures.
The Sinking of the Odradek
Stadium.
Tlooth.
20 Lines a Day.
JOSEPH MCELROY,
Night Soul and Other Stories.
ROBERT L. MCLAUGHLIN, ED.,
Innovations: An Anthology of
Modern & Contemporary Fiction.
HERMAN MELVILLE, *The Confidence-Man.*
AMANDA MICHALOPOULOU, *I'd Like.*
STEVEN MILLHAUSER,
The Barnum Museum.
In the Penny Arcade.
RALPH J. MILLS, JR.,
Essays on Poetry.
MOMUS, *The Book of Jokes.*
CHRISTINE MONTALBETTI, *Western.*
OLIVE MOORE, *Spleen.*
NICHOLAS MOSLEY, *Accident.*
Assassins.
Catastrophe Practice.
Children of Darkness and Light.
Experience and Religion.
God's Hazard.
The Hesperides Tree.
Hopeful Monsters.
Imago Bird.
Impossible Object.
Inventing God.
Judith.
Look at the Dark.
Natalie Natalia.
Paradoxes of Peace.
Serpent.
Time at War.
The Uses of Slime Mould:
Essays of Four Decades.
WARREN MOTTE,
Fables of the Novel: French Fiction
since 1990.
Fiction Now: The French Novel in
the 21st Century.
Oulipo: A Primer of Potential
Literature.
YVES NAVARRE, *Our Share of Time.*
Sweet Tooth.
DOROTHY NELSON, *In Night's City.*
Tar and Feathers.
ESHKOL NEVO, *Homesick.*
WILFRIDO D. NOLLEDO,
But for the Lovers.
FLANN O'BRIEN,
At Swim-Two-Birds.
At War.
The Best of Myles.
The Dalkey Archive.
Further Cuttings.
The Hard Life.
The Poor Mouth.
The Third Policeman.
CLAUDE OLLIER, *The Mise-en-Scène.*
PATRIK OUŘEDNÍK, *Europeana.*
BORIS PAHOR, *Necropolis.*

FERNANDO DEL PASO,
News from the Empire.
Palinuro of Mexico.
ROBERT PINGET, *The Inquisitory.*
Mahu or The Material.
Trio.
MANUEL PUIG,
Betrayed by Rita Hayworth.
The Buenos Aires Affair.
Heartbreak Tango.
RAYMOND QUENEAU, *The Last Days.*
Odile.
Pierrot Mon Ami.
Saint Glinglin.
ANN QUIN, *Berg.*
Passages.
Three.
Tripticks.
ISHMAEL REED,
The Free-Lance Pallbearers.
The Last Days of Louisiana Red.
Ishmael Reed: The Plays.
Reckless Eyeballing.
The Terrible Threes.
The Terrible Twos.
Yellow Back Radio Broke-Down.
JEAN RICARDOU, *Place Names.*
RAINER MARIA RILKE, *The Notebooks of*
Malte Laurids Brigge.
JULIÁN RÍOS, *The House of Ulysses.*
Larva: A Midsummer Night's Babel.
Poundemonium.
AUGUSTO ROA BASTOS, *I the Supreme.*
DANIËL ROBBERECHTS,
Arriving in Avignon.
OLIVIER ROLIN, *Hotel Crystal.*
ALIX CLEO ROUBAUD, *Alix's Journal.*
JACQUES ROUBAUD, *The Form of a*
City Changes Faster, Alas, Than
the Human Heart.
The Great Fire of London.
Hortense in Exile.
Hortense Is Abducted.
The Loop.
The Plurality of Worlds of Lewis.
The Princess Hoppy.
Some Thing Black.
LEON S. ROUDIEZ,
French Fiction Revisited.
VEDRANA RUDAN, *Night.*
STIG SÆTERBAKKEN, *Siamese.*
LYDIE SALVAYRE, *The Company of Ghosts.*
Everyday Life.
The Lecture.
Portrait of the Writer as a
Domesticated Animal.
The Power of Flies.
LUIS RAFAEL SÁNCHEZ,
Macho Camacho's Beat.
SEVERO SARDUY, *Cobra & Maitreya.*
NATHALIE SARRAUTE,
Do You Hear Them?
Martereau.
The Planetarium.
ARNO SCHMIDT, *Collected Stories.*
Nobodaddy's Children.

SELECTED DALKEY ARCHIVE PAPERBACKS

FOR A FULL LIST OF PUBLICATIONS, VISIT:
www.dalkeyarchive.com